After graduating from Leicester University, **Mark Haysom** had a thirty-year career in newspapers – starting as a trainee journalist on a local weekly and ending up as managing director of Mirror Group. In 2003 he moved into education as head of a large government agency. In recent years he has served on the boards of a number of charities dedicated to overcoming poverty, disadvantage and addiction. He was awarded an honorary doctorate from Leicester University in 2005 and the CBE in 2008. Mark lives in Brighton with his wife, Ann. His first novel, *Love, Love Me Do*, was published in 2014. In *Imagine*, the story continues.

Also by Mark Haysom
Love, Love Me Do

MARK HAYSOM

piatkus

PIATKUS

First published in Great Britain in 2015 by Piatkus
This paperback edition published in 2015 by Piatkus

1 3 5 7 9 10 8 6 4 2

Copyright © 2015 by Mark Haysom

The moral right of the author has been asserted.

*All characters and events in this publication, other than those
clearly in the public domain, are fictitious and any resemblance
to real persons, living or dead, is purely coincidental.*

A CIP catalogue record for this book
is available from the British Library.

ISBN 978-0-349-40391-5

Typeset in Sabon by M Rules

Printed and bound in Great Britain by
Clays Ltd, St Ives plc

Papers used by Piatkus are from well-managed forests
and other responsible sources.

MIX
Paper from
responsible sources
FSC® C104740
www.fsc.org

Piatkus
An imprint of
Little, Brown Book Group
Carmelite House
50 Victoria Embankment
London EC4Y 0DZ

An Hachette UK Company
www.hachette.co.uk

www.piatkus.co.uk

For Theo
A boy in a hurry who made a sudden
and early entrance into the world as this
book was being written

SATURDAY 3 AUGUST 1963

1

Saturday afternoon:
Crawley New Town

O ne behind the other, the two men lead the way from the bus station with the battered leather suitcase hoisted high above their heads. They are identically dressed in long drape jackets with velvet-trimmed collars, suede shoes with thick crepe soles, drainpipe trousers and bootlace ties. One has a cigarette that bobs dangerously from the corner of his mouth; he squints as the smoke snakes into his eyes. In sashaying polka-dot circle skirts and sling-back heels, their bottle-blonde girlfriends follow on in single file. Behind them are the children, Megan and then Baxter. Christie brings up the rear, carrying the baby.

And they are doing the conga.

A minute ago, everything seemed beyond her, everything seemed hopeless, and Christie felt tears coming to match those gathering in Megan's eyes. But now they are doing the conga with strangers through a strange town and Megan and Baxter are giggling and kicking out their feet in time to the breathless voices.

♫ Let's all do the conga,
La la la *la*,
La la la *la*

It's difficult for Christie to take it in, to adjust to what's happening. They have nothing in the world and nowhere to go and yet here they are, dancing through the streets with people she doesn't know, people she would normally usher the children across the road to avoid. And they are dancing her joyously, recklessly towards an unknown future.

♫ La la la *la*,
La la la *la*

Baxter turns to look up at her. She holds the baby close with one hand and waves to him with the other. He stumbles. Almost falls. Kicks out his leg again and laughs.

2

Earlier that day:
Ashdown Forest, Sussex

It's madness. Even as she drags the suitcase on to the bus and fumbles for the fares for herself and the children, Christie keeps telling herself that it's an entirely ridiculous idea.

And, if it's ridiculous then, it becomes even more obviously so when she sits down, shakes out her purse and finds she has just five shillings left in the world.

Madness.

There are so many reasons why she should be doing the safe and sensible thing, the only rational thing, however difficult and distasteful that might be. And of the three that matter most (in the end the only three that matter at all) two are sitting in the seat in front of her and the third is screwing up his face in complaint in her arms.

She leans forwards, puts her head between those of Megan and Baxter.

'OK, everyone?' she says.

They half turn towards her and nod. Megan manages a small smile of reassurance.

They have no idea where they are going or what to expect when they get there and yet still they are trying to be brave for her. They sit close together and in silence, staring intently ahead as the bus pulls away from its stopping place in the forest. They look so small, Christie thinks; so heartbreakingly small, so pale and tired.

As the bus manoeuvres steeply around the first bend, Christie glances back to the potholed track that leads to the clearing far in the woods. The branches of a great twisted oak hang in a dense forbidding canopy over its entrance; brambles spill menacingly from its tangled verges.

Christie shivers, closes her eyes and holds the baby tightly.

They left the clearing just a few hours ago, but so much of what took place there seems like a dream; it's as if it happened long ago and to someone else, not to her and the children. It's impossible to believe that they lived in that cramped and ugly caravan for six weeks. And for a moment, it's as if the storm that broke yesterday at sunset is something she imagined.

Leaning against the window with her eyes still closed, Christie can feel the August sunlight playing on her face as the bus slowly follows the meandering twists and turns of the road through the forest. She breathes deeply, letting the warmth soak into her. She is strangely calm, drifting almost towards sleep.

The bus turns a sharp corner and the sunlight disappears behind a tall hedgerow. Christie's eyes snap open.

The ache in her arms from hauling the suitcase reminds her. None of it is a trick of her imagination. None of it is a dream. They *did* live in that caravan for six weeks. The storm *did* rage all around them. Truman is gone. They have no home to go to. All that they own, all that they have left, is in that suitcase. And everything in her life has been a lie.

Everything except the children.

And now?

Now, instead of doing the difficult, distasteful, *rational* thing and going straight to her mother, she and the children are heading for a town she doesn't know. And her only plan when they get there is to turn up on the doorstep of a woman she has never met; who she knows absolutely nothing about; who, until yesterday, she thought had been dead for twenty years. And who has no idea that any of them exist.

And if it doesn't work out, if this woman turns them away (and who can blame her if she does?), then Christie will have just five shillings to feed the children and find shelter for them tonight.

It *is* madness.

3

On the bus

The truth, of course, is that Christie knows exactly what kind of life they could expect at her mother's house.

Her mother would be mean and hateful. She wouldn't want Megan and Baxter there and certainly wouldn't want the noise and fuss of the baby. Christie's twin sisters would have to move in together and share a room to create just a small space for her and the children. The house would be crowded and full of resentment.

With Truman's mother it's at least possible that it might be different; and that possibility is better than the certainty that otherwise awaits them.

And that, Christie tells herself as the bus lumbers along the narrow winding lanes, is why, however ridiculous it might seem, it's worth trying.

But what will she say to her? To this woman she doesn't know. How can she even begin to explain it to her?

How will she begin?

'Hello, Mrs Bird, you don't know me but—'

No, that won't do at all. That's how someone bringing bad

news might begin. Or it's a door-to-door salesman's opening patter.

'Hello, Mrs Bird, my name is Christie and I've brought your grandchildren to meet you.'

Better: to the point.

'Grandchildren?' she'll reply. 'You must have made a mistake, dear. You've got the wrong house. My son's not married.'

She'll try to close the door on them, send them on their way. Christie will have to be strong.

'There's no mistake, Mrs Bird. We've been married ten years.'

'Ten years?'

'And this is Megan, who is nine. And this is Baxter, and he's eight. And the baby is—'

'*Ten years?*'

Ten years. And only now does Christie know that they were ten years of cheating and lies. Ten years when she'd been afraid; too afraid to try to discover the truth.

'I know it's a terrible shock for you, Mrs Bird. It's a shock to us too.'

One of the lies: he said he was an orphan. Christie's eighteen-year-old heart had broken for him when he told her.

'He said you died years ago. When he was growing up.'

'But how could he?'

Yes. How could he?

'We're here, Mrs Bird, because we need your help.'

More than that. Much more.

'We're here, Mrs Bird, because your son has left us with no home and no money and nowhere else to go.'

Better.

'Mrs Bird, all we've got in the world is five shillings and the clothes in this suitcase.'

It's not perfect, but it's the best Christie can do. The truth is so new to her that she doesn't fully trust herself to speak it aloud. But she will have to find the words when they get there; these words or words like them.

And then either the door will slam in their faces, or it will open and she will let them in.

4

Mid-afternoon:
Crawley New Town

Christie isn't sure what she'd imagined; but it isn't this. As the bus finally makes its halting way through the cheek-by-jowl housing and industrial estates on the outskirts of Crawley, and then as it goes on to the bus station in the centre of the town, there's one thought that keeps running through her head. How can she and the children live in such a place? Everything is newly built and yet it looks so grey, anonymous and worn.

Reality comes rushing back to her when, with a hiss of its brakes, the bus finally comes to a stop. What has she been thinking? She doesn't know whether they'll be able to live there at all, let alone choose to do so. She's going to have to beg charity from a stranger. And beggars most certainly can't be choosers.

It is mid-afternoon when Christie shepherds the children off the bus, hands the baby to Megan, passes the carry-cot to Baxter and goes back to heave the suitcase to the pavement.

She has shown the bus driver the address on a slip of paper

and he has chirpily pointed them in the right direction. It's not far, he says, they can walk it in fifteen minutes.

Checking the address again and making sure it's safely secured in her purse, Christie bends to take the suitcase by the handle.

She tries to lift it. It was hard before; now the tiredness in her arms makes it impossible.

She tries dragging it. It moves a yard. Two.

She looks at Megan and sees tears coming, her lip begin to tremble.

'It's OK,' she says quietly. 'It's OK.'

Baxter puts the carry-cot down and comes to help.

They pull together. Another yard.

She feels a tap on her shoulder.

'Here, love,' a man's voice says.

She turns to look at him. A cigarette dangles from the corner of his mouth.

'I think me and my mate should give you a hand with that, don't you?' he says.

It's seeing the men carrying the case, one following the other, that starts their girlfriends dancing behind. Megan and Baxter quickly join in and Christie, reluctantly at first, follows on.

♫ Let's all do the conga . . .

As they jig around a corner, Christie manages to glance quickly about. There's nothing grand or beautiful to be seen, it's still the same grey dreary place, yet somehow it's no longer quite so dispiriting. People in the street smile at them and wave as they conga on.

At the bottom of a concrete flight of steps they pause.

Christie had hoped, had prayed, that Truman's mother would have a large house with plenty of space for her and the children. Shielding her eyes against the sun and looking up to the top of the steps, all she can see is a drab terrace of small council flats.

As they climb the stairs, their voices hush to a whisper.

♫ Let's all do the conga ...

Outside the door the men deposit the suitcase and then the four strangers dance away. The two women kiss Megan and Baxter on their cheeks and wave goodbye to Christie.

♫ La la la *la*,
La la la *la*

There's been no time for Christie to ready herself. She had planned to keep rehearsing what she was going to say as they looked for the address. But suddenly they are here and she can feel Megan and Baxter's eyes on her, waiting for her to do something.

She knocks on the door.

What were those words? The words she prepared on the bus?

No money and nowhere else to go.

That's it.

She can hear someone coming towards the door, a bolt being slid, a chain being released.

The door opens, just a crack, and a small grey-haired woman peers out.

'Mrs Bird?' Christie says.

Her hands are trembling as she holds the baby; she can feel the colour coming hotly to her cheeks.

'Yes, dear, that's right,' the woman says uncertainly.

'Mrs Bird,' Christie says. 'We've got no money and—'

It's not how she should have begun; she can see it in the woman's eyes, in the dismissive shake of the head. She thinks they're there to beg for money. The door begins to inch to a close.

Megan and Baxter are standing by Christie's side. As the door slowly closes, Megan reaches urgently for Christie's hand. Baxter though takes a small step forward.

'We've been doing the conga,' he announces to the woman.

'Have you, indeed?' Mrs Bird says.

A smile coming to her face.

The door opening wider.

TEN YEARS LATER

MONDAY, 1 OCTOBER 1973

5

Baxter

*Eleven o'clock: Lecture Theatre One,
Attenborough Tower basement,
University of Leicester*

Leaning forwards on the hard plastic edge of his seat, Baxter sits with his neck cranked and craned uncomfortably to the left as he looks back and along to the far end of the row.

It's the only way he can see her.

He's been sitting like this for so long that part of him has forgotten what he's doing here, what they're all doing here.

She is half turned towards him and talking to her neighbour in this totally intense, completely absorbed way that Baxter has decided is uniquely hers. From time to time she runs her heavily ringed fingers through the long silky gloss of her hair and laughs; and when she laughs, the small silver stars clustered on her right temple dance under the neon brightness of the lecture theatre lights.

Her fingernails are painted black to match her hair; Baxter

noticed them while they were waiting in the corridor outside. Everyone had arrived early because it was the first time and finally it was to begin. It was crazy out there, all shivers and whispers and sudden shouts of laughter. You could feel it running through the air, how jittery they were. Not that anyone was actually coming out and saying it, of course; not that anyone would have admitted how wound up, how wired they were.

No way.

He'd been among the first to arrive and had watched as she came down the stairs to the corridor below. She came down slightly sideways, minding her feet to make sure she didn't step on the wide bottoms of her flared jeans with the platform soles of her boots, and her long black coat fell open just enough to show the purple velvet top she's wearing.

It was then that Baxter forgot to breathe.

It was like she was wearing it for him, as if she rifled through the hangers in her wardrobe and put it on because he thought she'd looked so amazing in it when he saw her that time before. The previous week. On the first day of Freshers' Week. In the Union coffee bar. After they all queued for registration. That time.

Then suddenly and just for a moment – not long enough for him to be able think of anything to say, his mind a complete frigging blank – suddenly she was at the bottom of the stairs, standing close by. Close enough for him to reach out and touch her hair if he wanted to. Which he did – did *want* to. But which he managed to stop himself doing. Just. But that's when he saw them, the fingernails painted black; and that's when he noticed the silver stars.

He should have said something about the stars.

'Nice stars,' he could have said, pointing, smiling.

No.

'Stars. Far out.'

Not smiling.

Better.

But he didn't say anything, couldn't say anything, and then she recognised the girl she's now sitting next to and went through the crowd to greet her.

As she moved away, he saw she was carrying her books in a black Biba carrier bag, the ornate filigreed logo and lettering standing out in dulled gold.

'Biba. Far out.'

He should have said that. She would have liked that.

Despite the stiffness accumulating in his neck, Baxter continues to stare along the row. There was a moment earlier when he thought he caught her eye and was rewarded with a half-smile of half-recognition. He's waiting for her to smile again.

Her name is Abby. He knows that now.

Abby: it's written on the folder sticking out of the top of the Biba bag.

'You've got no chance there, man,' Josh says, leaning forwards, following Baxter's gaze along the row.

From the beginning, Baxter hasn't been sure whether he truly likes Josh. They were thrown together from the first. They'd boarded the same minibus at the station, helped each other with their cases and then, sitting side by side, had quickly discovered they were on the same course. It had been inevitable that their rooms would be on the same corridor of the same hall of residence. Later, Josh knocked on Baxter's door and they went together to the high-ceilinged bare-brick Junior Common Room bar. Baxter was glad of his company, glad of any company, on that first day, and they've stuck together ever since.

Josh sits back in his chair, cups his hands behind his head.

'Way out of your league, brother,' he says.

Reluctantly, Baxter settles back in his seat. It's only then that he becomes aware of the buzz of conversation swelling all around. The lecture theatre seats more than two hundred and it's very nearly full.

He glances at his watch. It was a present from Nanna Bird; because of his grades, she said. It's not the LED digital he would have chosen – but he didn't tell her, of course. She'd saved for it for so long.

'We should have started ten minutes ago,' Josh says, anticipating his question. 'But there's something going on out there.'

Baxter follows Josh's pointing finger to where the lecture theatre door is being held ajar by a large, round, uniformed security guard. In the corridor beyond, a woman in a black academic gown is standing on tiptoe, unnaturally close to a tall man with immaculately groomed, steely-grey hair. He is bending towards her, lowering his head, and she is whispering urgently into his ear.

Baxter slumps further into his seat and watches as the woman takes a half-step away and the grey-haired man slowly shakes his head, turns towards the doorway, turns again as though for confirmation and then comes sweeping into the room to take his place behind the lectern.

The room falls silent.

'Good-morning, ladies and gentlemen,' he begins. He has a vicar's melodious voice, rising and falling. 'My name is Professor Arthur Humphreys and I must apologise for my tardy arrival on the occasion of our first meeting.'

He pauses and peers eagle-eyed at those seated nearest to him. Baxter sees them shift uneasily in their seats, too close for comfort.

'In a few moments I will begin to map out the great voyage of learning and discovery that we will be embarking on in the coming weeks and months.'

A low murmur of anticipation runs through the room.

'But before we begin ... I regret to say there's some distressing business that I've been asked to conduct.'

Another murmur, this time rising as a question. Distressing?

'This is most unfortunate ... most unfortunate on any day, let alone on our first,' he says. 'I'm afraid ... I'm afraid I must ask one of your number to make himself known to me.'

Baxter feels something clench inside him. It's the old fear: the old fear of being picked on in the playground, picked on by a teacher in the classroom. He pushes it away from him, turns to Josh and smiles. It isn't him, the smile says. It can't be him.

The professor looks down at the untidy sheaf of notes he has deposited on the lectern.

'Is there a Mr ... ?'

He looks down at his notes again.

'Is there a Mr Bird with us today?'

Baxter's smile falls away, his heart races.

He tries to steady himself. No, this is crazy. It can't be him. It's a common enough name: among two hundred students, there's sure to be more than one.

21

People begin to turn in their seats.

'A Mr Baxter Bird?'

Josh looks at him, his eyes widening in question and surprise. Baxter meets the question with a small bewildered shrug of the shoulders.

'Mr Bird?' the professor says again, scanning the packed rows of the lecture theatre.

Slowly, Baxter raises his hand.

'Ah, Mr Bird, there you are,' he says.

Distractedly, he tidies his sheaf of papers.

'Mr Bird, I'm afraid I must ask you to make your way outside. A member of the university staff needs to speak to you on a matter of great urgency.'

Baxter could not have been sitting in a more difficult place from which to make a premature exit. He'd positioned himself in the very middle of the row at the very centre of the lecture theatre. At the time it was the obvious choice – safely at the heart of things, not exposed on the periphery like those at the front.

Aware now of the weight of silence that has settled on the room, feeling that every eye is on him, he pulls himself upright.

As the colour surges to his cheeks, he picks up his bag and sets off, nudging and shuffling past first Josh and then, one by one, everyone else in the row. Some stand to let him through, others merely pull their knees to one side to let him struggle by. With every apologetic step he takes, he can feel people turning away from him, as though embarrassed to meet his eye.

A moment ago he was one of them. Now he's been singled out, he's tainted, suddenly less than them.

Less than them?

His heart plummets.

That's it, that must be it. It's the only explanation. They must have decided that there's been some kind of a mix-up; that his grades aren't good enough for the university after all.

And he's worked so hard to get here. It's what he has imagined for so long: his dream, his mother's dream.

'One last question, Mr Bird . . .'

The university admission interview is coming to an end. It hasn't gone well. It's been a tough two hours: the three of them firing questions, the one of him stumbling flush-faced through answers. There have been long pauses. Embarrassed silences.

The room is hot. Baxter fingers his collar, squirms in his chair. He just wants it over now.

The well-padded, world-weary man with a cut-glass voice who has asked most of the questions consults his notes and peers over his heavy horn-rimmed spectacles. He sighs.

'Mr Bird, I'm going to be merciful and give you a final chance. And this time I want you to amaze us, dazzle us; I want a glimpse into your soul. Can you do that?'

Baxter manages to nod. Dazzle?

'Tell us then, I beg you,' the man sighs again, 'in words that will both astonish and inspire, what a place at university would mean to you.'

Baxter may have struggled with some of the questions – how would he describe himself? How is that different from

23

the way others would describe him? – but he knows the answer to this one. He just hasn't been confident enough to give it.

What does it mean?

Everything.

He hesitates.

Should he say it? Should he tell this plush, polished, condescending man what five people in a cramped council flat and no money is like? About sharing a bed with your brother, having no space of your own. Should he tell him about Pauper Bird with his second-hand school uniforms, second-hand clothes, second-hand football boots, jumble-sale books? About being cold because there's no money for the meter. About being hungry and not showing it, because there's no point, because there's no more. About his mother always doing her best for them, on her own; worrying, working every hour, urging them on. About Megan.

Tell the truth, his mother had said to him as he set off that morning. Just answer honestly and you'll be fine.

Quietly, hesitantly, he begins. At the beginning. In the forest.

And he does tell him.

All of it.

And then – more confidently, finding his stride – he closes his eyes and tells him what getting to university would mean. He can see it, imagine it.

It would mean long days in the sunshine, reading; long nights in the bar, talking. His own room. Friendships. Girls. Rock concerts; discos; dancing; laughter.

Escape.

Freedom.

He's never spoken so long, said so much.

When he stops, amidst the silence like a presence in the room, the horn-rimmed man takes off his glasses and starts to polish them. And then he stands up. And shakes Baxter's hand.

And smiles.

But now the dream is over and he'll have to go home and tell his mother he's been kicked out before he's even got started. He hasn't even made it through one lecture.

Not one frigging lecture.

Not that he's entirely surprised. All through Freshers' Week, he didn't believe he truly belonged. He felt weird, self-conscious, like he was acting a part. Look, this is Baxter being a student registering for his course; being a student drinking in a bar; going to a freshers' disco; listening to music; hanging out with Josh; playing his guitar in his room, practising the same song over and over.

♫ Imagine there's no heaven . . .

All week he felt like an impostor, waiting to be discovered at any moment.

Well, now he has been.

And what's worse, what puts the cherry on the icing on the very top of the frigging cake, is that with every step he takes, with every clumsy apology he makes as he bumps his bag into someone's arm, as he treads on someone's foot, he knows that he's getting closer to the end of the row, closer to her.

He may not have made much of an impression on her before but she sure as hell isn't going to forget him now, is she?

There she is. So amazing, so composed, so totally together; with her rings and her stars and her hand running through her glossy black hair. And here he is: a blushing, clammy loser.

'I'm sorry,' he says, when he finally reaches her.

She'll never know it but it's much more than an apology for having to stumble past her. It's an apology for having the audacity to breathe the same air as her, for thinking even for a moment that he belonged in the same room, for ever having looked at her and dreamed, for talking to her now, for not talking to her before, for wanting to touch her hair, for never now having the chance to touch her hair. For everything.

As she pulls her knees to one side to let him through, she looks up. In the entire row, she's the only one who has looked up. And as she does so, there's a question in her eyes and a small frown on her face that crinkles the stars on her temple.

A small frown, as though he has disappointed her.

26

6

Abby

Lecture Theatre One

Mechanically Abby pulls her knees to one side to allow the boy to push past. She looks up quickly at the sound of his voice but doesn't really see him, doesn't focus. Because she'd been so lost in her own thoughts, she didn't catch what the professor said and she's not sure who the boy is or why he's leaving. In any case, he's not someone she knows, anyone she's seen before.

She's got other worries.

It's the stars: they're too much. She can see that now, of course, now it's too late.

She imagined they would say something new about her – or rather, say something about the *new* her. And it turns out that she was right. They're eloquent; they speak volumes. But they say all the wrong things.

They're meant to suggest she's this free spirit – that she's different, somehow original, artistic, daring, confident, perhaps even a bit quirky. And these *are* all part of her true persona that can finally reveal itself now that she's free of Pontlottyn.

But as soon as she came down those stairs and saw Georgie and the others, saw how they were dressed, she realised that what the stars actually said, what they shouted from the nearest mountaintop, was 'TRYING TOO HARD.'

No, it's much worse than that.

What they shouted was 'JUMPED-UP TARTY VALLEYS GIRL TRYING TOO HARD.'

What they screamed was 'TRIVIAL, LIGHTWEIGHT, VACUOUS.'

Most of all what they said was '*Stupid.*'

Stupid.

Georgie's friends were polite about them, of course.

'Stars. Far out,' someone said.

But Abby could see what they really thought.

And if she could see it so clearly then, why in heaven's name hadn't she seen it before, when she could have done something about it? After all, she'd had time enough.

She'd been up since before dawn; there was simply no point in lying there any longer with her eyes wide open and her mind turning like the wheels of an express train, always on the same fretful track, over and over, faster and faster. She'd hardly slept a wink; she'd been too nervous and excited to sleep. It was only natural, she'd told herself – it was the sort of thing her mam would say and there had been comfort in that – only natural to be nervous. First day at college. First proper day, anyway.

So she was up before the first yellow glimmer of daylight and, while the rest of Leicester still slept, she tried on everything she had in her wardrobe. Twice. She'd already decided what she was going to wear, had laid it out the night before so as not to have to worry about it in the morning. But she'd had second thoughts. And then third. After that, she read through the introductory course notes for what must have been the hundredth time. She checked and rechecked the time and the place of the first lecture. She did her make-up and did it over again. And then, at the very last moment, when she was almost out of the door, she decided on the stars.

Twenty pence from that tacky stall in Ebbw Vale Market and only thrown into her suitcase as an afterthought, they came into her mind from nowhere. She rushed back through the door, delighted with the sudden inspiration, stuck them on, admired herself in the mirror and smiled.

Smiled!

So stupid.

And the rings? Far too many rings. And the black nail varnish? What on earth was she thinking? She's dressed for a disco, not a lecture hall.

And, of course, the accent makes everything worse.

She didn't realise how strong it was until she arrived in Leicester and found herself surrounded by the likes of Georgie and her friends: all these posh kids from Guildford and Woking and Winchester and wherever.

Abby has liked Georgie from the start. They sat at the same table in the Union coffee bar on the first day, got talking and they haven't really stopped since. About everything, all at once.

Even now, sitting waiting for the lecture to begin, they've skipped through South America and Asia: Allende's suicide in Chile and the last bombings in Cambodia. They've hopped to Europe: Black September and Athens Airport. From there they leapt to Mary Whitehouse and what she said about *Last Tango* – how dare she, when she's never even seen it?

Sanctimonious blue-rinsed cow, Georgie said. They then quickly moved on to the way the girl's head swivelled in *The Exorcist* – and wasn't it the grossest thing ever when Regan threw up? And it was green! – and then on again to Mike Oldfield and 'Tubular Bells' – you had to love it or hate it; they both love it.

Once they'd started talking they'd gone tumbling from one subject to the next. Or rather, Georgie had. Thinking about the stars had distracted Abby, kept her quiet. The stars and the accent.

Abby shakes her head: perhaps all this new-persona business is just so much tosh after all. Maybe she's destined for ever to stay plain Abigail Evans, Little Miss Mouse, Little Miss Diligent, Little Miss Prim-and-Proper from Pontlottyn.

Pontlottyn ...

Long ago Abby discovered that if you grow up in a scattering of houses in the shadow of a pit in the fold of a valley, the few people you know make assumptions about you. And that soon enough you are making the same assumptions about yourself. It's as if, in the small drama of village life, you're given a role, you play that role, you become that person.

So, because no one can put from their minds what happened on her eleventh birthday – and because she's an only child, living halfway up the hill, always on her own, her nose buried in a book – people assume they know who she is.

There's Abby: she's the quiet one, the serious one.

And she is! She *is* quiet, she is serious. But that's not *all* she is.

She also has it in her to be that free spirit – she's sure she does. But she could never show it in Pontlottyn because that's not who they permitted her to be. To have suddenly become someone else there would have shocked and disappointed all those people who think they know her best, and it would have embarrassed her, mortified her.

So getting to university, getting away, was meant to set her free.

But she hasn't escaped at all, has she?

Because in one day, she's somehow managed to transform herself from one person she isn't to another. Because in just that one day she's stopped being Pontlottyn's Little Miss Prim-and-Proper and has become the University of Leicester's Vacuous Welsh Tart.

Stupid.

7

Baxter

Attenborough Tower basement

Waiting in the corridor outside the lecture theatre are the portly security guard who had held the door ajar and the woman in the academic gown, the one Baxter had watched as she stood on tiptoe and whispered urgently in the professor's ear.

As the guard pulls the door to a close behind Baxter, shutting out the accusing silence of the lecture theatre, it's the woman who takes a step towards him.

'Mr Bird?' she says.

When he'd watched her from a distance, Baxter had thought there was something flirtatious in the closeness with which she stood next to the professor, in the stretch of her body, her upturned head. Because of that, he'd assumed she was a postgraduate student, not much older than himself. But now, as she moves towards him, holding her black gown tightly to her, he's surprised to see that she is older than he imagined, old enough to be his mother.

His mother?

He blinks. This isn't about grades.

Something has happened, something bad: he can see it in the woman's every anxious gesture as she comes closer. Her eyes go to his but can't stay there: she looks away, looks down; her hand goes nervously to her hair, gathered in an unruly bun.

It's happening again, Baxter thinks – he feels the familiar sinking rush of guilt when he thinks of his sister, the appalled heaviness in his chest – it's like Megan's day, the day they called him out of school. That's it; that *must* be it. Something has happened. To his mother, or his brother, or Nanna.

'Mr Bird?' she says.

He nods, a numbing panic rising.

'Mr *Baxter* Bird?' she says, frowning, seeking confirmation.

He nods again.

'Mr Bird, I'm afraid I must ask you to come with me.'

Before he can say anything, ask anything – before his mind can kick back into gear – she turns and leads the way along the corridor. He trails behind, the security guard walking beside him.

To the left of the stairs is a glass-panelled door. The woman pushes it open and holds it for him. For a moment, Baxter hesitates; whatever it is that she's about to tell him, he suddenly doesn't want to hear it. He *has* to know, he *needs* to know urgently, but at the same time he wants to put it off for as long as possible. The guard takes him gently by the elbow, nods reassuringly and steers him through the door before taking up position outside.

It is a small windowless room with a distant smell of stale

cigarettes. A pine-topped table on thin chrome legs stands in the middle and against the far wall are four red plastic stacking chairs. The woman pulls one of the chairs to one side of the table, pulls another to the other and gestures to Baxter to sit. She then takes her place opposite him.

'Mr Bird,' she begins earnestly. 'My name is Dr Rosetta Paulizky—'

Baxter gives a small laugh; he can't help it.

Doctor *who*?

'But you must call me Rosetta,' she adds reassuringly.

Baxter is dimly aware that he has closed his eyes, that he is slowly shaking his head and that his mouth has fallen open. This is getting unreal. *Surreal*. It's as if he has been catapulted into this dream, the weirdest frigging dream.

He opens his eyes. She takes this as her cue to continue.

'I work for the university's student-counselling staff,' she says. 'And I've been asked to speak to you ...'

She pauses, leans forwards, briefly rests the tips of her fingers on her temples.

'Forgive me, Mr Bird,' she says, flustered. 'This is most unorthodox and I'm not entirely sure it's the right thing ... I mean, I'm not sure *I* should be the one to tell you ... but he was most insistent, most persuasive.'

He?

She composes herself and begins again.

'Mr Bird, there is someone here to see you and he has some bad news. Very bad news indeed.'

Once more she pauses. Closes her eyes.

'You see, he thought it would be easier for both of you if I were to tell you. And if you then had a few moments ... before you meet.'

Baxter finally manages to speak, his voice no more than a whisper.

'Who is it?' he says.

Dr Paulizky leans across the table, her eyes now open and locked to his. She holds out a hand towards him; Baxter can see what she intends. It's for him to take, should he need it.

'You must prepare yourself,' she says softly.

'Who is it?' Baxter whispers again.

'I'm afraid . . .' she says. 'I'm afraid it's your father.'

What?

'My father?' Baxter almost shouts.

Startled, Rosetta raises her hand to quieten him.

'Mr Bird, there's no easy way to put this. Your father is here and he has asked me to tell you that he's had the most terrible news.'

She looks down at the tabletop. There's a white ring left by a carelessly placed coffee mug; she begins to trace the circle of it with her finger.

'He has asked me to tell you . . .' she says, 'that he doesn't have long.'

'Long?' Baxter says, mystified.

'That he's come to say goodbye,' she says.

'Goodbye?' he parrots.

'That he's dying.'

'*Dying?*' Baxter splutters.

Dr Paulizky nods, still looking down, tracing the ring.

'The doctors say he has only a few months . . .'

She looks up, puts her hand beneath her breast and taps at her heart.

In the long silence that follows, what breaks over Baxter

35

in an exhilarating rush, what runs through him in shivering waves, is a feeling of profound, undiluted relief.

It's not like Megan after all. They are all safe: his mother, his brother, Nanna. Everyone is safe.

'Dying?' he says, laughter starting to bubble.

Dr Paulizky looks up, alarmed by what she hears in his voice.

'But he can't be dying!' Baxter says.

'I know this must be very difficult—' she starts to say.

Baxter leans back in his chair, folds his arms across his chest and makes no attempt to conceal the broad smile that has fixed on his face. They are all safe. He hadn't realised until now how important that is, how much he depends on them all just being there. They're all safe and they've got the wrong student. It's not him who should have been called from the lecture theatre; it's some other poor unsuspecting sap. It's all a mistake, a colossal cock-up, a cosmic balls-up.

'You don't understand,' he says. 'My father *can't* be dying.'

'Why ever not?' she says.

'Because . . .' he says, stifling the laughter, 'because you can only die once, can't you?'

'*What?*' she says.

Baxter leans forwards to explain.

'You see, he walked out on us, ten years ago. I was eight years old—'

'But that doesn't mean—' she tries to interrupt.

'He walked out on us,' Baxter persists. 'And then, a few months later, he managed to step off a kerb without looking. Right under the wheels of a giant pantechnicon.'

It wasn't quite a *pantechnicon*, because strictly speaking a pantechnicon is for furniture, but it's one of the words he's been wanting to use. Like *panegyric*, *paradigm*, *polyphonic*.

'This enormous lorry,' he says, in case she didn't understand.

Dr Paulizky raises her hands, in shock, in protestation. She tries to speak but Baxter cuts across her.

'And do you want to know the best of it?' he says delightedly, slapping the tabletop with the flat of his hand. 'It was a Hovis lorry!'

Again Dr Paulizky attempts to interrupt. But Baxter is having none of it. They're all safe and he's on a roll now; he's rocking, he's rolling, he's freewheeling, he's free.

'So, don't you see?' he says, the hysteria rising unstoppably. 'Don't you see?' he says, giggling like the schoolboy he was when his mother first told him his father had died.

'It's like a Cockney rhyming thing,' he says, his eight-year-old self explaining the best joke he's ever heard.

'He can't be dying,' he says. 'Because my father is just like Hovis.'

Rosetta looks at him blankly.

'He's brown bread, Dr Paulizky. Dead,' Baxter says. 'Truman Bird has been brown bread for years!'

8

Truman

Rosetta Paulizky's office, Fielding Johnson Building, University of Leicester

Truman Bird sends the swivel chair rolling idly backwards and hears its low creak of complaint as it takes his full weight. He shifts position, lifts one cheek from the seat and releases a long rippling trumpet-blast of breaking wind. With a small grunt of satisfaction, he raises his feet to the polished mahogany surface of the desk, loosens his tie, undoes the button of his shirt collar, settles back and pats at the roundness of his stomach.

There's no denying it, no concealing it, is there? He *is* carrying a few pounds too many. It's all that Bella's fault – stupid cow, never did learn to cook. Chips with bloody everything.

He fishes in his jacket pocket for his cigarettes and taps one from the packet. A grin breaks on his face. Still, a few extra pounds is a small price to pay, isn't it? For a year like that.

He reaches for his lighter, flips it open, steadies his hand to hold the flame to the tip of the cigarette, draws deeply, tilts his head back and sends a ring of smoke to the ceiling.

OK, so he was down on his luck when he met her and it looked then like Margate had run its course for him – what with that business at The Hope & Anchor and the taxman sniffing around.

It had felt like time to head for pastures new. He wanted a fresh start, somewhere where no one knew him; a place to lie low and lick his wounds.

Because, in truth, he did need that bit of time these days. Because it *is* taking longer to bounce back: it *is* harder to come up smiling every time life knocks you about, knocks you down. When you're twenty or even thirty it doesn't matter, of course; nothing matters. Whatever life throws at you, you can just laugh it off, put a drink in your hand, start again. But at forty-one, every stumble feels like a fall and every fall is that much heavier than the last.

It's the same with a hangover.

When he was a kid, after a skinful the night before, he'd have a sore head in the morning, but he'd soon get over it. These days, though, there's a curdling sickness in the stomach and an ache of tiredness behind the eyes that lasts all day. Or at least until the first pint hits the spot.

And let's face it, he knows a thing or two about hangovers, doesn't he? On *Mastermind*, they'd be a specialist subject.

After all, he's had more than his fair share. He's had more than his share of knocks and setbacks too, come to that. Some days it feels like he's had his share and the next man's – and the next man is the unluckiest bugger you'd never want to meet.

But even though he was down at that time, he didn't give up, did he? Like he always does, he kept thinking, kept looking for a way out, kept trying to stay one step ahead. And then – bingo! – just when his luck seemed at its lowest, just when he was about to pack his bags and limp away, there was Bella on a barstool at The First & Last.

Easing further back into his chair, pushing the blotter on the desk to one side with his heels, Truman looks around the room. It's not the sort of place where he's ever felt comfortable. With its honeyed smell of beeswax polish, the heavy mahogany of the desk, the dark leather chairs and the glass-fronted bookcases, it has too much the feel of the headmaster's study or the office of an unfriendly solicitor.

He blows another smoke ring towards the moulded plasterwork of the ceiling, closes his eyes, settles back to his thoughts.

All in all, though, Margate was good to him. He'd pitched up there one summer's day with a suitcase in his hand and just thirty quid in his pocket and he had a rare old time for the next ten years. Ten years for thirty quid. You can't complain at that, can you?

A good few of those years were with Cilla at The Welcome, playing the piano in the snug, seeing the punters rolling in, trippers down from the East End, looking for a good time, having a right old knees-up night after night.

It came to a bad end, of course, when she found out he was helping himself to a few bob from the till. Well, what else was he supposed to do? She was never going to pay him what he was worth. And he was good for that place: before he waltzed in and started livening it up, it was on its knees.

He was good for her too. Only she was too dozy to know it, to appreciate what she'd got between the sheets.

40

After that he went back into the insurance game for a while, working for a broker down Cliftonville way. Did all right too, out on the knocker again. More than all right. Always did have the gift of the gab and a twinkle in the eye for the lonely housewives.

Then, just when the money was really starting to roll in, when he'd got a good few quid in his pocket for the first time in a long time, he met Sol.

He was in import-export. Buying this from someone who knew someone in Hong Kong or Taiwan; selling that to a trader on the High Street market. Always cash in hand. Not totally kosher. Not totally dodgy either. Somewhere in between.

They got talking one long lunchtime and – by the time they left the pints behind and were on to the shorts – they shook hands on a partnership. Truman immediately jacked in the insurance game and put all his cash into the business. This was his chance, he was sure of it. Finally, he was going to make it big, just like he'd always imagined – detached house in the country, new motor, flash bird on his arm, champagne on tap, life of Riley here we come.

For a while, it *was* good. They ran the business from the saloon bar of The Hope & Anchor, using the phone behind the counter, doing deals between rounds. Couldn't be better. But after a few months the taxman started sniffing around; Sol got nervous, wanted out; Truman demanded his cash back; there was a bit of a ding-dong, a bit of a barney; they were chucked out on the street; and Sol disappeared.

And that was that.

That was when he thought he ought to move on, make that fresh start, and that was when he found her, his Bella.

He only went into The First & Last for a quick one and there she was, sitting on that barstool, cigarette in hand, white mini-skirt tight around her thighs, stockinged legs crossed, balancing one of her red stilettos on her toes. Nice.

'You're a bit of all right, aren't you, princess?' he says to her, buying her a brandy and Babycham.

'You're not so bad yourself,' she says.

She reminded him of someone from years back; of Doll. He had a good thing going with Doll, a special thing. A special thing until he was ratted up about Christie and the kids. When he saw Bella sitting there like that, all the memories came flooding back and just for a moment he thought it really was Doll. Except Bella was much younger, of course.

A little belter she was: Bella the belter. He could hardly keep up with her; night after night, at it like knives.

He told her all his cash was tied up; he was waiting for this deal to come through. Import-export. She said she'd sub him until it did.

Well, she didn't need to know the business was finished, did she?

And anyway, he was sure that something would turn up. It always did if you stayed on your toes, kept your wits about you.

Except this time nothing did turn up and, after they'd been shacked up together at her place for almost a year, she finally cottoned on that there *was* no big deal he was waiting for; there *was* no cash on its way.

It was then that she lost it with him, really flipped. Launched all his stuff into the street through the bedroom window. Stupid bloody cow.

Then she told her brothers – ugly broken-nosed sods, the pair of them – how she'd subbed him to the tune of hundreds over the year, about the deal that never was. And that was when Truman knew there was no choice.

This time he really did have to get the hell out of Margate.

Truman glances at his watch and wonders how much longer they'll be. She was pretty agitated when she went off, the woman in the black gown, Dr Rosie something. In quite a state.

She was a real snooty bitch to begin with; looking down her nose at him like he was something she'd stepped in. She's one of those women's libbers, most likely, he thought. Man hater. Like that Germaine Whatsername. One of those burn-your-bra types. These universities are full of them, aren't they? He's read about it in the *Daily Mail*.

But the more he talked and met her eye, the more he told her the story, the more the colour rose in her cheeks. He enjoyed that. Watching the colour rise, knowing he was getting to her.

When she was younger, she must have been quite something; she hasn't lost it, you can still see it in her, in the way she holds herself. You can see that she's used to being looked at, likes being looked at. But she's let herself go a bit. No make-up, hair all over the place. Pity.

Truman closes his eyes; pictures her trying to compose herself, trying to work out exactly how she's going to break the news to the boy. It'll take a while.

Still, there's no hurry. He's comfortable enough with his feet up. He's got nowhere else to go.

43

Truman removes the watch from his wrist and examines it closely, weighs it in his hand. It's OK, he thinks, not bad; a present from Bella. Or was it Cilla? It's OK but it's nothing compared to the watch he used to have, the one with the gold bracelet and his name engraved on the back. Now *that* was a watch; that was something special.

He closes his eyes, unable to repel a surge of bitterness.

They took it from him, of course, the watch. Just like they took the car and everything else. And not content with taking every last thing he owned, they drove Doll away from him. His family too, come to that.

Bastards.

It was all more than ten years ago but the hurt suddenly feels new. There's no justice, is there? All he was trying to do then, all he's ever tried to do, is make a bob or two, get on in the world, get his share.

In the end – and it's hard to believe that it was only last Friday, given what's happened since – he disappeared from Margate in a hurry, with nothing in his pocket.

Ten years before, he'd arrived in a dazzle of sunshine. He left under a sky of unremitting grey and in steadily falling rain. It seemed about right. A metaphor for his life.

Standing by the side of the road, with his suitcase in his hand and his thumb out, he had the half-hearted thought that he might as well try his old mum first. He hadn't seen her for ten years, hadn't been in touch, but she'd forgive him that. She'd forgive him everything else too, everything that happened before. Of course she would. He's her only son; she'd forgive him anything.

At any rate, she wouldn't throw him out on the street. He'd have a roof over his head for a week or so, if nothing else.

Then, climbing into the cab of a van that stopped to pick him up, he had another thought. After he'd let his mum feed him up for a few days, she could lend him a few quid and he'd take a wander down to Brighton.

The idea of that made him feel better.

It would be good to go back. And it was sure to be safe now, after all this time. Ten years on, they wouldn't still be after him; it's all too long ago, no one would be interested.

The more he rolled it around in his mind, the more he liked it.

While he was down in Brighton, he'd track down Christie – Christie and the kids – and try to sweet-talk her into picking up where they left off. Well, that wouldn't be so bad. After all, they were all right together, weren't they? OK, she was mad with him at the end – fair enough – but they'd had good times along the way. And it was about time he had a place where he could settle down, have his family around him, take it easy, put his feet up. And she was still his wife. She owed him.

Failing that, he'd try to find Sally. The one who worked at The Salvation. He'd bought her jewellery in one of those expensive shops in The Lanes. A gold necklace, pearl earrings. She owed him too.

He shifts again in his seat, reaches over and stubs the cigarette out on the inner rim of a gunmetal-grey waste-paper bin.

Once more he looks at his watch.

45

There's no rush, he repeats to himself. It's not as if he's in that much of a tearing hurry to see the boy.

To be honest, he's not really sure what he thinks about that, hasn't really got his mind around it. Well, they weren't exactly close when he was a nipper, were they? And he's only up here seeing him now because he reckons it'll do his chances with Christie no harm. When she hears about it, it'll give a tug at her old heartstrings; him showing a bit of fatherly interest, devoting himself at the end to his son. He's left it late, she'll think, wiping away a tear, opening her arms and her heart to him, but not too late.

That's the idea. That sort of thing.

He's proud, of course, proud that a son of his has made it to university. The boy must have inherited his father's brains; that would explain it. A chip off the old block: like father, like son. Not that Truman was much good at school – he wasn't there long or often enough, wasn't interested. No, it was the University of Life for him, the University of Hard Knocks. But he's smart enough; he could have gone to university if he'd wanted. Could have done anything.

Like father, like son: Truman finds himself warming to the sound of that.

If the boy has inherited his father's brains, he reasons, perhaps he's turned out like him in other ways. Maybe he's not like he was when he was a kid.

He used to stare up at him, the boy did. As if he was accusing him of something. Stare at him with his mother's eyes.

The chair creaks again as Truman shudders at the memory of it.

*

It didn't take long to travel up to Crawley from Margate; just half a dozen lifts and a short walk from where he was dropped near the station. And before he'd had time to work out what he was going to say to her, he found himself standing at his mum's front door.

As he stood on the doormat, gathering himself, the thought suddenly came to him that she might no longer be there. It'd been ten years, she might have moved. Or worse. At her age, anything could have happened.

Looking around for reassurance, he saw the familiar curtains at the window, the same flowerpots beneath it. Relieved, he rattled at the door without another thought. Hearing the shuffle of footsteps inside, he stepped back, put a smile on his face and held his arms wide. She'd see him, burst into tears, fall into his arms. Her son, returned. No need for words, no need for an apology.

Job done.

But when the door swung open, it wasn't his mother standing there.

It was Christie.

9

Christie

A hundred and forty miles away, the Planning Department of Crawley Urban District Council

Christie is sitting at her desk, absently nursing a cup of coffee that she has allowed to go cold without taking a sip. In front of her, the telephone rings. She ignores it; somehow doesn't hear it. From behind a bank of sea-green metal filing cabinets, across the brightly lit room, someone shouts to her to pick up the call. She ignores them; doesn't hear them. Eventually the ringing stops.

What she can't work out is how on earth she let it happen. How, within seconds of him knocking at the door, they were sitting at Nanna's kitchen table, chatting like long-lost friends.

She even talked to him about herself! About her plans for the Open University course, having a different life. Because, with the children growing up, she could now start to think about herself, a little.

Madness. Why did she tell him *that*?

48

It's nothing to do with him, she thinks crossly.

Nothing.

It's *her* life; the life she made without him. On her own.

She corrects herself.

Not quite on her own. Because from the beginning, Nanna was there too.

'We've been doing the conga,' Baxter says.

A smile comes to the woman's face and the door opens wider.

'Have you, indeed?' she says.

Recovering herself, Christie seizes the opportunity. Still slightly breathless from dancing through the streets, she speaks rapidly and in a voice low enough that prying neighbours can't hear.

'We're here, Mrs Bird, because we've got nowhere else to go.'

It all comes tumbling out of her; she blurts out everything – or at least as much as she can in front of the children.

'All we've got in the world is five shillings and ...'

She isn't sure how much of what she's saying is being heard, being understood by the small grey-haired woman in her apron and carpet slippers clinging to the doorframe, leaning in to it for support, gripping hard.

Christie can see her eyes, clouded with questions, going slowly from Christie to the baby, to Megan and then to Baxter.

Finally, letting go of the doorframe, she reaches out and – with the lightest trembling touch of her fingertips – gently brushes first Megan's cheek and then Baxter's.

As if to be sure they are real.

Without a word she turns, leaving the door open in invitation. Christie follows her through the dark hallway, seeing immediately its worn shabbiness, feeling at once that it's all impossible.

They can't stay here, it isn't fair; the place is too small and this woman obviously has little enough to keep herself. How can they ask her to take four strangers in?

In the kitchen Truman's mother sits them at the blue Formica-topped table and wordlessly sets about cooking a meal – beans on toast with bacon, washed down with Robinson's Barley Water. Megan and Baxter eat hungrily in wide-eyed silence while she stands with her back to the stove and watches. From time to time she gives a small disbelieving shake of her head and a tense smile of encouragement to the children.

Afterwards she hurries through to the spare room and makes up the bed as Christie changes and feeds the baby. It's only when she is busily tucking the children in that finally she speaks. She bends and kisses them on the forehead, in turn, tentatively.

'What shall we call you?' Megan says, her voice tired and small.

'What would you like to call me, dear?' she says.

'Nanna,' Baxter says sleepily.

'Nanna Bird,' Megan corrects him.

It is later, at the kitchen table as they sit talking through much of that first night, that Christie tells Nanna the whole story.

And there is anger; alternating from one to the other.

There are shared tears.

And there are hugs, the like of which Christie has never felt before.

50

10

Truman

Rosetta Paulizky's office

Truman eases his feet from the desk, stands slowly upright, stretches, yawns loudly and ambles across to the tall sash window.

The ivy-clad Georgian elegance of the Fielding Johnson Building, where the administrative offices are housed, is in striking contrast to the towering glass-and-brick modernity of the rest of the university. It's as if what speaks of permanence and power has been reserved for those who run the university, whilst what is brash and new has been given over to the students.

Dr Paulizky's office is on the first floor, facing a narrow road that leads to the heart of the campus. Below, as Truman looks down, a boy with lank shoulder-length hair and a wispy beard walks by, his arm around the shoulders of a tall blonde girl in a long Afghan coat. As Truman watches, the boy suddenly breaks free and springs playfully away. The girl chases him for a few steps before he comes back to her and puts his arms around her waist. For a moment, under the grey October sky, they sway together like lovers on a dance floor.

Truman shakes his head.

So this is university, is it? This is what it's like. Not exactly breaking sweat, are they? Don't exactly walk around with their noses buried in their books. It looks more like a holiday camp, an excuse for putting off having to work for a living for as long as you can. That and the chance to get your leg over at every opportunity.

As the couple walk away, hand in hand now, Truman doesn't know whether to resent or envy them.

Watching as they turn the corner, it occurs to Truman that Christie didn't show him a photograph of Baxter; he doesn't know what the boy looks like.

Truman walks across to the desk, settles back into the chair. It's too late now but he should have asked. He's missed a trick there: Christie would have liked that, showing off her photographs of her precious boy.

When the door to his mother's flat opens and Christie appears, he stands there like some kind of idiot, with his arms still wide, a lunatic grin frozen on his face and his brain bouncing like a needle stuck in a deep scratch across a record.

He can't make sense of it.

Christie?

It's as if he's been going along a certain groove, confident of what's coming next, and then somehow that groove is no longer there to follow, somehow he's hit a wall he hasn't even seen and for a long moment he can't get past it.

Christie?

Just seeing her out of the blue like that after ten years is a shock in itself, of course. But it isn't that.

You see, he can't work out what the hell she's doing there, in his mother's doorway; the point is she's no *right* to be there.

Before everything came to an end, she didn't even know his old mum existed; he made sure of that. His mum didn't know about Christie and the kids; they didn't know about her. They didn't need to, did they? It was best that way.

And yet here she is, breezing out of his mother's flat like she owns the bloody place.

'Hello, princess,' he finally manages to say.

She doesn't say anything. She just reaches for the door and starts to close it. Close it in his face.

'Wait!' he says.

She pauses. Can't help herself, can she? The same old Christie, deep down she's still soft on him. Hasn't changed a bit.

'I need to talk to you,' he says.

She shakes her head. Reaches for the door again.

'No!' he says. 'Please?'

Again she pauses.

Just get her talking, that's the trick. Get her talking and she'll come round. Just like always. She needs time; that's all. It's understandable. Him just turning up like this.

'We've got to talk, princess,' he says.

Again she shakes her head. Only this time he sees the determination in her eyes. The door is closing. If it shuts completely, there will be no way back.

And that's when he comes out with it.

It's the one thing that's sure to stop her and it pops into his head from nowhere, almost without him thinking. He's always been like that, knowing the right words, *finding* the right words; quick on his feet, quick with a story.

'Christie?' he says.

The sound of her name stops her, just for a second.

'Christie, let me say one thing.'

She looks up at him with her big eyes, holding the door open just a crack. She hasn't lost it, he thinks; ten years on but still a looker.

He speaks softly.

'Christie,' he says. 'I've just come back to say ... to say goodbye.'

She opens the door a little more.

'Goodbye?' she says.

Bingo! He's got her talking.

'The doctors ...' he says.

'Doctors?' Christie says.

He nods. The door opens wider.

'They say it's just a matter of months,' he says, putting his hand to his chest, tapping at his heart.

And that's enough.

She can't resist that.

11

Christie

The Planning Department

The telephone rings again. Once more Christie ignores it. How *could* she have let him in? After all, she'd vowed to herself a hundred times, a thousand times, that if he ever showed his face she would slam the door on it. Without a word.

Why *didn't* she just do that?

She's tempted to blame it on the shock. She hadn't even heard anyone knocking, she was so preoccupied, going round the flat, trying to think of all the things Nanna would need in hospital. Dressing gown. Nighties. Slippers. Flannel. Toothbrush. Hairbrush. Toilet bag.

She was still going over the list in her head when she opened the door. And he was standing there. With that lop-sided smile of his and his arms thrown wide.

It *was* a shock. Such a shock that she took a step backwards and her hand went to her mouth.

Then, of course, once she got over that, he just came out with it, said what he'd come to say.

And that was a shock too. Despite the fact that it shouldn't matter to her. Not now.

But even that doesn't account for it, not entirely. It doesn't explain why she invited him in, made him a cup of tea, talked with him like that.

It certainly isn't that she has forgiven him. She will never, *can* never, forgive him for what he did. All the cheating, all the lies; leaving them penniless. And it most certainly isn't that she still feels anything for him.

She shudders.

The telephone continues to ring. Gradually a voice finds its way into Christie's thoughts.

'The thing is, Christie . . .' the man is saying.

She looks up.

'Sorry, Ray?' she says.

'The thing is, this strange-looking grey object on your desk is something called a tel-e-phone . . . a *tel-e-phone*. And sometimes it rings. Which is not surprising really, it being a *tel-e-phone*. And when it does, you're meant to pick it up by this handle thing here.'

He's talking loudly, not just for her but for the whole office to hear.

'I know, Ray. Sorry.'

'I know it's the most terrible inconvenience. But, what with you being the office receptionist and administrator, that's your job. To answer the *tel-e-phone*,' he says.

From behind the filing cabinets, she hears muffled laughter.

'I know,' she says quietly.

He leans over the desk. She can smell his aftershave, feel his breath. He's too close; people will notice. Any closer and

56

his drooping moustache and long sideburns will tickle her cheek.

'Sorry, I'm miles away this morning,' she says.

'Are you OK?' he whispers.

'Yes, I'm fine,' she says.

'Well, consider yourself thoroughly bollocked,' he says with a smile and an exaggerated wink.

'Drink, later?' he says.

'Perhaps,' Christie says.

'So remember,' he says, raising his voice again. 'If it rings ...'

'Pick it up,' she says obligingly.

As he walks away, Christie pulls the key-and-lamp unit and the handset of the telephone closer to her and tries to clear her head, to concentrate, to stop herself tumbling straight back into her thoughts.

But what makes it worse is that she talked about the children.

She doesn't want him anywhere near them. They've done just fine without him blighting their lives. Better than fine.

Perhaps she'd had no choice but to tell him about Nanna; she is his mother, after all. And it *was* right to take him to the hospital to visit her. Despite everything, Nanna would have wanted that.

And she *did* have to tell him about Megan. Or at least some of it.

But she shouldn't have told him about herself and she most certainly shouldn't have said anything about the boys.

Not that she thinks for a moment that he'll try to contact them. At least there's nothing to worry about on that score.

He was never interested in them before, he wasn't suddenly going to start to be now.

No, the boys will never need to know that their father has reappeared. And that's a relief. At least she won't have to go back on what she and Nanna told them all those years ago.

Her flesh creeps at the memory.

Anyway, Harry, poor scrap, is in Brighton with her mother – recovering from having his tonsils out – and Truman certainly won't go there. Even Harry isn't too keen, and he's always been her mother's favourite.

As for Baxter, he's safely miles away at university.

Safely? She's been so worried, she's hardly slept.

Just weeks before there had been more terrible IRA bombings in London – this time at the very stations Baxter had to go through on his way to Leicester. She'd kept close to a radio the day he left, nerves jangling, listening to every news item, convinced it would happen again. She'd been worried too about his journey to a city he didn't know; apart from to school, he'd never travelled anywhere on his own before. She'd worried about the trains, whether they would run at all with the railway workers always out on strike; about how he would find his way; what his room would be like; whether he'd make friends. About everything.

But her boy: up at university!

She's so proud.

Just think: she had to leave school at fourteen – *fourteen!* – and yet here's her boy at college. It's been her dream for so long that he'd get there; it's what she's imagined for him all along. He worked so hard, crouched sighing over his books at the kitchen table doing his homework, his revision, hour after hour, day after day.

She worked so hard to make it possible. Year after year.

From the start, there was never any money. She'd gone without so that he could have his books, his uniform. Gone without things that didn't matter – new clothes, shoes, make-up – and without meals too sometimes, pretending she'd eaten at lunchtime, to keep a few more shillings by.

'OK, Nanna?' Christie says, coming through the door, dropping her handbag to the floor, dropping to her knees to hug Megan quietly in one arm and Baxter noisily in the other.

It's dark already outside; cold. She hates this time of year: going to work before sunrise, coming home after sunset.

'Have you eaten?' Nanna says, looking up, smiling, bouncing the baby on her lap.

'Had something at lunchtime,' Christie says, admiring the drawing of a horse that Megan is showing her, listening to Baxter's quickfire account of his school day.

'Are you sure?' Nanna says, suspicion in her voice.

'Sure,' Christie says, taking her coat off, straightening Megan's ponytail, picking up her handbag again.

'Shall we?' she says.

'Best get it over with,' Nanna says grimly, hauling herself from her chair, handing the baby to Megan.

It's Thursday: pay day and pension day. Christie takes a small brown wages envelope from her handbag, tears it open. She's working as a filing clerk, going to night school to learn to type, to try to get a better-paid job.

'Four pounds,' she says, putting the money on the table, pulling out a chair.

Nanna reaches into the pocket of her apron for the pension money she queued for at the post office this morning.

'Three pounds, seven shillings and sixpence,' she says, handing it to Christie.

Christie takes the money, holds Nanna's hand.

'You sure?' she says.

Nanna laughs.

'You said the same thing last week,' she says. 'And what did I say in return?'

Christie smiles.

'That it all goes in the pot.'

'That's right,' Nanna says.

'Oh, almost forgot.' Christie takes her purse from her handbag. 'Family allowance.'

She adds the one pound and six shillings to the pile.

They sit at the table together and Christie reaches for a small notebook. Every penny they spend is recorded here, every penny they save. Quickly she separates the money into smaller piles – for rent, for food, for the electricity meter. She knows the price of everything; she *has* to know. It's the only way they can budget to survive through the week.

When she is done, a small heap of coins remains unallocated.

'Not much is it?' she says, biting her lip.

'We'll manage,' Nanna says, reaching for Christie's hand, giving it a squeeze of reassurance. 'We always do.'

Christie scoops up the coins and hands them to Baxter. It's his turn to drop them into the old glass vase that sits on top of the fridge like an accusation. There's never enough for what they need. The children have to wait for new clothes, new shoes, treats, sweets. Christie and Nanna wait longer.

But it was worth it, Christie thinks, putting her elbows on her desk, staring at the now-quiet telephone.

Every last exhausting minute of it was worth it.

She raised him on her own (she's only recently found out that they now have a name for her, for them. She is a single parent, they are a single-parent family); *she* did it – with Nanna's help, of course. And now he's up in Leicester, rubbing shoulders with the sons and daughters of solicitors and bank managers.

Her boy, her wonderful boy.

Perhaps he'll ring later and tell her how his first day of lectures is going. Or perhaps she'll try to get a message to him about Nanna and the hospital?

12

Baxter

The Attenborough Tower basement

When Baxter finally stops laughing, stops rocking in his chair, slapping at the table, Dr Paulizky leans forwards, a frown creasing her forehead.

'Baxter ...' she says. 'May I call you Baxter?'

He nods, still smiling. She can call him what the hell she likes as long as she lets him out of there. She can call him Iggy Pop or Ziggy Stardust or Richard Milhous Nixon; she can call him Monty frigging Python, for all he cares.

'Baxter, I don't pretend for a minute to understand what's going on here,' she says. 'I don't understand any of it—'

'It's simple,' Baxter interrupts cheerfully. 'There's been a mistake, that's all. It's no big deal. My father's dead and—'

'No, Baxter,' she says.

He sits back in his chair and gives a small, irritated shake of the head. Why isn't she listening to him? Does she think he's stupid or something?

'I can assure you, Dr—' he starts to say.

She raises both hands to stop him.

'No, Baxter. I can assure *you* that if your father is Truman Bird, then he's very much alive and at this moment sitting in my office.'

'No—' Baxter says.

'Yes,' she insists.

She stops, suddenly flustered again.

'Of course, when I say very much alive …' she says. 'Oh dear. What I mean is that he's very much alive *now*. Because, with the news from the doctors …'

She talks on. But Baxter is no longer listening.

'NO!'

He's awake now. He can see the light coming through the window of the flat. Can hear Megan's breathing at the other end of the bed.

He's awake. But he knows *he* is still there. Somewhere in the room. Waiting.

'NO!' he screams again.

He'd been dragged by the arm through long grass.

'I'm only eight,' he told him, pleaded, begged.

He was thrown into the back of a car. The car became a house. Empty. Echoing. He walked through a door and into a forest; running, falling. Rain plastered his hair, his shirt shivering to his back. His father limped after him. Chasing. There was lightning. Thunder. His father limped away. He had a suitcase in his hand.

But he's here. Now. In the room.

Under the bed?

Megan is awake: shouting.

'Mummy!'

63

And then she's there, his mother. Holding. Holding him. Until it all goes away.

Dr Paulizky's voice gradually comes back to him.

'Baxter?'

She holds out her hand towards him once more; he lets it lie there, open on the table.

'I think we should go to him now, don't you?' she says.

His head bowed, Baxter walks self-consciously beside Dr Paulizky. They leave the subterranean lecture theatre beneath the Attenborough Tower behind and make their way the few hundred yards across the university campus to her office. As they walk, and then as they climb the wide mahogany staircase and follow a dimly lit corridor, Baxter's thoughts are gradually reduced to one.

His father, back from the dead?

No way.

It makes no sense. He can't accept it, can't believe it, can't absorb it.

Dr Paulizky hesitates outside the panelled door of her office. She turns to Baxter.

'Ready?' she says.

Baxter feels the thump of his heart; he hears it somehow too inside his head. It's all a mistake, he tells himself again.

He nods.

Rosetta Paulizky reaches for the handle and pushes the door open.

It takes a moment for Baxter's eyes to adjust to the sudden

brightness that floods through the tall windows and into the office. When finally they do, he knows the truth at once.

There is no mistake.

Sitting with his feet on the desk, squinting through the smoke of a cigarette that hangs from his lips, is a man who can be no one else but his father.

It makes no sense.

Baxter remains rooted in the doorway as his father removes the cigarette from his mouth, swings his feet from the desk and hauls himself upright.

'Hello, sport,' he says, with a lopsided smile and an outstretched hand.

To Baxter, he somehow looks bigger and smaller at the same time. Bigger because he's heavier than he remembers, carrying extra pounds. Smaller because Baxter no longer has to look up at him as he did when he was eight years old. In his platform boots, he now stands inches taller.

Baxter ignores the outstretched hand. When he speaks, he says the only words that are in his head.

'I thought you were dead,' he says.

It sounds like an accusation. *Why didn't you stay dead?*

His father looks at him quizzically, raises an eyebrow.

'Not quite yet, sport,' he says, tapping at his heart. 'Not quite yet.'

Baxter shakes his head; still trying to take it in.

His father was dead.

And now here he is. Back in the land of the living.

And worse than that.

He's dying.

13

Christie
Lunchtime: The Boulevard, Crawley

As the minutes count slowly down towards lunchtime, Christie knows that the only place she wants to be is beneath Megan's tree.

Gathering her coat and handbag and hurrying from her desk, she tells herself that she needs time alone, time for herself. To fight off her thoughts, her memories.

The early-October afternoon is cool and grey. As Christie waits on the pavement outside the council offices for a gap in the traffic and an opportunity to cross The Boulevard, she knows that few people are likely to venture into the park on such a day. She's glad; she will have it almost to herself.

As she waits, she watches a middle-aged man in a raincoat and a trilby hurry across to help a young mother struggling with both a child in a pushchair and an unfeasibly large parcel, wrapped in brown paper and string.

The kindness of strangers, Christie smiles. It's what has kept her here all these years.

In that first moment, when she and the children stepped off the bus that had scooped them from the forest, Christie decided that she hated this town. As she fought to shuffle and drag the suitcase along the pavement, she wanted to be anywhere but here. Ridiculously, she even considered taking the first bus back to where they'd come from, to the caravan in the clearing in the woods.

But then those four strangers came by and led her dancing to the door of Nanna Bird's flat. To the same door that Truman appeared at ten years later.

In a daze, Christie leads him through to the kitchen. Once there, he looks around the room with a proprietorial smile and runs his hand over the pale blue Formica of the tabletop, greeting it like an old friend.

There's an unread copy of the *Daily Express* on the table; he picks it up, glances at the headlines and tosses it untidily back. He goes to the sideboard and picks up a framed photograph of Megan.

Christie wants to cry out.

She wants to shout at him to leave the photograph alone, to put it back where Nanna positions it so precisely, looking towards where she always sits at the table.

He doesn't know, of course, but putting his hands on it, smearing his careless fingerprints on the silver frame and the polished glass, is a violation.

But he doesn't know; he can't know.

So instead of shouting, Christie does the only thing she can think of doing – she goes to the sink to fill the kettle.

'What I don't get,' he says, holding the photograph as if

67

any minute it will slip from his fingers, 'what I don't understand, princess, is how come you're here?'

As Christie turns to face him, she feels a wave of anger break inside.

It's the way he's juggling the photograph. It's the fact that he's in Nanna's room, treating it as if he belongs there and she doesn't. It's the way he's talking to her, his old familiarity, as if the intervening ten years haven't happened, as if he's popped to the corner shop for cigarettes and has come back and picked up the conversation where he left off.

She fights back the anger, breathes deeply. He's told her he's ill, he's dying. It's all too long ago anyway. There's no point in going into any of it: the lies, the cheating, the hurt. Not now.

'I'm here because of Nanna Bird,' she simply says.

'*Nanna* Bird?' he says with a small mocking laugh.

Christie feels another sharp spike of anger. He always did ridicule her, he always had to spoil everything.

Again she swallows the anger back.

Carrying mugs of tea to the table, she changes the subject. She asks him about his life, where he's been living. In Margate, he says, on his Jack Jones, alone and lonesome. She asks him about his work. He's got own business, he says, import-export, it's doing well.

She closes her eyes, bites her tongue. He's been doing well and she's spent years struggling to put food on the table for his children. He could have found them, helped them.

She asks him about his illness. He brushes the question aside.

'Never mind about me, princess,' he says stoically. 'Tell me about you. About the kids. Tell me how you're here.'

Finally Christie relents. She tells him how Nanna loved the children from the start.

'She bloody would,' Truman says with a small laugh. 'Always nagging at me for grandchildren, she was.'

Again Christie bites her tongue, resists the temptation to say something on Nanna's behalf. She ploughs on: they stayed with Nanna until three years ago, when finally Christie was earning just enough to afford the rent on a place of their own, not far away, in Pound Hill.

In the tiny two-bedroomed flat, Nanna slept on the sofa. At first, Christie and the baby had one bedroom, Megan and Baxter the other. Later, when the baby was older, he moved in with Baxter and she and Megan shared. They lived like that for six years and Nanna Bird never grumbled. Not once.

'Where is the old bird?' Truman says. 'Be back soon, will she?'

'No, Truman,' Christie says. 'Not soon.'

For years, every Tuesday and Thursday lunchtime, Christie and Nanna had met at a small, noisy, neon-lit café in the Martletts where the windows always steam whatever the weather outside. The tables are rickety on their chrome legs and the chairs are cushionless and uncomfortable but Edie behind the counter is friendly, the tea is good and the sandwiches are freshly made.

Nanna Bird loved it there and could always be relied upon to be sitting at their table in the window when Christie came through the door.

Last Thursday, just as Christie was leaving the office, the

telephone rang and delayed her. She was a few minutes late arriving at the café.

Christie already has her apologies and a smile prepared as she runs the last few yards and pushes at the door.

But there is no smile from Nanna to greet her at their table.

'She's not here, love,' Edie calls across, with a questioning shrug of her shoulders. 'She hasn't been in today.'

Christie knows at once that something is wrong.

Nanna Bird is so reliable. If she says she's going to be somewhere, she is; on time and waiting. It's a matter of pride. It has always seemed to Christie so unlikely that Nanna could have raised a son as completely *un*reliable as Truman.

Running up the stairs towards the drab walkway outside the terrace of flats, a memory of the day she first knocked on the bottle-green door comes to Christie's mind. Then she arrived with a mixture of hope and trepidation. Now she feels nothing but fear.

She turns her key in the lock and calls out.

'Nanna?'

There is no reply. Christie's heart races.

'Nanna?' she calls again as she pushes open the kitchen door.

It's then that she finds her.

Not sitting in her place at the table with the newspaper spread; but in an untidy twisted heap on the lino by the sink. She is still in her nightclothes.

'No!' Christie says, falling to her knees beside her.

*

70

The tall oak with the broken branch has always been Megan's tree. The bench beneath it is where she and Christie would sit together for fifty precious minutes every Friday lunchtime during the school holidays.

Megan would make sandwiches at the flat, wrapping them carefully in the white linen napkins from the bottom drawer of the sideboard and carrying them in Nanna Bird's wicker shopping basket to the park. Christie meanwhile would hurry from her desk at the town hall at exactly one o'clock, and run across The Boulevard to join her five minutes later.

Megan always had to be there first though; it was part of the ritual. One time something delayed her and Christie – seeing the empty bench, her heart gripped with a mother's sudden terror for a missing child – waited in a shop entrance across the road until Megan appeared. Only when Megan had sat down where she always sat and arranged the wicker basket on the bench as she always arranged it did Christie emerge with the smile on her face she reserved exclusively for her daughter.

Once Christie started work, it took only a few weeks for these small rituals to become established. And then for the following six years they never varied. Even in the rain they would sit there, huddled close under an umbrella, pressed so tight they were joined at shoulder, elbow, hip and knee.

Such rituals were important to Megan. They were the fixed points in her life in which she found certainty, from which she drew strength.

Only the sandwiches changed over the years. To begin with they were the clumsy efforts of ten-year-old fingers – imprecise, flattened and punctuated with crumbling buttery holes. By the end they were perfect crustless triangles. They were always cheese and tomato though; even though Christie gently teased her, once she had begun with cheese and tomato, Megan would allow nothing else.

For six years they sat on this same bench under the tree.

Afterwards – long afterwards – when she could finally bring herself to, when she was strong enough to go there without everything falling apart, Christie committed to another ritual.

Whenever she could, she would come alone to the bench beneath the tree. Just to be with Megan. To be close, to shut her eyes and hear her voice and feel again the press of her.

Megan is sitting in the armchair, pressed into the small gap beside Nanna. Christie is listening from the kitchen. They've been at Nanna's for only a few weeks and Megan hasn't settled. She asks about her daddy. Constantly. When is he coming? When?

Nanna is trying to distract her with a story.

She's telling about a long-ago September morning when she was a girl and went brambling with her father. They are on a quiet sunny country lane and her fingers are purpled with the berries; more have found their way into her mouth than her basket.

Bees buzz low in the hedgerow, blackbirds hop busily along the verges, white butterflies dance, and Nanna carries on dreamily picking and eating until she hears her father's voice.

'Well, blow me!' he suddenly says.

She thinks she's in trouble for eating all the blackberries

and for the tell-tale stains around her mouth and on her blue pinafore dress.

She looks up and sees he's scratching his head beneath his flat cap with one hand and pointing to something behind her with the other. At first she doesn't understand.

'Look, girl!' he says. 'Look behind you!'

Slowly she turns, her mouth still working on the last of the sweetest, juiciest berry. Her jaw falls open.

Nanna nudges Megan next to her.

'And what do you think I saw?' she says.

Megan doesn't answer.

'What do you think was coming down the lane towards me?' Nanna says, trying again.

Again Megan doesn't reply.

'An elephant!' Nanna exclaims. 'The biggest elephant you ever did see!'

Megan is still silent.

'In the middle of Surrey,' Nanna says, 'an elephant! With big flappy elephant ears and the longest trunk!'

He is being led by his keeper on his way back to a circus that has set up in the next village. He is out for his morning constitutional.

'What do you think of that?' Nanna says, nudging Megan again. 'What do you think of that, Little Miss Megan?'

It's what she calls her.

Megan finally looks up at her.

'You were with your daddy?' she says, her voice small.

Sitting now beneath Megan's tree, Christie pulls her coat tightly about her and plunges her hands deep into the pockets.

73

The park is empty but for a solitary boy teaching himself to juggle. Tall and bony-thin with long fair hair, he has something of the look of Baxter, Christie thinks. He dresses like him too; or rather he is dressed as Baxter was on the day he left for university.

It was quite a shock. Nanna Bird had given him money for his birthday and he took himself to the High Street market to buy clothes. He left looking like a schoolboy and came back every inch the student in his platform-soled boots, wide-flared loon pants, collarless grandad shirt and army-surplus great coat. He stood self-consciously while she and Nanna Bird fussed around.

It is only after Christie has been watching the boy for some minutes that she recognises him from the supermarket on the corner. There he stacks shelves with the cares of the world etched into his face. Now, though, as the balls fly from hand to hand, as they arc through the air and dip and spin, he is utterly alive. He dazzles. He shines.

He is the only thing in the park that does.

Autumn has come early and the leaves are already clinging to the trees in their washed-out colours. Tired yellows, dull browns, faded reds.

Megan would have loved it. Christie has always longed for spring, but Megan liked autumn best.

Christie takes her hand from her pocket and slowly strokes the bench beside her. Where her daughter always sat.

'It was because of me,' Megan says.

Christie is at the sink, washing up. It is a late Sunday afternoon and Nanna has taken Baxter to the park.

74

Winter sunlight is streaming drowsily through the window of the flat, the surprising warmth making Christie dreamy.

'What was?' she answers distractedly.

'It was because of me that Daddy went.'

Christie turns, sees the tears in Megan's eyes.

'It was, wasn't it?' Megan says.

She has asked about her father every day. But not like this. Never before.

Peeling the rubber gloves from her hands, Christie drops to her knees and pulls Megan to her.

'No,' she says, rocking her. 'Why ever would you think such a thing?'

'Because he said.'

Christie doesn't understand.

'When?'

'He said in the forest.'

'Said what?'

'He pointed and said.'

'Pointed?'

'And he shouted.'

'Shouted what?' Christie says, desperately trying to make sense of it, holding Megan close.

'That I'd pay.'

Christie remembers, remembers the forest. When the storm came, Truman wanted to go into the caravan. Megan stood in his way. 'You'll pay for this!' he shouted, pointing. Not at Megan but at her, at Christie.

'No—' she says.

'That because of me we'd all pay,' Megan says.

'But he didn't mean—'

Megan isn't listening, can't hear.

'I'm sorry, Mummy,' Megan sobs. 'I'm so sorry.'

'But it wasn't you, my beautiful girl,' Christie says, over and over. 'It wasn't you ...'

Christie doesn't hear the voice calling to her across the park at first. When finally she looks up, the juggling boy has gone and striding towards her along the path is Ray.

She has never been able to finally settle on what she feels about Ray. But at this moment she is absolutely sure. She doesn't want him there. In her park. In her thoughts.

'Thought we were going for a drink?' he says as he comes near.

And then – before she has a chance to say anything – he sits down.

In Megan's place.

14

Abby

University of Leicester campus

As soon as the morning comes to an end, Abby goes clopping noisily down the steps of the lecture theatre in her platform boots and manages to be first out through the door.

'Need the loo,' she whispers urgently to Georgie.

She runs along the corridor, pushes open the door and, watching herself disgustedly in the mirror, plucks the stars from her temple one by one. She then slips the silver rings from her fingers and into her Biba bag. The black nail varnish will have to wait until later.

She feels better immediately.

She has to stop trying so hard, she tells herself; and she has to leave this new-persona nonsense behind. It confuses her, doesn't suit her. Instead, she will just get her head down and work hard. It'll be better that way. She will be who she's always been: the quiet one, the serious one.

Georgie is waiting for her on the steps outside the Attenborough Tower. They are going to the Union café to swap gossip and notes from their first morning of lectures.

'You've lost your stars,' Georgie says as Abby emerges through the swinging glass doors at the foot of the tower.

Abby shakes her head. She'd hoped her friend wouldn't notice, or at least wouldn't say anything.

'Ridiculous, they were,' she says.

Georgie laughs.

'Oh, say that again!'

'What?' Abby says, confused.

'"Ridickerless, they were." Say that!'

Abby blushes.

'You're teasing me,' she says. 'You're taking the mickey. About my accent.'

'No!' Georgie says. 'I love the way you speak. I'm so jealous.'

Abby hesitates.

'Oh, come on, Abby,' Georgie says. 'Don't take it wrong. It's just that when you live your whole life in sodding Surrey, you long to be from somewhere else. Somewhere real. You're so lucky.'

Lucky?

Abby has never felt lucky about where she comes from. Living in the long shadows of the slagheaps of a pit that once employed five hundred men but has stood idle for decades, she isn't sure anyone in Pontlottyn does. And Georgie, with her big house and her private school, she *isn't* lucky?

Georgie looks at her pleadingly and Abby responds with a small forgiving smile.

They turn together to walk towards the Student Union building. They take only a few steps before Georgie grabs Abby by the arm and points.

'Look,' she says. 'It's that boy.'

For a moment Abby isn't sure who Georgie is talking about.

'The one who had to leave,' Georgie explains. 'Something *distressing*, the professor said.'

Across the campus a tall fair-haired boy is walking gloomily beside a man in a slightly crumpled suit.

'They don't look very happy, do they?' Georgie says. 'Whatever do you think has happened?'

Abby shakes her head uninterestedly. She doesn't know the boy; she'd forgotten about him having to shuffle out of the lecture theatre and she wouldn't have recognised him again.

'It sounded serious, didn't it?' Georgie says. 'Do you think he's going to have to leave the course?'

'I don't know,' Abby says.

'Only it would be such a pity,' Georgie says.

'Why's that?' Abby says, her curiosity aroused.

'Because ...' Georgie says archly.

'Because what?'

'Because I do believe he was staring longingly in my direction just before he had to leave,' Georgie says delightedly.

'And ...?' Abby says.

'And because I could quite go for him too.'

'Georgie!' Abby says, pretending to be scandalised.

Abby looks up and focuses on the boy for the first time. With his head shame-facedly bowed and his shoulders slumped, it's difficult to see why he holds any interest for her friend.

The man and the boy walk on. Georgie takes Abby enthusiastically by the arm and they set off again.

'Anyway, I *do* think it's a shame,' Georgie says.

'About what?' Abby says.

'About the stars.'

'Hmm,' Abby says, suspiciously.

'No, I liked them,' Georgie says. 'I thought they made you look like Carly Simon.'

'Really?' Abby says.

'Really.'

It's an irresistible cue. They nod, one to the other, and walking arm in arm they begin to sing.

'*You're so vain, you probably think this song is about you . . .*'

15

Baxter

University of Leicester campus

Baxter walks on, his hands plunged deep into the pockets of his greatcoat. It has been the weirdest frigging morning and it's getting weirder still. It was meant to be the first day of his new life. Instead he's ended up with a dead man – a dead man walking, a dead man dying – and now he's on his way with him to a pub.

Going for a drink with a frigging zombie.

Unreal or what?

And he's got nothing to say to him, this man who is his father. Nothing. In Dr Paulizky's office they just stood there looking at each other like two punched-out boxers, trying to work out what the hell to do next. In the end, his father sat down, lit a cigarette and launched into a mind-numbing story about imports and exports. Not that Baxter was listening. Not that he needed to listen. Because the story wasn't being told to him. The story was for Rosetta Paulizky and she kept giggling like a teenager and turning to Baxter to try to involve him. Because she thought she should.

In the end, his father announced he needed a drink and the next minute they were out of Dr Paulizky's office and trudging across the campus. Where everyone could see them.

Baxter and his zombie father.

The sound of voices singing somewhere in the distance makes Baxter look up. He immediately wishes he hadn't.

♫ You're so vain, you probably think this song is
about you ...

It's Abby and her friend and they are walking arm in arm and singing at the tops of their voices as if they want him to hear, want him to look up and at them. Have they seen him? Are they singing *for* him?

No. Why would they sing for a sorry loser like him?

Baxter hunches smaller, as if by doing so he'll somehow make himself invisible.

Leaving the office, Baxter's father had held the door open and with a courtly flourish tried to usher Rosetta Paulizky through.

'Come on, Rosie,' he says. 'Come and have a quick one with us.'

It's *Rosetta*, Baxter thinks irritably, wanting to correct him. Her frigging name is *Rosetta*.

She raises her hands in modest protest.

'Oh no, Mr Bird,' she says. 'I think you and Baxter need time alone, don't you? You must have so much to talk about.'

His father looks at Baxter and shrugs.

'OK,' he says. 'Maybe you're right. See you later then?'

'Perhaps, Mr Bird,' Dr Paulizky says.

When they are almost through the door, Truman turns and leans close to her.

'I just wanted to say thanks, Rosie,' he says. 'Thanks for talking to Baxter for me.'

'You are most welcome, Mr Bird,' she says, touching his arm reassuringly.

'Only, I thought it would come so much better from you,' he says.

She looks at him quizzically.

'What with you being a doctor,' he says, tapping at his heart.

She gives a short, nervous laugh.

'Oh, Mr Bird,' she says, flustered again. 'I understand now why you were so determined that *I* should do it. But I'm afraid you've made a mistake. I'm not that kind of doctor.'

Truman stops. Shakes his head.

'What other kind of doctor is there?' he says.

'I'm a doctor of philosophy. It just means I've got a PhD.'

'A what?' Truman says.

And at that Baxter cringes, looks away. Embarrassed that this man should be anything to do with him.

It takes some time to get to The Old Horse on London Road. They have to make a detour on the way. To Baxter's bank. Where his grant cheque was deposited just last week.

'I'm really sorry about this, sport,' Truman says, patting at his jacket pockets for his wallet. 'I must have left it in Rosie's office. I'll pop back for it a bit later.'

'I'll forget my own head next,' he says, tapping at his heart, as if that is to blame.

Baxter has budgeted carefully. He knows he has fifteen pounds a week to survive on until Christmas and from that he has to buy his books, food, everything else he needs.

'Get thirty out for me, son,' Truman says. 'I'll pay you back later. And I'll give you a few quid extra to help you out.'

Despite that promise, Baxter hands the thirty pounds over with a shrinking heart. The grant is all the money he has and he knows that when it's gone there can be no more. His mother and Nanna Bird won't be able to help. It's difficult to part with.

Truman goes through the door of The Old Horse rubbing his hands in anticipation. The low-beamed room is welcoming: a log fire burns in the grate, the walls are decked with cheerful prints of hunting scenes and with horse brasses burnished until they gleam. At the bar, Truman strikes up an immediate conversation with two of the lunchtime regulars. One is a cadaverous, glassy-eyed salesman in a shiny blue suit, the other a retired butcher in a brass-buttoned blazer, sweating and florid-faced. Within minutes they are trading jokes and Truman has bought a round of drinks and a packet of cigarettes. Cheered on by them, he downs his pint in one and buys himself another.

Baxter does the sums. Eighty-six pence gone already.

'I was ready for that,' Truman says, wiping his mouth with the back of his hand.

'Who's this then?' the butcher asks, nodding towards Baxter.

Truman wearily raises his eyebrows, as if he's been asked the question a hundred times before.

'My boy,' he says resignedly. 'One of those long-haired layabout students, I'm afraid.'

The salesman and the butcher exchange glances.

'That's all we get around here. Bloody students,' the salesman says.

'The country's going to the dogs,' the butcher says. 'Everyone on strike all the time. Bloody football hooligans. Bloody students and coloureds.'

'Coloureds?' Truman says.

'Ugandan Asians,' the butcher says. 'Thousands of them.'

'Same bloody everywhere now,' Truman says, shaking his head. 'The country's full of them.'

Baxter cringes again. It turns out that he's got Enoch Powell – or even Alf frigging Garnett – for a father. But he chooses not to react, not to say anything. Instead he sips cautiously at his beer. He wants to keep a clear head and he's aware that alcohol is still new to him; he doesn't trust it. Before Freshers' Week, he could count on the fingers of one hand the number of times he'd held a pint glass.

As Baxter sips, he says a silent thank-you to the butcher and the salesman. Whatever planet these weirdos have landed from, he's glad he doesn't have to be alone with his father. As they'd walked together to the pub, he'd been dreading the silence he knew would quickly settle between them. Once his father had dispensed with the obvious questions – about his course, where he was living – there would be nothing else to say.

'Have you heard this one?' his father is saying. 'There's this Englishman, an Irishman and a Scotsman . . . '

Now, in the company of these strangers, Baxter can at least spend some time trying to get his head around what he feels about his father's Lazarus act, his miraculous rising from the mouldering dead.

Not that it will take long.

Because beyond a prickling embarrassment at every moment he has to spend in his company; beyond resentment at the way his father has assumed the role of the long-suffering parent; and beyond irritation that he's suddenly appeared and caused this seismic interruption to his new life, what Baxter feels is nothing.

A big fat zero.

Zilch.

He has no feelings for him. He's not even afraid of him, as he was when he was eight years old. In fact, watching him clown around for the salesman and the butcher, it astonishes Baxter that he was ever afraid of him.

All those nightmares. For this?

And, Baxter realises as he raises his glass and takes a deeper swallow, it's because of this absence of feelings that he has no curiosity about him, no questions for him, nothing to say to him. He doesn't want to know where he's been, what he's been doing, why he hasn't tried to contact him or his brother. He doesn't want to know him at all.

To new shouts of laughter, it's the butcher's turn to tell a story. Baxter doesn't listen.

It's not quite true to say that he has *no* questions, he corrects himself, the last inch of his beer turning warm as he nurses the glass in his hand. On reflection, he does have two. One for his father and one for his mother.

Two simple questions.

From his mother he wants to know what on earth is going on. She and Nanna told him his father was dead. They'd lied to him all those years ago. *Lied*. And they never lie. It's one of the certainties in his life, one of the things he's always been able to depend on.

So why? He doesn't get it.

And the question for his father?

That's even simpler.

All he wants to know is, when is his zombie father going to get the frigging hell out of his life again?

Baxter glances at his watch. It can't come soon enough.

16

Christie

Mid-afternoon:
The Planning Department, Crawley

All afternoon the same half-completed letter has been in Christie's typewriter. On any other day she would have rattled through it in no time. Today she has ripped the paper and carbon copy from her machine twice already as one clumsily hit key has followed another. At one point all the keys leapt up and jammed together; the tips of her fingers are now a faded inky blue from teasing them apart.

She shakes her head.

Why did Truman have to come back?

The October late afternoon had grown gloomy around them as she and Truman sat at the kitchen table talking.

Finally noticing the fast-fading light, Christie looks up at the clock on the wall and tells him they must hurry.

Leaving the flat, they walk briskly to the hospital through streets that have become so familiar to her during the past ten years. It feels strange, disconcerting, now to be walking those same streets with Truman. This is *her* place; he has no right to be here. It's disconcerting too to be side by side again after so long. Christie had forgotten the feel of it; it makes her jittery, ill-at-ease.

Once on the ward, Truman takes up a position at the end of the bed; Christie can't coax him closer. She goes to Nanna's side, kisses her forehead and takes her hand.

'It's only me, Nanna,' she says, reaching across to smooth the hair from her face.

Nanna's eyes are closed, she doesn't move, her breath is shallow and ragged.

'I've brought someone to see you,' Christie says.

At the end of the bed, Truman shifts his weight uncomfortably from one foot to the other.

'I'm no good at this, Christie,' he says. 'Hospitals give me the creeps.'

'Just talk to her,' Christie says encouragingly. 'It might help her, to hear your voice.'

Finally Truman leans forwards, gripping at the metal bar of the bed.

'Hello, princess,' he says. 'It's your boy. Come home.'

Nanna doesn't stir and Christie continues to hold her hand. A short silence settles. It's Truman who breaks it, with a long sigh.

'Christie?' he says.

Still holding Nanna's hand, Christie looks up.

'I'd better make a move,' he says.

She is shocked, momentarily angry. This is his mother lying here. He hasn't seen her for a decade and he can't bring himself to stay for more than two minutes?

'But you've only just got here,' she says.

He taps at his heart.

'It's been a long day,' he says. 'And I don't know where I'm going to sleep tonight.'

She'd forgotten about his illness; she's been thoughtless; she feels a stab of guilt.

'You haven't got anywhere?' she says.

Truman shrugs.

'I'd hoped Mum would put me up.'

Christie lets go of Nanna's hand and picks up her handbag.

'Here, take this,' she says, handing him a key. 'It's a spare to your mother's flat.'

It is what Nanna would want her to do; she's sure of it. However hurt she's been by him, she wouldn't want him to have nowhere to go.

'You could stay a few days and come and see her again over the weekend,' she says.

Truman takes the key from her. He bends towards Christie, as if to kiss her goodbye. She pulls away from him.

'OK,' he says. 'Too soon, I understand.'

Then he turns to his mother.

'Good-night,' he says softly. 'Sleep tight, princess.'

Christie tugs the paper and carbon from the typewriter, screws it into a ball and deposits it in the bin beneath her desk.

Truman didn't return to the hospital over the weekend. She was there day and night and he didn't show his face.

Again she'd been angry and disappointed with him: however ill he is, he could at least have found an hour to spend with his mother.

But again she'd been wrong.

When she called at Nanna's flat on her way back from the park at lunchtime, there was no sign of him or his suitcase. He'd gone.

Once more she'd felt a stab of guilt; she had judged him too quickly. He'd said he'd only come back to say goodbye. He must have stayed just that night and then left in the morning. He'd been true to his word.

Christie can't quite work out why his sudden departure – which should have simplified her feelings – has somehow made them more complicated still. He'd gone; that was the end of it. Before, that was exactly what she wanted: never to see him again. But now she knows that the next time she will hear anything of him will be the last time. One day she will receive word from a stranger that he has died.

'It would be better if he was dead,' Nanna says.

They are sitting at the kitchen table late at night, desperately trying to think their way through. The children are sleeping. Nanna and Christie are wearing their coats: there's no point in wasting money on heating at this time of night.

Christie and the children have been at the flat for a few months. Baxter's nightmares are getting worse: running through tall grass, running and falling, his father chasing. Megan is still asking for her daddy every waking hour. *When is he coming? When?*

Every day is a new battle in a long war: to stretch the

money out, to put food on the table, to find a way to live together in Nanna Bird's cramped, cold, damp council flat.

It's impossible to establish any kind of routine. The children have started at school, but they hate it. They don't yet have the right uniform – Christie can't afford it – and they are being teased relentlessly. Every morning is a fight to get them out of bed and on their way. At home they argue constantly; they've no toys to play with, few books to read. The baby is teething; his wail of discontent that evening had made the children cover their ears and shout.

'It *would* be better,' Nanna says again. 'If he was dead at least there'd be no more nightmares for the boy and no new heartbreak for Megan.'

Christie reaches across the table, pats Nanna's hand. She doesn't want her to get any more upset than she already is.

'But he's not, Nanna, is he?' she says. They have to deal with reality, not wishes.

Nanna looks up. Meets her eye.

'But he *could* be,' she says.

Weeks later it is decided. It's as if a kind of madness has gripped them both, won't let them go. They know it's insane, know it's wrong, but it draws them on. Irresistibly.

It *feels* like an answer – or, at least, part of an answer – but it's more than that. It's intoxicating, seductive. There's excitement in it; it's dangerous, reckless. There's revenge too: they're punishing him for what he's done to them.

'We'll tell them tomorrow,' Nanna says. 'We'll say it was an accident. He was knocked down by a lorry. We'll even have a ceremony to say goodbye.'

By then Christie is no longer capable of argument.

'It will break Megan's heart,' she says.

Nanna nods.

'I know, dear,' she says. 'But her heart's broken already. And it breaks again every time she asks for him.'

Christie takes Nanna's hand in hers.

'Are you sure, Nanna?' she says.

Nanna hesitates.

'I'm as sure as I can be about anything now.'

The following day, Christie calls the children to the kitchen table.

'We've got something to tell you both,' Nanna begins.

Christie sees Baxter smile at the sound of Nanna's voice. He looks up at her and the smile falls away. He can see in her face she's going to say something serious.

It's for Christie to tell them.

'It's about your daddy,' she says.

'Daddy?' Megan says. 'Daddy's coming?'

Her voice is excited, anxious.

Nanna shakes her head.

'We need you both to be very brave,' Christie says.

She knows already that it's a mistake. They should stop. Now.

'Brave?' Megan says, the excitement gone, only anxiety remaining.

'There's been a terrible accident,' Nanna says.

It's too late. They will have to go through with it now.

'A lorry,' Christie says, quickly.

'A lorry?' Megan says.

'Your daddy didn't see it,' Nanna says. 'They took him to hospital but it was no good.'

Christie reaches across, takes one of Megan's hands, one of Baxter's.

'I'm afraid your daddy ...' she says.

Her voice trails away. She can't do it.

'What your mummy is trying to say is that Daddy ...' Nanna says. 'Is that your daddy passed away ... in the hospital.'

Megan's eyes go wide. Her breath comes in small suffocated trembles.

Baxter looks like he thinks he should cry too. He screws his eyes up, rubs at them. No tears come.

They stay like that for a long time. Megan crying; Baxter trying.

'Is there anything you want to know?' Christie finally says. 'Anything you need to ask?'

Megan can't speak.

Baxter raises his hand as if he's at school and asks what seems to be the only question that will come to his mind.

'What kind of lorry?' he says.

Christie and Nanna Bird exchange glances.

'A bread lorry,' Nanna answers decisively.

It is one of those still autumn days when the mist clings hauntingly low to the grey-green sea. They'd been up early to catch the bus from Crawley to Brighton and, having left the baby with Christie's mother, they are standing against the railing at the end of the Palace Pier. Each of them is to say their goodbye and Megan will then let drop a photograph of her father into the waves.

Nanna goes first.

'I remember one day when you were a boy,' she says.

She pauses, clears her throat.

'You fell out of a tree you were climbing in the garden and I hugged and kissed you until you were better. You smelled of apples and new-mown grass.'

She nods to Christie to go next.

'I remember you when you sang to me on our wedding day,' Christie says, surprised at the sudden catch in her voice. 'It was perfect.'

Megan is fighting rising sobs.

'I remember . . .' she says.

Christie bends to comfort her.

'It's OK, Megan,' she says. 'You don't have to say anything.'

But Megan swallows her tears, determined to finish.

'I remember the fair and when I was up high on your shoulders and we had candyfloss,' she says.

Christie is so proud of her; she squeezes her shoulder, holds her tight.

Baxter looks up at Nanna.

'I remember lots of things,' he says.

'Just choose one, dear,' Nanna says. 'One happy thing.'

Baxter closes his eyes and concentrates; Christie wills him to find the one thing.

'I remember Hornby Dublo Super Detail,' he finally says, his voice no more than a whisper. His father bought the train set for him.

The photograph is one that has sat for years on Nanna Bird's sideboard. She removed it from its frame this morning and gave it to Megan to carry on the bus.

'It's time, Megan,' Nanna says.

Megan leans over the railing, holding the photograph with both hands, staring hard into her father's smiling eyes. Finally she lets it go and they all watch as it flutters like a small bird in the air and then settles face-up on the water.

Within minutes the sullen slop of the waves carries it away and into the mist.

On the bus back to Crawley that afternoon, Christie shivers.

How *could* she have lied to the children? How *could* she have put them through that ordeal on the pier?

And there's something else.

Panic grips her.

'But what if he comes back?' she whispers to Nanna, beside her.

'After what he's done to you? To them? To me?' Nanna says. 'No man would dare to show his face again.'

96

17

Truman

The Old Horse, Leicester

It's a bit rich, isn't it? He's come all this way to see the boy, travelled halfway up the bloody country; he's got him out of having to sit through some boring lecture, got him a day off; he's bought him a drink and shown him how to have a few laughs; and for what?

The boy has absolutely nothing to say to him. Nothing. Not a dicky-bird.

All he does is stand there po-faced, disapproving, looking at his watch as if he can't wait to get away, to be shot of him.

It's more than a bit rich.

He might be six feet something tall now and in need of a bloody good haircut but it's just like when he was a nipper. He hasn't changed a bit, Christie's precious boy. Always looking at him with those eyes of his, of hers.

Well, Truman Bird isn't going to stand for it. He's not having his own son show him up in company. He'll be having a word later. And if Baxter doesn't buck his ideas up, show a bit of respect, it'll be more than a word. He'll feel the weight of his father's hand. He isn't too old or too big for that.

It isn't right, is it? To be treated like this after everything he did for him when he was a kid. Put a roof over his head, food on the table, clothes on his back. All the things he bought him. That train set. Other stuff. Everything. Ungrateful sod.

Truman takes a long gulp of his beer, stubs out his cigarette in the overflowing ashtray on the bar and immediately lights another.

He needs to calm down, get a grip.

Steady on, Truman old son, he tells himself. Carry on like this and you really will have a problem with the old ticker.

And it's not worth the agitation because it isn't all bad. Far from it. Baxter apart, he's come up smelling of roses.

First there's the flat. Who would have guessed the university would have a place for the likes of visiting bigwig professors? Rosie had called him back when he and the boy were halfway along the corridor and handed him the keys. Compassionate grounds, she whispered. Give him a chance to stay in Leicester for the week and spend some time with Baxter. She even insisted that he left his suitcase with her. Someone would deliver it to the flat, she said. How about that for service?

And then there's Rosie herself, of course.

She's given him the keys to the flat, right? So she obviously wants him to hang around. If he keeps playing his cards right, he's in with a chance there. He could talk to her about Baxter, tell her how hurt he is by the way the boy is despite everything he's done for him; that sort of thing. She'll like that, her being a doctor. They could discuss it over a drink or two. And then?

Bingo!

So things have worked out pretty well. They always do if you stay on your toes and keep your wits about you. And of course, in the long run, it doesn't matter how the boy is. It's worth putting up with a bit of his silence grief, because it's not about him; it's about winning Christie round.

A home to go to, a meal on the table, somewhere to put his feet up; he deserves that, right?

In fact, it's the least he deserves. After what she told him.

At the kitchen table, he gets her talking; asks about the kids. And she launches straight into telling him about her precious Baxter starting at university. She even starts going on about doing some daft university course herself. He'll soon put a stop to that nonsense when they're back together, he tells himself.

'And what about baby Truman?' he asks, when she pauses for breath.

Christie laughs.

'No longer a baby, I'm afraid,' she says. 'Ten years old now.'

'Yes, of course,' he says, smiling.

She hesitates, stares at her mug of tea.

'And he's no longer "Truman",' she says quietly. 'He's Harold. Harry.'

At first, Truman doesn't understand.

'I changed his name,' Christie says. 'After you went.'

After you threw me out, Truman thinks. Threw me out in the dead of night in the pouring rain with nowhere to go. But he bites his tongue, stays shtum. He needs to tread carefully, keep things sweet.

'Harry,' Christie says, not looking at him. 'After my dad.'

Truman doesn't say anything, but it hurts. It's a betrayal. The boy was named after him. She's got no right.

'And my little princess?' he says, trying to change the subject, to lighten the mood. 'How's my Megan?'

18

Baxter

The Old Horse, Leicester

Baxter is drumming the palms of his hands on the top of the old sit-up-and-beg piano as his father plays.

'This is what I've been telling you about, son,' Truman shouts. 'Delta blues, Muddy Waters. The daddy of them all.'

'*I got a black cat bone . . .*' Truman sings.

Baxter nods his head and drums on, shoulders hunched, foot tapping, letting the shock of the music run through him.

'All right!' he yelps.

'Your turn, son,' Truman calls to him, still thumping out the tune.

And Baxter, reading the words his father has scrawled on a beer mat, sways to the beat and sings. Muddy Waters-style. Born to the Delta. Born to sing the blues. And once he understands where the music leads, where it takes him, he closes his eyes and he's back there, back then, and it's just like his father told him. He's in the basement of Theresa's Lounge, South Side Chicago, and the lights are bright and there's sweat and smoke stinging his eyes and the sound is bouncing off the walls. He's there with Elga Edmonds beating out the rhythm, Little Walter Jacobs jamming on harp, Jimmy Rogers ripping it up on guitar, and Otis Spann playing loose on piano.

♪ Well you know I'm the hoochie coochie man
Everybody knows I'm him ...

'Right on!' someone shouts.
The whole bar is stamping. Whistles and applause ring out.

At two-thirty, when the landlord had rung the bell and called last orders, Truman had gone to him, whispered something in his ear and put five pounds behind the counter. It's one of the last things Baxter can remember with any clarity.

'We've got a lock-in,' Truman had announced, climbing unsteadily on to a chair. By kind permission of the landlord, and providing the Old Bill didn't take an unhealthy interest, the pub was theirs for the afternoon.

'And the first round's on me,' he'd said to loud cheers.

Later, Baxter can't remember how they got started. It's weird. One minute he was sipping his beer cautiously at the bar, the next he was keeping pace with his father and they were deep in discussion.

And it turns out, he's all right.
His father.
His dad.
More than all right.
He's totally frigging amazing.

And that's pretty confusing; almost as confusing for Baxter as discovering his mother and Nanna Bird had lied. His memories of him when he was young must be wrong; the nightmares must have been wrong. Somehow. And it makes no sense either that his mother ever left his father. Because everyone in the pub can see that he's this far-out guy. He makes people laugh; he can talk to anyone, about anything.

And he knows so much. His dad. About music.

'You wouldn't have any of them,' Truman says. 'No Stones, no Joplin, no Zeppelin, no Hendrix, no John Mayall. None of them, if it wasn't for Muddy and the rest.'

'The rest?' Baxter says, conscious that his voice is slurred and coming from far away.

He needs to slow down with the beer; he has to slow down.

'Big Bill Broonzy, Bukka White, Lead Belly, Son House, Honeyboy Edwards, Howlin' Wolf, John Lee Hooker ... So many more,' his father says.

Baxter is blown away. The names alone are like magic.

'How come you know so much?' he says.

'Got my own record shop in Margate,' his father says. 'Going to start my own label too – Charlatan Records.'

'I thought you were in import-export?' Baxter says.

'That too,' Truman says, turning away, taking his empty glass to the bar.

When his father returns with two more full pint glasses, Baxter tries to change the subject. Not because he doesn't want to talk music. He wants nothing more. But he needs to know.

'The doctors ... ?' he says, tapping at his heart.

His father shakes his head.

'Nothing to be done, son,' he says. 'It's just a matter of time.'

'But you seem ... You seem OK.'

'I'll be well until I'm not, they say,' Truman says. 'One day it'll just—'

He clicks his fingers.

'But surely—' Baxter starts to say.

'No buts,' Truman says, putting a brave face on it. 'I've just got to enjoy life while I still can.'

At some point that Baxter doesn't notice, the butcher and the salesman disappear. When he next looks up, the pub is loud with workers in overalls having a drink at the end of their shift. His father is talking to two of them. They are from the Wolsey knitwear factory at Abbey Meadows.

Baxter goes over to them; they are standing close to an old upright piano.

'You play?' one of them is asking Truman.

'You bet,' his father replies.

'He can play anything,' Baxter says proudly.

In some way, he's always known this; he has a distant memory of a day when he was sitting alone in a car outside a pub while a piano played and people sang. And he knows it for a fact now.

Hesitantly, self-consciously, Baxter had told his father how he taught himself to play the guitar.

'It's the piano for me,' Truman said.

'What do you play?' Baxter said.

'Pretty much anything,' Truman said. 'But given a choice, I play the blues.'

104

Muddy Waters. Daddy of them all.

The knitwear workers urge Truman on; he needs no encouragement. Grabbing Baxter around the shoulders, he steers him towards the piano.

'You sing?' he says.

'I was in the choir at school,' Baxter says apprehensively.

'Yeah, but do you *sing*?' Truman says.

He scribbles some words on a beer mat, hands it to Baxter.

'Well you know I'm the hoochie coochie man
Everybody knows I'm him ... '

'That's some voice,' Truman shouts approvingly as the pub roars. 'You can be the first signing on my new label!'

Not waiting for an answer, he lurches from Muddy Waters into B. B. King and then on to the Stones and Bowie and Elton John.

And Baxter?

That's some voice, his father said.

Baxter is rolling, he's reeling, he's crocodile-rocking. He's Jean Genie. Outrageous, he screams and he bawls. He's Jumping Jack Flash and everything is just this total mind-blowing gas, gas, gas.

He's up there. Out there. Out of sight. Gone.

If only Abby could see him now.

Because the world is this amazing spinning rush and he's at the centre of it, gliding on the surface, riding it like it's a giant breaking wave. He's fearless, reckless. He's dangerous.

In his whole life, Baxter has never felt so ...

So—

So abso-frigging-lutely ...

19

Abby

The University Library, Leicester

A bby has spent the afternoon hunched over a desk in the warm comforting hush of the library, reading her paper-back *Bleak House*, faithfully following the footnotes and appendices, making underlinings and annotations in the margin in careful black ink. She hasn't noticed the afternoon light beginning to disappear.

Finally she senses it's time to make her reluctant way out of the fog that hovers among Dickens's pages, that creeps and rolls along the great polluted river and through the Court of Chancery. Closing her book, she bids farewell to Lady Dedlock, John Jarndyce and Esther Summerson, picks up her bag and follows a small departing stream of students out through the main door.

She shivers as she emerges into the cool air, pulls her long black coat more tightly around herself and fumbles to fasten the buttons. Distracted by this, she doesn't notice the students in front of her giving a wide berth to an obstacle immediately outside the library entrance.

It's only at the last moment, as she almost trips over him, that she sees the man sitting on the ground in the middle of the paved pathway. Stumbling to a halt, her Biba bag slips from her hand and falls in front of him.

He doesn't move.

'Sorry!' Abby says, gathering herself, bending to retrieve the bag and then stepping quickly back in shock at the sight of him.

Apart from his saffron headband and the beads strung in rainbow swathes around his neck, he is dressed entirely in crumpled baggy white. He is barefoot despite the autumn day, his hair hangs grey to his shoulders, his beard reaches luxuriantly to his chest. He is sitting cross-legged with his feet on opposing thighs. His wrists rest on his knees with his palms facing upwards, the thumb and index finger of each hand forming a circle, the other three fingers extended. His eyes are closed.

'The yogi says: be afraid of nothing,' he says.

His voice surprises Abby almost as much as his appearance: it is high and fluting and softened by a hissing lisp.

'Sorry?' Abby says, taking another half-step backwards.

'I've been waiting for you,' he says, his eyes still closed. 'I knew that you would come.'

'Me?' Abby says, looking around, certain he's mistaken her for someone else. The stream of students has dried; suddenly she is alone with this man.

He nods.

'But we've never met before,' she says, confused.

He tilts his head backwards. If his eyes were open, they would gaze directly into hers.

'We have shared eternity together,' he says.

Abby doesn't know whether to laugh or run.

'Pardon?' she says, deciding on laughter.

'I have known you always,' he says.

Abby laughs again.

'But it's not true,' she says. 'You don't even know my name.'

She realises, of course, that she shouldn't get involved with this strange creature, that she should turn on her heel and leave at once. That's what her mam would tell her to do. But she's never encountered anything like him before. She decides that he must be some kind of a maharishi; like the one the Beatles met. A mystic. And not much that was mystical ever happened to her in Pontlottyn.

'Your name has been for ever on my lips,' he says.

Abby reconsiders and prepares to leave; maybe he isn't mystical, maybe he's just creepy.

'You are Willow Moon,' he says.

Despite herself, Abby laughs again.

'I wish!' she says. 'But that's far too exotic for a girl from Pontlottyn.'

He shakes his head and smiles; his eyes still closed.

'You are Willow Moon,' he says. 'And you are come to rid us all of fear.'

Abby has heard enough. He isn't just creepy; he's crazy.

'No,' she says. 'I'm Abigail Evans and I'm off to have my tea.'

Determined to leave, she finishes buttoning her coat and takes a step away from the man. At that moment though, his eyes flick open. They are a wild startling blue.

'Beneath the willow moon, the April rains restore the earth,' he flutes. 'Your tears, Willow Moon, shall be that rain; with those tears, the past shall be purged and washed away.'

He *is* crazy – but his eyes hold her now, his voice draws her in.

He speaks again.

'The yogi says: forget the past, for it is gone from your domain; forget the future, for it is beyond your reach; control the present, live supremely well now. This is the way of the wise.'

It *is* crazy. But some of it makes sense. Forget the past, live supremely well now. That's right, that's what she should do.

'Who . . . who are you?' Abby says, her voice faltering.

'I am Niloc,' the man says. 'I am the Messenger.'

Slowly, he unfolds himself and rises to his feet. He holds his hands to his sides, his thumbs and index fingers still forming their circles. He is a small man. In her platform boots, Abby stands taller than him.

He looks up into her eyes. There's something almost serenely beautiful about him, Abby thinks. Serene, beautiful, mystical.

Suddenly, from behind, Abby feels a firm arm around her shoulders. Before she knows what's happening, she finds herself being steered quickly away from Niloc.

'Hi,' a girl's voice says brightly. 'I'm Sarah. I thought I should rescue you.'

Abby isn't sure that she wants to be rescued.

'The same thing happened to me in my first year,' Sarah explains with a shudder, still holding Abby tight. 'For a moment back there I almost fell under Colin's spell too. It's that voice, those eyes . . .'

'Colin?' Abby says, bewildered. 'He told me his name was Niloc.'

'Colin,' the girl says. 'Backwards.'

109

Abby feels ridiculous.

'He was a lecturer here in the sixties,' Sarah says as they walk, clamped together.

'A lecturer?' Abby says, aghast. 'What happened to him?'

'Woodstock,' Sarah says. 'They say he went to Woodstock, started dropping acid, came back like that.'

'Acid?' Abby says, not understanding

'LSD,' Sarah says.

'Drugs?' Abby says, appalled.

'OK now?' Sarah says, letting go of her shoulder and turning back towards the library.

Abby nods, feeling a little defeated. How can she have been so stupid, so naïve?

'Thank you,' she calls distractedly after Sarah.

The sixties had passed Pontlottyn by. Some in the village said the whole decade somehow missed the turning off the Heads of the Valleys Road and carried straight on to Merthyr Tydfil – and even there it paused only briefly. It might have been peace, free love and flowers-in-your-hair elsewhere, but no one ever stood up in chapel and explained that to the congregation of Pontlottyn in their Sunday best. It's true that Hywel Crumpler read about the hippie trail to Nepal in the *New Musical Express* and set off on his eighteenth birthday determined to hitchhike all the way – but the furthest east he got was the public bar of The Levant Sun in Abergavenny and he was home again by bus in time for supper. And one day in 1968 Susan Stimpson and Caroline Crocker *did* wear carnations in their hair – until Susan's mam spotted they'd picked them from the front garden and gave them what-for. But apart from that, Pontlottyn had carried on as it always carried on. Letting the world go by.

As Abby walks across the campus, she shakes her head. What was that new persona supposed to be? Daring, confident, perhaps even a bit quirky? She's been kidding herself; she's none of those things. She's a little girl lost in a world she doesn't fully understand, that she's been kept sheltered from.

She's Alice blundering through a topsy-turvy Wonderland.

111

20

Christie

The end of the working day: The Planning Department, Crawley

On the stroke of half-past five, Christie scoops up her coat and bag and makes for the door. Hurrying out, she meets Ray coming in.

The afternoon has been long and Christie's head aches. She can't shake Truman from her mind. Even though he has now gone, something doesn't feel quite right; something is nagging at her like unfinished business.

And why does she have to deal with this now, when she can barely think straight because of Nanna? Phoning the hospital during the afternoon, she was told there'd been no improvement. Christie would need to decide tonight about telling Baxter and Harry.

'In a rush again?' Ray says, the droop of his moustache adding to his look of hangdog disappointment.

'Afraid so,' Christie says, buttoning her coat and managing just a thin smile for him. She hasn't forgiven him for seeking her out in the park and interrupting her thoughts; for sitting in Megan's place.

'Only I was hoping that we might ...' Ray says, taking a step towards her.

Christie glances around to make sure that they're not being watched. She tries to back away but he comes closer.

'It's complicated right now, Ray,' she says quietly, urgently.

'Complicated?' he says.

'With Nanna, with the children, with Truman coming back ...'

Ray takes a step back.

'Your husband?'

Christie nods.

'What the hell has he come back for?' he says hotly.

Christie pauses. She wonders whether she needs to explain it at all; it's nothing to do with Ray, none of his business. Finally, though, she relents. As well as being her boss, he's been a good friend to her over the years and – although he's always wanted something more and she has never been sure – she owes him an explanation at least.

'I think—' she begins to say. She stops; puts her hand to her mouth.

'What is it?' Ray says, concerned.

It's only now, when she has to explain it to someone else, that Christie knows what's been wrong, why she hasn't been able to shake Truman from her mind.

It's your boy. Come home. That's what he told his mother.

He hasn't come back to say goodbye and vanish again. That's not Truman; he isn't capable of something as simple and selfless. With him there's always some other motive. She'd lost sight of that, forgotten who he is, what he's like.

'I think ...' she says. 'I think he wants to come back to me.'

113

She *hasn't* seen the last of him. One day when she goes to Nanna's flat, he'll be there again on the doorstep with his suitcase and his lopsided smile. She's suddenly sure of it.

'*What?*' Ray says.

And it won't be some stranger sending her the news. It will be her who's there at the end. That's what Truman intends.

Christie shudders.

'I think he wants to come back to me to die,' she says.

21

Truman

The Old Horse

Standing alone as The Old Horse rocks and roars around him, Truman raises his glass in silent self-congratulation and smiles.

It's as if he's found this golden key, this magic key that unlocks anything. He should have thought of it years ago. He's Ali bloody Baba; a simple tap at the heart and all doors swing open for him.

It's the key to Christie's door, Rosie's office and a flat at the university's expense. It's the key to Baxter's bank account too. Although, of course, he'll have to pay the lad back some day. That's only right. Because it turns out he's OK; turns out he really is a chip off the old block. Likes a beer and a laugh, loves his music.

He shouldn't have spun the boy the line about Charlatan Records though. That was careless; the drink talking. Got carried away there; showing off a bit. Still, no harm done. He'll think of a way out of that. Anyway, over the years in Margate he spent so long hanging about in Charlie's shop on rainy afternoons, listening to the latest records, he's almost come to think of it as his own.

The key helped with the boy too. A tap at the heart and a brave smile finally won Baxter over. *I'll be well until I'm not, they say.* That's a good line. He'll use that again.

It *is* magic, the key. Pure gold.

And later it'll be the key to Rosie's knickers. He's sure of it; he can see it in her eyes.

Ali bloody Baba, he is. And all the treasure there, just waiting for him.

It can't fix everything, of course. It can't bring his Megan back. But he's trying hard not to think about any of that. It does no good to dwell on it.

And of course, he'll have to stage a miraculous recovery at some point. He'll have to beat the odds, defy the doctors. It'll be a chance in a million, that sort of thing. But he can make that work for him too. Everyone heartbroken one minute, over the moon the next.

Truman glances at his watch. They will have to be on the move soon. The landlord will need the pub back to get ready for the evening session. As the Wolsey shift workers come to shake him by the hand and say their goodbyes, he looks around for Baxter.

He hasn't seen the boy for some time.

22

Baxter

In the garden of The Old Horse

It's like he's hit a wall. Or rather it's like the wall has hit him. As if one minute he's standing there with a grin on his face and another drink in his hand, and then the next, the wall comes at him – rushing, roaring – so that he can't hear anything. Except the rush. The roar.

And then everything is suddenly reeling, turning cartwheels in the room, in his head. And when, in a moment of sudden lucidity, he decides he needs to get outside – urgently – when he tries to walk, he discovers he's going sideways. As much as he's going forwards.

He bounces off a shoulder. A chair. A table. Going forwards. Sideways.

Then, when he manages to locate the door, after he finds the handle – tugs at it, pushes at it, clings to it, prises it open, swings on it – he steps outside into a garden. And the air hits him. And the wall comes rushing at him. Again.

Roaring.

It's the weirdest frigging thing how he was so absolutely up

117

there one second – riding it, that beautiful mind-blowing wave – and then how he's like this, now, the next.

He closes his eyes. The world spins.

Lurches. Sways.

He bends double.

Vomits.

Into a flowerbed.

Voluminously.

23

Abby

Late afternoon: College Hall,
University of Leicester

After her encounter with Niloc, Abby feels a chill of lone-liness as she walks back across Victoria Park and climbs the hill of Queens Road towards her hall of residence. She is glad that she will soon be talking to her mam on the tele-phone.

On the day she left home, they decided that this was to be their twice-weekly routine. Every Monday and Thursday afternoon her mother would call from the telephone box on the corner near Pontlottyn Halt and Abby would be waiting by the payphone that clings to the wall outside the Junior Common Room.

Depositing her bag and books in her room, Abby hurries along the corridor, down the stairs and out across the quad to make sure she's there in time for the phone to ring. She feels a sudden flutter of excitement; until now she hasn't been prepared to admit to herself how much she misses home.

She picks up the phone after the first ring and hears her mother fumbling to feed coins into the box.

'Just a minute,' her mother says.

Abby can picture her in the phone box. The glass will be misting, the Cardiff train will be pulling slowly away from the halt opposite and the wind will be whipping around the corner. Because it always does. And it will be raining. Because, more often than not, it is.

The coins rattle and drop.

'Is that you, Abby love?' her mother says.

'It is, Mam,' Abby says, a smile at once on her face.

'It's cats and dogs down here,' her mother says.

Abby can hear the rain pounding on the roof of the telephone kiosk.

'It's always cats and dogs down there, Mam,' Abby says, laughing, imagining the rain coming in horizontal drifts down the valley, wishing she was there.

'So are you eating?' her mother says.

Again Abby laughs. She knew that would be the first question.

'Yes, Mam,' she says.

It isn't enough; she knew it wouldn't be.

'So what is it you're eating then?' her mother says.

'I had a sandwich at lunchtime,' Abby says.

'A sandwich is no good to you, is it!' her mother exclaims. 'For goodness' sake, girl, make sure you have something hot this evening.'

'Yes, Mam,' Abby says, six years old again.

'And are you sleeping?'

'Not too bad,' Abby says.

'No dreams?'

'No, Mam,' she says quietly. 'No dreams.'

'But you're sure you're sleeping? Because you know it just gets worse if you don't.'

'I am sleeping, Mam, I promise,' Abby says, looking around to make sure there's no one there to hear.

'But it's not too dark for you, is it? You've got a light you can leave on?'

'There's one on the desk,' Abby says. 'It's just right.'

'And can you have the door open? Like at home?'

'Try not to worry, Mam,' Abby pleads. 'I have the window open. And I only need it when I have the dreams, don't I?'

'And you don't have the dreams?'

'No. No dreams,' Abby says.

It isn't true. She's had the dreams every night and has woken fighting the blackness, fighting for breath. But it's best her mother doesn't know. She'd only worry more.

'How's next door?' Abby says, changing the subject. The latest news of the widow Gwen Talbot is always a guaranteed distraction.

'Duw!' her mother says. 'She's all fuss and feathers over some new dress!'

Abby laughs.

'Got it from Morgans's in Cardiff, she did,' her mother continues. 'Been going on about it something awful, she has.'

'What's it like on?' Abby says.

'On her?' her mother says. 'She's mutton dressed as. A proper dog's dinner, she looks.'

They laugh together.

'And how's Dad?' Abby says.

'Just the same ...'

'How's he coping?'

'The doctor's given him new tablets,' her mother says. 'But it's no different, not really.'

'But he's OK?'

The hesitation tells told Abby all she needs to know.

'He's talking even less,' her mother says. 'Just takes himself off to his allotment and sits there in his shed.'

'But you're OK, Mam?'

'Me?' her mother says. 'I'm right as rain!'

They are back to the rain. And they laugh briefly together as it drums louder on the phone-box roof, as the pips sound, the money runs out and the line goes dead.

24

Truman

Dusk: Queens Road, Leicester

At the kerbside, the taxi waits, engine spluttering, its exhaust belching mistily into the cool late-afternoon air. In the back seat, Truman lights another cigarette and winds the window down.

'All right, sport?' he shouts.

Baxter doesn't answer.

Slumped sickly pale, shivering and sweating, he supports himself against a lamppost in the murky half-light of the gathering city dusk. He groans, leans forwards, retches emptily.

It's just the same as when he was a kid, Truman thinks. Back then, the boy couldn't go a hundred yards in the Wolseley without needing to pull over. Now, in the short distance from The Old Horse to Baxter's hall of residence, they've had to stop three times already.

But, to be fair, it's only natural at the lad's age, it's all part of growing up. And he'll learn soon enough how to hold his drink; just like Truman did, up at Catterick on National

Service. Those were the days: staggering back to barracks with Ginger and Fitz, a belly full of Theakston's and pickled eggs, taking it in turns to throw up in the hedgerow. And then on the parade ground early the next day, head pounding like a jackhammer, eyes gritty and a mouth like a Turkish wrestler's armpit. It's one of the rites of passage, something every man has to go through. And Baxter's young; he'll toughen up.

Anyway, Truman thinks, looking at his watch, there's no rush. It's early yet. Still plenty of time to find the flat, get his head down for a couple of hours, freshen up and then give Rosie a call. She gave him her number. For emergencies, she said; in case he needed her.

Well, it isn't an emergency exactly. He doesn't *need* her. But he does *want* her. He smiles, closes his eyes, sees her pat at her hair; breathes deeply, smells her perfume.

Of course, they shouldn't be in a taxi at all; they should be walking. It's only a mile and the air would have done the boy good, cleared his head. But when Truman found him in the garden, it was obvious that Baxter couldn't hold a straight line. Legs all over the place, like bloody Bambi on ice.

At the lamppost, Baxter straightens. He steadies himself and then staggers the few paces back towards the taxi. Truman pushes open the door and slides across the seat to create space.

'Think you'll make it this time, sport?' he says.

Baxter doesn't answer. He stares grimly ahead, breathing hard and gripping tightly at the seat in front of him.

The taxi inches away from the kerb and crawls the remaining half-mile up the hill of Queens Road. Truman can see the driver's worried eyes glancing every few seconds in the rear-view mirror, watching to see if Baxter needs to make another hasty stop.

In front of a short flight of wide, paved steps, leading to a huddle of modern three-storey sandy-brick buildings, the car glides to a sedate halt.

'This it?' Truman says, peering out of the window.

Baxter nods and scrabbles at the door for the handle. Truman leans across, releases the door and pushes it open.

'Hang on, driver,' he says. 'Just let me get him to his room and we'll be on our way again.'

Baxter hauls himself up and out of the car, stumbles across the pavement and sits quickly down on a low brick wall. As Truman climbs out after him, he hears a voice call.

'Baxter?'

Truman looks round. A dark-haired boy carrying a guitar in a battered case is jogging down the steps towards them.

'You know Baxter?' Truman says to him.

The boy nods.

'Yeah,' he says. 'I'm Josh. I'm just down the corridor from him.'

'Hello, Josh,' Truman says, reaching out to shake the boy's hand. 'You couldn't take him to his room, could you?'

Baxter is sitting, head slumped, swaying as though buffeted by a playful wind.

'What happened to him, man?' Josh says. 'He smells like a brewery.'

'I'm his dad,' Truman says. 'We've been drowning our sorrows.'

Josh looks away from Baxter and up at Truman.

'Sorrows?' he says.

'I've had bad news, son,' Truman says, tapping at his heart. 'The worst possible news.'

Well, he doesn't want Baxter getting into trouble, does he? Turning up drunk as a skunk at this time of day is bound to make people talk. It's best to let this Josh know the lad has an excuse. Word will soon get around.

'That's what the professor dude meant this morning,' Josh says quietly. '"Distressing business" . . .'

Truman doesn't understand and he doesn't have time to work it out: the meter is running on the taxi, he's anxious now to be off.

'So you'll help him?' he says.

'Of course. No worries,' Josh says, putting his arm around Baxter, lifting him from the wall.

Truman rests his hand on Baxter's shoulder.

'A few hours' kip and you'll be fine,' he says.

Baxter doesn't answer. Eyes almost closed, he looks dead on his feet already.

Truman turns and hurries towards the taxi. But before he ducks inside, he pauses, leans against the open door and looks back.

Josh and Baxter are slowly climbing the steps towards the light spilling from the buildings above: Baxter, tall, gangling and unsteady, is leaning heavily against the shorter, thick-set boy. In his long greatcoat and with his head bowed, he looks like a wounded soldier being helped from the battle-field.

As Truman watches them climb, it comes at him like a lightning strike.

From nowhere, there's a surge of emotion, shocking and unfamiliar. He's *proud*. Proud of Baxter. That's his son, up

126

there, on those steps. His boy, his flesh and blood. His little nipper, grown six feet tall.

His throat tightens, his eyes prick.

He tries to push the feeling away. Steady on, Truman old son, he tells himself. It's a bit bloody late in the day for this. After all, he never had any time for the lad when he was young, did he?

At the top of the steps Baxter turns and raises an arm in forlorn farewell.

But the truth is, he's turned out all right, the boy. Tall; fine-looking; up at university; playing the guitar; liking a drink and a sing-song. He *is* his father's son.

Josh and Baxter are almost out of sight now; Truman watches until he can see them no longer.

And Truman has missed out on seeing him grow up, hasn't he? He regrets that now, suddenly and for the first time. That's part of the pricking at the eyes: it would have been good to have known him when he was a youngster.

Still leaning against the car door, Truman reaches into his jacket pocket for his cigarettes, taps one out and then immediately thinks better of it. He puts the packet away again.

But now maybe he'll get to have a second chance, with Christie, with the boys. A second go at all of it.

And perhaps that's what was really on his mind when the idea came to him of picking up with Christie again. Perhaps it's what he wanted all along. A second go.

Finally Truman lets go of the door and slides on to the back seat.

'OK, mate,' he says.

But whatever the truth of that is, it's for tomorrow. Or maybe the day after.

The smile returns to his lips.
Because tonight he's got other plans.
Sleep.
Shower.
Telephone call.
Rosie.
Drink.
Golden key.
Tap, tap, tap.

25

Abby

College Hall

A bby makes her way slowly back across the quad to her
room, singing softly to herself. As she walks and sings,
she smiles and shakes her head. She is, she has to admit, in
something of a daze; she's floating.

> ♫ Money, it's a gas
> Grab that cash with both hands ...

It's like a dream; she can't believe it.

One minute she's feeling homesick and lonely, and the next
she's in this crowd of people casually discussing a trip to the
Rainbow Theatre. *Casually!* As if that's how she spends most
weekends: going to see rock bands, in theatres, in London.

Yeah, amazing, far out, she says. Deadpan.

Ridiculous!

Inside, her heart is racing. She has never even been to
London before, except for a school trip to the National
Gallery when she was fourteen and Siân Bayly was sick at the

129

back of the coach. And she's certainly never been to a concert – except with her dad to see the Tongwynlais Temperance Band when they played show tunes at the community centre. And that definitely doesn't count.

But now, in a few weeks' time, with people she's only just met, she's going to see Pink Floyd. In London.

Pink Floyd!

She'd followed her mother's advice. She went early to eat in the refectory, dutifully seeking out the hot food counter. Carrying her tray, she looked around the unfriendly cold-concrete and bare-brick room for somewhere to sit. Finally, gathering her courage, she asked to join a group at one of the long pine tables.

It's the first time she has ventured into the refectory and the first time she's met anyone in this place where she will be living for her first university year. In the previous week she kept quietly to her room or spent time with Georgie and her friends on campus.

They go around the table introducing themselves with a jumble of accents. It turns out that not everyone at university is a posh kid from Surrey: they're from Bristol, Hull, Plymouth, Birmingham, Rochdale, Torquay, Sunderland.

They're planning a trip to London to see Pink Floyd. Does she want to go with them? They ask as if it is the most natural thing in the world; as if they've known her for ever.

Leaving the quad behind, Abby pushes through the door of the nearest residence block. Still singing, she starts to climb the stairs towards the first-floor corridor that leads to her room.

♫ Breathe, breathe in the air ...

A voice calls out to her from below.

'Hey!'

She pauses, looks back down the stairs. A dark-haired boy with an embryonic Frank Zappa moustache and a guitar case in his hand is looking up at her.

'I need some help,' he says pleadingly.

Abby hesitates. He doesn't look as if he needs help.

'It's my friend,' he says. 'He's in a bit of a state and I can't leave him on his own.'

Abby takes a step back down the stairs, taking care not to tread on the flares of her jeans.

'Only, I've got this gig,' the boy says, raising his guitar case. 'I need someone to watch him for a couple of hours.'

Abby comes further back down the stairs.

'But I don't know you,' she says uncertainly.

'I'm Josh,' he says, with a friendly smile. 'We were in the same lecture this morning.'

'What's wrong with your friend?' Abby says.

'He's had this totally bummer news,' Josh says. 'About his father. He's like, dying?'

Abby's hand goes to her mouth.

'Oh, how terrible,' she says, a picture of her own father at once in her mind.

'He's been drowning his sorrows,' Josh says. 'He totally shouldn't be left on his own. He might throw up again.'

Abby was raised in a near-teetotal household. Her father's quiet boast is that not a drop of drink has ever touched his lips; her mother's great indulgence, under her husband's disapproving gaze, is an occasional glass of sherry at Christmas or at weddings and funerals. Alcohol is therefore associated in Abby's mind with mortification and shame, fun and small acts of playful defiance. But it is more repellent than fascinating.

'I'm not sure,' Abby says. 'Is there no one else?'

Josh shrugs his shoulders.

'I've knocked on all the doors. No one's in.'

Abby shakes her head. She can't go to a boy's room. Especially not a boy who has been drinking. A boy she doesn't even know.

'I'm sorry,' she says. 'I've got reading to do ...'

'You can bring it with you,' Josh says, nodding towards the Biba carrier bag she has in her hand. She took her books to the refectory in case she had to eat alone.

'Honestly,' Josh says, 'he's asleep and totally harmless.'

He turns and walks back along the lower corridor, leaving Abby with little choice but to follow. Halfway along, at the door to the room that Josh has disappeared into, she stops and peers inside.

The room is furnished identically to her own: the curtains are drawn and the desk lamp glows. Lying asleep on his back on the narrow bed is a boy, pale-faced, mouth open, fully dressed, with long tousled fair hair. It's the boy Georgie liked, the one who was called out of the lecture.

She steps inside.

'This is Baxter,' Josh says, unzipping the boy's boots, pulling them from his feet. 'He keeps talking in his sleep, going on about his father. It makes no sense.'

As Josh tugs at the boots, Baxter stirs.

'He *was* dead,' he mumbles, eyes still closed. 'But *now* ... now he's dying.'

'See what I mean?' Josh says with a grin.

Baxter shifts again.

'It's a new frigging . . .' he moans, slurring, 'paradigm.'

Josh laughs.

'A new frigging what, man?' he says.

Baxter doesn't answer. Instead he flings himself on to his side.

'We should keep him warm,' Abby says.

Josh eases the bedcover from beneath Baxter and wraps it around him.

'So, you'll do it?' he says.

Abby nods. She'll do it for Georgie; keep him safe for her.

'Only for a few hours, mind,' she says.

'Yeah. Whatever,' Josh says, grinning again, picking up his guitar case. 'Got to run.'

As the door closes behind him, Abby decides on the armchair in the corner next to the window. She can watch Baxter from there, and there will be light enough from the desk lamp to read. She takes *Bleak House* from her bag.

Shivering, suddenly cold, she sees Baxter's coat hanging on the back of the door. Retrieving it from its hook, she settles into the armchair, tucks her feet under her and pulls the coat heavily about her. It smells faintly of beer and cigarettes.

In the cocooned warmth beneath the coat, she feels tiredness slowly settling on her. She needs to close her eyes. Rest them. She can read later. She reaches up to the desk and turns the lamp to the wall to dim the light.

Baxter shifts on the bed. Again he mumbles in his sleep.

'Stars,' he says. 'Far out.'

26

Christie

Pound Hill, Crawley

As Christie turns the key and pushes open the front door of her box-like terrace house, she is exhausted beyond tears. The house that greets her is cold, dark and silent: there's no welcoming light in the living room, no music playing in the boys' bedroom, no picture flickering on the television screen. She can't remember a time when she's felt so completely alone. There's no Baxter, no Harry. No one to tell what the doctor said. About Nanna.

They must prepare themselves for the worst, he said.

The worst.

She's not hungry but knows she should eat. Without taking off her coat, she sits at the kitchen table and forces herself to take two bites of the stale sandwich she bought earlier at the small hospital shop. Pushing the sandwich aside, she climbs the stairs, runs a bath. Afterwards, she wraps herself in the velvet dressing gown the boys gave her at Christmas.

Returning downstairs, she goes to the sitting room, turns

on a single bar of the electric fire and settles into an armchair with her feet tucked up.

'Nanna ...' she says to herself.

She closes her eyes. Remembers.

So many snapshots: Nanna snuggling into the sofa, reading to the children, telling them stories; down on the floor on her complaining knees, playing with them; holding them in her arms, rocking them, tickling them until she and they are weak with laughter. Taking them on long exploring walks, on adventures.

One special day: Christie is sitting on a park bench, holding Harry. Nanna, Megan and Baxter are on the far side of the park, playing pirates, Nanna leading the way, limping extravagantly on an imagined wooden stump leg and talking to a squawking parrot perched invisibly on her shoulder. Megan and Baxter following behind, doing the same.

In the park Nanna plays in goal for Baxter. And at low tide on a rare day out at Climping, she brandishes a bat and takes guard on the hard-packed sand.

'You can be Fred Trueman,' she tells Baxter. 'And I'll be Colin Cowdrey.'

'Who's Megan?' Baxter demands, pacing out his long runup, preparing to bowl.

Nanna thinks for a moment, her repertoire of cricketers obviously exhausted.

'She can be a pirate again,' she announces.

And Megan keeps wicket on the sand with a wooden leg and a parrot on her shoulder.

It's a hot summer's day; the sky is wide and cloudless. Nanna scuttles between the wickets, hoisting her skirt above her knees.

'You need to look after yourself, Nanna,' Christie tells her, concerned the children will exhaust her.

'Nonsense!' Nanna gasps. 'They make me young again.'

Another day: they are travelling by bus to the ice rink at Streatham. It's Nanna's birthday treat for Megan. Sitting on the top deck as they crawl stop-starting along the High Road, Nanna confesses that she's never been on skates before. Anticipating what's in her mind, Christie suggests softly that it's perhaps a little late to learn now. They can stand at the side and watch.

'Nonsense!' Nanna says. 'It's never too late, is it?'

Clinging to Baxter at one side and Megan and Harry at the other, she makes her precarious way around the perimeter of the rink – laughing at every slipping sliding step she takes. By the end of her circuit, she has collected a small excited army of children. They are following her every move; laughing when she laughs; cheering her on.

At home that night, Nanna puts the children to bed and sings them to sleep. Her voice is surprisingly young and pure. It's the lullaby her mother always sang.

> ♪ Sleep, my child, and peace attend thee,
> All through the night.
> Guardian angels God will send thee,
> All through the night.

And Christie, listening from the kitchen, has tears suddenly running down her cheeks.

*

She has tears now too. In the armchair. In her dressing gown, in front of the electric fire.

Remembering again. Remembering the promise.

'It's what I've always wanted,' Christie tells Nanna one Thursday in the café in the Martletts, waving to Edie behind the counter. 'To study, to make something of myself.'

Over lunch, she explains about the Open University.

'And I thought, now the boys are getting older, I could ...'

She stops, suddenly uncertain. Worried that she sounds self-indulgent and foolish. How can a girl who left school at fourteen imagine that it is possible to have a university degree?

Nanna encourages her with a fierce hug.

'Do it, girl,' she says. 'Do it for both of us.'

Both of us? Christie isn't sure what she means.

'Both of us, *all* of us,' Nanna says. 'For all us women that never had a bloody chance.'

Christie is taken aback.

'You're becoming quite the women's libber,' she says with an approving smile.

'It's true,' Nanna replies with a girlish laugh. 'If I didn't need the support, I'd be out there burning my bra with the rest of them!'

At the end of the working day, Nanna is outside Christie's office, waiting. To be there when the letter asking for the application forms to be sent is dropped into the proud red postbox at the corner of the road.

*

It would be so easy to let go of the dream. Especially with Truman back and Nanna not there to encourage her. Easy to let the doubts overwhelm her – it's been years since she left school, would she be good enough? Could she keep up? Will they even accept her?

Do it, girl. Do it for both of us.

That's what Nanna told her.

Christie pulls her dressing gown more tightly around her.

27

Baxter

Several hours later: College Hall

Baxter isn't sure how he got here. Somewhere in the rattling ache that is his head, he has a fractured memory of the journey back from The Old Horse, of clinging to a lamppost, being in a taxi. And he remembers Josh, there at the end.

As for the rest: nothing.

Zilch.

It's not meant to be like this, he thinks. He's worked so hard to get here: he's not meant to end up legless on his first afternoon. What if the university find out, kick him off the course, send him down? Could they do that?

But at least the room has stopped spinning. He can now stare at the ceiling and it no longer whirls, shifts and repeats like a jerky cine-reel loop. Earlier, when momentarily he'd opened his eyes, the world was lurching and churning as if he was adrift on a mountainous sea.

He doesn't know how long he slept.

On waking, he's found that every part of him hurts, starting with his hair and ending with his toenails. It feels as if he's been hit by a train. Two trains. His head is heavy, leaden; he doubts whether he will be able to lift it from the pillow. Ever again.

There's a light coming from the corner of the room. Distantly, groggily, he wonders why there's a light.

Propping himself gingerly on his elbows, he tries to bring the room into focus.

It's then that he sees her.

In the soft pool of light coming from his muted desk lamp, she is sitting in the armchair, her feet tucked up, with his greatcoat wrapped around her. The light catches the glossy black of her hair.

Abby?

It has to be a dream.

He closes his eyes. Disbelieving. Slowly he prises them open again. She is still there, her eyes wide, watching him.

'Are you real?' he says, his throat dry, his voice croaky.

Abby replies with a quiet laugh. It's like music.

'Oh yes,' she says. 'I'm quite real.'

Her voice is like a lullaby.

'I'm Abby,' she says.

'I know,' Baxter says.

He falls quiet, trying to work it out. There's something he's missing. Why is she there?

'I'm Baxter,' he finally says, realising his omission.

'I know,' she says, with another small musical laugh.

Again a silence settles. A long silence. Baxter can feel unhurried seconds ticking by.

'I like your laugh,' he says. 'And your voice.'

His head throbs. He eases it back to the pillow.

'I had too much to drink,' he says.

Again Abby laughs her quiet laugh.

'I know,' she says. 'Josh told me. That's why I'm here, watching you. He had to go to a gig or something. I fell asleep.'

In the dull muddle of his head, Baxter tries again to make sense of it; finds that he can't quite; gives up.

'It's my father,' he says, wanting to explain, not wanting her to think badly of him.

'You were talking in your sleep,' Abby says. 'Something about he's dead and he's dying.'

'It's complicated,' Baxter says, too tired to tell her all of it.

'You said it was a new paradigm,' Abby says. 'In your sleep you said it. I was impressed!'

It's Baxter's turn to try a small laugh.

'Were you?' he says weakly. 'That's *paradigm* and *pantechnicon* in the same day.'

'What?' Abby says.

It's strangely comforting, Baxter decides, to talk like this in the almost-dark. To say things you would never say in the daylight. To let a few words drift across the quiet void of the room. To let questions go unanswered. To let the half-awake, half-asleep minutes pass.

'And you said *frigging*,' Abby says sleepily. 'I didn't think anyone said frigging. I thought it was just in books.'

Baxter doesn't reply at once. Again the stillness of the night wraps itself around.

'*Billy Liar*,' he confirms, showing off just a little.

'*For Whom the Bell Tolls*,' Abby offers, trumping him.

Baxter suddenly realises he needs to see her properly. He *has* to see her. For days, she has been in his every waking thought; he's carried her with him every minute; he's longed

141

just to be near her. And now, miraculously, somehow, she's in his room. And all he's doing is lying on his back sending words into the darkness. He wants to sit close enough to her to watch her face, to feel her breath, to be able to reach out and touch her hair.

He sits upright and tries to steady himself before attempting to swing his legs from the bed.

'Don't move,' Abby says. 'Because if you move I will have to leave.'

28

Abby

Baxter's room

'And I don't want to go,' she says. 'Not just yet.'

She doesn't want to break the spell. She is so warm and cosy cwtched beneath the greatcoat, and she likes his deep voice coming to her from the darkness. He is strange, funny, interesting. And she has never sat talking into the night before.

'I just wanted to be closer to you,' Baxter says, settling back on the bed.

Abby laughs.

'You're close enough where you are,' she says. 'My dad would have a fit to see me here.'

She likes too the way they talk and then just stop and listen to the quiet. It's as if there is a rhythm between them; easy and exciting, safe and unsafe.

'I didn't know you lived here,' Baxter says, yawning just a little.

'Directly above,' Abby says, looking at the ceiling, stifling a yawn of her own.

She doesn't feel she has to say anything more. That's part of the sleepy magic of it.

'I was looking at you in the lecture theatre today,' Baxter says.

Something drowsily clicks in Abby's mind.

'I thought you only had eyes for Georgie?' she says.

She's keeping him safe for her. She'd forgotten that.

'Georgie?' Baxter said. 'Who's Georgie?'

For a while, neither of them speaks. That too is part of it, Abby thinks. They both know when there's a need for words and when there's not.

'What time is it?' Baxter says.

'I don't know,' she says. 'I fell asleep when it was still early.'

It's the best she has slept since she left home. No dreams. No waking, fighting the blackness, fighting for breath. No need for an open window.

She feels herself now drifting back into the dreamless, inviting embrace.

'My mother lied to me,' Baxter says.

He doesn't explain it any further, doesn't say where the thought came from, what the lie was. It doesn't matter, Abby says to herself. He will tell her in time perhaps.

She sleeps. Wakes again.

'Niloc said—' she begins.

'Who?'

It's too complicated to explain.

'He said to forget the past and the future, live well now.'

Baxter doesn't reply. She wonders whether he is sleeping, whether he has heard her.

144

'But I can't forget ...' she says, to herself.

Baxter isn't asleep. He props himself up on his elbows and turns towards her.

'What can't you forget, Abby?' he says, his voice low.

TUESDAY, 2 OCTOBER 1973

29

Strachan

*Dawn: The flat above
The Salvation Inn, Brighton*

Strachan leans heavily towards the bathroom mirror and supports himself against the washbasin with one outstretched oversized hand. With the other, he grips the electric razor tightly and works it back and forth across the polished dome of his head.

He goes deliberately, taking care not to nick his scalp; from the beginning he's vowed that, if he's got to do this thing every day, he'll do it right. He's not going to face those jokers in the bar looking like Lon fucking Chaney, his head covered in crusty scabs. He's got enough to put up with from them without that.

Every day begins like this now. He's up at first light and working meticulously at his head while Sally sleeps on in the warm hollow he's left behind in their rumpled bed.

The low complaining drone of the razor seems right for his mood: he's woken again with little enthusiasm for the day. It's been like this every morning for months now. He can't work out why, but it's like an unshakeable cloud has settled on him. It's not that he's unhappy: he's no cause to be unhappy. He's got Sal, he's got The Salvation – by any reckoning, he has so much more than he'd imagined was possible ten years ago.

Back there, back then, his life was going nowhere. Slowly.

Day after day he sat in that lousy bedsit just waiting for the telephone to ring, waiting to see whether he was still wanted, if he was still in the game. And towards the end, whenever it finally did ring, more often than not it turned out to be something and nothing. There was a quiet word to be had with some loser on Mr Smith's behalf; an arm to be twisted; a few teeth to be loosened; a pocket or two to be shaken out. Kids' stuff. And then it was back to more long days of waiting.

No, he's not unhappy. And it isn't that he's bored either. Not exactly. But what he can't figure out is, if he now has all this *more* in his life, how come it doesn't feel like it? How come it feels like he's got so much *less*; like something has been taken from him, something is missing?

He knows part of the answer, of course. Part of it is that he's growing so fucking old.

Dressed only in his vest, he steps back from the mirror and considers his reflection. Ten years behind the bar has taken a toll – he looks like some giant geriatric ape. Why on earth does Sally stay with him? He sucks in the sad sag of his stomach. It doesn't make him feel any better: it draws more attention to the wild thatch of grey hair on his chest. There's now more sprouting and spiralling through the string of his vest than there was left on his scalp when he started this daily head-shaving business.

It was Sal's idea.

He'd always been proud of his hair. From way back, when he was just a lad out on the town, he kept it Brylcreemed and slicked perfectly back. But in the end it betrayed him and he went from a full head to a wispy comb-over in just a couple of years. It got so bad that some of the punters started taking the piss.

Taking the piss out of Strachan? No fucking way. One lunchtime, he decides enough is enough and he comes round from behind the bar to pick two of them up by their collars, take them outside, give them a slap, teach them a lesson. Sally has to step in to stop him.

Later that same day she comes up with the head-shaving idea.

'It'll look good,' she says. 'Sexy. You'll see.'

She cuts his hair short as he sits like a disconsolate schoolboy on a kitchen chair and then leaves him to do the rest. For the next half-hour he works dejectedly at the stubble, smoothing it away little by little. His spirits are only lifted when he reveals the faded zigzag scar that runs across his crown.

Portsmouth, he thinks with a smile. He went into that club alone to have a talk with the slimeball owner. Four of them came at him and one by one he laid them out, spitting blood and teeth.

Great days. It was the summer of 1955 and he was cock of the walk. The best.

With his head half shaved, he stands in front of the mirror and gently caresses the newly revealed scar. He then does the same with the matching smaller one above his left eye.

With renewed enthusiasm he goes back to the razor.

Afterwards he puts on his best pinstripe, white shirt and silk tie. Just like he used to, back when he was someone, he stands in front of the mirror, flexes his shoulders and tugs at his cuffs.

Spick. Span. Not so dusty after all, he thinks.

That evening he goes down the stairs with something of his old swagger. At the door, he pauses and runs his hand over his head, feeling the brute unfamiliar tightness of the skin. No one's going to mess with him; no one's going to take the piss. He's like his old self. He's Strachan again.

But as soon as he steps into the room it starts. Wally Shott, perching on a stool at the bar, splutters into his beer.

'Blimey,' he says. 'It's Yul bloody Brynner!'

Without missing a beat, the whole pub launches into it: the theme from *The Magnificent* fucking *Seven*.

> ♫ Dum, dum da-dum
> Dum, dum da-dum ...

Strachan is just about to pick Wally up by the throat when Sally pulls him away.

'He's a customer,' she whispers. 'I've told you before, you can't go hitting the customers.'

Strachan's shoulders slump.

'Anyway,' she says, 'they're only having a bit of fun. Just laugh it off and they'll get used to it soon enough.'

But Strachan hasn't been able to laugh. And they haven't got used to it. And as he unplugs the razor and smacks aftershave on to his shining scalp, he knows he'll hear it again today and every day. Hummed mockingly low behind his back, every time he makes his way through the bar.

♪ Dum, dum da-dum ...

153

30

Christie

The house at Pound Hill

In the shadowy half-light, Christie's eyes blink open; her heart thumps. Strachan has woken her from a frantic dream.

It began with the excited shouts of the children playing hide-and-seek in the park beneath Megan's tree. It ended in a rising panic as Christie searched for them, lost in a derelict house in a clearing in a towering forest. She climbed a cobwebbed ladder, pushed open a creaking loft-hatch. And there he was.

Standing above her in a roofless attic, black against a bleached sky.

Strachan has often appeared to Christie in the dead hours of the night. She never sees his face, but knows it's him — because he's always the one who comes to tilt her dreams into nightmares.

She is on her father's knee, singing, or she's pushing hard on her pedals as she cycles the rolling green crest of the Downs towards Devil's Dyke, or she's tiptoeing down a steep pebbled beach to the water's edge. Or a long rope is turning and she and Megan are skipping, taking it in turns to jump in and then out.

Granny was in the kitchen. Doing a bit of stitching ...

And suddenly he's there. An inky-black shape, a heavy-shouldered dark presence; a suited, slick-haired silhouette picked out against a cloudless sky.

As her heart gradually slows, Christie sits upright in the armchair and remonstrates with herself. It's absurd at her age to be having childish nightmares about a hired thug like Strachan, a thug she hasn't seen for a decade.

In any case, she tells herself, not for the first time, she has more reasons to thank him than to fear him.

It's because of him that she found out the truth. He tracked them down to the caravan in the woods and confronted her and then Truman with all the lies. About the money. About someone called Sally. Someone called Doll. About everything.

And it's because of him that she found Nanna Bird. Sneeringly, he handed Christie her address. He did it with undisguised malice, taking pleasure in showing her how naïve and stupid she'd been. But it turned out to be the greatest gift he could have given. Unwittingly, he led her and the children to Nanna's love.

Yes, she should thank him, not fear him.

But telling herself this, reminding herself, doesn't help. Because it's not just her who is haunted by Strachan. He was always in Megan's mind too.

'The man came to the forest to hurt Daddy,' Megan says.

Megan had seen it all from the caravan step.

'Yes,' Christie says.

She's so tired, worn down by the questions. They've had the same conversation a hundred times.

'But why did he come?'

'I've told you,' Christie says: 'I don't know.'

She gives the same answer every time – she can't bring herself to tell her daughter the truth. Something tells her that she mustn't destroy the flawless picture of her father that Megan has constructed. She's too fragile for that.

'But why did the man come?' Megan says.

'I just don't know, Megan,' Christie says, as patiently as she can.

She knows Megan doesn't believe her.

It's absurd: Christie is keeping the truth about Truman to herself and, in doing so, is lying to her daughter. And every lie makes her daughter trust her less.

'But why did Daddy go?'

Christie sighs, tries again.

'It wasn't you, Megan,' she tells her. 'It wasn't anything to do with you. Daddy loved you.'

It isn't enough. It's never enough.

'But if he loved me, why did he go?'

'Because Mummy and Daddy just weren't happy.'

That much at least was true.

'But why weren't you happy?'

Megan has forgotten all the tears – hers, Christie's – has wiped them from her memory.

'Was it because of me?' she says.

As the early-morning light finds its way in a weak shaft through the half-open curtains of the sitting room, Christie's eyes are suddenly heavy. The night has been turbulent; she has slept little. Too many memories. Too many ghosts.

In the comforting embrace of the armchair, she lets her eyes close, putting off the moment when she has to face the day. Staying there, drifting in a cushioned space somewhere between waking and sleeping, it's as if none of it is happening, none of it is real. Nanna Bird isn't in hospital, hasn't fallen to the kitchen floor.

Finally, reluctantly, she forces her eyes open. She can put it off no longer.

She has to go to the office, to explain to Ray why she can't be at work. Not today.

She has telephone calls she must make.

And then she must go to the hospital. To wait.

157

31

Abby

Later that morning: Lecture Theatre One

A bby is sitting alone, shivering, shaking – she isn't sure whether it's with shock, hurt or indignation. At the far side of the lecture theatre, Georgie and her friends huddle noisily together, laugh showily. Moments ago, when Abby finally found the courage to walk through the door, they had deliberately, ostentatiously turned their backs.

'Slut!' one of them now whispers stagily – loud enough for everyone to hear, to prompt a new burst of laughter, to make her blush crimson once more.

It's the same word Georgie used, outside in the corridor.

They were waiting for her at the foot of the stairs, Georgie and her friends. Innocently, Abby greeted them with a wide, delighted smile. How wonderful they should wait for her like that.

The smile disappears instantly.

'Welsh slut!' Georgie leans into Abby's face and hisses.

'What?' Abby says, taken aback.

'You didn't even like him!' Georgie says. 'You didn't even know who he was!'

'I don't under—' Abby starts to say.

'But that didn't stop you, did it?' Georgie cuts across her.

'Stop what?' Abby says, taking a step backwards.

'And you knew *I* liked him!' Georgie says, ignoring her question, jabbing at her now with a finger to her chest. 'You knew!'

It's only then that Abby notices Josh, standing amongst Georgie's friends, with a knowing grin on his face. Hazily, she begins to understand. He's told them something. About her and Baxter.

'Is that why?' Georgie says tauntingly. 'Is that why *you* had to have him? Because *I* liked him, because he was looking at me?'

'Have him?' Abby says, not understanding.

'I thought you were my friend!' Georgie says.

'But I am your friend ...' Abby says plaintively,

'*But I am your friend,*' Georgie mimics, her voice a cruel sing-song.

'I am, Georgie,' Abby says urgently.

'Some friend!' Georgie spits.

'But what have I done?' Abby says desperately.

Georgie turns to her group of friends.

'She doesn't even know, Little Miss Innocent!' she says. 'With her stars and her rings and her painted nails.'

'But nothing hap—' Abby tries to say.

'Slut!' Georgie says again, turning away.

'Slag!' one of her friends offers in support, over her shoulder as they walk away.

'Strumpet!' says another.

'Trollop!' someone else volunteers, to laughter.

Josh glances at Abby, shrugs and hurries after them.

*

At dawn Abby slipped from beneath Baxter's heavy coat and crept smiling from his room. It was a night she'd never forget. Drifting in and out of sleep; sending words into the darkness, hearing his deep voice in reply. It had been strange and wonderful; magical.

She didn't want to be there though when he finally woke. They would both be embarrassed, wouldn't be able to meet each other's eye, wouldn't know what to say. The magic would be lost.

Making her way up the stairs to her corridor above, Abby's hand goes to her mouth to stifle her scandalised laughter.

Little Miss Prim has spent a night in a boy's room!

She did it at first to keep him safe for Georgie. But she stayed because *she* wanted to. Nothing happened, of course, nothing bad; it was more *Swallows and Amazons* than *Lady Chatterley's Lover*. But it was the greatest adventure of her life.

And she slept! Wonderful dreamless sleep.

Back in her room, Abby sits on her bed trying to put a name to the feelings bubbling in her stomach, her chest, her throat. Finally she decides that one word won't do. She needs three.

What she's feeling is *surprise, exhilaration, delight*.

No, that's not it, not all of it, she realises. She needs a fourth.

What she's feeling is *happiness*.

And there's something more. There's anticipation too. She can't remember a time when she's been so excited about a day beginning.

*

The lecture theatre is filling up now. No one comes to sit beside her.

'Slattern!' someone turns and shouts from the other side of the room, to renewed laughter.

At school, Abby always stood on the edge of playground arguments; girls falling out over boys. Who likes Tommy Williams; who fancies Gareth Watson; who kissed Hywel Crumpler; who stole Billy Keates from Caroline Crocker at the school disco.

She, of course, was never involved. Always alone, always at the periphery of things. That was how she lived her life.

And that's part of the unfairness now. She's eighteen years old and she's never even been out with a boy! No one has ever asked her – they'd all been warned off. And even if they had asked, her dad would never have allowed it. Because he never let her go anywhere. Eighteen years old and she's never even held a boy's hand – not since she was ten, walking home one day from school with Brynmor Roberts. And yet she's being accused of ... of this!

She can't even find the words for it.

Happiness. That's what she'd felt. But now it's mortification. Mortification and guilt. And that's entirely ridiculous. Because she has nothing to feel guilty about.

But she's been humiliated. She feels degraded, somehow unclean. And she's an outsider again.

Only one thing can possibly make it worse, she thinks. And that's Baxter walking through the door, sitting next to her and confirming it all in their minds.

32

Baxter

The Attenborough Tower

Baxter's eyes are sticky, gritty, swollen. As he stumbles down the wide, lurching stairs towards the lecture theatre, they are hurting. Like someone is putting pins through them. From the inside.

And they're untrustworthy. They don't focus. Can't. Not properly.

But it's not just his eyes that are unreliable, he thinks as he hangs on to the handrail to steady himself. It's all of him. Every last sore, nauseous inch. At The Old Horse nothing seemed beyond him; he was Jumping Jack Flash, super-human, invincible. Now though he feels uncertain of his body. As if, in the sobering dawn, he has somehow disowned it. Or it him.

He hurries along the corridor. Despite his fuddled brain, his rebellious guts and every aching part of him, he has hauled himself from his bed and he's determined not to be late for the lecture.

His university life is finally, belatedly, beginning.

He may not be capable of much, but he's determined to be there. He *has* to be there. He can't miss two lectures in a row. The university will begin to notice. He'll be hauled up before some professor. Warned.

And he's determined too to see Abby, to thank her for watching him, to apologise for her having to watch, to explain.

No, it's simpler than that. He just wants to be with her.

He'd imagined it, dreamed about it and it had happened. She was there all night. In his room – *in his frigging room!* – and yet he didn't even manage to hold her hand. And in the morning she was gone.

But I can't forget ...

That's what she'd said – as though she wanted to tell him something and then couldn't. What did she mean?

At the door to the lecture theatre, he pauses, closes his eyes, breathes deeply, beats back a new tide of nausea. The lecture hasn't begun. He is only just there in body – and barely at all in mind and spirit – but at least he's made it on time.

As he steps inside, for a moment, in the sudden brightness of the amphitheatred lecture hall, his eyes send messages his slow brain can't decode. An unsettled sea of faces swims in a vast, steep-stepped room of impossible whiteness.

He sways, grips the doorframe. From somewhere on the far side of the lecture hall there is a piercing wolf-whistle and a quickfire burst of laughter.

The room gradually shifts into focus. Scanning the rows in front of him, Baxter desperately seeks Abby out.

Just when he has decided she isn't there, he finds her.

She is sitting towards the back of the room. There's an empty seat beside her. She's waiting for him; she has even kept a place for him.

Baxter begins to climb towards her. As he climbs, he starts to feel better: the sickness falling away from him with each step, his eyes opening wide for the first time that morning. He looks up and smiles.

She meets his eye.

Doesn't smile.

Bites her lip.

Shakes her head.

Turns away.

Defeated, Baxter slumps into the nearest empty seat. It's obvious: she doesn't want him anywhere near her.

He can't make sense of it. They'd had this thing, this totally amazing connection, when they talked into the night. She could have left at any time; but she chose to stay. How can he have got it so wrong?

He closes his eyes. His head begins to throb again.

The room falls quiet. Baxter raises his eyelids just enough to see.

Behind the lectern, where the eagle-eyed professor stood yesterday, is a chubby middle-aged mop-haired man, wearing a black jacket, black T-shirt and black bell-bottom jeans. He looks like a middle-aged, paunchy Paul McCartney.

'Good-morning,' he says with a chirpiness that cuts through Baxter, makes him wince.

'A quick message before we get under way, I'm afraid,' he

says. 'One of you lot has got to leave us before we begin. There's been an urgent telephone call for ...'

Urgent?

'Hang on a sec,' he says, fishing in his trouser pocket for a slip of paper. 'I've got the name somewhere here ...'

That doesn't sound good for someone, Baxter thinks as he settles queasily further into his seat, closes his eyes. But at least it won't be him this time. It was his turn yesterday. It's some other poor sucker today.

'Do we have a Mr Bird with us?' the mop-haired lecturer looks up and says. 'A Mr Baxter Bird?'

33

Abby

Lecture Theatre One

Abby watches as Baxter rises reluctantly from his seat. Yesterday she didn't know he existed; now she's gripped with anxiety.

Urgent? What now?

'Mr Bird?' the lecturer says again.

Baxter answers him with a shocked half-hearted nod.

'Mr Bird, you'd better fly,' the lecturer says.

He looks up at his audience, raising his eyebrows, grimacing, hamming it up like a second-rate stand-up comedian, extracting the small embarrassed laugh that dutifully follows. Bird. Fly. Geddit?

'Sorry,' he says. 'Couldn't resist. But you really should hurry, my friend. Someone's got a message for you outside.'

Abby feels a tightening in her stomach. His father is dying. Isn't that enough for anyone?

Preparing to leave, Baxter half turns towards her. As he does so, she realises with a small shock that until then she hasn't really looked at him. She'd seen him only in the distance when

Georgie pointed him out, she'd watched him on his bed in the half-light and, moments ago, she turned her head away as he climbed towards her.

He looks now, she thinks, like the boy he is inside, not the man he was trying to be, climbing the steps towards her. Awkward, uncertain, his long fair hair dishevelled, his face ghostly white, he's a schoolboy being called from a class-room. A schoolboy who loves long words. *Paradigm. Pantechnicon.*

She feels her heart breaking a little for him and a thought comes that surprises her – wherever he now has to go, he mustn't go alone. He shouldn't have to face whatever the message is by himself; he needs someone with him, to hold him, take care of him,

Her hand reaches for her Biba bag on the floor at her feet. Should *she* go with him? Would he want her to?

She makes a decision.

If he looks at her, if he asks her with his eyes, she *will* go. She'll have to. Ridiculously, childishly, she's let him down once already by not letting him sit next to her. She can't disappoint him again.

Baxter turns fully towards her as if to say goodbye. Forcing a thin weary smile, he raises his shoulders in a questioning, apologetic shrug.

Abby reaches once more for her bag and readies herself.

But then she hears the imagined hiss.

Welsh tart. Slut. *Slag.*

She sits back, feeling her courage ebb away.

Incapable of movement, she stays exactly where she is as Baxter makes his solitary way back down the steps and then as he hesitates for a moment in the doorway.

167

Breaking the silence of the lecture hall, the mop-haired lecturer begins.

'"Parting is all we know of heaven/And all we need of hell",' he intones as the door finally swings to a close behind Baxter. 'Who can tell me where those lines come from?'

34

Christie

Crawley District General Hospital

Nanna Bird is half sitting, half lying in her hospital bed: a frail, reduced figure barely disturbing the surface of her plump nest of pillows. Her eyes are closed, her breath rasping and erratic.

During the past five days, each time Christie has come to her bedside, it has been a new shock to see her like this. In Christie's mind, she remains such a presence, full of life and laughter. It's difficult to believe that this is the same woman.

So much has been taken away from her, so quickly: Baxter and Harry would hardly recognise her now.

Nanna's head has fallen to one side and her hair has been eased forwards by the pillows into a grey unruly fringe. Christie brushes the hair lightly away from Nanna's forehead with her fingertips. Absorbed by her task, glad to be able to do some small thing for her, she keeps gently brushing until Nanna is looking a little more like herself.

It's important that Nanna does look like herself. For her own sake, of course. But mainly for Baxter's.

Christie had gone early to the office and waited for Ray to arrive. He let her use the telephone to make her calls.

'Give Nanna my love,' he then said foolishly, self-consciously as Christie hurried back out through the door. Although he'd never met Nanna, he knew what she meant to Christie and the boys.

She did give Nanna his love. As soon as she arrived, as she chatted to her. Holding her hand. Fighting tears. Trying to pretend Nanna could hear. Imagining her reaction to a man she didn't know, sending her love.

'Well, it's never too late!' Nanna would say. Laughing.

The telephone calls were quickly made. A message left at the university for Baxter – how soon would he get it? When would he be able to come? – and a brief conversation with her mother. Nothing would be said to Harry yet. He is too young to come to the hospital; it would just upset him to see Nanna like this. It's better he remembers her as she was. Christie will go down to Brighton to speak to him as soon as she can.

The only person she hasn't been able to get a message to is Truman. She doesn't know where he is, how to contact him. But at least he saw his mother in the hospital, said a goodbye of sorts.

Good-night, he'd said. *Sleep tight, princess.*

He knew then, perhaps, that she wouldn't come out of hospital. Christie wasn't ready to accept it. She still isn't.

She reaches again for Nanna's hand, strokes it, pats it.

'Nanna ...' she says. 'Whatever will I do without you?'

35

Truman

Forty minutes later: Leicester Station

Breathlessly, Truman sits down opposite Baxter as the train pulls away from the platform. He takes a handkerchief from his pocket and mops at his forehead. He had to run down the long station steps as the guard's whistle blew and only just managed to yank open a carriage door and swing inside as the train moved off. He then walked the length of the train to find Baxter's compartment.

'Only just made it!' he says, collapsing into his seat.

Baxter doesn't answer. He looks paler than death, Truman thinks. There's something in his eyes though. Something hostile. Angry.

'Everything all right, sport?' Truman says, reaching for his cigarettes.

What the hell's wrong with the kid now? They'd been getting along just fine, hadn't they?

'Did you know?' Baxter says, challenge in his voice.

'Know what?' Truman says, clicking his lighter, inhaling deeply.

'About Nanna?'

Truman frowns: he doesn't understand what the boy is going on about.

'About her being in hospital?' Baxter says.

So that's it. They'd spent all yesterday together and he hadn't told him about his precious '*Nanna*' being in hospital. But the fact is that it hadn't occurred to Truman to tell the boy about it. The truth is, he still hasn't got his mind around this connection between Baxter and his old mum. He'd made sure to keep it separate: mother in Crawley, wife and kids in Brighton. Neither knowing about the other. It worked best that way. It's not his fault they've now got themselves tangled up. So there's no point in the kid getting surly; he can't be blamed for not telling him.

'I thought you knew,' he says. 'I thought your mother must have told you.'

That's right: if it's anyone's fault, it's Christie's.

He settles back in his seat, takes another long drag on his cigarette, closes his eyes and lets the smoke slowly escape as he listens to the rhythmic clackety-clack of the wheels on the track.

The silence between them now is good. He can do without talking. He can certainly do without grief from the boy. It was quite a day yesterday; and not the night he'd expected.

After the taxi dropped Baxter at his hall of residence, it delivered Truman a few minutes later to the driveway of a grand Victorian house, illuminated by a pair of ornate black cast-iron lamps. A broad flight of tiled steps swept steeply up to a porticoed, brass-furnitured door.

'This it?' the taxi driver says.

'Guess so,' Truman answers, scarcely believing his luck.

The flat is on the first floor and, as Truman pushes open the door, he lets out a low whistle.

When Rosie handed him the key, he'd thought it was enough that he'd have somewhere to lay his head. He hadn't expected this. The place is straight out of *Ideal Home*: all antique polished walnut, Turkish carpets, gilded picture frames, crystal glasses and silver plate. Truman has never seen anything like it.

This'll do nicely, he thinks with a grin.

He goes through to the bedroom, sits on the bed, tries it for softness, imagines Rosie beside him between the sheets.

Very nicely indeed.

On the bedside table there's one of the new white Trimphones. The closest Truman has been to one before is an advertisement in the newspaper. He lifts the receiver, enjoys the feel of it in his hand. The new amidst the old.

He looks around the room, taking it in.

This, he thinks, *this* is the life he should always have had. This is what he deserves. It's what he's chased for years, with this scheme or that. And now he's been handed a taste of it. For nothing.

He takes a slip of paper from his pocket and dials Rosie's number.

'Oh, Mr Bird,' she answers anxiously. 'Is everything all right? Are *you* all right?'

Everything's more than all right, he thinks.

'Not really,' he says, tapping at his heart as though she might hear. 'I was hoping we could talk.'

'Talk?' she says.

He likes her voice. He thought she was stuck-up at first – but he likes her being posh, he decides. She's even posher on the phone.

'I thought we might meet up,' he says. 'Talk about Baxter.'

'Baxter?' she says.

'I need your help,' he says.

That'll do it. With any woman, that'll do it every time.

They meet at a pub not far away, The Black Dog. He'd expected her to doll herself up a bit: best frock, bit of mascara, squirt of hairspray, dab of perfume, that sort of thing. Instead she's wearing jeans and a baggy jumper and her hair is down. He's in a suit; she looks like some bloody hippie just back from a concert on the Isle of Wight.

Truman is disappointed. She might have made a bit of an effort.

But then Marvin Gaye starts up from the jukebox.

♫ Let's get it on, oh baby
Let's get it on, let's love baby . . .

And Truman forgives her. He leans across the table, puts his head close to hers. They talk about Baxter. He tells her about the way the boy was with him – the way he was at first, of course. He was cold, he says. Silent. Antagonistic.

It's amazing what you can do with just a bit of the truth.

She says what he expects her to say. He has to give it time. He has to let the boy get used to him being around. And he's got to let Baxter come to terms with his . . . his condition.

He watches as she taps at a spot below her breast. Nice. He makes his move.

'He's not the only one who has to get used to it, Rosie,' he says, looking dejected, broken.

'Oh, Mr Bird,' she says. Reaching across the table. Patting his hand.

Bingo!

'There's so much that I haven't done in my life,' he says, putting his hand on hers.

She leaves her hand where it is. Smiles supportively.

'Perhaps there's still time,' she says.

'I don't know . . .' he says, unable to carry on.

'What is it?' she says. Meeting his eye. Encouraging him.

'It's just . . . I've been on my own so long . . .' he says.

'On your own?'

'There's been no one else, you see,' he says. 'Not since Baxter's mother and I broke up.'

He pauses, picks up a beer mat, plays with it, lets Marvin sing.

♪ Let's get it on, oh baby . . .

'I don't know how to say this, Rosie,' he says, leaning closer.

'Say what?' she says, patting at her hair.

He looks down at the tabletop. Coy.

'That I was too loyal. Even after we'd parted.'

She shakes her head, not quite understanding.

'You see,' he says, 'I've never been with another woman . . . only Baxter's mother.'

'Oh, Mr Bird,' she says. Flustered.

175

'And I guess, now, I never will,' he says, his hand going slowly to his chest.

Tap. Tap. Tap.

He's got her. For a moment, he's sure he has. But then a woman's voice trills across the bar.

'Rosetta, darling!'

And he loses her.

The trilling woman comes across to join them and for half an hour he listens to this toffee-nosed bitch of a friend of hers go on about some poxy play she's been to see. She's all *fin de siècle* this and *belle époque* that and post-Impressionist iconoclastic something else. Like she's swallowed a dictionary. He smiles at first, pretending to show an interest. But when he can't stand it any longer, he makes his apologies and heads back to the flat.

When the Trimphone wakes him in the morning, he expects it to be Rosie, apologising. But instead she tells him about Baxter heading off on a train to see his nanna.

The train rattles on and Truman keeps his eyes closed. That way, he reckons, they won't have to talk.

He's wrong.

'Why did you leave?' Baxter says.

What does he mean, *leave*? He took him to where his room was. He didn't leave him anywhere.

'Leave?' he says, yawning, eyes still closed.

'Leave us,' Baxter says, the challenge back in his voice. 'Ten years ago. Why did you just walk away and leave us?'

Truman opens his eyes. So that's it. That's what's narking the boy. Well, he's not having it. *Leave*? He didn't leave:

176

Christie threw him out. He's not the one the boy should be having a go at.

Irritably, he clicks open the lid of the small metal ashtray in the armrest of his seat and stubs out his cigarette.

'That's another thing you'd better take up with your bloody mother,' he says bitterly.

Baxter looks at him, the anger suddenly gone from his eyes.

'She told us you were dead,' he says.

'*What?*' Truman says.

'She told us you were dead . . . ' Baxter says again, his voice trailing away.

36

Baxter

On the train

Baxter stares out of the window, not really focusing as the train cuts between rolling green fields and then snakes briefly alongside a motorway. He feels bad. He hadn't meant to be angry with his father; it just happened. He'd started talking and it came spilling out.

It's his mother he should be angry with. She lied to him, lied to all of them, about his father being dead. And now she's only just got round to letting him know that Nanna's in hospital. She's been there since last Thursday, Dr Paulizky told him.

She was waiting for him outside the lecture theatre.

'Hello, Baxter,' she says, with a small quick smile. 'It's Rosetta Paulizky.'

As if he could forget.

'Shall we go to the room?' she says, turning to walk down the corridor.

Baxter doesn't budge. He's not going through all that hair-patting and hesitation again, all that hold-my-hand-if-

178

you-want-to. He doesn't feel up to it. In any case, he knows it's going to be about his father. It has to be. He's taken a turn for the worse. Or, more likely, he's gone, disappeared again. Just as he's getting to know him. That'll be it.

'Whatever it is,' he says, 'just tell me, please.'

Dr Paulizky walks back to him, comes close.

'It's your nanna,' she says quickly, quietly.

Nanna?

'She's in hospital,' she says. 'Your mother rang and left a message. You need to go home. Right now.'

'Home?'

He isn't quite getting it.

Nanna?

'Your grandmother had a stroke,' Dr Paulizky says, speaking more slowly, more deliberately now. 'Last Thursday. It doesn't look good, I'm afraid.'

Dr Paulizky reaches out and takes his hand. Squeezes it.

'I'm so sorry, Baxter,' she says.

179

37

Strachan

Lunchtime: The bar of The Salvation

Strachan is standing behind the bar, slowly looking around the room, studying it. He likes it like this: empty, ordered, polished, the moment before opening. It's one of his favourite times of the day.

And the pub, *his* pub, looks good. He and Sal are right to be proud. It was a dump when they took it on. Shabby battered tables and chairs, scuffed parquet flooring, peeling red flock paper on the walls; it was a place you only went to when nowhere else would have you.

They'd had them all back then. Drunks, low-lifes, no-lifes; bent coppers looking for a mark; twitchy weaselling ex-cons just out from the Scrubs; bent-nosed hard-cases; peroxide blondes in leather mini-skirts and laddered fishnets, fifty years old, dead-eyed and still on the game.

Within weeks of Strachan taking over, they were gone. All of them. He enjoyed that. Clearing them out with a look, a stare, a twisted arm, a hand to the throat, a swing of his fist or of the baseball bat that's now propped by the door behind the bar. And not one of them had dared to show their face again.

He'd been the big fella cleaning the fucking stables. Hercules: the one they taught him about at school.

In the following months, they had the place scrubbed, decorated, carpeted. They had new furniture, lighting, the lot. And quickly a better class of punter started to put their head around the door and venture in. And then word had got round and pretty soon they had a hit on their hands.

One of the most popular boozers in Brighton: on a busy night now, it roars.

That's part of the problem, of course, Strachan thinks. It was too easy, too quick. It isn't just that a geriatric ape stares dimly back at him from the steamed bathroom mirror every morning; it's that the excitement of sorting the place out has gone.

He checks his watch, runs a hand across his shaven head, pulls at his cuffs, walks across the bar, straightening a beer mat on a table as he goes. At the door he slides the bolts and then makes his way back behind the counter.

Wally Shott will be first in. He always is. You can set your watch by him.

'Morning, landlord,' Wally shouts as he pushes through the door, cigarette hanging from his mouth. 'Pint of your finest, if you please.'

As Strachan angles a straight glass beneath the pump and pulls at the ivory handle, he tries again to work it out. What does he mean, the excitement has gone?

He doesn't mean that he wants to go back and do it all again. Why the fuck would he want to do that? And it's not that he wants to do it somewhere else: he's not ambitious, he doesn't want a second pub, a bigger pub. No, that's not it. It's more straightforward than that.

He just misses who he was back then.

Because back then he felt like what he was, what he'd always been. He felt like a man. *The* man.

38

Abby

The Union coffee bar

Georgie pushes her cup to one side, leans back in her chair and glances distractedly around the room as if looking for inspiration, seeking help. She doesn't find it; the near-empty coffee bar is echoing, dingy, dimly lit. When it's full, it buzzes; now only a few tables are occupied. She turns back to Abby.

'I'm so sorry, Abby,' she says. 'Honestly, I feel terrible.'

She reaches across the table and takes Abby's hand.

'Just terrible,' she says again. 'I've been a real cow.'

Abby shakes her head, offers a fleeting smile. She will never feel about her the same way again, never really trust her; but Georgie doesn't need to know that.

'I can be like that,' Georgie says, shame-faced. 'Sometimes.'

Abby gently withdraws her hand.

'Friends?' Georgie says.

'Friends,' Abby replies.

She'd made the decision halfway through the mop-haired

lecturer's talk. By then, she was calmer, the shaking had stopped. She'd heard her mam's voice telling her: either she was going to have months of misery being taunted by Georgie and her friends or she could swallow her pride and confront her.

What's it going to be, Abby?

There was no decision to make. What was happening was childish, stupid, ridiculous. There was Baxter with his father dying and an urgent message he'd been called out to take – and here she was, having to deal with ... with *this*.

In the corridor outside the lecture theatre, she taps Georgie on the shoulder.

'Whatever it is, I don't want to hear it,' Georgie snaps, swinging round.

'No, Georgie,' Abby says, gathering her courage, her determination. 'You've got to listen.'

She tells her story deadpan: quickly, quietly.

I didn't want to go to his room. I'd never even spoken to him before. Josh begged me because someone needed to watch him; because he'd had too much to drink; because he'd found out his father is dying.

'*Dying?*' Georgie says, shocked.

Abby carries on. When I saw it was the boy you liked, I thought I should watch him. For *you*.

'Oh, Abby,' Georgie says, softening, apologetic.

Nothing happened, Abby says. I watched him. I went.

Georgie hugs her.

'Oh, Abby,' she says. 'I'm so sorry.'

Abby gently pulls herself free. She isn't finished yet.

'I'm so hurt you thought of me like that, Georgie,' she says. 'I'm not that kind of girl. I don't ... I don't sleep around.'

Sleep around? Is that what you were supposed to say? Is that what Bronwyn Chaffey screamed at Dilys Battrick in the playground? Abby has never spoken like this before. Too much the Little Miss Prim.

'Not a wanton hussy then?' Georgie says. Trying to make a joke of it. 'So you haven't got your claws into my Baxter . . .'

Her Baxter? Georgie has never even spoken to him.

'No,' Abby says. Feeling she is somehow betraying him.

'It's because you stayed all night,' Georgie says apologetically. 'That's why I thought the worst. Josh was coming out of his room and saw you this morning.'

'I fell asleep,' Abby says. 'In the chair. When I woke up I just left.'

It isn't quite true; it isn't quite all of it, of course.

She's left out the magic.

39

Christie

Mid-afternoon: Crawley Hospital

A young man with long straggling hair and a thin moustache hobbles in on crutches, his embarrassed smile
revealing two missing front teeth; a heavily pregnant mother
comes reversing in, pushing at the stubborn doors with her
backside, trailing a pushchair, her child pale and sleeping; a
middle-aged bespectacled man in a city suit holds his wife's
arm and impatiently steers her through; a porter briskly
pushes an empty wheelchair along the corridor, whistling as
he goes; a nurse rushes out, coat flapping, her cigarette packet
already in her hand; a stooped balding man shuffles in on his
stick, his face bloodied and bruised from a recent fall.

Christie isn't sure how long she has been sitting in the hospital's small comfortless reception area, watching the glass
doors open and close, waiting for Baxter to arrive.

She rests her eyes to ease an ache of tiredness.

The door swings again on its hinges and she feels the chill
air of the October day on her face. She looks up as a small
grey-haired woman hesitates in the doorway. The woman's

186

dark knee-length raincoat is tightly buttoned and she wears a Paisley-pattern headscarf knotted under her chin. Christie recognises the scarf. She bought an identical one for Nanna from British Home Stores last Christmas.

'Nanna,' she whispers, letting her eyes close again.

Once more the door swings open.

'Mum?' a voice says.

Nanna didn't wait for Baxter. She spared him; hurrying towards the end.

Christie was sitting by her bedside, holding her hand, stroking her forehead, unable to chat any longer, reduced to speechlessness by the mutinous screech that Nanna's breathing had become.

When her breathing starts like this, alarmed, Christie calls for a doctor. He answers her urgent questions with a shake of the head: there is nothing to be done. A nurse then pulls the curtains around the bed and leaves the two of them alone.

Half an hour later it is over.

And it is Nanna's last broken gasp of breath and the abrupt appalling silence that follows that astonishes Christie.

That buckles her.

Collapses her.

Christie rises from her chair, spreading her arms wide to hug Baxter, to hold him.

'Baxter—' she starts to say.

'Where's Nanna?' he says sharply, ignoring the offered hug. 'Is she all right?'

Christie lets her arms drop to her sides. It's only then that she realises Baxter isn't alone.

'Truman?' she says. Shocked to see him; not understanding. Shocked to see the two of them standing side by side, looking so alike, Baxter taller, skinnier than his father.

'I was up visiting the boy,' Truman says matter-of-factly, leaning in to her, pecking her on the cheek before she can think to stop him.

She told Baxter his father is dead. Years ago, she told him.

'But—' she begins and then quickly stops.

It doesn't matter now. She will try to deal with it later.

'Is she all right?' Baxter says again.

'We need to go somewhere to talk, Baxter,' Christie says quietly.

He shakes his head.

'No, I want to see her now,' he says. 'I've come all this way, I want to talk to her.'

Christie bites her lip.

'Is she worse?' Truman says.

Christie looks up at him, unable to find any words. She sees sudden understanding cloud his eyes.

'She's not—?'

Christie nods.

'NO!' Baxter shouts.

She spreads her arms for him once more, her son: she can see him fighting tears, refusing to let them come. But he doesn't take a step towards her. Instead he turns to his father.

'Come here, boy,' Truman says gruffly.

He pulls Baxter towards him. Holds him close.

And once more Christie lets her empty aching arms drop. Defeated. Done.

40

Truman

Crawley Hospital

Truman hadn't expected the boy to turn to him, hadn't expected to be holding him like this. And he certainly didn't think he'd end up blubbing. He can't remember the last time he cried. Back when he was a nipper, probably. Up to mischief; falling out of some tree or other.

And it's not his old mum going that starts the tears. That's bad enough, of course. They've not been close – not for a long time, perhaps not ever really – but he never wanted anything bad to happen to her. It'll take some getting used to: her not being in the world somewhere, somewhere he can just go if he wants to, if he needs to.

But that's not what starts him off.

It's the feel of the boy in his arms. It makes him blub like a baby.

It feels like nothing else, nothing before. This tall, bony, broad-shouldered lad of his in his arms. It's difficult to put into words without sounding soft. There's the feeling itself of the boy being there; solid and strong. There's the way they sort of fit together, lock together, as if they were always meant to. And then there's this other extraordinary thing. The boy *wants* to be there. He turned to him, his dad; chose *him*.

He looks over the boy's shoulder and sees Christie. There are tears rolling down her cheeks too.

And that's something else, of course, he thinks. It will do him no harm in that department, will it? Christie seeing how he is with Baxter now, how they are together. It's all grist to the mill.

The tears subside. He's feeling more himself again. He eases the boy away, holds him by the shoulders.

'All right, sport?' he asks.

Baxter nods. He looks ashen but his eyes are dry, he is keeping everything in. He's made of strong stuff, the boy.

'Then give your mum a hug, son,' he says. 'I think she needs one.'

Baxter turns, stoops and takes Christie into his arms. For long moments they stand together, rocking.

Truman looks on and smiles. It's good to see his boy looking after his mum; it makes a man proud. She doesn't deserve it, of course. But now isn't the time, is it? So he's done the right thing, the boy. A real chip off the old block, he is.

She's a lot to answer for though. She's only gone and bloody killed him off, told his children he's dead! Why the hell would she do a thing like that?

It's just vindictive, plain nasty. You wouldn't catch Truman Bird pulling a stunt like that. He might stretch the truth, make it work for him, tell a story or two. But a lie like that? That's out of line.

Slowly mother and son part.

'All right, Mum?' Baxter says.

She looks up and shakes her head.

'I'm so sorry, Baxter,' she says.

'What for, Mum?' he says gently.

She pushes the tears from her cheeks with the heel of her hand.

'For Nanna,' she says, ' ... for everything.'

'It's OK, Mum,' Baxter says, holding her briefly again. 'It's OK.'

Once more they part.

'All right, princess?' Truman says.

Christie's eyes go to him and then to Baxter. Again she shakes her head as if she's struggling to make sense of it, seeing them together.

'Would you like to see her?' she says to them both, a catch in her throat.

Truman blinks, swallows, holds his breath.

See her? Why would he want to see his old mum stretched out cold on a hospital slab? It gives him the creeps just to think about it.

He turns to Baxter. The boy looks unsure, bites his lip.

'You don't have to,' Christie says to him softly, reaching out to hold Baxter's hand. 'It might be best to remember Nanna the way she was.'

She's let the boy off the hook; let him off too. Truman breathes again. He doesn't want Christie to think badly of him though.

'I'll go to see her later,' he says. 'To say goodbye.'

Christie looks at him. A question in her eyes.

'I can't do it now, princess,' he explains.

'Why not?' Christie says. 'It might be better now.'

Why not? He looks at his watch, taps at his chest, sees the way through. He doesn't know where he's going, but he's not staying here.

'I've got this appointment,' he says. 'For tests.'

Baxter turns to him.

'You didn't tell me,' he says.

'Didn't want you to worry, sport,' Truman says. 'Thought you had enough on your mind.'

He looks at his watch again.

'Got to run,' he says. 'Don't wait for me. I'll come back later.'

'When will I see you?' Baxter says.

'Tomorrow,' Truman says. 'I'll come up to Leicester tonight and meet you at lunchtime tomorrow. At The Old Horse?'

Baxter nods.

Truman punches him lightly, affectionately, on the arm.

'Take care of your mum, sport,' he says.

Once more he bends to kiss Christie on the cheek. She recoils a little, but again she doesn't stop him. It's all working like a charm.

As he turns and makes for the glass doors, an idea comes to him. That's what he'll do! It will help take his mind off his mum and that slab.

He fishes in his pocket for his cigarettes and lighter; there's the start of a new spring in his step, the beginnings of a grin on his face. Well, why not? He's got the afternoon free now, hasn't he? It's been ten years, so she probably won't still be there. But he can track her down. She'll be somewhere in Brighton.

Sally at The Salvation.

He'll hitch down, have a wander around town and be at The Salvation for evening opening time. He'll find her, tell her about his mum; she'll hold his hand, comfort him. They'll have a drink or two, a stroll on the pier for old times' sake, a few laughs.

And with this golden key of his, this magic key?

They'll go back to her place. Tap. Tap. Tap.

41

Baxter

Two hours later: On the train

What was it he heard as the door to the lecture theatre closed behind him?

Parting is all we know of heaven
And all we need of hell

Baxter struggles with the idea of heaven, but if hell is every last part of you being completely wiped out, being left totally wrecked, if it's a pain that burns in your eyes and a gnawing ache that hollows you from inside, and if it's Jagger singing the same words over and over in your head, then it's right enough.

♫ I see a red door and I want it painted black
No colours any more, I want them to turn black ...

On the journey down, during the long silences shared with his father, Baxter hadn't been prepared to entertain the idea that Nanna was dying. Somehow he managed to keep it from his head. Dr Paulizky had said it didn't look good – but that didn't mean anything, did it? No: he would go to the hospital, he would sit by her bed, they would talk as they always talked, then he'd return to Leicester and in a few days she'd be out and everything would be back to normal. That was as far he'd allowed his mind to travel.

He certainly hadn't thought he would be on a train again, just hours later, heading to Leicester, knowing that he would never be with her again; knowing it but not nearly ready to accept it.

Every so often, tears have threatened. Threatened but not come. He can't remember ever crying, not even on Megan's day. Part of him wants to cry now, longs for the release of it. But a bigger part knows that it's best stay strong, hold it in.

Instead of tears, a tightness in his chest, his throat, had gripped him; the same tightness and heaviness he feels every time he thinks about his sister. He had to stop and fight for breath as he walked from the hospital to the station and again as he waited on the platform for the train.

They threaten again now, the tears, and he fights them back as the train pulls away from the platform with Baxter alone in his compartment.

After his father goes out through the hospital's glass doors, Baxter and Christie find chairs in the quietest corner of the reception area. He buys scalding murky coffee in thin plastic cups from a wheezing vending machine.

'I'm so sorry, Baxter,' Christie says again, holding her cup by the rim, sipping absently. 'I should have called you earlier.'

'Why didn't you?' he says. He can't keep the resentment from his voice.

'I thought there was more time,' she says. 'I didn't want to worry you when you were just starting in Leicester.'

'I'm not a kid,' he says, feeling anger rising again.

'I know, Baxter,' she says, apologising, sounding exhausted.

But she doesn't know; she's never known.

There are times – and this is one of them – when it seems to Baxter that she's always been the same: fussing over him, treating him like a child, screwing everything up, sending him to the wrong school, leaving him with no friends, going on about the future she imagined for him.

Baxter knows he's being unfair. She fusses because she loves him. Her dreams have become *his* dreams. And if it wasn't for the wrong school, he wouldn't have got to university.

'You told me Dad was dead,' he says, changing the subject.

'I know,' she says, staring at her coffee. 'It was wrong . . .'

Her voice is small: it trails away to nothing.

'But why?' he demands.

'You were having nightmares,' she says. 'Megan was asking for him all the time. It was breaking her heart.'

'So you lied?' he says angrily.

She says nothing. Just lets her head hang. As if she's taken too many blows. Can't take any more.

'And you made us say goodbye to him like *that*!' Baxter says, not letting it go. 'On the pier . . .'

'It was stupid,' she says. 'But at the time, I thought it was for the best.'

For the best? A lie?

'But I don't get it,' he says. 'Because Dad is such a great guy.'

She keeps her head bowed low; doesn't look at him.

'You don't remember,' she says quietly.

She's right: he doesn't remember. Not clearly. Somehow it has got jumbled, muddled. Before, all his memories of Dad were of being dragged, thrown, shaken, shouted at. But now?

'I thought I did remember about Dad,' he says, wondering aloud. 'But getting to know him in Leicester . . .'

'I don't think we should do this,' his mother says. 'Not here. Not now.'

She's right: he should be thinking about Nanna. He feels suddenly ashamed. But still he can't let it go entirely.

'And now he's dying,' he says, like an accusation. 'Did you know?'

She nods.

'Will you stay tonight?' she asks. 'We can talk about it properly. All of it. We can talk about Nanna too.'

If he stays, he knows it will be a way of forgiving her. And he isn't quite ready for that.

'No,' he says, seeing the hurt register in her eyes. 'I should get back.'

He's missed too much already.

'Will you be all right?' she says.

He's not sure. But he isn't going to admit it.

'Will *you*?' he says.

She bites her lip, nods once more.

And then he does forgive her. A little. By holding her again, swaying with her.

*

197

Outside the school gates, his mother crouches low and straightens his cap and tie; she adjusts the strap of his new satchel.

It's his first day.

He looks at her accusingly. His tie is too tight, his collar feels itchy, his blazer is making him hot, the satchel is too big and heavy. He feels sick.

'I feel sick,' he says.

'It's just nerves,' she says. 'It's the same for everyone.'

Some older boys, bigger boys, go by. They point, laugh.

'You know, I'm so proud of you,' she says, ignoring the laughter. 'Just imagine: if you work hard here, anything is possible. You can do anything. You can make all your dreams come true.'

Dreams? he thinks. All he wants is to be with Megan at her school.

When the letter arrived, his mother and Nanna didn't make much of it in front of Megan.

They hug him, whisper excitedly to him but there is no celebration, no jelly and cakes: Megan failed her 11-Plus the year before and it isn't fair on her to have a party because he has passed his.

So Baxter doesn't think too much of it at first.

He's pleased – because there's never been a letter about him before and because he likes to be good at things – but he doesn't believe it means very much. Not really.

He's wrong. It changes everything.

Throughout that long hot summer holiday when he is eleven years old – as he and Megan go on adventures with

Nanna and play cricket on the sand – the truth slowly sinks in.

Because of some stupid test, he has to go to a different school – a grammar school. And because of that same test, Megan is already at a secondary modern. And that means their life together is over. They'll go to different places, have different friends, do different things. Just because of some stupid test.

It's like they've come to a fork in the road that they've always travelled together. They've got there walking hand in hand, but now they have to go in different directions. And – although he will still see her as she goes her way and he his – the roads will keep diverging, keep taking them further apart.

It isn't fair.

But then suddenly it's all right after all: he and Megan are reprieved.

Almost as soon as he starts at the school, it's decided that the whole system will change: there will be no more stupid grammars and secondary moderns, no more roads forking. Everyone is going to be the same, everyone is on the same road, just some going faster than others.

And he and Megan will be at the same school again, a new school. A 'comprehensive'.

Baxter doesn't know what it means exactly but he runs home happy on the day they announce it at assembly.

But then the worst thing happens. A few weeks later his mother comes back from work and sits with him at the kitchen table.

'I've got the most wonderful news,' she says.

Baxter is excited. Wonderful?

'You won't have to go the comprehensive after all,' she says.

He doesn't understand.

'I've fixed it that you can still go to a grammar school!' she says. 'So you can still make your dreams come true. Like we talked about. What do you think about that?'

What he thinks is that she's got it wrong. There aren't going to be grammar schools. The headmaster said.

'No, Mum—' he starts to explain to her.

'I've fixed it!' she says, delightedly. 'I've fixed it for you to go to the very best school for miles around!'

She's begged a favour of friends at work, at the council. They've agreed that Baxter can go to school in another town; in Reigate, where there will still be a grammar. He will have to go by bus every day, and it will take an hour to get there, but it will be worth it.

'What do you think of that?' she says.

What he thinks is that it's the biggest screw-up of his life.

He protests, he sulks.

'She's so proud of you, Baxter,' Nanna tells him, taking him to one side as his first day approaches. 'She wants only the best for you.'

'But Nanna—'

'No more buts, my brave Baxter Bird,' she says, tickling him, trying to make him laugh. 'It'll be fine, you'll see.'

She calls him that, 'my brave Baxter Bird', whenever he has to do something he doesn't want. Like go to the dentist.

Or 'my busy Baxter Bird'. She calls him that too. When he does his homework.

Roland Roberts holds his nose, like there's a bad smell suddenly in the classroom. All the boys around him do the same.

'Here comes the Pauper,' he says.

Baxter shuffles between the desks. They elbow, jostle. Push.

On the first day – when he'd had to stand blushing, humiliated, in front of the class and be introduced – they'd spotted the patched blazer from the second-hand shop, the darned jumper, the faded school cap, his worn shoes.

'Go away, Pauper Bird,' Roland Roberts hisses in his ear. 'And take your stink with you.'

In the playground they circle him, jab at him.

Baxter says nothing, avoids their eyes, tries to stand his ground.

And he doesn't tell the teachers, doesn't tell his mother or Nanna. There's no point. He knows it will only make it worse.

As time goes by, the taunting becomes less – although it never ends entirely – and he begins to enjoy some things about being at the school. Most of the lessons, the football, the cricket.

But it's still a screw-up.

Because Pauper Bird makes no friends.

'How can I?' he mutters to himself darkly on his long journey home at the end of each day. When he's a pauper amongst the rich boys. When he's the only boy on the bus. When the bus arrives just minutes before the start of the school day. And when he has to pick up his satchel and run to catch it after the final bell. When he can't even stay to kick a ball in the playground.

It *is* a screw-up. No possibility of friends in Reigate, where he doesn't belong. And none in Crawley.

There he is a pariah. The only boy in a different school uniform. The boy who leaves early and comes back late. Megan's brother. Stuck-up. High and mighty. With his posh school and his la-di-da voice.

He's a bad smell in Reigate; posh in Crawley. It's like a half-life; he doesn't really have a life anywhere.

'Why don't you go out and play?' his mother says as he lies on his bed at the weekends reading one book after another.

Because there's no one to play with. Because he doesn't know anyone. Because they don't want to know him. That's why. That's what he should tell her. But he never does.

And what makes it even more of a monumental screw-up? What's the final stroke of cosmic genius in the whole let's-send-Baxter-to-school-in-a-different-town plan? There are no girls.

Reigate Grammar is an all-boys school.

It doesn't matter at first, when he is eleven. But a few years later, suddenly it does start to matter. And then, as the months creep by, it matters more. It matters a lot.

It becomes an obsession; Baxter thinks about it all the time. Waiting for the bus, on the bus, during lessons. How is he ever going to meet girls, *a* girl, *any* girl? Certainly not in Reigate. In Crawley? His only hope, he eventually decides, is one of Megan's friends.

But just when he's plucked up enough courage to ask Megan to help him, Che frigging Guevara walks into her life. Their eyes meet across the Pick 'n' Mix counter at Woolworths, where she's doing a Saturday job, and that's that. After Che, there is never any talking to her again.

And then the half-life is over. Finally.

As he waves goodbye to his mother and Nanna at the station and climbs aboard the train that is to carry him to Leicester, Roger Daltrey is screaming in his head, the orchestra soaring behind him.

> ♫ I'M FREE – I'm free,
> And freedom tastes of reality ...

It's not an easy journey. *En route*, he has to travel across London, heaving a heavy suitcase on and off trains, up and down wooden escalators. And it's just weeks after IRA bombings at Victoria Station, at King's Cross and Euston.

But he doesn't notice the load he is carrying and, despite his mother's fretting, he doesn't worry about the bombs.

Because, finally, he *is* free.

The dream, the university dream has come true: he's free of Reigate, of Crawley. Free to start again in a place where he can be the same as everyone, part of everything.

*

Roger Daltrey fades. Jagger begins again.

♫ I see a red door and I want it painted black

Baxter settles back into his seat on the train, plunges his hands into the pockets of his greatcoat.

But it hasn't turned out that way. Because so far, he hasn't managed to sit through a single lecture. First because of his father; now because of Nanna.

And it feels like the dream is slipping through his fingers, slipping away from him.

The light is going from the afternoon; the train rattles on. Why is he thinking about all of this? Why now?

He knows the answer.

Because Nanna is the one he talked to. Nanna is who he talked to whenever there were things he couldn't say to his mother.

And because Nanna was there for him. After Megan. In a way that his mother couldn't be, because she was only just holding it together for herself and for Harry.

Because Nanna was *always* there for him.

And because she never will be again.

42

Abby

Outside the Union building, Leicester

After Georgie made her apology, she hurried away from the Union building; Abby though has remained in the coffee bar throughout the afternoon.

From time to time she has forced herself to read a few pages of *Bleak House*, but her attention has quickly wandered. For the most part, she has simply sat alone and watched as the tables around hers have emptied and filled again, as ragbag battalions of students in faded denim and crumpled cheesecloth have come and gone.

Each time the coffee bar fills, the jukebox kicks into life: David Bowie, Mott the Hoople, Fleetwood Mac, the Carpenters, Tina Turner.

♫ They call it Nutbush city limits ...

With the comings and goings, it's as if a continually changing tide is swirling around Abby. She is the only constant, somehow unable to bring herself to move.

A kind of sadness settles on her.

It isn't self-pity, she tells herself. It's just that she had been ridiculously happy; the night had been full of magic and she was so excited about the day as it began. Just for a moment, she *wasn't* Alice blundering about in a world she didn't understand. For that brief moment she felt she was starting to belong.

Slut. Slag.

With those words, Georgie destroyed the magic, made it something cheap and tarnished. And – however much they might pretend otherwise in the coming months – she took away the best part of their friendship too: the unconditional part, the part where you trust each other entirely.

So it isn't self-pity. Not exactly. It's more like a small grief for two small deaths. For the loss of the magic; for the loss of her friend.

No, it's three deaths, she corrects herself.

There's the failure of courage – that too had felt like something dying inside. She should have let Baxter sit with her; she should have gone with him when he was called out of the lecture hall, when he needed her.

Baxter: she wonders where he is, what the message was.

In all the swirl of the coffee-bar comings and goings, Abby hasn't seen a single person she knows. It seems to sum it up: she's on her own again, magic gone, friendship gone. She isn't even sure now that she wants to go to London to see that concert. The others probably won't talk to her; she will only end up disappointed.

Now *that*, she tells herself, that *is* self-pity. It's time to get a grip, girl; definitely time to make a move.

The scraping of chairs being pulled from a table on the

other side of the room announces the arrival of another wave of newcomers. Once more the jukebox comes alive. There has been more Bowie than anything else during the afternoon.

♫ It's a god-awful small affair
To the girl with the mousy hair ...

Picking up her Biba bag, Abby makes her way from the room, pausing at the door to listen to the last few bars.

Outside, the chill autumn air surprises her – just as it did on leaving the library the previous day. What somehow doesn't is the sight of the first person she has recognised all afternoon.

Please, not this, not now, she thinks.

'I have been waiting for you, Willow Moon,' Niloc says.

Dressed as before, in saffron headband, rainbow beads and baggy white, he is standing on one leg in the middle of the path, the sole of his right foot tucked into his inner left thigh. His hands are held above his head, clasped together, pointing upwards. His eyes are closed.

Despite herself, Abby stands for a moment, transfixed. Sarah, the girl who rescued her yesterday, warned her about Niloc, but there is something about him that draws Abby irresistibly in. It's as if he casts a spell on her. He looks strange and exotic, speaks in riddles, says mystical things. And he has singled her out. It's as if he is watching over her.

'The yogi says: forget the past, forget the future,' he says. 'Live supremely well now.'

The spell is broken. That's where she went wrong, she thinks! She'd listened to him, believed him. She *had* lived for the moment, agreeing to watch over Baxter. And look where it got her!

'You told me already,' Abby says dismissively, boldly, preparing to walk past him. 'It doesn't work, boyo.'

He blinks open his eyes.

'"Boyo"?' he says, still on one leg, wobbling slightly, his head now cocked to one side.

Abby blushes, her boldness falling away.

'Sorry,' she says, 'it's a Welsh thing.'

He looks her in the eye, as if trying to find the answer to a question.

It's difficult to work him out, Abby thinks: you can't really see what's going on in his mind. And it isn't mysticism, it's all the hair. All you can see of his face are those wild blue eyes lodged between his bushy eyebrows and his long, grey-streaked beard. You can barely see his mouth when it moves.

Niloc closes his eyes once more. She guesses that whatever the question was, he has found his answer.

'Look only for the good in everything,' he says, 'so that you absorb the quality of beauty.'

'*What?*' Abby says, suddenly losing patience.

She's had this . . . this shitty day and he's going on about looking for the *good* in everything. Where's the good in being called a slut?

'If you permit your thoughts to dwell on evil,' he says as though answering her, his voice high, fluting, 'you yourself will become ugly.'

Evil? Ugly? It's ridiculous. *He* is ridiculous. Why is she even listening to this?

She's had enough, heard enough. She pushes past him, making him wobble more.

'Oh, piss off, Niloc!' she hears herself say, using words she's never used before.

43

Strachan

The flat above The Salvation, Brighton

Strachan stares impatiently at his watch; it isn't the first time he's done so in the last hour. Sally is late: if she isn't back soon, she won't be there for opening time.

He heaves himself from his armchair, paces across the living room, twitches back the curtain, peers out to the street below. The light is nearly gone; streetlamps are flickering into life.

Where the fuck is she? She's been out all afternoon.

He clenches his right hand, makes it a fist, smacks it into the palm of his left and paces back across the room. He stops suddenly and his weighty shoulders slump; he leans on the dining table, rests heavily on his knuckles, breathes deeply.

He's kidding himself: he knows why she's late. It's happening, like he's always known it would.

He's losing her.

He'd always thought it couldn't last for ever; that one day she'd find someone else. He's twenty years older than her, for Christ's sake! She still looks the same – at least she does to him – as the day he met her. His Audrey Hepburn; his girl with flashing grey-green eyes.

And him? A miserable superannuated gorilla; a fucking silverback with a sagging gut. That's what he is now.

It's a miracle she's stayed with him as long as she has. Let's face it, it's a miracle she's ever been with him at all.

The first time they kissed, he bent towards her and held her lightly, cautiously, in his arms. She felt so small, fragile; as if at any moment she would snap in two.

'I'm not made of glass,' she whispers, encouraging him, reassuring him, her breath hot in his ear. 'I won't break.'

He squeezes her. But not tightly. Just enough to feel the press of her body against his.

They walk along the seafront; she makes him take his jacket off and roll up his sleeves. She's wearing a short summer dress and her highest heels but still she doesn't come up to his shoulder. She jokes about it; dancing around him as they walk, she teases him about his height, about the muscled breadth of his shoulders. She measures her hand against his. Her giant, she calls him. Her eyes big. Flashing.

He feels clumsy next to her; clumsy taking her into his arms.

The first time they make love, she says it again. He's scarcely able to believe that she's there, with him, that she could possibly want him as much as he wants her. He moves, carefully, tenderly, attentively; keeping his weight from her.

'I told you,' she says, slightly breathless, moving with him, against him, 'I won't break ...'

They move more urgently towards the end. But still he takes care.

Afterwards, wrapped together, he feels her tears warm on his chest. He's hurt her. Or worse: he's disappointed her.

But no.

'My giant,' he hears her say. 'My gentle giant.'

Strachan goes back to the window, yanks the curtain to one side: there's still no sign of her. Again he checks his watch and as he does, he sees it – the shake, the tell-tale shake of his hand.

Fuck it.

It hasn't happened for years. Not since Sally made him go to the doctors, not since the blood-pressure tablets. He can feel his heart racing. He needs to calm down, get a hold of himself.

He understands it now though.

He understands now why he's been waking up every day with a cloud hanging over him. It's been about Sal all along. He must have known, somehow sensed, that something is wrong, that she's found someone else.

Fucking Sal, he'll—

No, he *does* need to get a hold of himself: it might be over, but he's not going to fall apart. Not in front her. And whatever she's done, whatever she's up to, he won't hurt her. He's made his living with his fists – but he can't hurt Sal.

He loves her. He should never have allowed himself to love her so much. Again he sends his fist smacking into his palm.

But he'll hurt *him*, the bastard, whoever he is. He'll find him, take him apart. Piece by fucking piece. He'll—

He hears a voice calling from the stairs.

'It's only me,' Sally shouts.

She comes through the door, unbuttoning her coat.

'It's turned cold out,' she says, not meeting his eye. 'Sorry I'm late. I lost track of the time walking around the shops.'

He can hear the lie in her voice.

'Are you OK, Strachan?' she says.

He doesn't answer.

She's always called him by his name. Over the years, she's tried all the usual terms of endearment but none them ever seemed right: *darling, love, lover, sweetheart* – none of them seemed to fit.

She glances at her watch, slips off her coat.

She has a new blouse on, he notices. A favourite skirt. Her best shoes.

'Look at the time!' she says. 'I'd best go down and open up.'

It's their routine: he does lunchtimes on his own, she opens up in the evenings and he goes down later, when it starts to get busy.

She makes for the door, turns, looks back at him, frowns and finally meets his eye.

'There's something—'

She pauses, starts again. She's nervous, not herself. He can see it in those grey-green eyes.

'There's something we need to talk about,' she finally manages to say.

Strachan tenses, holds his breath. This is it. This is how it ends. Still he says nothing.

'Later,' she says. 'We need to talk later. OK?'

She turns again, walks quickly through the door and back down the stairs.

And only then does Strachan allow himself to breathe.

44

Truman

Opening time: The Salvation Inn, Brighton

T ruman turns his jacket collar up against the cold wind that gusts from the sea and sinks his hands deep into his trouser pockets. Shivering, he stays only a few moments at the top of the steeply banked pebbled beach.

Well, he's never been one for the great outdoors, could never see the point of it, the fun in it. He's more the indoors type, he tells himself with a smile as he struggles across the shifting pebbles and back up to the esplanade. His recreational activities are confined to the warmth of a bar, a bedroom, a bed.

Standing in a lay-by outside Crawley, he'd stuck his thumb out for no longer than a minute before a car pulled over.

MGB Roadster: brand-new, red, soft top. Nice.

The driver though is no more than a kid. He works in the City; a stockbroker. Truman can barely bring himself to say two words to him. Well, there's no justice in the world, is there? A spotty kid driving a motor like that and him still having to rely on his thumb.

But the compensation is that they purr south along the A23 and in no time he finds himself walking down North Street from the Clock Tower.

It's like coming home.

For old times' sake, he goes into Hannington's, to the haberdashery department where Christie worked before they were married. He'd drop in there sometimes back then, to surprise her. To ask her for knicker elastic, just to see her blush.

Twenty years on, nothing much has changed: brightly coloured rolls of fabric are still lined up side by side, some fat, some thin, but all military-correct on sloping shelves; the long dark wooden counter for measuring out is still there; the drawers behind still hold their buttons and pins, tapes and loops, hooks and fasteners, silks and threads. And everywhere there is that same smell of ironed and laundered cotton.

He pauses, closes his eyes, breathes deeply in. It's Christie's scent: fresh, seductive. It was always with her back then. Back when they were young together.

Walking through the department brings it all back to Truman. Her boss was old Manny Bonfield; a miserable bugger with a long face and dark suit. And Mrs Ashmore was the supervisor; a proper dragon.

But now there is no one there whom Truman recognises. It's all too long ago.

From Hannington's he goes to the old house: white-stuccoed, mid-terraced, on a road that runs steeply down to the sea. He stands outside, lights a cigarette, and remembers the day they left in a hurry – getting Christie and the kids packed and out in double-quick time – remembers going back, finding it stripped bare.

Ten years ago it was, but sometimes it still feels painfully like yesterday. Today, though, time has softened it.

They were good times, weren't they? Most of them. Well, some of them.

Finally, he pulls himself together. Blubbing with the boy at the hospital and now coming over all nostalgic? It's not like him. Maybe it's his old mum going that's making him like this; making him lose himself in the past.

But there's no point in that. Live for the moment, always look forward. *Carpe* the bloody *diem*: that's his rule.

From the house, he goes to the beach. To clear his head.

The light is fading, the streetlamps coming on, as he makes his way from the esplanade towards The Salvation.

He jogs across the road, through the slow-moving traffic.

There were good times too with Sal. OK, so she was none too pleased with him at the end, but she'll be over that now. In any case, he'll soon talk her round. Always could.

He doesn't expect to find her still at The Salvation, behind the bar. She'll have moved on by now, found somewhere better; it always was a dump. But it's the place to start; he can have a pint there and ask around. Someone's bound to know where she is now.

Outside, he checks his watch. Perfect. Bang on opening time.

He pushes open the door and steps inside, reaching in his jacket pocket for his cigarettes and lighter as he does so. The bar is empty, he's the first in. He spots at once that the place has been done up. Nice. He looks towards the bar.

Bingo!

She's behind the counter, busy with something on the shelves. She has her back to him, but he recognises her at once. It's the curve of her, the shape of her, the way her hair is pinned up. He'd forgotten just how special she is. He was a mug to ever let her go.

'Hello, princess,' he says, not moving from the doorway.

She turns, her eyes widening, like she's seen a ghost.

'*You?*' she says.

He answers with a lopsided grin.

'You're not welcome here,' Sally says, leaning forwards on the counter. 'I don't want to see you in here. *Ever.*'

He can hear the shake of anger in her voice. No problem. It'll just take some time, that's all.

He taps a cigarette from the packet, puts it to his lips, clicks his lighter, takes a long drag and releases the smoke towards the ceiling.

'Don't be like that, princess,' he says. 'I can explain everything. About before.'

'You've got some nerve,' she says, 'coming back like this.'

She's still angry – but at least she's talking. He smiles, cocks his head.

'Nerve?' he says.

He walks towards the bar. Close enough to breathe her perfume. She backs away.

'I thought you owed money,' she spits at him. 'I thought that's why you vanished.'

'That was years ago, Sal,' he says evenly. 'No one's interested now.'

She shakes her head.

'I wouldn't be so sure about that,' she says, a sneer in her voice.

Of course they're not interested, Truman thinks. Ten years is a long time. He'd borrowed the money from the old man, Mr Smith – and he's probably dead and buried by now. And his thug, Strachan? He'll be well past it.

A shout from the door interrupts his thoughts.

'A pint of your finest, Sally my dear.'

Sally moves towards where the newcomer has perched on a barstool.

'How's things with you, Wally?' Truman hears her say as she pulls at the pump handle.

'Never better,' Wally says, watching the glass fill.

Sally glances back towards Truman. He can see her trying to come to terms with him being there, trying to figure out what she really feels.

She looks good. No, better than that: it's as if the years haven't touched her. The beer looks good too.

'Got one of those for me?' he calls to her.

Sally hands Wally the pint, pulls another and walks back towards Truman. She's forgotten already about chucking him out. He can see in her face that something's softened in her. She's probably been thinking about all the good times they used to have.

See? He knew she'd come round.

'So, what have you been up to?' she says, passing him the pint.

Fair enough, she still isn't quite her old self. She's tense, jumpy; checking her watch, watching the door. But it's progress.

'I've done OK for myself,' he says, taking a first sip. 'Got my own business. Import, export. Record shops. I've even got a record label.'

'Sounds good,' she says.

He can see she's impressed.

'But you're still here,' he says, looking around. 'The place is a lot better though.'

'It was a dump,' she says, forcing a quick smile.

'It certainly was,' Truman laughs.

For a moment there's silence between them.

'Listen, Truman—'

She's used his name.

'Listen, I can't stand here chatting,' she says. 'I've got this telephone call to make . . .'

He reaches across, tries to put his hand on hers. She pulls away.

'Don't go,' he says softly. 'Not yet. I've got something to tell you.'

'What's that?' she says.

He looks her in the eye. Says it slow.

'Just that I've missed you, princess,' he says. 'Missed you so much.'

She flinches; her head going to one side with a question.

'Oh yes?' she snaps. 'What about your wife? Your children?'

It's what that bastard Strachan told her at the end. That's why she's spent all these years being mad with him.

'Forget about them, Sal,' he says. 'I told you, I can explain.'

'Can you?' she says, disbelieving.

'I should have told you the truth back then,' he says. 'Only I was too stupid, too proud.'

He worked it out in the car, while the spotty kid was driving. It's perfect. A hook on the end of a line she'll have to bite on.

'Too proud?'

See? Can't resist.

'The truth is, Sal, I made a bad marriage,' he says, studying his pint. 'I picked a wrong un. Turns out Christie was carrying on behind my back. I ended it as soon as I found out. It was over long before you and me.'

He looks up, meets her eye again.

'So you don't see her?'

'No, I told you,' he says. 'It's over. Divorce. Everything.'

'And the children?'

He's worked that out too.

'I can't even be sure they're mine,' he says bitterly, looking down at his beer again. 'I see one of the boys – he's the one most like me. A chip off the old block. Up at university.'

She's not rushing off to make that call now, is she? He's got her. She's on the end of the line; he only has to play her, gently reel her in.

'So what brings you back here?' she says.

'You do, Sal,' he says, his voice low.

'Me?'

He nods.

'I thought we could have a walk on the pier later, like we used to,' he says. 'I've got something else I need to say.'

Her eyes narrow.

'Can't you say it now?' she says.

'No,' he says, tapping at his heart, giving her a clue. 'It's best we're alone.'

For a moment she seems uncertain. Finally, though, she nods.

'OK,' she says. 'Let me make that telephone call. You stay here and we can make the arrangements later.'

Hook, line, sinker!

The telephone is at the far end of the counter. He watches as she sashays towards it, like she doesn't want him to take her eyes off her, doesn't want him to move an inch from where he is.

Women: you have to love them. It's been even easier than he thought. He hasn't lost it, see? He can still charm the birds from the trees.

'Oh, hello, Mr Black,' he hears her say as she glances back to him, smiling. 'I'm phoning to confirm that order.'

45

Strachan

The flat above The Salvation

When the telephone starts to ring, Strachan is sitting in an armchair by the window. Sunk so deep in his thoughts, he isn't aware of it at first.

She's lied to him – and he's never known her lie before. It confirms everything, that lie: she hasn't been to the shops, she's been somewhere else, with someone else. That's what the new clothes are about, the best shoes.

And there's no avoiding it, no pretending it isn't happening. Later they'll have to talk, the truth will come out and it will all be over.

Over.

Finally, the ringing of the phone cuts through his thoughts. Irritated, he snatches up the receiver.

'What?' he barks.

'Oh, hello, Mr Black,' he hears her say. 'I'm phoning to confirm that order.'

*

It's their signal. Sally needs him downstairs. In a hurry.

It's been years since she's had to use it. Since he cleared the place out, got rid of all the scum, there's rarely been trouble. But she needs him now.

She needs him.

Suddenly his body remembers.

He springs from the chair and is across the room in three powerful strides and out through the door. He moves like an athlete, like a boxer, light on his feet, the adrenalin pumping, taking the stairs two at a time. At the entrance to the bar, he picks up the baseball bat he keeps propped in the corner and pushes the door open a crack.

He hasn't felt like this for years. He's watchful, alert, poised.

In the bar all is quiet. Wally Shott is on his usual stool; Sally is chatting to a punter further along the bar.

It makes no sense. Why the signal?

Strachan focuses again. His eyes go to Wally, to Sally, to the punter. And then he understands.

It's the lying toerag: the one who owes the money. The one who had a thing with Sally. He's come back. Truman something? Truman ... Truman Bird! That's it.

Strachan grips the handle of the baseball bat, flexes his shoulders, juts his chin.

Oh yes. Time to play.

He turns and walks quickly along the corridor, out through the back door and on to the street. Once outside, he sets off in a loping run around the building. He's going to come in through the front and give the toerag something to remember. Something he'll never forget.

Stepping inside, he closes the door softly behind him and reaches down to quietly slide the bolt.

Wally half turns on his barstool towards him. Strachan raises a silencing finger to his lips.

The toerag hasn't heard him come in. He has his back to him and is still chatting to Sally. Strachan can see she's taking care not to look in his direction. He creeps towards the bar, baseball bat in hand.

'Like I told you,' Truman is saying, 'business is good. Imports. Exports. That sort of thing.'

Strachan reaches out with the bat and taps Truman on the shoulder.

'What the—?' he says as he turns.

Strachan steps towards him. They are close enough that he can see the sudden panic in Truman's eyes.

'Who the hell are you?' Truman says.

'Don't disappoint me,' Strachan growls. 'Don't say you've forgotten me.'

46

Truman

The Salvation

ruman recognises the voice first, then the baseball bat: It's the psycho, it's bloody Strachan!

What his mind is struggling with is the rest of him. There's something, something different. He can't put his finger on it.

Finally he gets there: it's the hair, or the lack of it. The psycho bastard is bald now; bald as a bloody coot, and even uglier with it.

'I haven't forgotten . . .' Truman says, his voice trailing off. Strachan smiles.

'I'm glad,' he says, leaning closer. 'I'd have been hurt if you didn't remember me.'

Remember him? He had bruises for weeks after the last time they met.

'So, sunshine,' Strachan says, sneering. 'What brings you to The Salvation?'

I could ask the same, Truman thinks. What the hell is Strachan doing there? Where has *he* sprung from?

'Just popped in,' Truman says lamely. 'For old times' sake.'

Strachan comes closer still. Truman can feel his breath on his face.

'For old times' sake, is it?' he says. 'That's nice. It's always good to see old friends at The Salvation.'

The mad bastard is talking as if he owns the place.

From behind him, Truman hears Sally's voice.

'Leave it now, Strachan love,' she says softly. 'Just throw him out on his ear and make sure he doesn't come back.'

'Strachan *love*'? So that's it! It *is* his place. He and Sally are together. And that's why she'd kept him talking – just long enough that Strachan could appear.

'I thought you might have come back to pay what's owed,' Strachan says, ignoring Sally.

'Owed?' Truman says, as innocently as he can.

'The five thousand,' Strachan says.

'But you took everything,' Truman says, holding his hands palms upwards as if to show they're empty. 'Everything from the house, the car, my watch—'

'We took pennies,' Strachan snarls. 'You still owe us big.'

Truman starts to back along the bar to where Wally is sitting watching open-mouthed.

'You,' Strachan barks at Wally. 'Out!'

Wally immediately drops from his barstool and scuttles across the room. At the door, he bends low and slides the bolt before disappearing out into the darkness.

Weighing up his options, Truman glances towards Sally and then towards the door. Strachan tracks his every move.

Sally will help him, Truman thinks; she might have stitched him up but she won't want to see him hurt.

'Tell him, Sal,' he says. 'Tell him I haven't got it.'

Sally laughs.

'That's not what you were saying just now,' she says.

He was wrong. She *does* want him hurt.

Strachan raises the baseball bat, braces, prepares to swing.

'Is that right?' he says. 'Is that what you were saying?'

The bat hovers, twitches.

'No!' Truman shouts. 'WAIT!'

His hand goes to his heart. It's a reflex now. He taps.

'Don't!' he says. 'The doctors—'

'Doctors?' Strachan cuts across him.

Truman points to the bat.

'It could kill me,' he says. 'I could go just like that . . .'

He tries to click his fingers but his hands are wet with sweat. He keeps backing around the room, towards the door.

'It'd be murder,' he says. Tapping again. 'You'd get life.'

Strachan lowers his arm, lets the bat fall to his side. Truman can see he's got to him, has put just enough doubt in his mind. The magic key: not only does it open every door, it's a get-out-of-jail-free card too.

'Let him go,' Sally says urgently to Strachan. 'We don't want trouble.'

Truman reaches the door. Fumbles for the handle. Stumbles out into the night.

47

Strachan

The Salvation

Strachan continues to stare at the door long after it closes behind Truman. For just a few moments, it was like it used to be. The weight he's been carrying had lifted, the cloud had gone, the blood had pumped. It had felt good.

He'd felt fucking good.

But the toerag slipped through his fingers; had gone before he could finish with him. Strachan is left disappointed: he'd wanted to feel the thud of the bat into Truman's guts, wanted to see him lift, fold. There's an ache in his arms that hasn't been satisfied.

Finally he turns to face Sally. She is still behind the bar, hasn't moved from the spot.

'I should've—' he starts to say, brandishing the bat.

'You could have bloody killed him,' she says, cutting across him, shaken.

She takes a glass from a shelf and a tea-towel from a hook behind the counter, begins polishing furiously.

'I just wanted him gone,' she says hotly. 'Thrown out. That's all.'

Strachan shakes his head, blinks. She's angry. With *him*?

'I've told you about that bloody bat,' she says, pointing. 'I've always said you'd end up killing someone.'

He'd wanted to have it on the shelf behind the bar where everyone could see it. She took it down as soon as he put it there.

'You never know when to stop,' she says.

But he *had* stopped.

'If I hadn't been here ...' she says.

So that's it. She's worried how he'll be when she isn't there, after she's gone. It's her way of starting to prepare him.

Well, he doesn't want to hear it.

'What did he want?' he says, changing the subject.

She turns away, puts the glass back on the shelf.

'It was like he said,' she says. 'He'd come back for old times' sake.'

Strachan flinches.

'Old times?' he says jealously. 'With you?'

Sally looks at him steadily.

'There's no need for that,' she says. 'I didn't want him here. That's why I called you.'

She's right. There's no cause to be jealous. Not of the toerag anyway.

'What did he say?'

'He was just talking big,' she says. 'Showing off.'

Why is this so difficult? He tries again.

'What did he say?'

She sighs, as if sick of talking about it.

'That he's got a business or something,' she says. 'It's going well. He's got a boy at university.'

She's not telling him all of it, he can see that. Truman had tried to sweet-talk her, that's the truth.

'Is that all?'

She nods. He lets it go. He has to. He's not going to row with her. How would that help?

He makes a decision.

'I'm going out,' he announces. 'You'll have to cope on your own tonight.'

Sally looks shocked. He never goes out in the evening; he's never left her on her own.

'But where are you going?' she says.

To see an old friend, he thinks. For old times' sake.

'Out,' he says.

He goes through the flap in the counter to the door behind the bar. His navy-blue Crombie overcoat is hanging there. He always feels good wearing it: nice bit of cloth, scarlet lining, velvet collar. He lifts the coat from its hook, puts it on, pulls at the cuffs.

'But I told you,' she says, 'there's something we need to talk about.'

And that's why he's going, he thinks. Because he doesn't want to fucking hear it.

'Not now,' he growls. 'Not tonight.'

48

Baxter

Nine o'clock: Outside Leicester Station

Baxter has decided to walk from the station back to his room at College Hall. Standing beneath one of the four giant archways of the station entrance, buttoning his coat, turning up his collar, he tells himself he needs the air, the exercise, something to slow his mind and stop the low ache that's once again gnawing at his head. It's as if his hangover of the morning has been waiting mockingly in Leicester for his return. It fell away the moment Dr Paulizky told him that Nanna was in hospital; he was reunited with it as the train pulled slowly back through the dark outskirts of the city.

Walking will help, he tells himself.

In truth, though, it's his only option: he's not sure of the buses. Watching from the archway as they pass, all their destinations are utterly unfamiliar: Kirby Frith, Highfields, Braunstone. Every baffling name is a reminder that he's only been in the city for ten days. He's an outsider, he doesn't yet belong here; he wonders now whether he ever will.

So there's no choice, no decision to make. He will have to walk.

'But how will we get there?' he once asked when Nanna announced they were off on a new adventure.

'Shanks's pony,' she said.

He frowned, puzzled. A pony?

Laughing, she pointed to his feet.

And Shanks's pony it has to be now, he says to himself, stepping out from beneath the arch, trying to shrug off the memory of Nanna's laugh.

Or rather Shanks's pony it *will* be, if he can work out the route. He was driven away in a minibus with Josh when he first arrived in the city; Dr Paulizky put him in a taxi this morning.

He hesitates, uncertain whether to turn left or right. He closes his eyes, trying to remember the roads the taxi took. If he can find the university, he knows his way to College Hall.

Uphill, he finally decides; it has to be uphill.

The rain that blearily streaked the windows of the train for much of the journey to Leicester has driven people inside. Although it has now stopped, the streets remain unnaturally quiet. The silence is only broken by occasional distant hostile chants of football fans returning from a match.

They're angry, Baxter thinks as he walks, making sure they're not coming his way. But then, everyone seems angry these days. On the train, there had been skinheads running along the corridor, kicking at the doors. At the station, the ticket collector had argued with a red-faced man. A taxi driver had screamed abuse at a cyclist as he pulled away. Everywhere you go, people are angry. There are all these songs about peace, Baxter thinks, but it's all bullshit. There's no peace: there's only shouting, kicking, fighting. There's war. Death.

♫ I see a red door and I want it painted black . . .

Recognising nothing as he walks, seeing so few people, Baxter feels a pall of loneliness settle on him. Perhaps his mother was right, he thinks; perhaps he should have stayed with her. After all, there's little enough to hurry back to in Leicester.

Not now; not after this morning with Abby. She'd wanted nothing to do with him in the lecture hall. A loser, that's all he is. Nothing but a loser.

No more buts, my brave Baxter Bird, Nanna tells him.

He walks on and finds a shadowy side-road with a sign-post pointing towards the university. Arriving at the campus, it too is disconcertingly quiet. There are lights high in the Attenborough Tower but only a few ghostly silhouetted figures to be seen flitting behind the windows.

♫ No colours any more, I want them to turn black . . .

From the university, he strikes out into the enveloping dark-ness of Victoria Park, striding quickly across the wet grass, aiming for the streetlights on the far side. He then follows the slow drag of the Queens Road hill. In the past ten days, he has walked the hill half a dozen times. Still, though, the unbroken terraces of cramped red-brick Victorian houses that front directly on to the narrow pavements seem alien to him. It's an industrial city landscape he's only seen described in books before. It's one more thing that makes him feel out of place.

Finally College Hall comes into view. It should be a welcome sight – but the prospect of spending the rest of the night sitting alone in his room with Nanna's voice in his head fills him with dread.

He has to talk to someone, be with someone.

Wearily, he starts to climb the wide, paved steps.

If he knew where his father was, he could go to him. But he doesn't. Josh? No, he doesn't want to hear anything Josh might have to say.

So who else is there? Who else does he know? No one.

Only her.

And that, of course, is where his mind is inevitably taking him. Because whatever happened this morning, he wants to see Abby, needs to see her.

Only her.

My brave Baxter Bird, Nanna says.

Turning the key in the lock, pushing open the door, Baxter flicks on the light and gloomily surveys his room. The bed is an unmade tangle of sheets and blankets, there are clothes and books scattered in small unruly heaps on the floor. It's what he left behind as he hurried out, determined not to be late for the morning lecture.

It can wait, he thinks; he's not going to tackle it now. He hangs his coat on the hook behind the door and goes back out to the corridor.

Her room is directly above, that's what she said.

Tucked to one side, immediately before the door that leads to the stairs, is a small windowless kitchen. There's a tall yellow-doored larder cupboard, a small fridge, a kettle, a white Baby Belling cooker on the crowded worktop. Baxter has never seen anyone in there. Until now.

'Hey, brother,' Josh calls to him as he tries to slide past unseen. 'Making toast, man. Want some?'

Baxter goes into the kitchen. He hasn't eaten since he and his father stopped for a burger at a van parked outside the station on their way to the hospital. The smell of the toast under the grill awakens sharp pangs of hunger now. But he doesn't want to be there with Josh. He wants to be with Abby. Perhaps *she* will make toast for him.

'No, you're all right,' he says to Josh, anxious to move on.

'Everything OK?' Josh says, determined not to let him go.

'OK?' Baxter says.

'The message, man?' Josh says. 'Being called out of the lecture like that?'

There's no escaping it: Baxter will have to tell him.

'It's my grandmother,' he says. 'I had to get to the hospital. But I was too late ...'

Josh slowly, sadly shakes his head. He reaches up and puts a comforting hand on Baxter's shoulder.

'That's a bummer, man,' he says. 'A real bummer.'

Baxter had been right: there *is* nothing Josh has to say that he wants to hear.

'Yeah, well ...' he says.

'I hardly ever see my gran,' Josh says. 'Were you close?'

Baxter knows he can't handle this. Not now. It's a betrayal, it's cowardly; but it's the easiest way out.

'No,' he says, shrugging his shoulders, 'not really.'

My brave Baxter Bird, Nanna whispers again, disappointed.

A black billow of smoke emerges suddenly from beneath

the Baby Belling's grill. Baxter sees his opportunity: pointing urgently towards it, he makes his escape through the door and on to the stairs.

'Shit,' he hears Josh shout, 'the toast!'

Baxter counts and re-counts the doors along Abby's corridor until he's confident that he has it right. He doesn't want to choose the wrong one and have some stranger answer. He can't cope with that: having to explain.

He stands in front of the door, breathes deeply. Hesitantly, he raises his hand and holds it poised, about to knock. But then he stops, shakes his head, lets his hand drop, glances quickly to his left and then to his right. His heart beating faster.

This is frigging stupid. He wants to see her, *needs* to see her, but now he's here, he doesn't know what to say to her.

He can do this, he reassures himself. He can do this.

My brave Baxter Bird.

He raises his hand once more. Knocks softly and gently calls her name.

49

Abby

College Hall

A bby hears the knock and recognises Baxter's deep voice at once.

She doesn't answer. After the episode with Georgie, she doesn't want him within a mile of her.

No, that isn't it at all, she corrects herself. She doesn't want him within a mile of her, like *this*.

She *does* want to see him: she needs to know that he's all right. She also wants to apologise, to tell him that she's been stupid and cowardly. And – yes, OK, she admits – it's true as well that she'd like to spend more time with him, to find the magic again.

But she can't have him coming into her room – because someone is sure to see him and it would start again.

Slut. Slag. All that nonsense.

And in any case, she thinks, excusing herself, she can't possibly answer the door. Because all she is wearing is the long silk Biba kimono that her neighbour, the widow Gwen Talbot, gave her as a present on the day she left.

A kimono.

With nothing underneath.

She can't stand there and speak to him dressed like this. *Un*dressed like this! She'd be mortified. Excited – her flesh tingles at the sudden surprising thought of it – but mortified none the less.

'Abby,' Baxter calls again. More insistently, but still softly.

Her old Dansette is playing low in the corner. She struggled all the way from Wales with it in one hand and her oversized suitcase in the other. Her dad gave it to her for her fifteenth birthday.

Her dad! He'd be horrified: a boy coming to her room like this. Abby pulls her kimono more tightly about her.

Stevie Wonder is singing.

♫ Don't you worry 'bout a thing
Don't you worry 'bout a thing, Mama …

Abby tiptoes across the room, turns the volume down, bites her lip and holds her breath. That's easy for him to say, she thinks. Easy for Stevie Wonder. Don't worry about a thing? He's not a girl from Pontlottyn, alone in her room, wearing a silk kimono for the first time and nothing else, with a boy knocking urgently on her door and her father looking over her shoulder.

She's frightened to move: at every step, the kimono gently rustles. She was thrilled by the soft sound of it as the silk moved sheer against her when she first put it on earlier this evening. Now she is afraid it will betray her.

*

The widow Talbot had come running to the station after her and handed over the Biba bag with a knowing look in her eye.

'Open it when you get there, lovely,' she said, as Abby's dad looked on disapprovingly.

When she opened the bag in Leicester, Abby didn't dare try it on at first. It was too beautiful; she'd never owned anything like it. She ran her hand over the silk, folded it carefully and put it away in her wardrobe.

Absorb the quality of beauty, Niloc said.

And she, Little Miss Mouse, who has something that truly is beautiful, was keeping it tucked away in her wardrobe. She proudly uses the carrier bag for her books, of course – but the thing itself she keeps out of sight. Stupid.

After eating in the refectory and taking a long bath, she slips it on. It wraps itself shimmering around her, it sweeps to the floor and its long sleeves swing as she twirls in front of her mirror. The silk is golden and it has a geometric pattern that suggests a Japanese garden, picked out in muted blues and soft pinks.

The look of it, the touch of it, *is* truly beautiful. It makes *her* feel beautiful.

Baxter calls again.

'Abby,' he says. 'Please answer.'

There's something in his voice. Something desperate.

Whatever she's wearing, she can't just leave him standing there, can she?

She steps forwards and reaches for the door handle. But at that moment a scrap of paper emerges through the gap at the foot of the door. She bends, picks it up.

It was my nanna, he has scribbled. *I couldn't get there in time.*

239

50

Christie

Pound Hill

Even as she pulls her raincoat on and walks beneath her umbrella through the gleaming wet streets to the phone box to make the call, Christie knows it isn't a good idea. But she knows too she can't be alone – she just has to be close to someone.

'Ray?' she says.

It's all she has to say.

'I'm on my way,' he says.

More off than on, over the years, they have tried to make it work between them; or rather, Ray has tried and Christie has never felt ready, has hesitated, hasn't felt quite right about it.

Their last attempt fizzled out a few months ago. In the weeks before, they had been to the Embassy cinema to see *The Day of the Jackal*, had tried ten-pin bowling in the centre next door, had gone for a drink at The White Hart, been for a meal at The George Hotel, gone dancing in the Starlight Ballroom. After the dancing, he had walked her home. They had held hands, self-consciously. On her doorstep, they had kissed. Briefly.

She likes him, of course. How can she not? He is the kindest, most genuine, solid, faithful man she has ever known. He cares about her. But, every time they try again, it is this solicitude that she begins by welcoming and ends up resenting.

After that brief embarrassed doorstep kiss, she had told him that she still didn't feel ready. She needed more time to think about how she felt. He had walked away, his shoulders hunched with disappointment.

But tonight she needs him – his genuineness, his solidity – and no one else.

He is there within twenty minutes.

'I can't promise anything,' she tells him as soon as he arrives.

'I don't care,' he says, with a face that says he does. 'I'll always be here for you, Christie. Whenever you need me.'

They talk into the night, or rather she talks – about Nanna, the boys, Truman, about Megan – and Ray holds her hand and listens; takes her into his arms when she cries; makes her mugs of tea; wipes away her tears with his hand; smiles when she smiles; laughs briefly, encouragingly, when she laughs.

'I'd better be going,' he finally says, after the tea, the tears, pointing at the kitchen clock.

'No,' she says, shaking her head, taking his hand.

She has never felt so close to him, never truly wanted him before.

She thinks maybe she's been wrong all this time. Maybe they are right for each other after all?

But then she thinks, Perhaps I'm kidding myself? Perhaps I'm trying to justify why this one night I need someone, need him?

In all her years alone, she has never missed having a man next to her in bed. After Truman and the way he betrayed her, why would she want a man? But tonight she can't let Ray go.

She leads him upstairs, leads him to her bed.

She is shy; suddenly nervous. He is tender, loving, kind. Everything she knew he would be. Everything she wants. Everything she needs.

And afterwards she cries again.

Because of the tenderness. The gentleness. The fierce, urgent closeness.

She can feel his breath on her neck now, the weight of his arm around her and the rise and fall of his chest against her back.

Ray murmurs in his sleep, adjusts his weight and holds her more securely.

She relaxes into his arms; she can't remember being held like this, feeling so safe. Before, she would have railed against it, the loss of independence it implies, having someone else looking after her. She has been too long alone; being strong, making her own way. But now it feels right.

The rational voice in her head tells her that she isn't being fair; that even now, having come this far, she still can't be confident about how the future will work out for them, whether there will be a future. But for this one night she's beyond being rational. She's allowed that, isn't she? Just once.

Closing her eyes, she feels the warmth coming from Ray's nakedness. She is wearing nothing but the silver heart-shaped locket that she always wears around her neck. She reaches for it now, brushes it first with her fingertips and then clasps it tightly.

It belonged to Megan.

Christie once stood and watched a blacksmith work, beating hot yellow-orange iron into shape on an anvil. Sparks flew, the hammer fell and a molten rod became a curlicue to adorn a gate.

After the lie, that's the way Megan is.

She holds the memory of her father burning close and hammers at it, twisting it, distorting it, turning it from one shape to something else entirely.

Her father loved her. Her father left. Because – although she loved him – she disappointed him, let him down.

On she hammers.

So anyone she loves and disappoints will leave her.

'Hush now,' Christie says.

But there is no hushing Megan. Not this time.

It's because of the test. She'd found it difficult to settle into her school. The 11-Plus had come too quickly for her.

With a frown, Christie puts the letter back into the envelope. Megan is at her side.

'You won't ever leave me, Mummy, will you?' she says.

The question lands like a blow; it takes Christie's breath away.

'*Leave* you?'

She is appalled, ashamed. What has she done to her daughter that she can have such thoughts, ask such questions?

'Because of the test,' Megan says. 'Because I let you down.'

Her tears are wild, frantic, uncontrollable.

'But you didn't,' Christie says, kneeling in front of her, wrapping her into her arms. 'You didn't ... it doesn't matter ... Hush now ... It's just a silly test.'

Christie's eyes are open: Ray's breath on her neck is suddenly bothering her, the weight of his arm across her is oppressive. She shifts away, frees herself from him. Fully awake, she lies staring into the shadows of the bedroom as if searching there for answers.

Before the forest, Megan was carefree, happy. She skipped and ran like any other girl. She was always singing.

♫ Love, love me do ...

Christie can hear her voice as clearly as if she's in the room. With her. Now.

When she was tiny, there were tears, of course, tears and upset. With Truman as a father, how could it be any other way? But Megan seemed resilient, the way that children can be. She would be high on her father's shoulders and laughing, almost before her eyes were dry.

But did Christie fail her? Even then. Is there something more she should have done?

Megan loved her father – and the depth and ferocity of that

244

love surprised Christie. It shouldn't have done. After all, Christie had loved her own father absolutely, unquestioningly. But she'd been so angry with Truman, she lost sight of that.

Turning restlessly on to her back, Christie focuses on the ceiling. There's no question. She *did* fail her daughter.

The lie was meant to help, was meant to take away the heartbreak. But all it did was to extinguish hope. Replace it with emptiness and fear.

Christie moves again in the bed, turns on her side and faces Ray.

It's a good face, she thinks, open and honest, lightly creased with laughter lines. But suddenly she can't look at him; she's too disappointed with herself. Again she turns on to her back.

How quickly her feelings, her thoughts have shifted. Just a few hours ago, she thought that maybe there was a chance for them. But now she fears what she has done, what this night will mean to him. She *has* been unfair. She was lonely, hurting because of Nanna, and used him to take away the hurt. Is that the truth of it?

And, if it is that simple, what a stupid, stupid mistake it was. He will think he has found the lover he has waited for all these years; she fears she has lost a friend.

She has to try to stop thinking. About Ray. Most of all, about Megan. It takes her on a path that leads to the very edge of madness; she has been that way too many times before. She has to try to concentrate on the day ahead.

There's much to do: she has to go back to the hospital to collect the paperwork and then she has to register the death. How does she go about that? Ray will know; she'll ask him in the morning.

Ray: she will have to try talk to him, try to explain – she thought she was ready, she isn't, doesn't know whether she ever will be, she's so sorry, he'll have to give her time. Those laughter lines will crumple into a frown.

Later she will have to go to Nanna's flat. Nanna may have left instructions for her funeral somewhere.

The funeral: she needs to find an undertaker, choose a coffin, select the hymns.

It's Nanna's voice she hears now, young and pure, singing the children to sleep.

♪ Sleep, my child, and peace attend thee,
All through the night . . .

Christie feels her eyes fill; pushes away the memory.

And after the undertaker, she must make sure that Baxter has got back safely, that he's all right: she will telephone College Hall and leave a message, asking him to call her at work.

If only she'd been able to convince him to stay, she could have taken care of him.

She shakes her head. That's not the half of it: she'd needs him as much as he needs her. If he'd stayed, this thing with Ray would never have happened.

And then there's Truman: there's no choice now. She *will* have to let him move into the house and look after him in his final few months. She doesn't want him in her house, in her

246

life – Christie shudders, pulls the sheets and blanket around her, the idea repels her – but she'll do it for Nanna. She owes her that, and so much more.

It was strange to see them together, father and son. A shock. And Truman had held the boy; Baxter had turned to *him*. That's yet another thing she needs to think about. She doesn't want Truman in Baxter's life; where Truman is, trouble is close behind.

Her eyes are heavy now.

Beside her, Ray murmurs once again; in the distance a door slams and a car pulls away into the night; from the streetlamp on the pavement outside the house, light glimmers dully through the curtains.

She lets her eyes close. Tries to sleep.

It is raining again; she can hear it against the window.

WEDNESDAY, 3 OCTOBER 1973

51

Baxter

Ten o'clock: Lecture Theatre One

When the older, taller of the two policeman turns Baxter, twists his arms behind him, propels him against the wall and forces the handcuffs to his wrists, a shocked gasp runs through the lecture theatre.

'*No!*' someone shouts from a place high and behind.

A girl's voice. Abby's?

Baxter's face is crumpled against the wall; he can see nothing, no one. The policeman is leaning in to him, wheezing into his ear; his breath coming sour, smelling of tea and tobacco. His uniform is noxious too: he has doused himself in aftershave and there is a distant smell of mothballs, but neither can mask the rank odour of something rotten, something rotting, that hangs about him.

Baxter closes his eyes; tries to ignore the sharp pain in his wrists and his arms, tries to blot it all out – the pain, the rub of the wall against his cheek, the stench of the policeman, the gasp in the hall.

It's Dr Paulizky's voice he hears next.

'Is that entirely necessary?' she demands of the policeman.

She's angry; it doesn't help. The policeman leans harder into Baxter, levers his arms higher. The pain is in Baxter's shoulders now.

'Tell you what, darling,' the policeman snarls at her, 'you do your job – leave me to do mine.'

After pushing the note under Abby's door, he'd gone back down the stairs to the kitchen. Once more, Josh offered him coffee and toast; this time he accepted.

'A real bummer,' Josh says.

Baxter looks puzzled, wondering how Josh can have known that Abby didn't answer the knock on her door.

'Your gran, man,' Josh explains.

'Oh, yeah,' Baxter says, awkwardly.

It's the extent of their conversation. After that, they stand in uncomfortable silence, taking an occasional bite at the toast, slurp of the coffee.

Suddenly, Abby appears at the kitchen door.

'You—' she starts to say to Baxter.

'I—' he begins to reply.

Josh intervenes.

'Best be going,' he says, aiming a consoling punch at Baxter's arm. 'Hang loose, brother.'

They talk through the night, the way they talked before: snatches of conversation drift across the room between them, from Baxter on the bed to the armchair where Abby sits, snuggled beneath the greatcoat.

Abby insists on it being that way; it's her condition for agreeing to come to his room. She doesn't let him come close to her, hold her hand, touch her hair. Kiss her.

No matter.

She stays through the night and he tells her about Nanna Bird and the hospital; about his father, come back from the dead; about his mother and the lie.

'She did what she thought was best,' Abby says.

'It was still a lie,' Baxter replies.

'But a lie because she loves you,' Abby says.

'Does that make it all right?' he says.

Later she sends a question into the darkness:

'Were you close to your nanna?'

He was right about her voice: it *is* like a lullaby.

'She was my friend,' Baxter says, surprising himself with the truth of it. Until that moment, he hasn't thought of Nanna in quite that way.

Abby must have heard the surprise in his voice.

'Friend?' she says.

Baxter considers the question.

'I think, perhaps, my only friend.'

It's a statement of fact: he isn't feeling sorry for himself, doesn't want Abby to feel sorry for him.

'Only friend?' she asks.

He doesn't answer. It's too complicated to explain about the school in the wrong town. About Megan.

They fall quiet. Minutes pass.

'My best friends were Dylan and Cissy,' Abby says.

Again a silence. It's Baxter who breaks it.

'What happened to them?'

Abby doesn't reply.

He tries again. Gently.

'What happened, Abby?'

It's good to say her name.

'I can't talk about it,' she says, so quietly, so quickly he can hardly hear. 'I've never talked about it.'

He hears the same tone in her voice as the previous night.

'But I can't forget ... ' she'd said.

There is something he doesn't understand, some hurt here. He doesn't feel capable of pursuing it, though; doesn't trust himself not to be clumsy, to blunder about, hurt her more.

He lets it lie. Perhaps another time, she will explain.

Abby had planned to depart unseen at first light – but Baxter lets her sleep on, not wanting her to go.

He leaves it until he can leave it no longer.

'Abby,' he calls softly to her.

She wakes, stretches luxuriantly, yawningly checks her watch and then springs from the chair and hurries to the door.

She waits until there are no voices to be heard in the corridor and eases the door open a crack, peering anxiously first in one direction and then the other. Finally she steps out – only to step smartly back in again.

'It's Josh again,' she whispers urgently to Baxter. 'He saw me.'

Baxter, still lying on his bed, props himself up.

'He *saw* me,' Abby says despairingly. 'It'll all start again ...'

Baxter swings his legs from the bed.

'Abby—' he starts to say.

He wants to tell her that it's all right, that he will tell Josh to keep his stupid mouth shut.

'No,' she says. Stopping him from coming closer.

She opens the door again, looks out, glances back to Baxter poised on the edge of the bed, and then slips out into the corridor.

After Abby leaves so hurriedly, Baxter begins to ready himself for the day. Finally, at the third attempt, he's going to make it to a lecture.

He uses his greatcoat as a dressing gown – just moments before it was shaped around Abby, holding her warmth, her promise – and goes along the corridor to the bathroom. As he stands beneath the shower and lets the water cascade over him, he has her lullaby voice in his head.

With his mind still full of her, still in a dream of her, he walks back along the corridor, gets dressed for the day, picks up his books, closes the door behind him.

Josh is waiting outside the kitchen.

As Baxter walks towards him, Josh starts to applaud.

'Far out, man!' he shouts. 'Far out!'

Baxter shrugs; he doesn't understand. He reaches Josh and the applause stops.

'So?' Josh says.

'So?' Baxter replies, puzzled, frowning.

'So, I saw her!' Josh says, with an admiring grin. 'Leaving, this morning!'

'So?' Baxter says defensively.

'So, did you get it, man?' Josh says, aiming a congratulatory punch at Baxter's chest.

These punches are getting wearing, Baxter thinks. No, *Josh* is getting wearing.

'Get what?' Baxter says, confused.

Josh looks at him in disbelief.

'"Get what?" the man says!'

Baxter shakes his head.

'Get what, Josh?' he says as patiently as he can.

'The sympathy shag, of course,' Josh says gleefully.

Baxter still doesn't quite understand. Again he shakes his head.

'The sympathy fuck, man!' Josh exclaims.

'*What?*' Baxter says, finally understanding but now not prepared to believe what he's heard.

'What was it, brother?' Josh says his grin delightedly widening. 'A hand down her knickers for a dying dad? All the way for a dead granny?'

The policeman lets go of Baxter's arms, grabs him by the collar and grinds his face abrasively to the wall.

'Right, Sonny Jim,' he whispers in Baxter's ear, 'we're going to move off now and you're going to be a good lad and behave.'

Baxter keeps as still as he can.

'Understand?' the policeman says.

Baxter manages a grunt in confirmation.

'Good boy,' the policeman says.

Still holding him by the collar, he yanks Baxter away from the wall and pushes him stumbling out through the lecture theatre door.

52

Abby

Lecture Theatre One

As the door closes behind Baxter, behind the two police-men, a shocked buzz immediately starts up in the lecture theatre.

The same question is on a hundred lips.

'What the—?'

Georgie is saying something to Abby.

Abby doesn't hear it. She's too busy trying to make sense of what she's just seen.

When the woman in the black academic gown arrived flanked by the two policemen, the lecture theatre had quickly fallen silent.

At first Abby was grateful for the distraction: it stopped Georgie asking questions. Abby had been trying to explain what happened the previous night. She'd decided it was better for her to say something about being in Baxter's room; better than waiting for Georgie to find out from Josh.

At the back of the lecture hall, someone was laughing loudly. They were the last to notice the uniformed arrivals; when they finally did, their laughter was cut short, it hung in the air.

The woman went immediately to the podium, the policemen arranging themselves either side of her, grim-faced.

'There's nothing to be alarmed about,' she announced, patting nervously at her hair. 'My name is Dr Rosetta Paulizky and these gentlemen just need to have a word with one of you.'

'It'll be Baxter Bird,' someone behind Abby jokily whispered to their neighbour.

'It always is,' came the giggling reply.

Abby swung around in her seat to silence them with a glare. How dared they! They didn't know what he was going through – with his father, his nanna.

'Baxter?' Dr Paulizky said.

No!

Abby turned towards Baxter as he rose to his feet three rows in front of her. He was wearing the greatcoat that for two nights she'd wrapped around herself as a blanket. She had almost begun to think of it as hers.

Baxter made his way along his row and down to the front. The resigned slump of his shoulders told Abby that he was prepared for another terrible blow. Something else had happened. The policemen were there with yet more bad news.

It was only when the policeman grabbed Baxter and forced him against the wall that she knew differently.

'*No!*' she shouted out involuntarily.

*

Abby can't make sense of it. Why would the police want Baxter? Why would they do *that* to him?

'Well?' Georgie demands. 'You spent the night with him. What the hell's lover boy done now?'

53

Baxter

*Ninety minutes later: The interview room,
Leicester City Centre Police Station*

The room is small, windowless, bare, grimy-white; there is space enough for a table and four worn tubular chairs and little else. The table, coming at a right-angle from the wall, is oblong, narrow, its wooden surface scuffed and scored. Baxter is sitting on one side ; the two policemen are facing him. The older of the two lights a cigarette and sips noisily at a mug of pallid, milky tea.

It's the younger one who speaks first.

'So, are you going to tell me about it, son?' he says.

Baxter has been holding himself tense, bracing himself, ready for a barrage of hostile, threatening questions. But the policeman's voice surprises him. He is a genial uncle putting a comforting arm around him, encouraging him to talk.

Baxter's eyes fix on the tabletop. He's finding it difficult to think.

'You're in deep water, son,' the policeman says. 'If you don't talk now, it'll only go worse for you.'

Baxter looks up. Deep water? He's so far out of his depth, he's drowning.

His only experience of any of this is from watching television when he was growing up: *Z Cars* or *Softly, Softly* flickering in black and white, the suspect sitting, saying nothing – pale and twitchy, refusing to talk – until Inspector Barlow snarls at him thumps the table and the truth comes out.

'Take a big breath, son,' the policeman says, 'and just tell us what happened.'

Baxter had never hit anyone before; had never previously contemplated hitting anyone, even when the 'Pauper Bird' taunts had rung every day in his ears. He'd steered clear of playground scuffles, had avoided Mad Jimmy Spaull who could pick a fight in an empty classroom, had crossed the street whenever there was a hint of trouble ahead.

But with Josh, he doesn't stop.

Can't stop.

'What was it?' Josh says, his grin leering and wide. 'A hand down her knickers for a dying dad? All the way for a dead granny?'

Baxter feels the sudden anger rise.

Without thinking, almost as a reflex, he throws a single punch at Josh – and Josh goes down and backwards, as much in surprise as under the impact of the glancing blow to his chin.

But Baxter isn't done.

Seeing Josh fall to the corridor floor, he leaps on him, sits astride him, pins him down. Hits him again.

And then again. And again. His fists pummelling, over and over, at Josh's face.

Drawing blood. Breaking bone.

Hauling himself to his feet, he swings a platformed boot hard into Josh's ribs.

Josh groans, stays down.

That, Baxter thinks, that's for my father, dying. Again the boot swings: That's for Nanna. Then once more: For the lie. And lastly – lastly for Abby.

He stops, looks down at Josh. There's no feeling of satisfaction: it's just over, that's all. He is done, spent.

Baxter bends double, shaking, trying to regain his breath, his hands on his knees, his chest heaving.

Finally, he straightens and walks unsteadily along the corridor, leaving Josh where he lies.

An hour has passed since Baxter told his story. For much of that time he has sat alone in the interview room, his mind numbed and his body unaccountably aching.

When the policemen return, they have Dr Paulizky with them. She sits beside Baxter, holds out her hand on the table, inviting Baxter to take it. He ignores it.

'You had something you wanted to say to us on Mr Bird's behalf,' the younger policeman says to her.

'I know it doesn't excuse him,' she says, pushing a wayward lock of her hair behind her ear, 'but it's been a difficult few days for Baxter.'

Speaking quickly, she explains about his grandmother, ill in hospital.

Baxter shakes his head, eyes still fixed on the table.

'Not ill,' he mumbles.

'Oh, Baxter, I'm so sorry,' Dr Paulizky says, taking his hand, whether he wants it or not.

'I was too late,' he says.

Dr Paulizky momentarily closes her eyes, then carries on, talking directly to Baxter now.

'This is very serious, Baxter, I won't pretend otherwise. With an assault on a fellow-student, there are bound to be consequences.'

'Consequences?' Baxter echoes.

'Disciplinary action,' Dr Paulizky says. 'There's going to be a hearing on Friday afternoon.'

She hands him a letter.

'A hearing?' Baxter says, bewildered.

She nods, bites her lip.

'It's all in the letter,' she says. 'It really isn't good, Baxter. You should prepare for the worst. You could be expelled. Sent down.'

'Sent down?' Baxter says, his world, already collapsed, now falling apart entirely.

She nods again, continues.

'But the good news is that I've spoken to Josh in hospital. He'll be OK. He doesn't want to press charges, and—'

The younger policeman raises his hand, as if stopping traffic.

'That, madam, is not for Josh to decide,' he says. 'We're talking Actual Bodily Harm here – and that makes it a police matter.'

He exchanges a confirmatory glance with his colleague.

'But,' he says, 'under the circumstances, we'll not punish the boy twice – we won't take Baxter through the courts. We're going to leave it to the university to take action.'

Baxter looks up, relieved about this at least. He feels exhausted, emptied, ashamed.

Dr Paulizky smiles, tries to thank the policeman.

'That's wonderful news, I'm—' she says.

But the policeman isn't finished.

'We've already spoken to Josh,' he says. 'And we've told him he needs to mind his tongue in future.'

He leans forwards, rests his elbows on the table.

'As for you, son,' he says to Baxter, 'you've got to learn that life's full of prats like Joshua Hurlstone. But you're a bigger prat still if you think you can deal with them with your fists.'

'I know,' Baxter says, hanging his head.

'This time, then, we're going to let you go with a caution,' the policeman says. 'Next time you won't be so lucky.'

'A caution?' Baxter says.

'Your parents will be informed,' he says, 'and a record of the incident will be kept on file.'

Baxter flinches. What will his mother say? What will his father think?

'Thank you,' he manages to say, preparing to stand.

Again the hand comes up.

'Not so fast, son,' the policeman says. 'It's for the duty sergeant to issue the caution – and if your father's in Leicester, we'd like him to be present. Do you know where he can be reached?'

Baxter closes his eyes: all the good things that have been starting between them will be wrecked by this. And his father only has months to live: there will be no time to make it right again.

'Don't worry if you don't know,' Dr Paulizky says, squeezing his hand. 'I'll find him.'

'He'll be at The Old Horse at lunchtime,' Baxter says weakly.

'In that case, sunshine,' the older policeman says, leaning across the table towards him, 'it looks like you'll be staying with us for a while longer.'

As the policeman leans forwards, Baxter can smell it again – it smells like the end of everything, like death.

54

Truman

Late morning: His mother's flat in Crawley

Truman turns on to his back and tucks one hand behind his head, bolstering the pillow on his mother's bed; with the other he scratches idly at the stubble on his chin. He's come without a razor – without a change of clothes too. He didn't expect to be staying over.

By the time he'd finally found his way out of Brighton though, there was no choice. After scarpering from The Salvation, he'd gone hot-footing it through The Lanes, ducking down shadowy back-streets, diving along the dark twitterns and narrow alleyways that criss-cross the town, flitting from one unlit shop doorway to the next. All the time looking over his shoulder to see if Strachan was following him.

He scratches again, enjoying the rasping sound of finger-nails on stubble.

The plan was to spend the night with Sal. Failing that, he should still have had plenty of time to get back to Leicester and give Rosie a call.

But when eventually he got a lift from the outskirts of the town, he looked at his watch and realised that Leicester was out of the question; it would have to be Crawley. He'd have to put his head down at his mum's place for the night. He still had the key Christie gave him in his pocket.

It was creepy going back to the flat in the dead of night, turning the key in the lock, stepping into the silence of the dark hallway. Creepier still climbing into her bed – what with her stretched out cold on a slab somewhere. But it was either that or pass another night tossing and turning on the lumpy spare in the other room. He'd done that at the weekend; he wasn't about to do it again.

Her room and her bed still had her powdery old-lady smell. It gave him the willies at first, that smell. But he got used to it soon enough. Head on the pillow, he went out like a light and slept the sleep of the innocent. Beautiful deep, dreamless sleep.

Which was a surprise. Because the thought of that psycho bastard coming at him with a baseball bat should have kept him awake for hours. Either that or given him nightmares.

But he fooled him, didn't he? Outwitted him. Got out, got away, stayed one step ahead. And now, as long as he doesn't set foot in Brighton, he never has to think about the psycho Strachan again.

Truman smiles; scratches once more.

But who would have believed that Sal would take up with Strachan? No accounting for taste, is there?

No accounting for the way women are, that's for sure, he thinks bitterly. First Bella the belter kicks him out and then

Rosie slips through his fingers. Now he's lost out on a night with Sal – lost her to a fat, bald old bastard with a baseball bat in his hand and a mad glint in his eye.

A thought suddenly strikes Truman.

Perhaps he's losing his touch.

He puts both hands behind his head, stares at the ceiling, considers the idea; rejects it.

No, it's not down to him; it's got to be them. They don't know what's good for them, what they're missing out on.

That said, he can't remember ever having gone so long without a woman. Even during the last week with Bella, he went without, didn't he? She started coming over all moody about the money, turning her back in bed at night. Stupid cow.

No, it's far too long and he needs to do something about it. It's what they say: it's like an itch, it needs scratching.

And he has the time today, doesn't he? And the more he thinks about it, the more he certainly has the inclination.

So, he ponders, staring again at the ceiling; what are the options?

Option one: he could stay in Crawley and give it a try with Christie. But – and it's a big *but* – he doesn't want to be at the flat a moment longer than he has to. It really does give him the creeps. And anyway, he can tell Christie isn't nearly ready yet. A peck on the cheek at the hospital is one thing; going any further is something else altogether. It will take time: but a bit longer playing the doting father with Baxter, a bit of sweet-talking and eventually she won't be able to resist.

But not just now, not yet.

Option two: he can head back up to Leicester and give

Rosie a ring. Another tap at the heart, a few tears for his old mum.

But then again, it seems a shame to hurry back. Rosie won't be free until the evening, after work – and he doesn't want to spend the whole day kicking his heels waiting for her, does he?

Option three isn't an option at all. He can't go back to Brighton – not with the psycho on his tail. Same goes for Margate, where Bella's broken-nosed brothers will still be after him.

So if it's too early to go back to Leicester, and if he isn't going to Brighton, can't show his face in Margate, doesn't want to stay in Crawley, where is he going to go?

He closes his eyes and then opens them wide with a smile.

What's called for, he thinks, is a quiet drink in a nice little boozer in the country. And he knows just the place.

It's been ten years but it's her pub, isn't it? So she's sure to still be there. And with the way they used to be together and with this magic key of his, *she* won't turn him away, won't turn him down.

He moves his hand from his chin to his chest, as if to rehearse it. Slowly. Tap, tap, tap.

They never could keep their hands off each other, could they?

It's perfect. He'll swing by there for opening time; they'll have a drink or two, a bit of a sing-song if the piano is still in the snug; and then, after last orders, he'll lead her upstairs to her bedroom and he'll scratch that itch.

Scratch it good.

He closes his eyes, pictures her in the bed next to him; he

can smell her perfume. Chanel No. 5: she won't have changed it.

Suddenly, it's going to be a good day. The best.

He'll have to tidy himself up as best he can – freshen up the shirt, put a crease back in his trousers. He can't do anything about the stubble though: he'll have to say he's thinking of growing a beard. She might even like it, rough against her cheek.

He sits upright and then, with a bounce and a spring, he launches himself from the bed and on to his feet. It's an old trick, from when he was a boy – up and out of bed in one movement.

This time, though, he lands much more heavily than he used to. There's a pain that runs from his ankle to his knee, another that shoots to his lower back.

He staggers, winces, smiles ruefully. Steady on, Truman old son, he says to himself; you're forty-one, not fourteen. Don't want to put the kibosh on the day before we start, do we?

He makes his way to the bathroom – limping slightly with the pain now twitching in his knee – and studies himself in the mirror above the sink.

Not so dusty, he thinks.

He reaches for the toothbrush that stands in a glass next to the tap – and then pulls his hand away, appalled.

What's he thinking of? Using a dead woman's toothbrush. Still shuddering, he squeezes toothpaste on to his index finger and uses it as a makeshift brush.

And then he remembers.

Damn it! He's supposed to meet the boy at The Old Horse at lunchtime.

He stops brushing; thinks it through. Lunch with the boy in Leicester or an afternoon scratching that itch in Doll's bed?

No contest.

Well, he can't be in two places at once. And it's not as if the boy is that desperate to see him, is it?

55

Baxter

In the cells, Leicester Police Station

Baxter doesn't know what time it is: they've taken away his watch. He can't stand without having to grab at the waist of his jeans: they've taken his belt too. If there'd been laces in his shoes, they would have taken them as well.

Standard procedure, they say, slamming the cell door behind them. Leaving him on his own.

There is a smell of disinfectant in the cell: Jeyes Fluid. Baxter recognises it at once; they used the same at school. But, however much the cleaners have slopped on to the cell floor, there is still an underlying odour of putrefaction, of decay. Baxter puts his hand to his nose – he's been there too long, it seems to be leaking out of him too now. It's as if the smell has worked its way into his skin, just as it had with the older of the policemen. It's the smell of failure and disappointment, Baxter tells himself gloomily. Of remorse and regret. The mouldering smell of hope being slowly eaten away.

There's going to be a hearing. He could be sent down. It could all be over. Gone.

He needs to be out of there, he needs a shower, he needs to see Abby, he needs—

No, what he needs is to cool down, stay calm.

He takes a deep breath and tries to steady himself. Sitting on the edge of the low bed, he rubs at his knuckles, studies them. The skin is reddened, sore.

He shakes his head. What the frigging hell came over him? It's as if he'd been infected by all the anger he'd felt around him the previous day, like he'd caught it.

He feels suddenly sick. He's frightened too: he's scared himself. He's never been like that before, never lost control, never hurt anyone. He didn't know he was capable of hurting anyone.

My brave Baxter Bird. Nanna's voice is sarcastic now.

And it may have cost him everything. The university dream. His future. Everything.

Closing his eyes, he sees himself pinning Josh to the floor, sees his fists swinging, connecting. Madly. Uncontrollably.

The policeman is right: Josh *is* a prat. But however much of a prat he is, he didn't deserve *that*, did he?

And what was it that Josh said that had got to Baxter so much? Was it the *dying dad* or the *dead granny*? Or was it talking about Abby like that? Making her cheap. When she's the most perfect . . .

It was all of it, he decides. All of it. Jumbled together.

Once more he tries to stop his mind. Chill. He looks around the cell: there is nothing to see. The brick walls are dirty white; there is a barred window up high and out of reach.

A new picture comes into his head: his boot swinging hard into Josh's ribs.

How can he have done *that*? Over and over.

Again Baxter shakes his head.

He shouldn't be let off with a caution. He deserves to be sent down. He deserves to be there in the cell. He frigging deserves it. They should let him rot here.

Breathe deeply, Baxter, tells himself again. Breathe deeply.

56

Strachan

The esplanade in Brighton

The tide is full and high, waves are lifting, breaking, frothing; gulls feverishly work the shoreline. But as Strachan walks the two miles of the esplanade from the Palace Pier to the King Alfred Leisure Centre, he doesn't once glance seawards.

The leisure centre is clad in scaffolding and workmen are hoisting buckets of mortar noisily to the roof. Up high a radio plays: Karen Carpenter fighting the beseeching cries of the gulls.

♪ Just like before,
It's yesterday once more ...

Leaning over the scaffold, one of the workmen lets out an extended wolf-whistle at a passing mini-skirted girl in knee-high white patent-leather boots. Strachan doesn't hear the whistle, doesn't see the girl.

He's intent on just one thing: killing time.

He wants to make sure he arrives back at The Salvation just moments ahead of lunchtime opening and not before. That way he won't have to face Sally, won't have to talk. He doesn't want to hear it, doesn't want to see her stand in front of him and say the words.

Sliding back the cuff of his Crombie overcoat, he looks at his watch. He still has an hour. It's a forty-minute walk back; he'll sit on one of the benches that face the sea for the remaining twenty. Sitting will do him good: his head is still aching from the night before.

It's the poncey colour that fools Strachan. He might have his own pub, but he never was a cocktail man – never much of a drinker at all, in truth. And he reckons anything that colour can't do him too much harm.

He's wrong.

'Tequila sunrise,' Mr Smith says gleefully. 'You don't serve these at The Salvation?'

'No,' Strachan growls.

'You really must, darling,' Mr Smith says. 'I drink them like pop these days.'

Strachan had turned up on Mr Smith's doorstep unannounced. He hadn't seen him in ten years, hadn't even spoken to him on the telephone, but Mr Smith clucked and fluttered an enthusiastic greeting.

'Come in, my dear boy, come in,' he says, ushering an uncomfortable Strachan into the hallway. 'How simply wonderful to see you – and with that shaven head! How divine!'

Strachan has never visited Mr Smith at home. In all the years of working for him, taking care of business, they'd always met at the same table at a Victorian tea room on the seafront. Time has taken a toll on the tea room – Sally had dragged Strachan in there one afternoon and the panelled walls were neglected and worn, the gilded ceiling had lost its lustre – but it has been kinder to Mr Smith. The shock of white hair is as elaborately coiffed as ever, his face only a little more lined.

He is wearing a floor-length electric-blue dressing gown with quilted black lapels. At his neck is a purple Paisley silk cravat. He has an unlit cigarette in a long black-enamelled holder.

'Do you like the ensemble, darling?' he says, striking a pose and then giving Strachan an unsteady twirl. 'Quite the Noël Coward, don't you think?'

Strachan doesn't know what to say – he'd forgotten just how discomfited Mr Smith could make him – so he tells him straight off that Truman has shown his face at The Salvation.

'The toerag?' Mr Smith says, his voice high, eyebrows arched. 'Well, the cheeky little shit!'

'He still owes you,' Strachan says, his voice travelling lower as if to compensate for Mr Smith's shrillness.

'He does indeed ...' Mr Smith says, remembering.

'Do you want me to collect?' Strachan says.

'Tell you what,' Mr Smith says, patting him on the arm, 'why don't you come and have a drink and we can talk all about it.'

He leads the way to the living room. There are two large white damask sofas facing each other across a blue Persian rug, and between them is a low table of polished creamy-yellow

277

marble. Matching lamps at either end of the sofas are held aloft by pairs of slightly wistful, puff-cheeked *putti*; a chandelier, cascading icicle drops of crystal, hangs in the centre of the room. On one wall is a large canvas, painted in oils, framed in filigreed antique gold: two young men are stretched sunbathing naked in a verdant meadow.

Strachan glances towards the painting; turns his eyes quickly away again.

Mr Smith goes to an ebony cabinet at the far end of the room and fusses over the preparation of the cocktail – three ice cubes, a generous slosh of tequila, a precise measure of orange juice, a quick slurp of grenadine syrup, a slice of a whole orange and a glacé cherry, both perched delicately on the side of the glass for decoration. He explains each step to Strachan. Strachan doesn't listen: if he lives to be a hundred, he knows he'll never make a cocktail. His hands are too big, his fingers clumsy, his patience short. If anyone asks for anything fancy at The Salvation, it's Sally's job.

Sally: Strachan closes his eyes, tries not to think of her.

'So,' Mr Smith says, looking up at him with a smile, 'what *are* we going to do about the toerag?'

He hands a glass to Strachan, takes a sip from his own. Strachan examines the cherry, the orange slice; considers what to do with them. Finally, he plucks them from the side of the glass and drops them inside. The cherry bobs against his lips as he takes a gulp.

'He's got money,' he says, concealing a grimace at the sweetness of the drink. 'Got his own business.'

'Has he, indeed?' Mr Smith says, his smile vanishing.

They both drink again in silence.

'So?' Strachan says.

'So,' says Mr Smith, 'I'll get one of my boys to take care of him.'

Strachan shakes his head.

'No,' he says.

Mr Smith looks at him, eyebrows raised in question.

'I thought you were out of it?' he says.

Strachan meets his look with another slow shake of his head.

'Are you sure?' Mr Smith says.

Strachan swallows the remainder of his drink.

'He's mine,' he says, all the old menace back in his voice.

One last time: that's what he'd promised himself as soon as he saw Truman standing at the bar. One last swing of the bat. One final fucking hurrah.

In just a couple of hours, he and Mr Smith see off one bottle of tequila and start on another. After the first glass they dispense with the decoration, after the second they abandon the sunrise in favour of neat tequila. After the third they keep the bottle between them on the marble table to avoid having to make the walk to the ebony cabinet.

At some point, Strachan phones Sally, says he'll be late. At some other point, later, when his legs are no longer quite his own and his words are coming slurred and disjointedly, he goes to the hallway and telephones again, says he won't be home.

'But where are you?' she says, alarmed.

He's never stayed away before.

'Mr Smith,' he says, carefully.

'Mr Smiff?' she says.

He tries again.

'Misser Smith,' he giggles.

And Strachan never giggles. Never has.

'But we were going to talk,' Sally says pleadingly.

He doesn't answer. Instead he puts the phone down. Deliberately. Carefully. Best that way, he tells himself, putting his finger to his lips, as if to hush her, hush himself. Best to leave it all unsaid.

He goes back to the living room and finds that Mr Smith has put a record on his stereo and is dancing, gliding around the damask sofas with his eyes closed and cigarette holder aloft.

♫ Mad about the boy
I know it's stupid to be mad about the boy . . .

Between drinks they reminisce. They swap old stories, relive old battles, celebrate old victories and talk about all the scores that Strachan settled on Mr Smith's behalf.

Settled with his fists. With a word. With just a look.

Back when he was the man.

Strachan looks again at his watch and rises from the bench where he has spent his twenty minutes staring vacantly out to sea.

Walking along the esplanade, starting to focus on the afternoon ahead, his head finally easing, he is suddenly aware of being alone. He so rarely walks alone now: when Sal isn't with him, he feels self-conscious, like part of him is missing. From the beginning, they'd fitted together. He'd been so long on his own, he doubted they would at first. But he was wrong: they were made for each other.

Or at least that's what he thought. Until now.

He focuses again, on the toerag.

Find him, sort it: that's what he's promised Mr Smith. Just like the old days.

He has a plan: after the lunchtime shift at The Salvation he'll be out and away before Sal can collar him. And then he'll begin to track Truman down. He'll start with the toerag's mother; he knows where to find her from the last time.

Strachan walks on, feels a little better.

He lifts his head – but his heart quickly sinks again.

Because coming towards him, in a bustling hurry, is Sally.

57

Christie

Midday: The Planning Department, Crawley

The post arrived after Christie had hurried Ray out through the front door and just before she left the house an hour later. The letterbox clattered and the package landed with a small thud on the mat. She knew at once what it contained.

Dreams.

The plump brown envelope is stuffed full of her dreams – at least, that's what she tells herself, knowing she's being overdramatic but having to fight off a surge of regret none the less.

Retrieving the envelope from the doormat, she tests it in her hand. They don't weigh much, do they?

Dreams. Hopes. Brave intentions.

Christie shakes her head: despite the promise she made to herself – the promise to Nanna too – she now knows the Open University dream has to be put on hold.

And she knows too that putting it off means there's a good chance it will never happen at all. Because after this, something else will get in the way. And then something else.

Follow your dreams, that's what she always tells the children – it's what her father told her when she was a girl. But she's never been able to: life has always managed to get in the way.

Her mother's domineering, then Truman's lies, then the children. And after Truman, of course, dreams were a luxury she couldn't afford. When they arrived penniless in Crawley, all her thoughts were taken up with just getting through each day. Dreams were put aside.

Put aside. But not forgotten.

Leaving the house, Christie balances the package on the narrow hall table, glancing back at it as she closes the front door behind her. There's no point now in even opening the envelope and studying the application forms.

On the bus to work she wrestles with it.

It had seemed the perfect time, *her* time. Baxter was away at university; Harry would soon start secondary school. And she was as strong as she'd ever be, after Megan.

She was going to do it, Christie told herself. Because finally she could. Because she'd earned it. Because it was 1973, for goodness' sake, and a different world for women. The newspapers were full of it: women marching, women striking, women standing up for women. She'd even read – in a copy of *Spare Rib* she'd found at the office – about an ordinary mother, just like her, who had done the same thing. She'd left school at fourteen but now she had a university degree and a job working for a trade union.

But in just a matter of days, everything has gone from perfect to a total mess.

Despite the promise she made to Nanna, she couldn't possibly consider enrolling on the course now. Not with the funeral to come. Baxter angry with her. Ray in her bed. The inevitable poisonous gossip at work.

Not with Truman back and taking over life again.

However ill he is, it's hard not to resent him. She wishes now she'd divorced him during the years they were apart – but she hadn't known where he was, didn't know how to begin.

Not that it would have made any difference, she thinks bitterly: he would still have come back and ruined everything.

She stops herself, reminds herself. She's made her decision. There's no point in bitterness. She *has* to take care of him. For Nanna's sake.

And for Megan's too.

At her desk, the telephone rings. Someone from behind the filing cabinets picks up the call, answers it immediately. Ray has told everyone in the office about Nanna: when Christie arrived they crowded around, not knowing quite what to say, hesitant voices low.

Thankfully no one appeared to suspect anything about Ray. Christie knows it won't stay that way: the world of the Planning office is too small, nothing goes unnoticed or unremarked.

She has made her telephone calls – the message left at College Hall for Baxter, an appointment arranged with the funeral director, another with the registrar. She is waiting now until it's time to go to the hospital, to collect the paperwork she will need to register Nanna's death.

She is waiting. Thinking.

*

It was a day of mixed emotions when they finally left Nanna's flat after all those years. Sad to leave Nanna and so many memories behind; proud that finally Christie could afford a rented house of their own. It wasn't much, but it was theirs, she told herself.

It was what *she* had earned. Christie. Alone.

They have a special celebratory meal in the kitchen the first night. Nanna joins them; Baxter and Harry clown at the table, excited; Megan helps with the food, quiet and withdrawn. A new neighbour knocks on the door and gives them a welcome-gift of a bottle of wine. Liebfraumilch; even Harry is allowed a sip.

Christie goes to bed that night with her hopes high. Megan will be happier: she's sixteen, and finally she has a room of her own; she can invite friends round. Baxter has more space to study. Harry at last has a garden to run in.

Two weeks later, in the dark small hours of a summer morning, it's not a neighbour who is on the doorstep. It's a woman police constable.

Hearing the rattle of the letterbox, Christie is at the door in a moment. She has been striding back and forth across the lounge carpet, waiting for Megan to come home, growing more desperate as each hour of the night passes.

'Mrs Bird?' the police constable says.

Seeing the uniform, immediately fearing the worst, Christie is too shocked to answer.

No, she tells herself. This isn't happening. Not my Megan. *No.*

'Mrs Bird, we've found Megan.'

Christie breathes. They've found her.

Baxter comes down the stairs.

'What's going on?' he says.

'They've found Megan,' she tells him, her heart racing.

Christie can see the panic in his eyes.

'Is she all right?' he says.

'She's fine,' the policewoman says. 'She was sitting alone on the beach in the dark. We didn't want to leave her there – for her own safety.'

'The beach?' Baxter says.

'Brighton,' the policewoman says.

'Where is she now?' Christie says.

'Last time I saw her, she was lying on a bed in the cells,' she says, with a reassuring smile. 'We need you to come and collect her.'

It is three o'clock when Christie and Baxter set off for Brighton in the back of the panda car.

They have left Harry at Nanna Bird's – eight years old and rubbing at his sleepy eyes – not really understanding what is happening.

In the back seat of the car, Christie speaks to Baxter in urgent whispers, trying to make sense of it. She doesn't want the two police officers in the front to overhear.

'She didn't say anything to you?' she says.

Baxter doesn't answer.

Christie struggles to remember exactly what the police constable said. Megan was on the beach when they found her. Sixteen years old and alone on the beach in the middle of the night!

'What on earth was she doing on the beach?' she says, to herself as much as to Baxter.

As the car speeds towards Brighton, the police radio crackles into life: there's a domestic incident here, a minor accident there. Someone is drunk at bus stop near Preston Park; a lorry has broken down at Seven Dials.

And Megan is in the cells.

'Why Brighton?' Christie whispers.

'Perhaps she went there with him,' Baxter says.

Christie doesn't understand.

'Him?'

'Her weirdo boyfriend.'

'*Boyfriend?*' Christie says.

She thought they talked about everything, mother and daughter. Why doesn't she know about this?

Christie ignores a new ringing of the telephone, closes her eyes, rests her elbows on the desk and her head in her cupped hands. She has chased these same thoughts so many times before, like pursuing shadows flitting along endless corridors. They will never let her be. And in a way – although they lead to madness – she doesn't want them to. If she dismisses them from her mind, she will be turning her back on her daughter.

Christie lifts her head from her hands: Ray's voice has cut through her thoughts.

'What is it, Christie love?' he whispers.

He is leaning across her desk, too close again. Someone is bound to notice. She backs away. She has enough on her mind to worry about.

She should have told him this morning – that it should

never have happened, that she's sorry – but she couldn't do it, couldn't face the hurt in his eyes.

'Christie?' he says. 'What is it? Is it Nanna?'

'It's Megan,' Christie says. 'Nanna's going has brought it all to the surface again, I guess.'

Ray nods. Christie looks at her watch.

'I've got to go to the hospital,' she says.

'I'll see you later?'

'Yes,' she says, with a forced smile.

She will talk to him later, tell him them.

She stands, picks up her handbag.

'Christie,' he says. 'Last night . . . You know I love—'

She holds up her hand, shakes her head and stops him.

'Not now, Ray,' she says. 'We'll talk later. OK?'

58

Abby

Victoria Park, Leicester

There is a distance between them as they walk. Just two days ago they linked arms and sang as they went striding across campus. Now they keep a careful yard apart – as if that space between them holds something brittle and untrustworthy. Despite this, or perhaps because of it, Abby and Georgie have decided to go together to visit Josh. They need to know what happened with Baxter.

As soon as the morning lecture ended, the rumours and the speculation began. Someone had seen Josh being taken away in an ambulance. There'd been this major hassle between him and Baxter, they said: it got really heavy; they had a massive fight. It was about some girl, someone said; it had to be about a girl. No way: Baxter just freaked out, went wild. It was drugs: it had to be drugs, Baxter was dropping acid, it was a bad trip, the worst. No: he was pissed again. He was out of his skull on Monday afternoon, wasn't he? He's got a problem, needs help. Help? Dream on: he needs locking up, he's out of control. Too right: he's certifiable, a headcase. Cut him some slack, man: his dad is dying, he's under like this total stress. Forget it: it's Josh who's dying, it's Josh who's in hospital.

No, Josh isn't in hospital, Dr Paulizky tells Abby and Georgie when they knock at her office door to ask. The hospital patched him up quickly and he is now back in his room at College Hall, nursing cuts and bruises and a broken nose, feeling very sorry for himself.

She doesn't sound very sympathetic.

'Is one of you Abby?' Dr Paulizky says as they are about to turn to walk away.

'Me ...' Abby replies timidly, stepping out from behind Georgie. 'Why do you ask?'

'No reason,' Dr Paulizky says. 'Baxter mentioned your name at the police station, that's all.'

Georgie's eyes open wider. Abby sees at once what she's thinking. Somehow this is all her fault.

But why *did* Baxter mention her name? What *did* happen between him and Josh? Is it because Josh saw her leaving Baxter's room?

'Where is he?' Abby asks Dr Paulizky, ignoring Georgie.

'Still with the police, I'm afraid.'

'Is he OK?'

'No, not really,' Dr Paulizky says. 'We're trying to find his father. You don't happen to know where he might be?'

Abby replies with a shake of the head.

*

'Is *he* OK?' Georgie says, disbelieving and angry, as they set off across the park towards College Hall. 'It's Josh who's been beaten up by that lunatic.'

The sky is an unbroken blanket of grey cloud; heavy beads of last night's rain hang dismally from the autumnal trees that line the path.

'He's not a lunatic,' Abby says quietly, determinedly.

She was unable to defend him when everyone crowded around after the lecture. There were too many of them, too many questions, and she didn't know what to think. She still doesn't.

'He's not like that,' she says, as much to herself as to Georgie.

They walk on in a low-spirited silence that bothers Abby more at every step. She can't let it rest.

'Anyway, I thought you liked him,' Abby says. 'I thought you wanted to go out with him.'

'So did I,' Georgie says. 'But that was before I knew anything about him. I think I've had a very narrow escape.'

Amazing: how on earth does Georgie manage to make everything about her, Abby thinks. And how dare she think badly of Baxter, how dare she judge him? She doesn't know what he's been going through. She doesn't know about his voice in the night, the magic.

'Catawampus.'

'Cata-what?'

Baxter's laughter comes to her out of the darkness.

'Catawampus,' Abby says again, pulling the greatcoat warmly around her.

291

She likes the sound of the word, the rhythm of it, the feel of it on her tongue. And she knew it would make him laugh. Despite everything.

She explains.

'You've got your *pantechnicon* and your *paradigm*—'

'And my *panegyric* and *polyphonic*,' Baxter interrupts.

'And I've got *catawampus*,' she says. 'It's my new favourite word.'

'Cata . . . ?' he begins.

' . . . wampus,' she finishes for him.

'But where did you find it?' he says.

She can see from his dark shape that he is sitting upright now, enjoying it. His mind momentarily freed from his nanna, his father, his mother.

'At the dentist,' she says, giggling.

It's ridiculous: as soon as she speaks, the word assumes a shape, a presence, an identity – it's a big friendly creature, a female hippopotamus-type creature, wearing a loud floral-print dress, sitting in a chair in the dentist's waiting room, reading the *Rhymney Valley Express*. A catawampus. She has half-moon spectacles perched on the end of her broad hippo nose.

'You found a catawampus at the *dentist*?'

She can feel it starting to grip her, grip them both. Hysteria, rising.

'In the *Reader's Digest*,' she manages to say.

Hysteria: making her body shake with laughter, tears roll. He is the same; his voice comes strangled.

'The *Reader's Digest*?'

'It was one of their Word Power . . . thingies,' she says.

The laughter is stopping her brain.

'"Thingies"?' he says, teasing her.

'Thingies,' she replies defiantly.

'But what does it mean?' he says.

For a while she is unable to speak. The tears are running, her nose too. She sniffs, snorts. Not attractive, she thinks. The thought makes her worse. Makes her helpless.

'It means—'

She stops. Unable to continue. She tries again.

'It means askew.'

That sounds ridiculous too – it sounds like a kind of a bird or something: a skew. The laughter is hurting now.

'Askew?' he says.

She sniffs, snorts again.

'Awry,' she tries.

That's worse. A wry.

'Give me a sentence,' he says.

She takes a run at it.

'The world has gone catawampus,' she says.

He goes quiet. Remembers.

'It certainly has,' he says.

Halfway across the park, there is a junction of paths. It's there that Abby and Georgie find him: he is kneeling on a saffron cushion, his hands in his lap, his head upright, his eyes inevitably closed.

'What the—' Georgie says as they approach.

Abby's heart sinks.

'Just ignore him, Georgie,' she says, determined to walk on.

His voice stops them.

'You have come to me again, Willow Moon,' Niloc says.

Georgie laughs.

'Who the hell's Willow Moon?' she says.

'I am,' Abby says wearily. 'It's what he calls me.'

Niloc opens his eyes.

'You are not alone,' he says.

'This is Georgie,' Abby says. 'Georgie, this is Niloc the Messenger.'

Georgie stares at him, open-mouthed, taking in everything – the headband, the beads, the baggy white clothes, the long grey hair and beard.

'So what's today's message, Niloc?' Abby says, slightly testily.

'You are impatient, Willow Moon,' he says.

'We're in a hurry,' she says.

He doesn't move a muscle – but he manages to convey disappointment.

'Sorry,' Abby says.

And suddenly she is. She's sorry too for pushing past him yesterday.

Georgie's mouth is still open, her eyes wide; it's to her that Niloc turns.

There is something more accusing in his voice today, Abby thinks.

'There is a magnet in your heart,' he tells Georgie, his eyes burning, 'a magnet that will attract true friends. But only when you learn to live for others, will they live for you.'

He's telling Georgie off! Abby thinks delightedly. He's telling her to grow up and stop being such a selfish cow. He's taken one look at her and seen what she's like!

'Say it,' he tells Georgie.

294

It is a command, issued so softly that somehow Georgie can't refuse.

'Only when I live for others, will they live for me,' she says meekly.

'You must repeat these words until they become your truth,' he tells her.

Niloc turns back to Abby, meets her eye, smiles.

'And you must go now, Willow Moon,' he says. 'For you have your own truth to find.'

'Come on, Georgie,' Abby says, reclaiming her as a friend, taking her by the arm and steering her past Niloc and on down the path.

After a few yards they both stop and look back to Niloc.

Georgie's mouth has fallen open again, still trying to work out what just happened – but Abby feels differently, feels something warm and unfamiliar. What she feels is pride.

There's no denying it, she thinks as they turn and walk on, arm in arm: she does feel rather proud of Niloc. And, just at that moment, she feels proud of herself too, emboldened by knowing him. Little Miss Mouse and her friend the maharishi.

At College Hall, Abby and Georgie knock on Josh's door. He invites them in, wincing painfully as he walks, his hand nursing his ribs as he sits. His face is swollen, cut; he has a strip of white sticking plaster stretched across the bridge of his nose.

'So Baxter just went for you?' Georgie says, fussing around, plumping a cushion, putting it behind his back.

'It wasn't like that,' he says, trying to smile, enjoying Georgie's attention, barely noticing that Abby is in the room.

He pats the arm of his chair, inviting Georgie to sit beside him. She snuggles against him.

'Georgie!' Abby whispers. 'What are you doing? We're here to find out about Baxter.'

Shuffling even closer to Josh, Georgie speaks teasingly.

'I'm just doing what I was told,' she says. 'I'm living for others so they'll live for me.'

She turns towards Josh, runs her fingers playfully through his hair.

'Will you live for me, Joshie?' she says.

Joshie?

'I will,' he says, looking up at her with a puzzled smile, scarcely believing his luck.

'There, you see!' Georgie says gleefully. 'It works!'

Abby shakes her head: Baxter is lying in a prison cell somewhere and all Georgie can do is flirt with the boy who put him there.

'So what did happen, Josh?' she says.

Josh prises his eyes away from Georgie, turns to Abby. His hand goes to his face; he gently touches the plaster strip across his nose, winces again. Georgie tuts her concern, brushes his face with her fingertips.

'I was just messing around, that's all,' he says. 'I wouldn't have said a word if I'd known it was so freaking serious.'

'Serious?' Abby says.

What is he talking about?

'That he was so far gone.'

'Gone?'

'That his precious Abby is so bloody important to him,' he says.

296

Important? Somehow she's known it all along. She's tried to resist the thought, but she knew it was about her.

'What on earth did you say to him?' she says.

'You'll have to ask him that,' Josh mumbles.

'But he did that?' she says, pointing to Josh's face. 'He did that for *me*?' she says.

Horrified. Blushing. Embarrassed. Irritated. Frightened. Delighted. Her heart skipping a beat.

59

Truman

Lunchtime: The Hare and Hounds

It's as if a film has juddered to a halt and a single frame has remained frozen: it makes the hairs on Truman's neck stand on end and tingle with anticipation. It's as if time has stayed still for a decade – with him standing, watching from the shadows of the low gabled doorway of The Hare and Hounds.

He'd carefully pushed the door open and taken a half-step inside; he'd straightened his tie, plucked a comb from his top pocket and run it through his hair. It was only when he reached in his jacket pocket for his cigarettes and lighter that he looked up and saw her. Sitting where she'd always sat, perched high on a stool by the bar.

It's then that the frame freezes. It's one of those *déjà vu* things that people talk about. Where he's been there before, in that moment, knowing the feeling of it and knowing what's coming next.

A shaft of weak, dust-speckled October sunlight comes through a gap in the curtains, illuminating the welcoming gloom of the snug.

He sees her toss her head back, hears her laughter; he watches as she crosses and then uncrosses her legs; he imagines he can hear the soft rustle of her stocking-tops. He closes his eyes, breathes deeply. There's Chanel No. 5 in the air, mingling seductively with the maltiness of the beer and the rich heavy waft of cigar smoke: three kinds of heaven. She is holding court as she always did, surrounded by an admiring ring of lunchtime regulars.

It's wrong to say that nothing has changed.

There's a small tiredness around her eyes and something in the tense, disappointed set of her mouth that speaks of the years that have passed. Her hair is different too: it's no longer an elaborate lacquered beehive – but she still has it determinedly up and away from her face. And she still wears her familiar tight black skirt and a crisp white blouse with the top three buttons undone.

Still a looker, Truman thinks. That knowing promise in her.

Doll, his Doll.

Truman *does* know what's coming next: he's going to say what he said once before, long ago. He chooses his moment, waits for the bar to fall silent.

'There's a sight for sore eyes, if ever I saw one,' he says, staying back in the doorway, his voice low.

The heads of her admirers swivel towards him. Doll's eyes follow theirs, squinting into the shadows.

He hadn't noticed before: she is wearing glasses on a chain around her neck instead of the beads he remembered. She balances them now on her nose.

'*You!*' she says.

'Hello, princess,' he says. 'I—'

'*Out!*' she barks, pointing to the door, hopping down from her stool and coming clacking towards him in her high heels.

A lopsided grin comes to Truman's face.

'Don't be like that, Doll,' he says, holding up his hands in surrender, playing the schoolboy caught red-handed, up to no good.

He steps forward, feeling the twitch of pain in his knee, limping.

'Out!' she barks again, still pointing to the door.

He sees that she's noticed the limp, can sense the smallest hesitation in her.

'Just give me two minutes,' Truman says, dropping his hands, meeting her flashing eyes.

'Go!' she says. 'Now!'

'*One* minute then?' Truman says, still smiling. 'I've got something to tell you.'

A voice comes from behind her.

'You want him gone, Doll?'

It's one of the regulars: ruddy-faced, big, broad.

She turns.

'No, it's OK, Gerry,' she says. 'I'll handle it. I don't want trouble.'

She turns back to Truman.

'OK,' she snaps. 'You've got thirty seconds.'

Bingo! Can't resist, can she?

'That's all I need, princess,' he says.

He takes a cigarette from his packet, offers her one. She says no with a shake of her head.

'Is there somewhere we can talk?' he says. 'Somewhere a bit quieter?'

She leads the way to a table in the far corner. It's where he was sitting the first time he met her, when she came over and plonked herself on his lap.

'You're a bit of all right, aren't you?' he'd said.

'You're not so dusty yourself,' she'd said.

He lowers himself into a chair, exaggerating the limp, making sure she sees his grimace of pain.

'What's with the leg?' Doll says, choosing a chair opposite his.

It's a reflex, see: works like a dream. You can't see someone in pain and not ask, can you?

'Just had a bit of bother,' he says bravely, dismissively.

'Bother?' she says.

'Earlier today,' he says. 'Got clipped by a car.'

Well, there's no harm in it. She doesn't need to know the sad and sorry truth – how he sprang from the bed like a fourteen-year-old and came down to earth forty-one – not when he can make the limp work for him.

'This nipper ran into the road,' he says, looking down, rubbing at his knee. 'I saw a car coming, dashed after the kid. Pushed him out the way.'

'Oh, Truman,' Doll says, her hand going to her mouth.

'But the car clipped me,' he says, giving the knee a final rueful rub.

'I'm still a bit shaken up, to be honest,' he says.

He puts his cigarette in the ashtray, holds his hands out to show her. Makes them tremble.

Doll looks at him, suddenly doubtful, her head to one side, her eyes narrowing in a question.

'Is *any* of that true?' she says.

Truman blinks, disbelieving.

'Why would I make a thing like that up?' he says. 'Why would I lie to you?'

She takes the glasses from her nose, lets them fall on the chain. She is angry again.

'Why?' she says. 'Because you're Truman Bird, that's why.'

'But—'

'Don't "but" me,' she says. 'Everything you ever told me was a lie.'

It's to be expected, isn't it? She's bound to be upset. After what Strachan told her back then about Christie, about the kids. She's just got to work it through her system – it's just a small storm, it'll pass soon enough. He tries again.

'No, I can—'

'I don't want to hear it,' she cuts across him. 'Just say what you've come to say and then get the hell out of my pub.'

He picks the cigarette from the ashtray, draws deeply and releases a spiralling cloud of smoke.

'We had something special, you and me, Doll,' he says.

'I don't—'

It's his turn to stop her.

'Something special,' he says. 'I've thought about you every day for ten years . . .'

Well, she's gone through his mind from time to time, hasn't she?

' . . . and I lost you,' he says. 'All because of a misunderstanding.'

'A misunderstanding!' Doll splutters. 'A wife, three children! They were a *misunderstanding*?'

He takes another drag on his cigarette, lets the smoke escape as he speaks.

'I can explain all of that,' he says.

'I told you,' Doll says. 'I don't want to hear it.' She looks at her watch. 'Your thirty seconds are up,' she says, her patience exhausted.

He raises his hand, stops her again.

'That's not why I've come back,' he says solemnly.

Time for a bit of a speech.

'Life's been good to me,' he says. 'Got my own business now: import, export, record shops, you name it. I've got this pad up in Leicester. Beautiful place – straight out of *Ideal Home*.'

'Leicester?' she says.

'To be near my boy,' he says, playing the proud father. 'Baxter's at university up there. Real chip off the old block, he is.'

She looks again at her watch.

'Why are you telling me all this?' she says.

He takes a deep breath. Here we go, Truman, old son: time to make your move.

'Because we were special, you and me,' he says. 'And you were the first person I thought of ...'

He lets his voice fade to nothing.

'The first person?' she says.

'When they told me ...' he says.

Again he falls silent, bows his head, studies the tabletop.

'Told you what?' she says, her voice a mixture of impatience and apprehension.

He looks up, meets her eye. His hand goes to his heart.

Tap.

Tap.

Tap.

'What's with the tapping?' she says abruptly.

He looks up, shocked. What? She doesn't get it? Heartless cow, Truman thinks.

He tries again. Tap. Tap. Tap.

'It's the doctors, Doll,' he says sorrowfully, bowing his head again.

She doesn't answer.

'They say it's just a matter of time,' he says.

Again she says nothing.

'Just months,' he says.

Still she just sits there.

'So I thought,' he says, hesitation in his voice, looking up, 'I thought I'd come to say ... to say ... goodbye.'

Finally she speaks.

'And?' she says.

There's no softness in her voice.

'And?' Truman says, a little uncertainly. 'And I just thought we might have a drink together, for old times' sake.'

'And?' she demands again.

It's not just a lack of softness: there's a real edge to her.

'And maybe a bit of a sing-song round the piano, like we used to,' Truman says, lamely, ploughing on regardless.

'And?'

What is it with her?

Well, he's come this far: in for a penny and all that. He reaches across, puts his hand on her knee.

She slaps it away.

He manages to smile. Doesn't give up.

'And later,' he says, 'I thought we might ...'

He leaves the words unspoken.

Doll stands.

'Do you remember my Frank?' she says, fighting her anger, a suggestion of tears in her eyes.

Frank? Who the hell is Frank?

'My husband,' she says.

'Oh, yeah ...'

Truman suddenly recalls an old photograph behind the bar.

'My Frank died,' she says.

So?

'I know.' he says.

What *is* she going on about?

'My Frank died,' she says, spitting the words at him, 'of a heart attack!'

Oh hell, Truman thinks; he'd forgotten that.

'So I know,' Doll says.

What does she know?

'I know what someone with a bad heart looks like,' she says. 'I know the skin going grey, the tiredness, the sweating, the breath getting short ...'

She's not done. Not nearly.

'And you come here—'

'No, wait, Doll—' he says, getting to his feet.

'You come here with all your lies and—'

It's no good; she hasn't been fooled for a second. She always was savvy, Doll: he'd been a mug to think it would work on her. It's time to cut and run.

'Don't be like that, Doll,' he says, holding his hands up once more, attempting a smile again. 'You can't blame a man for trying, can you?'

There's a tap on his shoulder – it's happening again, just like with Sally at The Salvation. *Déjà* bloody *vu*.

Truman turns.

'Time for you to leave, sunshine,' Gerry says.

60

Baxter

Afternoon: The cells

Lunchtime has come and gone – they brought him grey, inedible food on a thin metal tray. He wasn't hungry anyway. The afternoon is now wearing slowly on.

Where is he, his father? He's supposed to be at The Old Horse, that's what they'd arranged. But he didn't show up at all at lunchtime. Is he all right? Has something happened to him?

The taller policeman looks as if he's enjoying himself when he collects the untouched tray and breaks the news to Baxter.

'Looks like your old man has gone AWOL,' he says. 'So you'd better make yourself at home. I think you're going to be with us for some time yet, sunshine.'

The door closes with a dead clang and Baxter settles uncomfortably back on the low bed, closes his eyes and wonders whether what he feels now – alone, drained, empty – is what Megan felt then.

*

At the police station, Megan doesn't speak until the police-woman makes her.

'Haven't you got anything to say to your mother?'

Megan doesn't look up; she speaks softly to the floor.

'Sorry,' she says.

'I've been so—' Christie starts to say, but then thinks better of it and just gathers Megan into her arms and holds her.

Baxter stands to one side, studying his sister. When you live with someone, sit with them every day in the kitchen, wait for them to finally emerge each morning from the bath-room, you don't really notice them; don't look at them as you look at other people. Baxter sees her now as if looking at a stranger: she wears a long floating black dress, a thin black velvet ribbon around her neck, her hair hangs black to her shoulders, she is thin – when did she get so thin? – pale. Beautiful.

They wait at the station for the first train of the morning to take them home, sitting on a bench, watching the sun rise inchingly, mistily, over the tracks.

'Was it him?' Baxter whispers.

Che frigging Guevara with his stupid wispy beard, his spotty forehead and his poxy bandanna.

'Who?' Megan says.

'Che— I mean, Jonathan.'

Megan puts a finger to her lips, looks at him pleadingly. She doesn't want her mother to hear.

'No,' she says.

Baxter can hear the lie in her voice.

But he has to stay loyal to her.

Doesn't he?

61

Strachan

Crawley New Town

The Capri is the only car Strachan has ever owned. It's a mark of how far he's come – how far *they've* come, him and Sally. They went to the Ford showroom together, excited as teenagers, the cash in a fat roll in his trouser pocket. He didn't want red – too flash, he said – but Sal insisted. She was right.

She's always right.

Climbing out of the car, he turns the key in the lock and runs his fingers along the paintwork of the door. Everything reminds him of her.

He has to put her out of his mind. Concentrate.

He can't.

Just for a moment, seeing Sally striding towards him along the esplanade, Strachan thinks about turning, walking the other way.

He isn't quick enough.

'Stay there!' she shouts, pointing.

He freezes.

She grabs his arm and tows him – five feet nothing tugging the arm of her giant – towards a bench facing out to sea.

'Sit!' she orders.

He sits. Obediently.

He's never really understood it: how no one else but Sal has ever made him feel special, how she can also make him feel so small.

She remains standing, hands on hips. Seated, he can still look her directly in the eye. He doesn't.

'What's going on, Strachan?' she says. 'You didn't come home.'

'No,' he mumbles, his head dropping, the hangover nagging quickly at him again.

'But why?' she says.

He doesn't answer.

'I needed to talk to you,' she says.

He looks up.

'That's why,' he says.

She frowns, shakes her head.

'I don't understand.'

He hangs his head again. Says nothing.

She steps towards him, cups his face in her hands.

'I love you, Strachan,' she says.

From the depths of him, a hollow laugh.

'But not enough,' he says.

She pulls away.

'What?'

'You're leaving me,' he says. 'That's what you're going to tell me.'

'*Leaving?*'

He nods.

'Leaving?' she says again. 'I could never leave you, you big lump. Why ever would you think ...?'

He raises his head. He's got it wrong?

'What, then?' he says. 'What did you want to tell me?'

How can he have got it so wrong?

She takes his face in her hands again, looks into his eyes.

'That I'm pregnant, Strachan,' she says, a sudden sob catching in her voice, a smile.

'I'm pregnant ... and I'm forty ... and I'm scared ... And I wanted to talk about it ... I wanted you to hold me and make it all right ... like you always do ...'

She is crying now.

Pregnant?

The new blouse, the favourite skirt, her best shoes: Sally was at the doctor. That's why she was late back.

'Pregnant?' he says. 'But how ...?'

She laughs, pushing away tears.

'I think you know how,' she says. 'But I messed up with the Pill.'

Pregnant?

'But I'm sixty—'

She puts her finger to his lips, presses her cheek against his, her breath is hot in his ear.

'You're going to be a father,' she whispers.

She pulls away again. An inch. The tears are falling. But she is laughing now and there is a wildness in her. A wild delight.

'You're going to be a father, you big lump,' she says

again, as he pulls her towards him, holds her fiercely to him.

In relief. Joy. Fear.

Flexing his shoulders, Strachan pulls at the cuffs of his shirt, looks around, reminding himself of the way to Truman's mother's flat. He's only been there once before, ten years ago, but he hasn't forgotten. She made quite an impression on him, Mrs Bird – a lovely old lady with a toerag for a son.

He reaches in his pocket for his sunglasses: the day is overcast but he's still nursing the remains of the hangover, hasn't been able to shake it off.

Even after what Sally told him.

Somehow – somehow, since she told him – he's been conscious of driving differently, walking differently, holding himself differently. Feeling differently. Somehow *everything* is different.

Not that he knows how he feels. Not exactly.

Most of all, it's relief. She's not leaving him; he hasn't lost her.

And after that?

He feels something he's never really known before. He feels afraid.

He's going to be a father. *A father?*

And it fills him with a dazed terror. There's going to be a baby to take care of. *His* baby. How the fuck is he going to do that? He's never held a baby; wouldn't know how. Never for a moment wanted to. Never imagined being a father, never wanted it. Strachan. A *father?* And he's sixty years old. Sixty.

Relief. Fear.

And pride.

He's going to have a child. It will be a boy. Big and strong. His boy. *Lewis.*

Lewis: the brother he never had. The brother who was always invisibly, indivisibly with him when he was nothing but a hungry snotty-nosed scrap of a lad; sharing his room, his dreams, everything.

Strachan tries to stop his thoughts. He shouldn't be here, doing this – Sally begged him to stay with her in Brighton. But he'd promised Mr Smith that he'd find the toerag and sort it. He has to see it through.

He'd promised himself something too – that last hurrah to remind himself of who he once was.

But now it's much more than that.

He knows it's crazy but he wants to spend time with his son on his own. He needs to get used to the boy; the boy needs to get used to him. He wants to show Lewis who his father is, who he was. Talk to him, explain some things.

Strachan climbs the steps to the drab concrete terrace of flats. Ten years on, it looks just the same: sad, run-down, dingy; dingier still through his dark glasses.

OK, Lewis? Let's do this, son.

He counts off the doors. Raps with his knuckles.

62

Christie
At Nanna Bird's flat

From the hospital, Christie has come directly to Nanna's flat. It isn't just that she needs to see if Nanna left a note of her funeral wishes; she also wants to be where she spent so much time, to sit where she sat. To hold her close.

But it hasn't worked out like that.

As soon as she steps into the kitchen, she knows that someone has been here. There are cups unwashed in the sink, the chairs at the kitchen table have been carelessly pulled out and left askew. A glance into Nanna's bedroom confirms that someone has slept there. Slept there!

Truman. It has to be Truman.

It feels like a new betrayal. He's been here, using Nanna's things, sleeping in her bed. How could he? How *dare* he!

She sets about making the bed, straightening the chairs, washing the cups; she has to return the flat to the way Nanna would have it. She is drying her hands on a tea-towel when she hears the sharp rap on the door.

A neighbour, come to offer condolences: that's Christie's

first thought. She doesn't want to talk about Nanna to anyone; she's not ready for that, she wants to keep her to herself. But it has to be faced.

She goes to the door, takes a deep breath to steady herself, opens it.

Takes a step back.

No!

He has stepped out from her nightmares. A dark shape in dark glasses, his bulk filling the doorway. She knows him at once.

We don't have time for this. I have. We're not to make a
you.
I'm looking for Mrs Bird, he says, leaving forwards, his

63

Strachan

In Nanna Bird's doorway

Hearing the footsteps coming to the door, Strachan arranges his face into a smile to greet the old lady. Or at least he thinks it's a smile but – holding it, waiting for her as she fumbles with the Yale lock – it doesn't feel quite right. More like a curled-lip scowl.

The door opens.

'Hello, Mrs—' he starts to say, his mouth still forming the words although he sees at once it isn't her.

Perhaps he has the wrong door, the wrong flat?

There is, though, something about the woman that he recognises. Recognises but can't place.

No matter.

'I'm looking for Mrs Bird,' he says.

The woman takes another step backwards. Her hand goes to her mouth. She shakes her head.

What the fuck is the matter with her? She looks scared witless, as if he's firing up a chainsaw, coming at her.

We don't have time for this, Lewis. We've got to move it on.

'I'm looking for Mrs Bird,' he says, leaning forwards, his voice a threatening growl.

64

Christie

In Nanna Bird's hallway

Christie's mind is working quickly, joining pieces, looking for a way out. He's come for her but he doesn't recognise her. What does he want with her?

She fights for composure.

She wants to run, knows she can't. If she runs, he'll follow. She forces herself to take a step forwards.

'I'm Mrs Bird,' she says.

He looks puzzled, smiles – a snarling smile – shakes his head. He is bald, his head shaved. He wasn't bald before, was he?

'No you're not, lady,' he says. 'Now why would you tell me a thing like that? Why would you lie to me?'

Lie?

'Let's try again, shall we?' he says, his voice deadpan. 'Only this time, don't disappoint me – I don't like to be disappointed.'

She doesn't understand.

'OK?' he says.

317

She manages to nod.

'I'm looking,' he says, slowly, leaning heavily on every syllable, 'for Mrs Bird.'

Christie closes her eyes, breathes deeply again. Should she lie? Tell him that she doesn't know a Mrs Bird?

It's no use: he'll track her down. Make her pay.

'I,' she says, as evenly as she can, 'am Mrs Bird.'

He flinches. Bares his teeth in anger.

'I am!' she says quickly. 'I'm Christie Bird.'

She doesn't expected the shake of the shoulders, the low effortful rumble of laughter.

'Of course,' he says, 'the toerag's wife . . . I *thought* I knew you from somewhere.'

From the caravan, the forest, the day when Baxter ran and Megan cried. A succession of snapshots run through Christie's mind.

'It's the toerag I'm looking for,' Strachan is saying. 'He still owes us. I thought I'd start with his old mum.'

Mrs Bird: Christie understands now.

'She's not here,' Christie says. 'She's—'

Why is she even telling him this?

'She's what?' he says.

She will have to tell him now, say the words that make it real.

'She had a stroke,' she says. 'She died. In hospital. Yesterday.'

It's Strachan's turn to take a step backwards. He looks shaken. Suddenly smaller. Almost vulnerable.

'I'm sorry to hear that,' he says. 'I only met her once but she reminded me . . .'

318

He leaves the words hanging in the air.

'Reminded you?' Christie says softly.

Strachan stares hard at the stained concrete of the terrace floor. He looks up.

'Of my mother,' he says.

It's the most unlikely of outcomes: one moment Christie was standing there in stark terror, but now she's grateful to Strachan, glad that he's come. Never again will she have nightmares about him. How can she, after seeing him like this? He's just a man, like any other man.

'You got to know her then?' Strachan says.

All the menace has gone from him.

'We came here after the caravan,' Christie said. 'She took us in.'

They are chatting like old friends – but it ends as quickly as it began.

'And the toerag?' he says, a sneer in his voice.

'Truman?'

Again he nods. This time abruptly.

'Why do you want him?' Christie says defensively.

She owes Truman nothing – but she doesn't want to see him hurt. And Baxter would never forgive her if she were to lead Strachan to his father.

'He showed his face in Brighton yesterday,' Strachan says.

Brighton? It must have been where Truman went for his tests.

'He's only just turned up again,' she says. 'We hadn't seen him for years.'

'So where is he?'

He was in the flat last night; she can't be sure where he is now.

'I don't know,' she says.

'Don't disappoint me ...'

He's leaning forwards again. His lip curled.

'I'm not,' Christie says. 'I saw him at the hospital yesterday. I honestly don't know where he is now.'

He'll be up in Leicester somewhere. With Baxter. That's what they'd arranged. Christie isn't sending Strachan to where her boy is.

'And he's sick,' she says pleadingly, tapping at her heart.

'Truman's dying. He's got just months left. Why can't you just leave him alone?'

65

Truman

*Early evening: In the cab of a lorry
on the road to Leicester*

As the lorry drags slowly away from the lay-by and on up the hill, the driver curses, pumps at the clutch and, finally finding an elusive second gear, graunches the long lever into position. The cab is suffocatingly hot and smells of the oiled rags that litter the floor and the damp dog that nestles amongst them – the rough-haired mongrel rests its head on Truman's knee, looking up with forlorn brown eyes. The cab seats are lumpy and torn and Truman shifts to try to find the least uncomfortable position: it's going to be a long slow haul back. At this rate of progress, he'll be lucky to be in Leicester by nine o'clock. He regrets now clambering into the cab; he'd only been standing in the lay-by with his thumb out for a few minutes before the lorry wheezed and shuddered to a halt.

Still, beggars can't be choosers, he tells himself. And there's no point in wasting money on train fares.

Truman rubs a round spyhole in the grimed passenger window and peers out. The light is disappearing from the day.

'Going far, mate?' the driver shouts above the concussive boom of the engine.

'Leicester,' Truman shouts back.

The driver nods.

'I can drop you,' he says, 'just outside.'

'Thanks,' Truman says.

He settles back, tries to ease the dog's head discreetly from his knee.

The dog lets him push its head to one side – and then immediately resumes its position, its expression unchanged.

'Nasty limp,' the driver says.

Conversation is difficult above the noise of the engine: it is reduced to a few shouted words.

'What?' Truman says.

'I noticed,' the driver says, 'as you climbed in. Nasty limp.'

Truman gets it: he's asking about the limp.

'War wound,' he said.

It's a gift, the way the stories just come to him.

'You were too young,' the driver says, incredulous.

'Blitz,' Truman says. 'I was just a nipper.'

'Blitz?'

Truman gives a single nod.

'What happened?' the driver says.

'Doodlebug,' Truman says.

'London?'

'Croydon.'

The driver is old enough to remember: Croydon got it bad.

'And?'

'Brought the roof down.'

'Nasty.'

'Got out,' Truman says. 'Went back in.'

'Back in?'

'Mum trapped inside,' Truman says.

He's enjoying this. He can see it all – the dust, the smoke, the heroic boy, face blackened, clothes torn.

'Tried to find her,' he says.

He goes quiet. Waits for the driver to ask; it works better that way, makes it more genuine. Volunteer too much too soon and it sounds phoney.

'So?'

'Bloody wall comes down,' he says. 'On top of me. Buggered the knee.'

He pushes the dog's head to one side again, rubs his knee. The dog looks at him accusingly, returns to its position.

'And your mum?'

Truman slowly, disconsolately, turns his head to his spy-hole, gazes unseeing through the window, lets the silence speak of his heartbreak.

'The bastards,' the driver says.

Well, Truman thinks, continuing to stare through the spy-hole, a smile now on his face, there's no harm in it, is there? Not really. It passes the time and no one's getting hurt.

Truman shifts again, this time to reach into his pocket for his cigarettes. He changes his mind.

'Got a cigarette?' he says. 'Been gasping all day.'

No point in smoking his own; not if he doesn't have to.

'Of course,' the driver says, reaching for his Players No. 6 on the dashboard, tossing them across to Truman. 'Keep the packet, mate.'

*

Truman lets his eyes close and relaxes into his thoughts. He's glad that it's too difficult to keep talking above the insistent reverberation of the engine. He needs time to get his head straight.

The itch remains unscratched; perhaps he *is* losing his touch.

The more he thinks about it, the more it looks like his plan to get back with Christie is the right one. It'll be good to settle down, have a place of his own, someone to take care of him.

He shifts in his seat again, imagining her warmth next to his.

Yes, that's what he'll do. He'll spend another couple of days with Baxter and then he'll head back south and sort things with Christie. A bit of billing and cooing. She'll come round.

He stretches. Yawns. Runs his hand over the stubble on his chin. The heat in the cab is making him drowsy.

But in the meantime, he thinks, drifting into his dreams, he'll have another crack at Rosie. He'll ring her from the flat when he gets back. Invite her over. Have a few drinks.

Lie down on the bed with her.

Turn the golden key.

66

Baxter

Evening: In the cells

B axter has tried sitting, lying, pacing – at one particularly distracted moment, he even tried a few perfunctory push-ups. Time has never moved more slowly; a day has never lasted so long.

But still his father hasn't come. Where the frigging hell is he?

He's practised the guitar in his mind, his fingers working at the frets.

♫ Imagine there's no heaven . . .

He's been Lou Reed joylessly taking a walk on the wild side.

♫ Holly came from Miami, FLA.
Hitchhiked her way across the USA . . .

He's been Bob Dylan listlessly knockin' on heaven's door.

♫ It's gettin' dark, too dark for me to see . . .

He's thought about the hearing, tried to picture what it will be like, what he'll say. But no words come.

He's tried to imagine how he's going to tell his mother. On the telephone. That he's been expelled.

'Mum, I've got something to tell you ...'

He's tried to work out where he will go afterwards, after Leicester. What he'll do. With the rest of his life. But his mind won't stretch to that.

He's thought about Megan, about Josh, Abby, Nanna, his mother, his father. About everything that has happened over the past few days.

He's thought about all of them and all of it until his head hurts so much that he can't think about it any longer.

But still his father hasn't come.

67

Strachan

Shortly after opening time: The Hare and Hounds

Strachan talks it through with Lewis.

The old lady is dead and the toerag is dying; so what's the point in going on? They could stop now, go back to Brighton, back to Sally. The boy could be with his mum.

They sit in the Capri in Crawley, discussing it.

Strachan explains why they can't walk away.

It's about duty, son; it's about being a man. You give your word on something, you see it through. You make a promise to someone, you don't let them down. You never quit. Every morning you've got to look yourself in the mirror and know you're not a quitter.

OK, Lewis?

The boy nods.

Good boy.

Strachan reaches for the key in the ignition. Just as he did ten years before, he drives from Crawley to the Ashdown Forest. Then it was under the glare of the summer's sun; now the last light drains from the October day as he negotiates the twisting country lanes. It's dark by the time he pulls into the car park of The Hare and Hounds and climbs wearily from his car.

It's a long shot, he tells Lewis – but it's the only other connection he knows the toerag has. He doubts though whether Truman will have had the balls to go back to The Hare and Hounds – and if he has, whether he managed to keep them intact for long.

'*I'll cut his fucking balls off and feed them to the cat!*'

Strachan smiles – remembering Doll, wielding a gleaming pair of dress-making shears screeching her message for Truman.

Whether Truman has shown his face there or not, it'll be good to see Doll. She's a real touch of class.

At the bar, Strachan removes his sunglasses, runs his hand over the cool tight skin of his head, and speaks just two words.

'Hello, Doll.'

She looks at him quizzically, trying to connect the voice to the face. She gets there; he sees it in her eyes, a light coming on.

'Here, I know you, don't I?' she says. 'You're Strachan, aren't you?'

He nods, smiles.

They never forget, Lewis.

'I like the head.' She nods towards him approvingly. 'Sexy.'

'You're looking great yourself, Doll,' Strachan growls.

'Drink?' Doll says, lifting a glass, tilting it towards him in enquiry.

'No,' Strachan says. 'Working.'

She looks at him, gets it at once.

'You're after him again, aren't you?' she says. 'Truman.'

Strachan flexes his shoulders, pulls at his cuffs.

'He showed up in Brighton,' he says. 'He still owes us.'

He looks along the bar, taking it in with a professional eye. She's good at her trade, Doll. He can see it in the way the glasses are laid out and gleaming, the counter polished, the towels carefully draped near the taps. There's pride in everything she does.

Look and learn, lad.

'Don't suppose he's had the balls to turn up here?' he says, turning back to her.

'He was here just this lunchtime,' she says.

'Here?' Strachan says, surprised.

Either Truman has guts or he's a fool.

'I sent him packing,' Doll says.

'I bet you did,' Strachan murmurs appreciatively. He can picture it.

'He started shooting me a line,' Doll says, 'some cock and bull story about his heart—'

Strachan cuts across her.

'He's got a heart condition,' he says. 'His wife told me. He's dying.'

Doll grimaces, snorts her derision.

'Dying, my arse!' she says.

'What?'

'He's no more dying than I am,' she says.

'But—'

'No "but"s about it,' she says. 'I know dying when I see it.'

'So what happened?'

329

'I called his bluff, faced him down.'

'And?'

'And?' she says, eyes flashing, angry. 'He just smiled that smile of his – it was all just a bloody try-on.'

So Truman's at it again, with the lies. He's lied to Christie, to Doll – even to Strachan himself at The Salvation.

Tap. Tap. Tap.

'The toerag . . .'

Doll shakes her head.

'*Toerag*'s too good for him,' she says.

For a moment silence falls between them as Strachan considers his options. Give it up, go home; keep going, see it through? There's no decision to be made: no one lies to Strachan.

Never let anyone double-cross you, son. Make them pay. And always tell the truth yourself. It's about honour. It's the code.

'You don't know where he's gone, do you?' he says.

Once more Doll shakes her head.

'Not for sure,' she says. 'He said he's got some fancy place in Leicester.'

'Leicester?'

'His boy's at university there.'

Leicester? Well, why not? He could stop on the way, buy a few things; pick up a shirt and a toothbrush.

'Thanks, Doll,' Strachan says. 'Looks like I've got a long drive ahead of me.'

'You're going after him then?' she says.

Too fucking right he is.

*

Doll lets him use the telephone on the end of the bar. He can hear the swell of voices and shouts of laughter at The Salvation as soon as Sally answers; it sounds like a busy night. He shouldn't have left her to cope on her own.

'This is stupid, Strachan,' she says.

'I'm working,' he says.

'*This* is your work,' she says firmly. '*Here*.'

'I won't be back,' he says. 'Not tonight.'

'*Again?*' she says.

There is anxiety in her voice now; she is alarmed, not angry. It cuts through him. He doesn't want to hurt her, doesn't want to disappoint her – especially not now, not with the baby. In all the time they've been together, he's always been there for her; reliable, dependable, rock-fucking-solid. It would be the easiest thing in the world to just drive back home to her.

But sometimes, Lewis, you've got to do what's right, not what's easy.

'There's no choice,' he says. 'I've got to see this through.'

He puts the phone down quickly. Before she has the chance to say anything more.

'Thanks, Doll,' Strachan calls along the bar. She is serving a customer, laughing, flirting, fluttering her eyelids at him, wetting her lips with the tip of her tongue.

'On your way?' she calls back.

He answers with a quick nod. Suddenly he isn't feeling great; the heaviness is in his chest again, his breath is coming short; if he stops to look at his hands, he knows they'll be shaking.

He doesn't want his boy to see him like this.

Doll finishes with her customer and comes towards him.

'Here, you feeling all right?' she says, a note of concern in her voice. 'You're not looking so good.'

He gives a perfunctory pull at the cuffs, a flex of the shoulders.

'Tied one on last night,' he says. 'That's all.'

That's what it is, the tequila.

'I'll be off,' he says.

'Well, give Truman my love, won't you?' she says mischievously.

Strachan makes a fist of his right hand, smacks it into the palm of his left.

She smiles.

At the door, Strachan stops, turns to look at her again.

'Dying, my arse!' she'd said.

Sheer class, Lewis lad. Sheer class.

68

Baxter

Ten o'clock: Leicester Police Station

The sallow-faced sergeant leads the way in hostile silence; he walks busily, self-importantly, on his heels, with a stride shorter than his height demands. Baxter follows behind, beside his father, head hanging, the long brightly lit corridor echoing to the clip of their leather soles on the unforgiving hardness of the tiled floor. Doors lead off at regular intervals on either side; from behind one of them comes a shout, an anguished scream of frustration or pain, and then a low condescending ripple of laughter.

Baxter stops, alarmed.

What kind of frigging place is this? Is this what he's seen on television? Where Special Branch bring their suspects and abuse them, torture them until they crack, spill the beans, confess all?

'Sports and social,' the sergeant barks over his shoulder in explanation. 'Playing pool.'

Baxter feels foolish, almost disappointed. He walks quickly on, catching his father up, taking care not to meet his eye. His father is limping. He didn't have a limp before, did he?

On the steps of the police station, the cold night air greets Baxter like a friend. He is out, free. He breathes deeply, closes his eyes and lets the air wash over him.

Ignoring Baxter, the sergeant turns to his father.

'It's been good to meet you, Mr Bird,' he says, offering his hand.

'Likewise,' Truman says. 'And apologies again for the boy. He's let me down – let the whole family down.'

His words are like blows to Baxter's guts.

'Just make sure we don't see him here again,' the sergeant says.

'Don't worry about that, Sergeant,' Truman says, shaking his head, raising his hand towards Baxter as if to strike. 'Trust me, I'll make sure he doesn't let any of us down a second time.'

Baxter feels weak, nauseous. He's eaten little and has sat too long in the cell. He can still smell it: Jeyes Fluid and decay. The sergeant's lecture and the subsequent caution were long and harsh. He'd sat beside his father, devastated.

The sergeant turns smartly on his heels, walks briskly back inside.

They stand a little apart, Baxter staring at the concrete of the steps. He sneaks a glance upwards as his father shivers, turns up the collar of his jacket, goes fishing in his pocket for a packet of cigarettes and a lighter.

Baxter feels the weight of the silence between them. It would be better if he spoke first. But there are no words, no excuse for what he did.

'I'm so sorry, Dad,' is all he can finally manage.

In one deranged moment, he has destroyed everything. His dream, his future and all the good things that had started to grow between him and his father. He has let him down.

'I'm so sorry,' he says again.

He can put it off no longer. Slowly he drags his eyes up and away from the steps. He is dreading the look on his father's face, the scowl, the grim set of his mouth, the angry flash of his eyes.

But what greets him instead is a smile. A broad lopsided grin. A pleased and playful punch to the arm. A bear-like hug that lifts him from the ground. A head thrown back. A helpless, doubling-up bellow of laughter. And a jig danced in delight.

69

Truman

Outside Leicester Police Station

'**W**ay to go, Baxter Bird!' Truman manages to shout through the gulps of laughter. 'Way to go, my boy!'

He stops, gasping for breath, rests, rubs at his knee: he shouldn't be dancing. But he can't stop himself. A real chip off the old block, Baxter is. Gets into a scrap, not a mark on him, puts the other lad in hospital. He's a son any father would be proud to call his own.

And that po-faced bastard of a sergeant droning on like it's the end of the world? Well, it had been all Truman could do to keep a straight face.

'I've been in some scrapes in my time,' he wheezes, 'but a day in the cells? That really takes the bloody biscuit!'

'But—' Baxter starts.

The boy had obviously feared the worst; thought his old dad would give him a proper seeing-to. That's his mother's influence, making him soft; he'll soon grow out of it.

'No "but"s, lad,' Truman says. 'I'm proud of you.'

He grabs Baxter by the arm, steers him away from the police station steps and towards Granby Street.

'Come on,' he says, looking at his watch. 'It's just gone ten. We've got time for a quick one before they close.'

When he'd finally opened his eyes, the dog's head was still on his knee, its mournful eyes still gazing up at him. It had given Truman the creeps. He stretched, yawned, aimed a sly dig of his toe into the dog's ribs, levered it away with his foot.

The lorry driver looked across at him accusingly.

'Hey, mind the bloody dog, mate,' he said.

'Sorry,' Truman replied, the picture of innocence.

He looked at his watch: they'd been on the road for more than three hours.

'Nearly there?' he asked, lighting a cigarette from the packet the driver had given him.

'Just coming up,' the driver replied.

He dropped him on the outskirts of the city and Truman found the nearest phone box and made a call. It was Rosie who told him that Baxter was at the police station. He arranged to meet her later and stopped a passing taxi.

The Barley Mow is a warm welcoming fug after the brief walk through the cold October streets. They find a table in the corner, close to the log fire.

'So what exactly happened?' Truman says, sipping his pint.

Baxter looks sheepish, raises his own glass, puts it down again untouched.

'Well, there's this girl . . . ' he says.

'Girl?' Truman says delightedly.

Like father, like son: there's always a girl. Has to be.

'So?' Truman says.

Baxter shifts in embarrassment, looks down at the table.

'Josh said some stuff,' he mumbles.

'About her?'

'Sort of,' Baxter says.

Truman takes a long gulp of his beer. The boy isn't much of a talker. He'll have to teach him – he needs the gift of the gab to get on in this world.

'So, what did he say?'

Baxter finally looks up.

'Well, Josh knows about you.'

A single tap to the heart.

'And I told him about Nanna,' Baxter says, 'and he knows that Abby stayed the night.'

Truman glows with pride, with approval.

'Stayed the night?'

Baxter looks down at the tabletop again.

'Sort of,' he says.

'And what did our friend Josh say?'

Baxter closes his eyes, looks pained.

'He asked me whether I'd got it . . .'

Truman understands at once; but's he's enjoying this, he wants his son to say the words, to make a man of him.

'Got it?' Truman says, playing dumb, picking up his pint, putting it to his lips. 'Got what?'

Baxter looks around, leans closer. Whispers.

'The sympathy . . .'

Truman laughs, spluttering into his beer.

'What?'

338

'The sympathy . . . you know,' Baxter says as if the words are a bad taste in his mouth.

Truman shakes with laughter.

'And you clobbered him. For that?'

Baxter nods.

'Defending the lady's honour?'

'Sort of.'

'And you end up in the cells all day?'

Baxter looks him straight in the eye for the first time since they left the police station.

'You were meant to be at The Old Horse at lunchtime,' he says in mild accusation. 'I could have been out then.'

'Sorry, son,' Truman says.

Tap. Tap. Tap.

'They kept me in for more tests,' he says. 'Didn't you get my message at College Hall?'

He should have rung and left one. But there's no harm done.

Baxter shakes his head and sips his beer.

'Were the tests OK?' he says.

Truman sighs.

'There's nothing to talk about,' he says.

Well, that's true enough, isn't it?

'I could be sent down,' Baxter blurts out, pained, devastated.

Truman doesn't understand.

'Thrown out by the university,' Baxter explains. 'There's going to be a hearing. On Friday. I've got a letter.'

The boy's making too much of it. That's his mother again. She's babied him, made him soft. So what if he does get chucked out – it's not the end of the world, is it?

339

'Don't worry about that, son,' he says. 'I'll be there. I'll talk on your behalf, get you off the hook. Just you leave it to me.'

Well, he's good at that. Good with a story.

'Will you?' Baxter says.

'Of course,' he says. 'No problem.'

For a moment there is silence between them.

'You're limping?' Baxter says.

Truman stretches his leg out and rubs his knee.

'It's nothing,' he says. 'Just an old football injury.'

Gift of the gab, see?

'Football?' Baxter says. 'I didn't know you'd played.'

'Played?' Truman says. 'I was just about to turn pro when this happened.'

He points at his knee. Gives it another reproachful rub.

'Pro? You were that good?'

'Better than Greavesie, they reckoned,' he says, waiting for the reaction.

'*Jimmy* Greaves?' Baxter says, not disappointing.

Truman nods, smiles.

'Jimmy and me were on the books together at Chelsea, when we were boys.'

The dates probably aren't quite right – but Baxter won't know that.

'Really? You never said ...'

Truman takes a diffident pull at his beer.

'Yeah, well, I've never been one to show off,' he says.

'So what happened with the knee?'

Truman puts his pint down on the table. He grimaces as if recalling a memory he's tried to banish.

'We were playing Leeds up at Elland Road.'

He pauses, gazes into the distance.

'I'd gone past two on the wing, put my head up, ready to cross, and this big fella clatters me from behind.'

He gives the knee another rub.

'Even as I went down I knew it was buggered for good.'

Baxter looks at him, eyes dancing with pride.

'What happened to the big fella?' he says.

Truman laughs bitterly.

'Went on to play for England,' he says. 'Name of Jack Charlton.'

They sit for a moment in silence. The new admiration for his father still alight in Baxter's eyes. Truman finally breaks the silence.

'Well, that's enough about me,' he says. 'What I want to know is: *did* you? What Josh said?'

Baxter's brow furrows. He blushes, shakes his head, turns away.

'I've never even held her hand,' he mutters.

What?

'But you said she stayed the night—'

Baxter cuts across him.

'It's complicated,' he says.

Complicated? It was never that complicated when I was a lad, Truman thinks.

'Well, my boy,' Truman says, 'if you want my advice ...'

He pauses. Baxter nods.

'Don't bother with all that holding-hands rubbish. You've got to come on stronger than that.'

'Stronger?' Baxter says, suddenly all ears.

'Say something nice to this Abby to get her in the mood,' Truman says. 'Then make your move. A woman likes a man to be in control. She expects it.'

'Something nice?'

'"You're looking a million dollars, princess,"' he says. 'That sort of thing.'

'Princess?'

'Yeah, they like that,' Truman says. 'Makes them feel special.'

Truman can see Baxter trying to take it in, trying to file it away. If he had a notebook and pen, he'd be writing it down. And so he should: pearls of wisdom, he's giving him.

'And then make a move?' Baxter says.

'Get close, put your arm around her waist, look into her eyes, pull her towards you . . . ' Truman says, 'then – bingo! – the rest will take care of itself.'

'Bingo?' Baxter says.

'Bingo,' Truman says in confirmation.

There is a sudden swell of voices at the bar; a handbell at the end of the counter is loudly rung.

'Last orders, gentlemen, please,' the landlord calls out.

Truman downs the final inch of his pint and hands the empty glass to Baxter.

'Drink up, son,' he says. 'Let's have another quick one – then I've got to dash.'

70

Christie

Eleven o'clock: Pound Hill

S he hadn't been able do it; she'd had her speech ready –
she likes him, has always liked him, but now isn't the
time for them – but one look at him loping down the garden
path with an unstoppably broad boyish smile had softened
her heart, brought a smile to her own face.

Earlier she'd gone to the phone box on the corner, invited
him to the house, told him they needed to talk; all this with
only one thought in mind – he'd always been honest with her,
she needed to be the same. He deserved the truth, however
painful.

Twenty minutes later, he is there. And she is surprised at
how glad she is to see him.

She has the same doubts, the same confusions – could
they be right for each other after all? Or is she just using
him?

He bends, kisses her. She doesn't pull away.

'You wanted to talk,' he says.

She shakes her head.

'Not really,' she says. 'Just wanted to see you.'

She is aware that every loving word, every gesture makes the way back harder. She can't stop herself.

He has a bottle of wine in his hand.

'Blue Nun?' he says, the boyish grin returning.

And hours later they are back where the day began.

In her bed.

But sitting with him at the kitchen table, drinking the wine, had been so good and she had felt so close to him. His voice was calm, strong, reassuring. And he listened. Perhaps most of all, it was because he listened.

Turning on to her side to face him, she smiles: two nights running, he's listened his way into her bed. The sly old fox.

Sipping at her wine, she'd told him again about Truman, explained that she owed it to Nanna to look after him for whatever time he has left.

'I don't think Nanna would see it that way,' Ray said. 'She'd want you to live your own life.'

She knew he was right, but it didn't change anything.

'I think it's what Baxter will want too,' she said. 'He's already angry with me; I can't let him down again.'

During the day, she had left three messages for Baxter at College Hall – two from work and one from the phone box as soon as she got home. She'd waited outside for half an hour for him to call back.

He hadn't.

She'd been hurt, disappointed, angry with herself. The

only reason Baxter didn't call was because he was still upset with her. How can she have done that to him?

At some point during the evening talking with Ray, she'd made a decision. It was no good *thinking* she knew what Truman wanted and what Baxter expected of her. She had to find out. And if Baxter wouldn't call her, she would have to go to Leicester to speak to him and confront Truman.

That is, if Truman was still in Leicester ... But where else would he be?

Ray shifts in the bed beside her and tiredness starts to overwhelm Christie. She slept so little during the previous two nights and it has been a long day of difficult encounters – getting the paperwork from the hospital, registering the death, making arrangements with the funeral director. Meeting with Strachan.

Yes, she thinks sleepily, it really has helped being with Ray. And because of him, she now knows exactly what she's going to do. Tomorrow she will go to Brighton to talk to Harry about Nanna. And on Friday, if she still hasn't heard from Baxter, she will travel up to Leicester.

Yes, that's it. Or ...

Hush now, she tells herself.

She regrets the words immediately. She knows at once it will now be another night of restless dreams.

Hush now.

It's what she used to say to Megan.

*

'Hush now,' Christie whispers.

She is holding Megan, just as she has held her all her life. As tightly to her as she can. Rocking her.

When they arrived home, after a tired wait at Brighton Station for the first train of the day, she asked her what happened on the beach.

For a moment Megan looks as if she is going to speak. Then she looks at her mother, looks at Baxter. Sees their drawn, anxious faces.

'I can't . . .' she says.

She collapses into tears.

Christie takes her into her arms.

'Hush now.'

'I let you down. It was stupid. I'm so sorry, Mum,' is all Megan says, between sobs.

In the weeks that follow, there is a new fragility in Megan. She is quieter than ever, more withdrawn, the darkness grows under her eyes.

In urgent whispered conversations over tea in the café at the Martletts, Christie and Nanna decide that what's best is to give her time and space.

And cuddles, Nanna says. Give her plenty of cuddles.

'She's just growing up, that's all,' she says. 'It's probably just a phase she's going through.'

'Are you sure, Nanna?' Christie says.

'I think so,' Nanna replies, squeezing Christie's hand, trying to reassure her.

But it isn't just a phase – and all the cuddles do is bring more tears.

'Hush now.'

As the weeks turn into months, Christie's worries intensify.

Megan isn't eating; the darkness under her eyes says that she isn't sleeping; she misses days at school.

But every time Christie tries to talk – treading gently, carefully – she is met by the same shake of the head and tear-filled eyes.

Christie worries too about Jonathan. She hadn't even known he existed before the night at the beach. They had been going out for three months – Baxter had seen them together – but Megan had kept him a secret from her.

It chips at Christie's heart when she discovers her girl has secrets she doesn't share. When did that begin? She'd thought they talked about everything, sitting side by side on their bench in the park.

He is older than Megan – she is only just sixteen and is still at school, he is twenty and at the local college. He's tall, slender, poised, narrow-shouldered; he wears his hair, dark and long, held back by a red bandanna; his eyes are a deep mysterious brown. Christie can understand the attraction but she worries that he is too old for Megan. And there's something about him – his self-possession, his cryptic smile – that makes her worry more.

She doesn't trust him.

The first time Christie speaks to Jonathan is when he comes to the door asking for Megan shortly after the night on the beach. Christie is bright and chatty with him: if her daughter likes this boy, then she must welcome him, she tells herself. But she is left strangely discomfited. He meets her eye but doesn't answer. Just smiles.

*

'Hush now,' Ray is saying.

He leans over her, folds her into his arms, holds her close.

'What is it?' she says, her eyes wide.

'You were having a bad dream,' he says.

71

Abby

Later: College Hall

'Hush now, Abby love.'

The weight is on her chest, her legs are pinned, she can't move her arms: it is dark, black, impenetrable. She fights for breath. The blackness is dense, viscous, almost solid: if she could move, she could cup her hands and hold it, feel its mass. It is gritty in her mouth, it clogs her nostrils. She fights it, fights for breath. She finds she can lift her head; just. She does so now. A thin shaft of light works through the darkness; a child's hand, Dylan's left hand, is all she can see of him. The blackness is heaped suffocatingly around him, on top of him. She fights for breath. The fingers of Dylan's hand are impossibly white – they were never so white in all the times when he and she and Cissy went running and rolling together in the meadow on the hillside. The fingers flicker, twitch; fall still. There's no sign of Cissy. She hears a child's cry, far in the darkness. A whimper.

She fights for breath.

'Hush now, lovely.'

Her mam's voice again: it is out of place, out of time, it doesn't belong there. She pushes it away. It is too soon. The calling has to come next; it always comes next.

She calls to him. *Dylan, Dylan.* Her voice is muffled by the darkness, it can't reach him. She calls again. *Cissy. Cissy.*

Nothing but the dead silence.

'Hush now.'

This time she doesn't resist. She lets her mother's voice reach into the blackness, pull her free.

She wakes. Fighting for breath.

She had fallen asleep on her bed with her copy of *Bleak House* on her chest. Stupid! It's like an invitation to the dreams to come back. They stayed away all the while she slept in Baxter's chair: they are back within minutes now that she is on her own. With the weight of a book on top of her.

Ridiculous.

She gets up from the bed, pushes open the window, swallows the cold night air.

Calmer, she goes back to her bed and pulls the sheet and blankets over her. The lamp on her desk gives out a dimmed light sufficient for her to see her watch. It is past eleven o'clock, and still there's no word from Baxter.

Earlier she'd gone with Josh and Georgie to the Junior Common Room bar. They teased her when she ordered a pineapple juice. Georgie insists that she tastes her barley wine – and laughs when Abby sips, gags and pulls a face.

The bar is alive with talk of Baxter. He's bound to be sent down from university, sent home in disgrace.

It isn't fair; they don't know the truth of it, what happened. Abby turns to Josh and tells him: 'Either you stand up and say something, or I will.'

She doesn't know where she will find the courage but she isn't put to the test. Nursing his bruised ribs, Josh climbs on to a chair and calls for quiet.

'Peace, brothers and sisters,' he says, milking the moment, as Georgie looks up at him admiringly.

'You've got to leave my man Baxter be. You've got to back off.'

He is quickly into his stride.

'Because believe me, brothers and sisters, none of this is down to Baxter Bird,' he says.

'I'm not proud . . . ' he says, his voice tremulous, 'of what happened this morning.

'I said some things I shouldn't have said. And Baxter? He took it wrong.

'I got what was coming to me, what I deserved. So don't you lay any of it on my man Baxter. He's got troubles enough – with his father having only weeks to live and his granny dying in his arms just yesterday. Baxter Bird is the good guy here. We need to reach out and support him, give him love.'

Abby sees Josh meet Georgie's eye as she helps him down: it has all been an act, just for her.

He steps down to whistles of approval and applause. Somehow he has managed to get himself off the hook for the things he said, and emerge as the hero. He and Georgie are made for each other, Abby thinks.

She can't stand it any longer. She's furious with Josh, with them both. She hurriedly finishes her pineapple juice and snatches up her bag, preparing to leave.

'Are you coming tomorrow?' Georgie says. She hasn't even noticed that Abby is angry with her.

'Coming where?' Abby says abruptly.

'There's a demo. A march against the National Front.'

Abby saw the posters in the Union coffee bar yesterday: FIGHT THE FASCISTS, SMASH THE NATIONAL FRONT. The National Front are holding a rally to protest at the Ugandan Asians moving into the city; the student union has organised a march against them.

'Perhaps,' Abby says. Over her shoulder. As she sweeps stomping from the bar in her platform boots.

Abby still can't quite work out what she feels about Baxter. He did *that* to Josh. For her?

And they'd never even held hands . . .

She needs to talk to Baxter about it, to understand.

All evening she hoped for a knock at the door or another note pushed under it. But there was nothing. Perhaps they are going to keep him at the police station overnight, locked up in the dark in a tiny cell?

She shudders at the thought.

She closes her eyes, hears his voice.

No, it isn't true that she can't work out what she feels. She does know: she's just reluctant to admit it.

'*Nos da, cariad,*' she whispers to him, wherever he is.

Good-night, my love.

352

72

Baxter

Minutes later: College Hall

Two quick pints on a near-empty stomach isn't the best of ideas for Baxter. They leave him feeling strangely disconnected – not drunk exactly, but distanced from the world.

It has been the weirdest of all the weird frigging days. And walking back alone from The Barley Mow, under a full moon, through the cold, dark, empty streets, only makes it weirder still.

Incoherent. Unreal. Surreal.

Like the world is suddenly in black and white. Flickering under the streetlights like some Fellini film, one of those that everyone says is totally amazing but no one ever really enjoys or understands; implanting images on his eyeballs. Images of a police cell, of Josh's blood on his hands, his father limping from a football field, a police sergeant scuttling along a corridor like a busy black beetle.

And time somehow stops working: the walk back lasts an exhausting lifetime and yet takes no time at all.

Baxter hears the stamp of his boots on the steps up to

College Hall. He looks down at them as he climbs, as though they belong to someone else. He looks up, surprised to be back.

He has only one thought.

Abby.

He reminds himself of his father's advice. He must come on strong, stronger: it's what a woman expects.

At the residence block, he pushes open the door, climbs the stairs, goes along the corridor. Counts the doors.

Knocks.

There's no answer. He knocks again. Loudly. The sound thunders along the empty corridor. He steps back. Uncertain.

The door opens.

Abby.

She is wearing a golden kimono. She floats, shimmers. Her hair is slightly ruffled, glossy black; she's been sleeping.

'You look—' he says.

He can't think of the words. Any words.

Say something nice.

Call her a princess.

'You look like a princess, princess.'

It's true, she does: a dark-haired princess, dressed in gold. He's never seen anyone, anything more beautiful.

'Princess?' she says, mystified, alarmed, holding the door, closing it slightly between them. 'Are you OK, Baxter?'

Say something nice. Make your move.

'Never better, princess,' he says, leaning towards her with a grin.

It isn't true. His head is swimming. His voice doesn't belong to him. But he's here. Now. Just. He has to make his move.

He lunges towards her.

Tries to grab her by the waist.

But she is too quick for him.

And stepping neatly back inside, she meets his forehead with the swiftly closing door.

THURSDAY 4 OCTOBER 1973

73

Christie

Morning: The beach at Brighton

I t's one of those rare October mornings when, after days of autumnal gloom, the sun briefly remembers summer. But despite the sudden warmth, Christie is fighting back successive waves of wild, fearful shivers. She's fighting to stop her tears too, refusing to let them come.

She must be brave for Harry.

As they sit tightly together, side by side on the pebbled beach, she doesn't want him to know what this place is, what it means to her. It's going to be a difficult enough day for him without that.

There are too many ghosts here. She'd vowed never to come back.

She'd travelled down to Brighton by an early bus and collected Harry from her mother. Setting off along the esplanade, she had left the choice to him of where on the beach they would sit.

'You be a Messerschmitt and I'll be a Spitfire,' he said.

Despite herself, Christie had laughed and spread her arms

aeroplane-wide and they had chased and circled, dog-fighting their way down past Hove Lawns.

Finally he had run ahead – engines whining, machine guns sputtering – and led them unerringly to this spot.

Too many ghosts. Today, she must keep them from him.

Beside her, Harry chatters on, explaining – he the expert teacher, she the novice pupil – that it was Spitfires that won the Battle of Britain. She smiles, encourages him. Doesn't tell him that she remembers: the sky alight above Brighton, the bombs falling. She'll tell him one day.

Just as one day, perhaps, she will tell him about this place.

It was here that she would come with her father. Down at the shore he taught her to skim pebbles, watch them bounce on the water; halfway up the beach, amongst the shingled smaller stones, they would hunt for the dully polished droplets of emerald-green sea glass that she so treasured when she was a girl; up here, up high, they would sit together and talk while sorting the pebbles around them by colour and size, searching for their greatest prize.

They had a rule: they were not allowed to leave the beach until they'd found a pebble run perfectly through with a hole. They were hagstones, her father said, magic stones: if you looked through them, you could see the future. At home, he would add each new piece of stony magic to one of the strings that hung in his shed like rows of cumbersome, over-sized beads.

Her father: he would have known what to say to Harry, how to tell him about Nanna. He would have found just the right words. She will visit his grave this afternoon. Talk to him.

It was here too that she danced down to the sea hand in hand with Truman, barefoot on the bruising, shifting stones.

They laughed together and grimaced and ouched at every painful step. It was twenty years ago and they were courting. It was a time when anything, *everything*, seemed possible. A time before she knew better; before she knew anything at all.

And later, in the early days of their marriage, it was to here that she ran, to be alone, so that no one else would see her tears.

Later still, it was to this same spot that she brought Megan and Baxter when they were young, for long, carefree days in the sunshine. If they timed it right, the tide was low, and, wearing floppy sun-hats and rubber sandals, they played together for hours by the gently lapping sea.

Every morning, after the night at the beach, Megan is up early and out of the door before breakfast, to spend precious minutes with Jonathan as he walks to college, making herself late for school. In the afternoons, she gets home, changes out of her uniform, hurries out again and isn't back before dark.

Christie waits in the kitchen for the sound of the key in the door and calls to Megan as she comes in.

'There's a cup of tea in here for you.'

Megan puts her head around the door and manages a thin, brief smile.

'No thanks, Mum.'

Christie tries to talk.

'Been anywhere nice?'

Megan shakes her head. She looks tired, pale; she is dark under her eyes.

Christie tries keeps it light: girl talk. Or rather, mother-and-daughter talk. What's Jonathan like? What's he studying? Where do they go? Where does he live? What do his parents do? Did he walk her home tonight? Is she being careful?

For weeks, the pattern remains the same. Megan out, Christie waiting. Christie talking, Megan not.

It's hard to bear, the silence. They'd been so close – sharing a room all those years at Nanna's, sharing their bench in the park. Megan's retreat into silence hurts Christie, unnerves her. It feels like a withdrawal of love.

And then it changes. Or at least some of it does.

Still Megan doesn't talk, but suddenly she stops getting up early, stops rushing out in the afternoons. Instead she takes to her room, to her bed, keeping the curtains closed. Jim Morrison sings the same sad song on her record player.

♫ This is the end, beautiful friend,
This is the end, my only friend, the end . . .

Christie taps at her door. Has anything happened? Is she all right? Does she want anything? Need anything? Can't they just talk? Please. Please, Megan. *Why* can't they talk?

♫ This is the end, my only friend, the end . . .

Alarmed, Christie goes to Megan's school and speaks to her form teacher. Megan has always been withdrawn, he says, she doesn't mix much with the other girls; recently her work has deteriorated, she has missed too many days. But Christie mustn't worry, it's probably just a phase.

Although Christie doesn't trust his patronising aloofness, his condescension, shrinks from the careless hand on her

362

knee, she tries to follow his advice, tries not to worry. But it's impossible.

And then one day, unable to bear it any longer, she catches the bus and goes home from work at lunchtime while Megan is still at school. She *has* to see inside Megan's room; it has begun to obsess her. She's sure there will be a clue there to tell her what's wrong. To allow her to help her daughter.

The room is in darkness; the bed is unmade; the curtains and windows are closed; the air is spent and stale but it still carries a distant reminder of the orange-blossom scent of the Aqua Manda perfume that Megan always wears. There are books and clothes lying in untidy piles on the floor. With a mother's unthinking habit, Christie begins to gather them up. But then she stops, puts them back. She doesn't want Megan to know she's been there.

It's then that her eye is drawn to something differently heaped, at the foot of the bed. She recognises all of Megan's scattered clothes, but not this. She goes over, picks it up.

It is a long black dress. Ripped apart, slashed at, shredded, torn. A pair of scissors lies on the floor nearby.

Shocked, Christie lets it drop where she found it.

It's only later, on the top deck of the bus that carries her anxiously back to work, that Christie remembers.

It's the dress that Megan was wearing that night on Brighton beach.

That evening, Christie taps at Megan's door. Has something happened? Is it about Jonathan?

'I'm sleeping,' Megan answers. 'I'm OK. Don't worry.'

Don't worry?

Christie talks about her endlessly with Nanna.

'Give her time. She's probably just fallen out with her boyfriend,' Nanna says. 'It'll be a teenage broken heart, that's all. It'll mend soon enough.'

It doesn't mend.

Christie asks Baxter to talk to Megan, to try to find out what's wrong. She won't tell him.

And then, one late afternoon when Christie gets back from work, she taps again at Megan's door. And this time there is no reply.

Heart racing, she pushes the door open.

When Christie was last in the room, she'd found it in darkness, the bed unmade, clothes and books spilled on the carpet. But now light floods in, the curtains are flung wide; the bed is pristine, perfect; the room is impossibly tidy. Even Megan's posters – Jim Morrison, Marc Bolan, David Bowie – have been taken down from the walls.

Megan has gone: that is Christie's only thought.

Panicked, she opens the wardrobe, fearing that she will find it empty. But Megan's clothes are all there. Neatly hanging, neatly folded.

Christie sits on the bed, trying to work out what has happened.

There *has* to be an explanation. The room has been stripped bare, it is sanitised, depersonalised, as if Megan has never been there. There is nothing of hers to be seen.

Except.

Christie gets quickly to her feet, goes across to the dressing table. Next to the folded posters is an exercise book. On top of it is Megan's silver locket.

Holding the locket tight, Christie picks up the exercise book, feeling suddenly guilty, as if she is betraying a trust.

There is a title on the cover: MEGAN'S JOURNAL.

Christie turns to the first page. It's blank.

She flicks on. Every page is blank.

Except the last.

At first Christie's eyes lock on the few words of the single sentence at the top of the page – but somehow her brain refuses to make sense of them.

She forces her eyes to move on.

Beneath that single sentence is a drawing that brings a smile to Christie's face. Megan has always been so good at art – she should go to college, Christie thinks. The same college as Jonathan; that would make her happy. And later she can get a job as a designer, or perhaps she could work in a gallery. She can do anything. Her daughter. Look how she's drawn herself. Fragile and beautiful in a long black dress.

Christie's smile falls away. Her hand goes to her mouth.

The dress that Megan is wearing is the one she wore on Brighton beach. And she has drawn herself fragile, beautiful. And pregnant.

The words at the top of the page suddenly make sense.

I'm so sorry, Mum.

NO!

Christie screams. She sees at once what has happened, what is about to happen. The apology, the locket, the sanitised room.

NO!

She runs down the stairs, out through the front door, along

the street to the telephone box. She calls the police, her hands shaking, fumbling at the dial, her words a panicked jumble.

Somehow she slows herself, starts to make sense.

Her daughter is missing. She knows where she will be. Where she was before. On Brighton beach. She's sixteen years old. *Sixteen!* They have to get to her, bring her home. They have to.

Christie goes back to the house, to Megan's room, and waits. And all the while, Megan's song plays inside her head.

> ♫ This is the end, beautiful friend,
> This is the end, my only friend, the end

A man with a wild shock of white hair tells the coroner what he saw that night.

It is late, moonlit; he is out walking his dog along the esplanade.

There is something moving slowly along the shoreline that attracts his attention. He pauses, leans against the cast-iron railings, peers out; he sees the silhouetted shape of a girl, picked out against the liquid gleam of the sea.

He worries for her at once – a girl alone on the beach so late at night. He calls to her.

'Everything all right there?'

He is too far away; the breeze from the sea carries his thin voice away. She doesn't hear him. Continues walking towards the sea.

Alarmed, he ties his dog to the railings. He goes down the steps, on to the beach. Slipping, sliding across the pebbles, he tries to go to her.

But he's too late. She is gone. Into the waves.

As the man talks slowly to the coroner, Christie closes her eyes and imagines her daughter in the darkness, with the vast empty sweep of the beach around her, watching the restless movement of the chill moonlight as it stretches across the sea into the distance.

She must have been sitting on that beach for hours, alone, thinking. Thinking about Jonathan, certainly. About her father, perhaps. About Baxter and Harry. About her mother. *I'm so sorry, Mum.*

What had Christie done to her daughter? Why couldn't Megan just talk to her like she always had? They talked about everything when they shared the room at Nanna's flat.

If they hadn't moved to the house at Pound Hill, they would have still been in that room, and they *would* have talked. And Christie would have held her, made everything all right. And she would still be alive.

Jonathan is at the inquest. The coroner gently quizzes him: is there anything he can tell the court?

'No,' Jonathan says.

They'd broken up weeks before, he says. He hadn't seen her, hadn't heard from her.

There is something in his voice that Christie doesn't trust, doesn't quite believe. But she dismisses the thought – because by then she doesn't trust anyone, anything, doesn't trust herself.

Returning to his seat, he meets Christie's eye and smiles that same superior smile she'd seen on her doorstep that time.

She shivers.

Christie is called to the stand. Does she know why Megan was on the beach that night?

367

She doesn't.

Can she think of any reason why her daughter might take her own life?

She can't.

She says nothing about Megan's journal and the drawing of the fragile pregnant girl. She keeps her secret to the end.

The coroner calls for the post-mortem report; Christie tries not to listen to the details. But at the same time she needs to know it all.

The sea temperature was low, the body was well preserved.

It had taken ten days for Megan's body to wash ashore at Cuckmere Haven, fifteen miles east of Brighton. Ten paralysing days when, although she knew there was no hope, Christie had still clung to it.

Christie can't stop herself picturing it, seeing it all: Megan floating, face-down, cold. So cold. Water filling her mouth, her ears. Her eyes open. Staring down. Seaweed tangling in her hair.

The report continues: there were no drugs to be detected in the body, no alcohol. Nothing unusual.

Christie holds her breath. Waits.

'Nothing?' the coroner says. 'Nothing at all?'

Nothing.

Absurdly, Christie's first reaction is relief: they didn't find anything. Megan wasn't pregnant after all!

A moment later it hits her.

The final injustice. The final insult.

Her girl, her beautiful daughter, was certain she was

pregnant and had convinced herself that she'd let everyone down, that there was nothing to live for. If she'd come to her mother … If they had talked about it … If they'd gone to a doctor … If …

The coroner records an open verdict.

A death unexplained. A death for no reason. And only Christie knows the truth of it.

Harry is sorting pebbles beside her, counting them into piles.

'Look, Mummy!' he says excitedly. 'There's one with a hole.'

He hands it to her: she grips it tight and looks down at him proudly. Unlike Baxter at the same age, Harry is fearless, reckless: he charges at life. Head-first. In the playground he is always in the thick of the noisiest army of marauding small boys: plastic sword raised, he leads the charge against the castle on the mound; he's the first to slay fire-breathing dragons, two-headed snakes and monsters from the deep; he's at the front of every daring raid and rescue.

To think that Christie had worried that he'd grow up cosseted and soft! He didn't know his father or either of his grandfathers, and Baxter – who Harry idolises, worshipped from the first – is eight years older and was too late home from school to play often with him. Yet somehow he has grown into this glorious rough-and-tumble boy.

He isn't quite that boy today though. The tonsillitis and a week with Christie's mother have left him pale, subdued, vulnerable. The aeroplane run along the esplanade has quickly spent his energy.

How will she begin to tell him about Nanna, her boy with

a head full of memories of her? Christie has made one decision: she will say nothing about his father – it would be too much to try to deal with in one day. But she has to find a way to begin with the rest. It will break his heart.

He looks up at her, a question in his eyes before it's on his lips.

'What is it, Harry?' Christie says.

He looks away, picks up a small pebble, throws it a few feet.

'I want to come home,' he says. 'I want to play with my friends.'

'Don't you like it at Grannie's?' Christie says. 'I thought she bought you cake and ice cream?'

Harry shrugs, squirms.

'I like Nanna Bird best,' he says.

This is Christie's moment. Now.

'Harry,' she says, 'there's something I've got to tell you about Nanna.'

He looks at her, squints into the sun and shields his eyes. There is a note of quiet determination in her voice that he hasn't missed.

'Is Nanna all right?' he says.

She puts her arm around him. He is bony-thin, just as Megan and Baxter were at his age, like she was as a girl. She squeezes him to her.

'While you've been down here, Nanna had to go to hospital, Harry,' she says. 'She was very ill.'

Harry's lower lip begins to tremble.

'What kind of ill?' he says. 'When will she be coming home?'

Christie shakes her head. There is no easy way.

'I'm so sorry, Harry,' she says.

'Sorry?' he manages to say.

'Nanna won't ever be coming home again,' Christie says, tears coming. Hers held in check, his streaking his face. Holding him, rocking him.

They stay until Harry's tears dry.

Christie shivers again. There *are* too many ghosts in this place and Nanna's is now amongst them.

In her hand, she still holds the stone that Harry found, the hagstone. There's no need to look through it though, she thinks: she knows exactly what the future holds. A funeral; more tears; putting off her dream of the Open University; taking Truman into her home.

She closes her eyes and lets the sun's warmth work on her.

Right now, she thinks, if she could be granted just one wish, it would be that the magic of the stone could work both ways. To be able to look one way through it and see the future; look the other and see the past. To see everything that has gone before. And then be able to go back.

And change it.

371

74

Strachan

Morning: Leicester University campus

He doesn't belong there – that's obvious. They don't want to know him and the feeling is mutual. He watches them warily as he crosses the campus, his lip curled; they move out of his way as soon as they see him coming.

Look at them, Lewis. Fucking students.

There he is: suited, booted, sharp. And there they are: anything but.

With his crisp white shirt and silk tie, his dark glasses and his slick polished head, he couldn't be more out of place.

They stare at him, with puzzled frowns, as he stands broad-shouldered in his velvet-collared, scarlet-lined Crombie at the foot of the Attenborough Tower. He glares back at them with unconcealed distaste.

They've got so much fucking hair, for one thing. Hair everywhere, halfway down their backs or falling over their eyes or ballooning out from their heads in giant afros. And that's just the boys. Hair on their faces too: long straggly sideburns and sparse fluff beards that Strachan knows he'd only need to blow on to remove. Like huffing at a dandelion clock.

If the hair's bad, the clothes are worse. They are jumble-sale refugees, the lot of them, in their washed-out denim, tie-dyed T-shirts, wrinkled cheesecloth and boots with plat-forms so high they can hardly walk in them. If they turned up at The Salvation looking like that, Strachan would show them the door.

Worse still, they are stick-thin. Beanpoles. He's bigger, wider, squarer than any two of them put together. Make that three. He hasn't seen a single one of them all morning he couldn't lift with one hand. By the throat.

With your mother's brains, you'll be here one day, son. But not like them. You'll be a man, not a boy. Sharp, strong. I'll make sure of that.

It was late when he arrived in Leicester the previous night and the only hotel he could find was an anonymous modern block in the middle of a roundabout. There was just one room left – a dingy double with a view of a bus shelter.

He doesn't mind, he tells the receptionist. He's not there for the view.

Sitting on the bed, he silently curses the night on the tequila. It has left him weak, weary, his hands shaking; there's a dull burning ache in his chest.

Gathering himself, he telephones Sally again. She sounds sleepy when she picks up the receiver but snaps awake at the sound of his voice.

'Where on earth are you?' she demands.

'Leicester,' he says.

'*Leicester?*' she says. 'What in God's name—'

'The toerag,' he cuts in. 'His boy's at university here.'

'But why . . . ?'

'I told you, I'm working,' he says.

'Come home, Strachan,' she demands abruptly. 'I don't understand what the hell you're playing at. I'm worried about you – about us. You're going to be a father. I need you here.'

'I need to do this, Sal,' he says.

'But why?'

He can't explain, not so she'd understand. Lewis gets it; she never will.

He spends most of the night with his eyes open, chasing the shadows thrown on the ceiling by the headlights of each car that circles the roundabout, trying to picture himself. Sally's giant. Pushing a pram. Holding a baby. Making sure that nothing hurts him, harms him, gets in his way.

Trying to imagine when the boy is ten, and he's seventy. When the boy gets to university. And he's eighteen. And Strachan is seventy-eight.

'Can I help you, sir?'

Strachan turns: there's a uniformed security guard coming towards him. He assesses him in an instant; knows the type. Thinks he's hard: he isn't. Thinks he can handle himself: he can't. Fat, slow, soft. A fucking powder-puff.

'I'm looking for someone,' Strachan says.

He'd been to the university office asking after Baxter. He reckons that if he finds the son, he'll find the father soon enough. They said they can't help him because he isn't family.

374

'Who might that be, sir?' the security guard says, coming closer.

Strachan had stopped some students and asked about Baxter. Did they know him? They'd responded with quick shakes of their head and hurried by.

'Name of Bird,' Strachan tells the guard. 'Baxter Bird.'

The security guard stops, scratches his head.

'Young Baxter?' he says. '*Again?*'

'Again?' Strachan says.

The guard ignores the question.

'I saw him this morning – going into a lecture,' he says. 'He'll be out in half an hour or so.'

Strachan isn't waiting that long.

We don't do waiting, Lewis.

'Where?' he says.

The guard points to the tower.

'Lecture Theatre One – down in the basement. But you'd best wait here, sir.'

Strachan steps forward, pushes at the glass doors and strides inside. The security guard follows, trotting behind.

'No, sir, you don't understand,' he says as Strachan finds the stairs and goes down to the basement. 'You can't come in here ...'

At the foot of the stairs, he puts a hand on Strachan's shoulder to stop him going further.

Look and learn, Lewis lad. Look and learn.

He shrugs the hand away and points at the door to the lecture theatre.

'That one?'

The guard doesn't answer. Instead he steps around Strachan to block him.

'I'm warning you,' he says, pulling himself to his full height, squaring up, puffing out his chest. 'You can't go in there, Mr—'

Strachan leans towards him.

'The name's Strachan,' he says, his voice little more than a whisper. 'Just Strachan.'

He's enjoying this, he's forgotten about the shakes, his blood is pumping.

The guard raises his hands, tries to shove Strachan backwards, away. It's as though his hands meet rock. He tries again, pushing harder, with all his weight.

Strachan doesn't budge.

Not an inch, Lewis. Never give an inch.

Shocked, the guard takes a step backwards. It's a mistake; it gives Strachan the room he wants.

Two punches. Like the old days. That's all it takes.

A left to the guts, to fold him. A right to the temple as he goes down.

Fucking powder-puff.

Strachan flexes his shoulders, pulls at his cuffs, rubs at his knuckles, steps over the guard's body and pushes open the door of the lecture theatre.

75

Baxter

Lecture Theatre One

'So *Pride and Prejudice* must of course be understood in the social context of—'

The lecturer stops in mid-sentence.

He'd carried on despite the earlier commotion in the corridor, a commotion that began with a raised voice and ended with a thud, like a sack of wet sand hitting solid ground. But now the door swings open and the frame is filled with the looming shape of a man.

Seeing the incongruous appearance of the man, the bulk, the dark glasses, the muscled twitch of his shoulders; forgetting at once about Jane Austen, the pinch-faced lecturer nervously adjusts his spectacles on his thin beak-like nose and clears his throat.

'Can I help you?' he offers uncertainly.

Glad of the distraction, all eyes in the lecture theatre turn towards the door. The lecture began just a quarter of an hour ago – but, at each slowly passing minute, the students had drowsily slumped further into their seats, sent there by the somnolent, lisping drone of the lecturer's voice.

Baxter though is attentive, buzzing, wired; he's hung greedily on every word that has fallen sibilantly from the lecturer's lips. Life isn't perfect, far from it – there's a bruise on his forehead, a mark of shame reminding him of his encounter with Abby's door, and he carries the threat of being sent down with him like a crushing load – but he's made it. Finally a lecture has begun and he hasn't been asked to stand up and shuffle out.

He'd arrived when the lecture theatre was already full.

He and Josh walk in side by side. In the doorway, they pause: Josh, wincing with pain from his bruised ribs, raises Baxter's arm aloft and he's greeted with a foot-stomping, whistling welcome. Every step of the way to his seat, he is applauded. By now they all know his story – his father, his grandmother, his fight with Josh, the day in the cells, Josh's forgiveness.

Somehow, in the midst of all of this, in a way he doesn't quite understand, he's gone from loser to celebrity, from villain to hero.

Taken aback, blushing, Baxter manages a small self-conscious wave of acknowledgement. He knows he doesn't deserve his new status but, as he takes his seat, he can't resist a sheepish grin.

After Abby closed her door on him, Baxter returned to his room, reeling.

378

What the frigging hell had he done?

He sleeps only fitfully, finally jerking awake, heart pounding.

Lying on his bed, eyes wide in the darkness, he realises that he's in danger of losing it altogether, losing the plot, losing himself. It truly wasn't like him last night with Abby – that's not the way he is. It wasn't him with Josh either. He's got to get a grip.

What he needs is a day, an ordinary day, with nothing weird happening. A day when he can sit through a lecture, read in the library, have an early night. A day when he can work out what he will say at the hearing and what his father could say on his behalf.

He's got to make it right with Abby first, of course. He has to know that he hasn't wrecked everything by lunging at her like some frigging maniac. He needs to apologise to Josh too.

But apart from that, what he needs is quiet.

He is up early and he leaves a note under Abby's door. Trying to apologise; trying to make sense of it for her.

Last night, that wasn't me, the note says. *Everything in my world really has gone catawampus. Forgive me.*

On his way back to his room, he meets Josh in the corridor. He's shocked at the damage he's done to him. His face is cut, bruised, his nose held in place by white tape.

'Josh, I—' he starts to say.

'No worries, brother,' Josh says, spreading his arms wide in forgiveness.

They embrace quickly, carefully, in an embarrassed manly hug.

'You've got a bruise on your forehead, man,' Josh says as they part. 'Was it the pigs?'

Pigs? Baxter doesn't understand.

'The fuzz, the filth,' Josh says. 'Was it police brutality?'

Baxter's hand goes instinctively to the tender spot.

'No,' he says self-consciously. 'I just walked into a door.'

The man takes a step into the lecture theatre.

There's something about him, Baxter thinks, something that seems oddly familiar. His size, his shape, the tug at the cuffs. Something.

'Can I help you, sir?' the lecturer says again, more apprehensively.

They can all feel it. It's not just the man who has entered the room: it's what he's brought with him. There's a sudden menace that runs in the air, a tension that's electric.

Josh tries to break it: he straightens in his seat, flexes his shoulders, makes as if to stand.

'I'm going to make him an offer he can't refuse,' he whispers, cheeks puffed, Marlon Brando-style.

That must be it, Baxter thinks. That's why I recognise him – it's *The Godfather*. He's Luca Brasi, he's Salvatore Tessio, Vito Corleone.

Someone volunteers from behind in a stage whisper, 'It's Yul bloody Brynner ...'

It starts softly. Low. But gradually it begins to swell until the whole lecture theatre threatens to rock with it.

♫ Dum, dum da-dum
  Dum, dum da-dum ...

The man scowls, removes his dark glasses, raises a hand, points, roars.

'Shut. The. FUCK. Up.'

The room falls silent instantly. The man replaces his glasses.

'Can I help you, Mr ... ?' the lecturer begins once more, his voice faltering.

'The name's Strachan,' the man says, quietly now, deadpan. 'Just Strachan.'

'And ... ?' the lecturer says.

Strachan raises his hand again, lets his pointing finger slowly scan the rows of students.

'And I've come for Baxter Bird,' he says.

76

Abby

Lecture Theatre One

This time Abby remains rooted, silent. She doesn't cry out at Baxter's name; the thought that she should go with him doesn't enter her mind. Like everyone in the lecture theatre, she is incapable of movement.

Everyone except Baxter.

Three rows below her, she sees him heave himself resignedly to his feet. It's happening again. How can it be happening to him again?

She watches, hand to her mouth, as Baxter starts to shuffle along his row.

'Mr Bird,' the lecturer says anxiously, 'I really don't think you need to—'

Strachan doesn't turn. His eyes follow Baxter's slow progress.

'Shut it!' he says to the lecturer.

'But—' the lecturer tries again.

Still Strachan doesn't turn his head. But he raises a hand, points sideways at the lecturer. Silences him.

'Don't make me say it again,' he says.

Until this man, this ... this creature, this Strachan, had spoken Baxter's name, Abby hadn't felt nearly ready to forgive what happened the previous night. In truth, she'd woken this morning not knowing whether she ever would feel ready. She'd spent a whole day fretting about Baxter, worrying about him in the cells.

And then.

Then, he'd thundered on her door, called her his princess, grabbed at her. Grabbed! And her in her silk kimono!

She'd been so angry with him. So hurt and confused.

And the note under the door had only made matters worse. *Catawampus!* If he thought he could simply summon up their word, *her* word, and all would be forgiven ... well, he had another think coming.

She'd stomped down the hill from College Hall still angry with him and had made sure he couldn't try to sit next to her in the lecture theatre.

And then everyone had applauded him! Like he was a hero. It had made Abby angrier still.

But now. Now?

Now, Abby feels suddenly faint, panicked for him.

The world is tilting dangerously. Askew. Awry. Catawampus.

77

Baxter

Lecture Theatre One

Hearing his name, standing, leaving: it's a reflex. He is Baxter Bird and this is what he does: hears his name, stands, leaves.

Every frigging day.

When Strachan called his name, he'd found himself on his feet and pushing, nudging towards the end of the row before he'd even had time to think.

Strachan? Should he know that name?

But this time it's different. This time – now that it's too late, now that he has shown himself, identified himself – he can clearly see that he should have stayed exactly where he was. Not just see it. Feel it. Everyone can feel it.

This guy is bad news. The worst possible kind of news.

And yet Baxter is going to him!

All those years at school, he'd avoided Mad Jimmy Spaull, crossed the street when there was trouble ahead, but now, as soon as Vito Corleone calls his name, he's up and cheerfully walking towards him.

Well, not cheerfully. But walking. Just. Because his legs don't feel as if they belong to him. It's as if they are leading and he has no choice but to reluctantly follow.

Strachan? Why does that name nag at him? And what the frigging hell does he want with him?

Is it about Josh? About what he did to him?

That's it. That *has* to be it. He's Josh's father – or he's been hired by Josh's father – and he's going to make Baxter pay for what he did.

He reaches the end of the row and Strachan, his face immobile, expressionless, points towards the door.

'Don't go!' someone whispers loudly from behind.

A girl's voice. Abby's?

But he has no choice. Strachan knows who he is now.

Baxter turns, looks at the rows of faces in the silent lecture theatre, turns again and goes out through the door. Outside, the body of the portly security guard lies across the corridor.

Baxter blinks. Swallows hard.

This is even worse than he thought.

78

Strachan

Outside Lecture Theatre One

Strachan is sweating, he can feel his shirt clinging wrinkled to his back; he's nauseous, his guts are churning. The fucking tequila. Two days after and he's still feeling it. It's not good for him, the booze. He won't make that mistake again.

It's a shame: without the sweats, the shakes, the sickness, he would have enjoyed it more. Silencing that roomful of cocksure jokers, calling the boy out, watching him struggle to the end of his row, scared witless.

Strachan looks at Baxter now. He's seen him once before, of course. Ten years ago when he was just a boy: big blue eyes, pale like a ghost. It scarcely seems possible this lanky long-haired loser is the same person.

'You don't remember me?' he says.

It's a statement as much as a question.

Baxter frowns, shakes his head.

'Should I?' he says.

Strachan can hear the fear catching in his voice.

'You were only this big,' he says.

Showing him, with his hand outstretched.

One day, Lewis, I'll be measuring you like this. Showing how tall you've grown.

Baxter shakes his head once more.

'Never mind,' Strachan says, his patience immediately exhausted.

He juts his jaw, sends the fist of his right hand smacking into the palm of his left.

'I'm looking for your toerag father,' he says.

Strachan can see shock register on the boy's face.

'My *father*?'

Who else?

'Who else?' Strachan says.

Again the boy shakes his head.

'I thought—'

He stops as soon as he begins.

'What did you think?' Strachan says with a snarl of impatience.

'I thought you'd come for *me*,' Baxter says quietly.

The boy is shaking. Strachan can see him shaking.

'Just tell me where he is and you can get back to your poncey lecture,' he says.

'Who?' Baxter says, trying to play dumb, play for time.

Strachan leans towards him.

'Don't jerk me around, sonny,' he says. 'I'm not in the mood.'

Baxter takes a step backwards. Strachan matches him with a step forwards. If the boy wants to dance, they'll dance.

Look and learn, Lewis.

'I haven't seen him,' Baxter says, unconvincingly.

Strachan reaches out, grabs him by the throat, lifts him to tiptoes.

'One chance,' he says. 'That's all you've got.'

A strangled sound is coming from Baxter. Strachan eases his grip.

'He's here,' Baxter wheezes, gasps. 'He's in Leicester – but I don't know where.'

Strachan lets go of the boy's throat. Pats him mockingly on the cheek.

'That's better,' he says. 'Much better.'

79

Truman

A little later: Victoria Park

Truman is striding across Victoria Park towards the university campus. There is a spring in his step, the sun is out and the itch has been scratched. Well and truly.

♫ Rosie, oh Rosie,
I'd like to paint your face up in the sky ...

He is shaved, showered, rested and on his way to talk her into coming with him to The Old Horse. Life can't get much better, can it? A couple of drinks at lunchtime and an afternoon back between the sheets.

♫ Rosie, oh Rosie ...

It had worked like a charm. After leaving the boy outside The Barley Mow, he went back to the flat, rang her again; she'd come over, they'd talked about Baxter and his day behind bars.

'I'm worried sick,' he says, sorrowfully shaking his head. 'I don't know what's going to become of the lad.'

'Become of him?'

'After,' he says, tapping slowly at his heart. 'After I'm ...'

Her hand goes to her mouth, she pats distractedly at her hair; as she does so, her T-shirt tightens across her breasts. Nice.

'There'll be time for you to speak to him,' she says reassuringly. 'He'll turn out fine, I'm sure.'

They talk about his old mum.

'She always meant the world to me,' he says, head bowed.

She comes closer, pats his hand, tears in her eyes.

They talk about the limp.

'It's nothing,' he says bravely, dismissively. 'It just flares up from time to time.'

'How did it happen?' she says, putting her hand to his leg, letting it rest there.

'Suez,' he says. 'I was out there before it all kicked off.'

'Before?'

'SAS,' he says.

She looks shocked, impressed, comes closer still.

'But what happened?' she says.

'Not allowed to talk about it,' he says, tapping his nose. 'Official Secrets and all that.'

'Does Baxter know?'

'No,' he says. 'I told him it was an old football injury.'

'Football?' she says.

'A white lie,' he says. 'Truth is, it's the other knee that got crocked that time.'

'You've had quite a life, Mr Bird,' she says.

'It's Truman,' he says. 'Call me Truman.'

He looks her in the eye, is about to tell her about Megan, about what happened to her, about what Christie had told him. Well, you've got to play all the cards, haven't you? But there's no need.

'I've been thinking about what you said the other day,' she says.

'What about?' he says.

'About not knowing any other women ...' she says, her voice trailing away.

Bingo!

'It's the truth,' he says, pulling her towards him.

♫ Rosie, oh Rosie ...

As he walks, where Don Partridge plays the harmonica, Truman breaks into a whistle. It's difficult to resist the temptation to break into a dance.

Oops.

Steady on, Truman old son, he thinks with a grin, remembering the limp, walking with a stiffened leg.

Halfway across the park he pauses contentedly to survey the scene. Ahead of him is the university, with its tall white tower and a lower glass-and-red-brick building set against a cloudless sky. In the distance to the right, a crowd is gathering in the sunshine. Coming towards him is a long-haired boy in a greatcoat.

Running.

'Baxter, my boy!' he calls delightedly to him, throwing his arms out, the grin on his face growing wide.

80

Baxter

Victoria Park

Baxter had given Strachan the slip. It had been simple. Too simple?

Once Strachan had elicited the strangled confirmation that Truman was in Leicester, he grabbed Baxter by the collar and propelled him away from the lecture theatre and stumbling up the stairs. Halfway up, Baxter tripped and fell forwards, and Strachan momentarily released his grip. Feeling the weighty absence of it, the sudden freedom, Baxter took off, scrambling at first on his hands and knees, then climbing to his feet and running. Running up the stairs. Pushing, through the door. Tumbling headlong out on to the campus. Into the air, the sunshine. Taking off again. Frantically looking over his shoulder.

Run, Baxter, run! he urges himself onwards now. Run like the wind! Run like there's no tomorrow.

His coat is heavy, hot; his platform boots are not made for running; he has a stitch, quickly in his side. He pauses – bends double, breathless – looks back again and sees a stretched smile on Strachan's face. He's smiling! Like it's all some frigging game! He hasn't even bothered to break into a trot to follow Baxter – he's simply quickened his stride, as though content to stalk him at a distance. *Smiling.*

Run, Baxter, run!

But where to?

Still doubled, struggling for breath, the only place that Baxter can think of is back to College Hall. But is that sensible? To risk leading Strachan to where he lives, his one place of safety? But then again, if he can get across the park and on to Queens Road … if he can then dive down one of those side-roads … lead him round and round in circles … he's sure to lose him.

That will work. Won't it?

And then Strachan won't find his father. His father? *What the frigging hell does this madman want with him?* Whatever it is, it isn't to exchange pleasantries, swap jokes about old times over a cup of tea. Baxter has to get away from Strachan, find his dad, warn him.

Straightening, he fixes his eyes on the far side of the park and sets off again.

Run, Baxter, r—

It's then that he sees him, limping across the park, throwing his arms wide.

And by now Strachan has surely seen him too.

No way!

With a plummeting heart, Baxter realises that he has managed to do the one thing he knew he mustn't do, the one thing he was determined not to do.

He has led Strachan to his father.

He's brought the hunter to the kill, the slavering hound directly to the hare.

81

Truman

Victoria Park

The boy comes closer, running harder across the park, legs pumping, boots thumping, his long hair flowing behind him, greatcoat flapping.

Run, Baxter, run! Truman says to himself, his arms still outstretched, the delighted grin still on his face.

It does Truman's heart good to see Baxter running like this, running *to* him. Once before – a long time ago – the boy had run away from him, into the forest. Now he can't wait to be with his old dad. That's a bit special, isn't it?

'Hey! Slow down!' he calls to him jokingly. 'What's the tearing hurry, son?'

Baxter comes to a gasping, untidy halt in front of him. He grabs Truman by the arm, chest heaving; he tries to speak, can't get the words out. Truman puts a steadying hand on his shoulder.

'What is it, son?' he says, a frown now replacing the grin.

There's something going on here, something he doesn't understand.

'I gave him ... I gave him the slip,' Baxter finally manages to say.

He half turns, still holding Truman's arm.

'But he's still ...' he pants, 'still behind me.'

'Who is?' Truman says, looking up, alarmed.

Truman knows the answer to his question almost as it leaves his lips; peering into the distance, his eyes settle on a tall, broad-shouldered, dark-coated figure. He's wearing sunglasses; sunlight is bouncing on his shaven head.

'He's after you,' Baxter gasps, pointing. 'Who is he?'

Who is he? More to the point, Truman thinks, how the hell did he get here? His mind is suddenly in overdrive, trying to find a way out, a way through.

Could the two of them take him on? Father and son, side by side, Butch and Sundance, swinging punches? He looks at Baxter, considers the idea for a moment. Dismisses it. Ten stone wet through, the boy might have floored Josh but Strachan will only need to look at him and his knees will give way.

Baxter lets go of his arm, straightens.

'He's a frigging loony ... he grabbed me by the throat,' Baxter says, the words coming fast and scared now. 'Why's he after you?'

What? He doesn't have time for this; it's not the time for bloody stupid questions, with Strachan strolling across the park, coming nearer, smacking his fist into the palm of his hand.

'It goes back a long way,' Truman says quickly, looking around, looking which way to run.

'What does?' Baxter says.

The park is open, flat; there's no cover. Whichever way they go, Strachan can easily follow.

Bloody Baxter.

'It was just business,' Truman says. 'He's a sore loser. He's never got over it. He's off his trolley, needs locking up.'

Bloody Baxter – useless bloody boy – why the hell did he have to lead Strachan here?

'What are we going to do?' Baxter says. 'We can't outrun him. Not with your heart – and your leg.'

The crowd in the distance to the right has swollen. It must be a hundred-strong now; they are carrying placards; it looks like the police are there too.

'What's happening over there?' Truman says urgently.

Baxter looks across the park.

'It's the demo,' he says. 'There's a march through Leicester.'

Truman looks right, left, behind him. There's no choice. Anyway, there's safety in numbers, that's what they say, isn't it? Even the psycho Strachan won't mess with a crowd like that. Not with the police there.

'Come on,' Truman says to Baxter, setting off. 'That's where we're heading.'

82

Abby

At the gathering point for the demo

When the door to the lecture theatre had swung to a close behind the Strachan creature, there was a small embarrassed burst of nervous laughter. The lecturer hesitated, trying to compose himself and decide what to do. Should he carry on? Should he call the police? In the end he simply picked up from where he left off, pretending that nothing had happened.

Ridiculous: when Baxter pushed open the door, everyone saw the security guard lying unconscious in the corridor!

Abby is angry. The lecture should have been stopped and the police should have been called: anything could have happened to Baxter. She thinks she should stand up and say something. Or perhaps she should leave and telephone the police herself? She doesn't listen to a word of the lecture, doesn't take a single note.

Finally, glancing at her watch, she realises that she has left it too late: the lecture is almost over. And that makes her wretched and guilty.

When the lecturer at last grinds to a hissing halt, she picks up her bag and goes rushing out into the corridor. The security guard has come to and is sitting at the foot of the stairs, holding his head in his hands, nursing his wounded pride, but there is no sign of Baxter.

Abby doesn't know what to do.

And when Georgie asks her to keep her company on the march, she can't think of a reason to say no.

There is some discussion about whether the march should set off or not. The National Front have cancelled their rally, word has quickly spread around the campus and only a hundred students have bothered to turn up. It seems pointless to continue.

Even Georgie, who had been so excited about joining her first demo, seems to have lost interest. Josh hadn't felt up to marching and she is missing him.

But the diminutive girl with a giant afro and dark-rimmed glasses, bristling with energy and indignation and brandishing a megaphone, isn't to be denied.

'*Smash! Smash! Smash!*' she yells as the megaphone whines and sings.

'Smash the National Front,' a few voices mutter in doleful response.

Undaunted, the afro-haired girl leads the way and a ragged column of half-hearted marchers form up behind her and start to shuffle forwards. Two bored-looking policemen shrug their shoulders, raise their eyebrows, straighten their helmets and follow behind.

'*Smash! Smash! Smash!*' comes the megaphone call.

'Smash the National Front,' Abby mumbles apologetically, looking down, wishing she wasn't there.

'*Smash! Smash! Smash!*'

Two voices, loud and deep, come suddenly from beside Abby.

'Smash the National Front!' they boom.

Abby looks up and sees Baxter smiling at her side and, next to him, the man she'd glimpsed once before across the campus. A man with a broad, lopsided grin on his face, who can only be Baxter's father.

83

Strachan

Victoria Park

Strachan finds a wooden bench at the edge of the park, sits heavily down and watches as the last of the marchers straggle into the distance and out on to the London Road. When they disappear from sight, he can still hear the determined strident voice on the megaphone.

'*Smash! Smash! Smash!*'

But he can no longer hear the reply.

Smash! Smash! Smash! That's about right, isn't it, Lewis? That's what he's going to do to the toerag once he finally gets his hands on him. He's slipped through his fingers once too often – next time he won't be so lucky.

Still, you have to hand it to him. It was a smart move to head for the demonstration. Anywhere else and he would have had him.

But it doesn't matter, not really. He might have missed him this time, but sooner or later he'll track him down. If he doesn't get him now, he'll get him later – when the demo's done, this afternoon, this evening, tomorrow, whenever. It's of no concern. Strachan isn't going anywhere until it's over.

If you've got a job to do, son, stick with it. Stick like glue. Watch and wait.

Strachan takes a handkerchief from his pocket and mops his face and his scalp; the handkerchief comes away sopping wet. The heat of the day has surprised him; he should have left the Crombie in the hotel. He feels light-headed, nauseous, suddenly tired like he's never been. He holds his hands out in front of him; watches the shake.

He thrusts them in his pockets. Hides them from his boy.

It's one fucking thing after another, he thinks. First the tequila laid waste to him; now the heat has knocked him out. He's like that other big fella ... not Hercules ... the other one ... Samson ... He's like Samson after he's been got at with the shears.

He runs his hand ruefully over his head, closes his eyes, lets the sun work on him, restore him. The sweat is rolling down his face. He wipes again with the handkerchief, feeling the cool wetness.

He can only just hear it now, drifting from the distance.

'*Smash! Smash! Smash!*'

That's what he's done all his life, isn't it? Smash, smash, smash.

That's who he's been. Strachan. Just Strachan. Breaking heads. Breaking bones. Without breaking sweat.

Until now.

His head is aching, swimming; he needs to get back to the hotel, rest up, call Sal, hear her voice.

84

Truman

On the march through Leicester

Truman can't help but laugh aloud. Here he is, bold as brass, swinging through Leicester in a crowd of kids, scot-free. One minute the psycho is closing in on him, fist smacking, snarling like a pitbull; the next, Truman has pulled a Dick Barton.

In one bound he's free.

But what he doesn't get, can't understand, is how come the psycho has tracked him to Leicester? No one knows he's here, do they? He can't remember telling anyone.

Only Christie.

The smile falls from his face.

Bloody Christie! That's it. She's only shopped him, hasn't she?

Here he is spending time with her precious boy – her long useless streak of a boy who managed to lead Strachan right to him – here he is at death's door, as far as she knows. And yet she sends the psycho after him!

There'll be words about this once they're back together.

Still, he won't let it spoil the moment, spoil his day. He is enjoying this, being here, being amongst the kids, breezing along in the sunshine.

'The National Front are the fascist front!' the girl on the megaphone shouts.

'Smash the National Front,' comes the desultory reply from the marchers.

Baxter is striding at his side and next to him is a girl, glossy-haired, a real looker; if Truman was twenty years younger he'd be shoving Baxter out of the way to have a crack at her himself.

Baxter turns to him.

'The leg seems a bit better,' he says.

He's forgotten the limp.

'It comes and goes,' Truman says, not missing a beat.

There is something wrong with the boy's forehead.

'What's with the head?' he says, glad to change the subject.

Baxter's hand goes to the bruise on his forehead; he touches it, winces.

'Walked into a door,' he mumbles, turning away from the girl.

They stride on in silence for a few yards.

'That Strachan—' Baxter begins.

Truman stops him. He doesn't want to have to explain it any further. The less the boy knows the better.

'Not now, son,' he says. 'Not the time, not the place.'

He walks closer to Baxter, nudges him with his elbow, gestures towards the girl, whispers.

'Is that—?'

Baxter nudges him back, stops him, embarrassed.

Truman grins.

'Did you . . . ?'

Baxter shakes his head, looks straight ahead, crimson.

'Aren't you going to introduce me then?' Truman says.

Baxter turns to the girl.

'Abby, this is my father,' he says. 'Dad, this is Abby.'

Truman stretches across Baxter, offers his hand; she reaches for it and they shake as they walk.

'Nice to meet you, Mr Bird,' she says, her voice lilting. 'I'm so sorry to hear about . . .'

Truman can see she doesn't know what words to use; she taps at her heart.

He shakes his head, brushes her concern aside.

'Good to meet you, Abby,' he says. 'You've got a lovely voice. It's like music.'

He can see her cheeks colour a little. She might be too young for him but it does no harm to try it on, does it?

'*Smash! Smash! Smash!*' comes the megaphone voice again.

'It's about time she changed the bloody tune, don't you think?' he says to Abby, pretending to use a megaphone, smiling, making her giggle.

'Tell you what, I'll go and see what I can do,' he says.

85

Baxter

On the march through Leicester

As Truman sets off, gently easing, snaking his way
through the marchers to the front, Baxter turns to
Abby, shrugs his shoulders. He doesn't know whether to be
proud of or embarrassed by his father.

Abby looks up at him.

'He's quite something, your dad,' she says.

Baxter decides that it's OK to be proud.

He resists a smile though, bites his lip: he knows he needs
to say something about last night. He needs to apologise, to
make it all right between them.

'Abby, I'm—'

A new voice suddenly comes over the megaphone, interrupting him. His father's voice.

'PARADE, *HALT*!'

The march comes to an unruly stop.

Peering through the dishevelled ranks of marchers, Baxter
can see his father at the front, standing beside the afro-haired
girl, megaphone in hand. The girl is frowning; his father is
answering her with a huge lopsided smile.

Baxter watches, pride giving way to embarrassment once more, as his father puts the megaphone to his mouth, tilts his head back.

'ARE YOU READY?' he yells.

Marcher turns to marcher: the same questions are everywhere. What the hell is going on? Who is this guy?

'I SAID, ARE YOU READY?!'

Some of them get the idea this time.

'Yeah!' a few voices shout, still uncertain.

'OK,' Truman says. 'Let's do it!'

He raises his arm, summons the marchers to move forwards, following him, and then his voice crackles and soars above them.

'*Power to the people ...*'

Suddenly he is John Lennon. Suddenly they are dancing.

'Far out!' someone shouts.

The chorus comes with a roar.

'*Power to the people, right on.*'

They link arms, marching, dancing, a hundred voices raised together.

'*Power to the people,*
Power to the people, right on.'

A little later *power* somehow becomes *peace*. Baxter can see his father bend and share the megaphone with the afro-haired girl. Yoko joining John.

♫ All we are saying is give peace a chance

As they march and dance and sing, people from the roadside begin to join them: students, mothers with pushchairs, children. The one hundred becomes two, becomes three, becomes more.

♫ All we are saying is give peace a chance

They dance on past the railway station and into the city centre; Lennon cedes the stage to Bob Dylan.

♫ The answer, my friend, is blowin' in the wind

Baxter looks down at Abby. He can't believe what's happening: he is arm in arm with Abby and his father is leading them through the streets of Leicester, through crowds of smiling, applauding shoppers. For a moment he has forgotten everything else: the hearing, Nanna, everything.

On they go, their numbers growing all the time, on past pubs where lunchtime drinkers spill on to the pavements, past offices where windows swing open and workers wave, past bus shelters packed with pensioners, and on past an ugly gathering of jeering skinheads.

In their checked Ben Sherman shirts and thin black braces, short blue jeans and Doc Martens boots, they are carrying a Union Jack and walking angrily away from the scene of the abandoned National Front rally. A few shout jeeringly at the marchers. Seeing them, Baxter's father madly, magically, mockingly metamorphoses into Chuck Berry.

♫ My ding-a-ling, my ding-a-ling,
I want to play with my ding-a-ling ...

The whole march picks up the chorus and drowns the skinhead taunts with laughter.

And Baxter?

Baxter thinks his chest will burst, his heart will break. That's his father up there, up at the front. That's his dad. His dad who is dying. Going singing, dancing to the end.

He has never felt more desperate. More proud.

86

Christie

An hour later: The cemetery on the Old Shoreham Road, Brighton

Christie begins with a silent apology: it has been too long since she visited her father's grave. There was a time when she would come often and sit with her thoughts and her memories in the shade of the old broken yew. In recent years, though, she has come to Brighton as infrequently as she can and every time has hurried quickly away.

Too many ghosts.

She rests a hand on his headstone, speaks softly to him.

'It's only me, Dad,' she says. 'Your best girl, come to see you.'

It suits him, she thinks, this simple no-fuss stone; it feels solid, reliable. It is tucked away, almost unseen, behind a forest of lofty ornate crosses and marble obelisks, beyond a showy rank of supplicating, genuflecting angels. He would have hated anything like that. He would have pulled a face, put on a la-di-da voice and made fun of the very idea of it.

'You're my only angel,' he would have said, tickling her, making her squirm on his lap, making her giggle.

He's been gone twenty-six years but his voice hasn't faded.

She has bought yellow roses from the florist on Church Road and she kneels now to place the bouquet on the grass of the grave. He always loved his roses. Closing her eyes, she can see him, pipe in mouth, deadheading contentedly in the sunshine.

'Hello, my best girl,' he says with a smile, seeing her coming around the corner, her satchel on her shoulder. 'How's tricks?'

She considers the question.

He taught her to keep her chin up, put on a brave face.

How's tricks? She shakes her head: there's no point in pretending, he always knew when she was hiding the truth.

'It's not been easy, Dad,' she says.

Christie has no clear memory of Megan's funeral. Only nightmare fragments: the curtains closing jerkily around the coffin at the crematorium; a sea of shocked young faces as Megan's classmates gather; Nanna stumbling, almost falling, as they leave the house; Baxter speechless, dry-eyed, drawn; Harry's frightened tears, the panicked feel of his hand in hers; the mocking brightness of the day.

She has few clear memories of the weeks and months that followed. All she knows is that somehow she survived them. That they all did. They clung together and came through. Each carrying a hurt that would never fully mend.

Nanna was so strong in those months; without her, Christie wonders how they would have coped. Nanna never talked about it – there was nothing that could be said. She just held Christie tight, stopped her from falling apart. She held Baxter too, looked him in the eye, helped him to stay strong.

Christie wonders about the toll it took on Nanna, the damage it did. Is that what later brought the stroke on? Did Megan's death lead to Nanna's? Is there no end to it?

One day haunts Christie from that time.

She is walking back from the supermarket, drained, numbed, leaden, plastic carrier bags in hand. Looking up, in the distance she sees Jonathan coming towards her.

She wants nothing to do with him but, trying to avoid one another, they come to an awkward stop facing each other. She looks up, meets his eye.

He smiles.

That smile.

And that's enough.

She drops the carrier bags and swings at him, slaps him hard in the face. She's never hit anyone before.

'DO YOU KNOW WHAT YOU DID TO MY DAUGH-TER?' she screams as he reels away. 'YOU KILLED HER … YOU KILLED MY MEGAN!'

She wants someone to blame.

But it isn't true: even as she says it, she knows it isn't true. What killed Megan began long before. With her father.

No, Christie corrects herself. It wasn't just her father.

It was the lie too.

How's tricks?

Apart from Megan? The ache of missing Nanna? The

worry that she hasn't heard from Baxter? That she's broken Harry's heart? That Truman wants to come back to her – to die? That she has to abandon her only small dream? Again. That she's confused about Ray, worried about Strachan?

'How's tricks, Dad?'

She rests her hand on the headstone, shakes her head, raises her chin, puts her brave face on.

Has to laugh.

87

Strachan

Early afternoon: The hotel in Leicester

Strachan stands in the narrow space between the bed and his hotel room window, gazing out across to the bus shelter, not focusing on it; watching the cars circle the roundabout, not seeing them. As he stands, a new rush of tiredness threatens to engulf him. He sits on the edge of the bed, holds out his hands. Looks at them. Waits for the shake.

Fuck it.

With a heavy grunt, he lies down on the bed, rests his head on the pillow. Maybe it isn't just the tequila and the heat. Maybe it's some poxy bug he's picked up that's wiping him out. What he needs is sleep: a few hours with his head down and he'll shake it off. And then he'll go looking for the toerag.

He lets his eyes close. Immediately blinks them open.

No, he tells himself, sitting up, swinging his legs from the bed, reaching for the telephone on the bedside cabinet. Sleep isn't what he wants – what he needs is to hear Sally's voice. Suddenly he misses her like never before.

He glances at his watch: she will have closed up after the lunchtime session, she'll be upstairs in the flat. He dials the number.

'Strachan?' she says crossly. 'Where are you?'

'Still here,' he says. 'Leicester.'

'But—'

He cuts across her.

'I've been remembering . . .' he says hesitantly, softly.

There's something he needs to say to her. She's told him she is pregnant, but he hasn't told her what she means to him. He's never been good with words.

It's not good, Lewis. Try to be different, son. Try to be more like your mum.

There's a silence at the other end of the line. He can hear her waiting for him. Finally she can wait no longer; her voice is hushed, gentle, urgent. No one has ever had a voice like hers.

'What is it, Strachan?' she says. 'What were you remembering?'

For a moment, he's not sure he can carry on. He lets more seconds of silence tick past.

'I was remembering the day we first met,' he says.

Again she waits. This time he continues.

'I was standing at the bar. I kept looking at you; you kept looking away from me.'

'I remember,' she says. 'I remember everything.'

She does. He knows she does.

'And later, I asked you for a walk along the seafront . . .'

'And I said yes,' she says. 'And made you take your jacket and tie off.'

That's right. The day was hot, he rolled up his sleeves and

swung his jacket across his shoulder. She danced around him as they walked.

'And I never told you ...' he says

Again the silence. Until she has to break it.

'What didn't you tell me, Strachan?' she says.

He takes a breath, swallows.

'That I was the proudest man alive that day,' he says.

There is a shake in his voice that even he can hear.

'Right, that's it,' she says decisively, breaking the silence. 'If you're not home tonight, I'm coming up there tomorrow to get you. I need you here. With me. Not chasing around in Leicester.'

'No, Sal—' he says.

'Yes, Strachan,' she says.

And this time it's her who puts the phone down on him.

88

Baxter

Queens Road, Leicester

This is what it would feel like, Baxter thinks, what it would be like. If they were together, if she was his.

Amazing.

Absolutely frigging amazing.

It's not quite right, of course: she isn't holding his hand; he doesn't have his arm around her shoulder; he hasn't lifted her up, swung her round; they haven't gone chasing across the park, laughing; haven't fallen to the ground together and gazed up at the sky; he hasn't seen the smile in her eyes, the promise when she looks up at him.

But they are walking in the sunshine, side by side, just the two of them. Baxter and Abby. She seems to have forgiven him and nothing weird is happening.

She makes the world tilt.

He can feel excitement surging, tumbling inside. She stops his mind, stops his breath. Almost.

And he's on this amazing high. Floating. Because of Abby and because of the march and his father leading them through the streets like some far-out Pied Piper; singing, dancing.

'Your dad was just fabulous,' she says.

He loves the lullaby way she says it – *fab-lous*.

'There must be a word for singing like that?' she says. 'All those voices coming together?'

She's leading him, providing him with a cue. He doesn't understand at first – but then he gets there.

'Polyphonic!' he says delightedly.

Yes! *Pantechnicon, paradigm, polyphonic.*

She looks up at him; not with a smile but with a question.

'But what happened this morning?' she says. 'With that ... that creature?'

Baxter shudders, feels Strachan's hand at his throat.

'He's just some nutter,' he says. 'He was looking for my dad.'

She frowns.

'But why, though?'

They walk on. It's strange how their strides match. He's so much taller – taller still in his platform boots – but they fit together. Perfectly.

Why, though?

'It's business,' Baxter says confidently. 'My dad got one over on him and the nutter has had it in for him ever since.'

They are climbing the long slow hill of Queens Road. Baxter doesn't want it to come to an end.

'We gave him the slip,' he says proudly. 'I don't think we'll be seeing him again.'

But even as he says it, he knows it isn't true. Strachan

417

wouldn't give up that easily. He'll be back. Snarling. Angry. Angrier.

The sun momentarily dips behind a cloud. There is a sudden chill in the air.

89

Abby

Queens Road

It feels strange to have this boy so tall beside her. Strange, exciting, dangerous.

She knows she likes him – how could she not like him, with the magic in the night? – but it's not that simple. Because all around him there is catastrophe, wildness: policemen appear from nowhere; gangsters interrupt lectures.

So she can't just reach out and take his hand, can she? Much as she wants to. Because if she does, anything could happen.

But at the same time, she doesn't want this hill to end; she wants it to stretch on for ever. Because she likes walking beside this tall thin boy and there is just the chance, isn't there? A chance that, somewhere along the way, she will find the courage to put her hand in his.

What is it that Niloc told her?

Control the present, live supremely well now.

If only she could. If she could control the present, right now, she would put everything else out of her mind and reach out and take this boy's hand and—

But how can she? How can she forget the bruises on Josh's face, the lunge?

If you permit your thoughts to dwell on evil, you yourself will become ugly.

Niloc said that too. And he told Georgie something.

Only when you learn to live for others, will they live for you.

That was it. Abby was glad when he said it to Georgie – but did he really mean it for *her*?

Control the present, live well now; dwell on good, not evil; live for others.

What he's given her is a prescription for living, Abby can see that. But it's too much, too big a leap from where she is. It feels beyond her.

Abby groans. This is their hill, today it belongs only to them: Abby and Baxter. But it's inevitable that thinking about Niloc would summon him; a genie appearing unwelcome from the bottle.

'What is it?' Baxter asks.

Abby points ahead.

'I told you about Niloc,' she says. 'That's him.'

She'd described him to Baxter, sitting lotus-position outside the library, balancing on one leg outside the Student Union. But this time is different. This time, although he is dressed in his beads and baggy white, he is emerging from a newsagent on the corner, pausing in the doorway to light a cigarette.

'That's not very mystical, Niloc, is it?' Abby says as they come closer.

Niloc looks up. From the crease of his eyes, Abby guesses that somewhere in the depths of his beard there may be a smile.

'No,' he says, glancing down at the cigarette, embarrassed. 'Sorry.'

'This is Baxter,' Abby says, anxious to move on, impatient to have their hill back. 'We're in a hurry, I'm afraid. Can't stop.'

Niloc looks up at Baxter, his eyes suddenly alive, startling and blue.

'The prophet says—' he begins.

Abby groans again, starts to move on.

'Not now, Niloc,' she says gently.

Baxter intervenes.

'No, let him,' he says, with a small laugh. 'I could do with any advice that's going.'

Niloc turns to Abby for confirmation. Reluctantly, she nods her assent.

He begins again, his voice high and lisping.

'The prophet says that the season of failure is the time for sowing the seeds of success,' he tells Baxter.

Who greets the news with a grin.

The top of the hill comes too soon and Abby hasn't found courage along the way. She is tempted to think it's Niloc's fault for interrupting them – but she knows she has only herself to blame.

'Will I see you later?' Baxter says.

'I don't know,' Abby says, not wanting to sound too keen. Ridiculous. Why can't she just say yes?

'My dad's coming over,' Baxter says. 'We're going to have a drink in the JCR.'

'JCR?' she says, not understanding.

'Junior Common Room.'

She feels stupid. How does she not know that? Alice in Blunderland.

'Will you come?' he says.

Abby glances at her watch and her hand goes to her mouth. At the mention of the Junior Common Room, she has suddenly remembered. It's Thursday: by now she should be waiting by the telephone on the wall.

'My mam!' she says, rushing off.

'Will you come, Abby?' Baxter calls after her.

'Perhaps,' she shouts back.

As she goes crashing through the door, the telephone is already ringing. She drops her bag and snatches up the receiver.

'Just a second,' her mother says.

Abby hears the coins rattle and drop.

'Is that you, Abby love?' her mother says.

'It is, Mam,' Abby says, smiling. She knows they will begin this way every time.

'You sound breathless,' her mother says.

'Been running,' Abby says. 'Didn't want to be late for you.'

'That's nice,' her mother says.

It is so good to hear her voice. Reassuring. After the bewildering last few days, Abby knows she can rely on her mother being just the same, that life in Pontlottyn will be going on as usual.

422

'The sun's shining up here,' Abby says. 'It's like summer today.'

Her mother laughs.

'It's stair rods down here,' her mother says. 'Listen.'

Abby can hear the rain bouncing.

'Everything all right, is it?' her mother says. 'Eating? Sleeping? No dreams?'

'Everything's fine, Mam,' Abby says.

It isn't true: the only place there are no dreams is in Baxter's chair.

'And you and Dad?'

'The same,' her mother says. 'What you been up to then?'

What has she been up to? Abby doesn't know where to begin. Best not to begin at all.

'I'm going to a concert,' she says. 'Pink Floyd.'

'A pop group, is it?' her mother says. 'That's lovely.'

Abby seeks other safe ground.

'I tried on that present from the widow Talbot,' she says.

'Oh yes. What was it then?'

'A dressing gown,' she says.

'That's nice, isn't it?'

She knows her mother is picturing candlewick, comfy – not silk, sheer, golden and clinging.

But maybe she's being unfair? Perhaps she should at least try to talk to her mother about Baxter.

'I've met this boy, Mam,' she says.

'A boy, is it?' her mother says. 'I'd better not tell your dad. He'll worry himself sick.'

Abby hesitates, bites her lip.

'The thing is,' she says, 'I don't know whether to go out with him or not.'

He hasn't asked her. Grabbed at her, yes; asked her, no.

'It's no use asking me about boys, Abby love,' her mother says warily. 'The only boy I ever went out with was your dad.'

'Oh,' Abby says, disappointed.

'But he's a nice boy, is he?' her mother says.

Nice? Abby isn't sure that *nice* is the word for him.

'He is, Mam,' she says.

'As long as he's sensible,' her mother says. 'That's the important thing.'

Sensible?

Drunk, fighting, behind bars, lunging, chased by a gangster.

'Oh yes, Mam,' Abby says. 'He's very sensible.'

90

Strachan

Early evening:
The hotel room

Strachan wakes with a jolt to discover the room in near-darkness, lit dimly by the glimmer of streetlights and intermittently, luminously, by the headlights of passing cars. It takes him a few moments to remember where he is; to piece together how he's got there, to convince himself that it isn't a continuation of the jumbled dreams he has been falling in and out of all afternoon.

He begins by kicking a ball. He feels big, uncomfortable; football isn't his game but Lewis wants to play. They are on a clifftop. The ball floats high, carried by a swirl of wind. Lewis chases it, scampering to the cliff-edge. And Strachan is there. In an instant, catching him before he falls. They are boxing now: Strachan is showing Lewis how. But the boy doesn't want to box. Strachan is disappointed, hurt. The boy turns his back on him. Walks away. They are talking now:

Strachan is promising he'll be there. To see Lewis score that goal. To pick him up after that dance. To see him graduate. To see him get married. To hold his child. They are running now: side by side, laughing.

The dream shifts: Strachan is with his mother now. They are not alone.

He has come back: his father. They haven't seen him for years and they don't want him there – not in the tenement, not in their lives, not like it was before.

They are on the shared landing outside the flat and his mother is tight behind Strachan, pressed close, her hands on his slim shoulders – he can feel the bony grip of her fingers – holding him to her, holding him back. His father can't get to her there. He is keeping her safe.

His father sways. Bellows. He is wearing his tweed Sunday-best waistcoated suit but his tie is loose, his stud collar is undone; he is unshaven, his eyes are bleary.

Strachan faces him.

He is thirteen years old, big for his age. But not big enough.

With a long careless sweep of the back of his hand, his father swipes him out of the way. Strachan bounces against the wall, falls to his knees, pulls himself up.

He puts himself in front of his mother again. Unsteady. But there. Keeping her safe.

His father nods, acknowledges him, smiles approvingly. And then – as Strachan flails at him with small fists – he grabs him by his shirt, lifts him, throws him casually down the stairs.

As Strachan falls, rolls, slumps, he can hear his mother scream. And the slap of his father's hand on her face.

Not safe.

Another car circles the roundabout, headlights playing across the ceiling. Strachan's eyes are still heavy; he lets them close and feels himself being sucked back towards the dream again. It's there, waiting for him behind his closed eyes.

He shakes himself awake, sits upright on the bed and waits for the next set of car lights to give him the light to glance at his watch.

Six-thirty: he's been on this bed for hours. He should have been out looking for the toerag but instead he's slept the afternoon away. It's the bug – it has left him weak, powerless.

He lets his mind drift. Sally said she would come, if he isn't home tonight. But he's sure she won't; she can't leave the pub. But it's not fair on her. He'll do it today, have the final hurrah, show Lewis how. He'll sort the toerag and head back to Brighton tomorrow.

His mind drifts on. Fucking Truman Bird: what a piece of work. He'd told Strachan he was dying, told Doll too – but she saw right through him. Trying it on with her, just like he had with Sal. But he'll pay for it; all of it. What he owes. More.

Strachan yawns, settles back, his eyes coming to a close again.

But there's no rush: he can take his time, get his strength back.

Because Truman Bird isn't a mug, he won't be going anywhere tonight – not now he knows Strachan is in town. He'll keep his head down, keep out of sight; he won't surface again until the morning.

91

Truman

Waiting for a taxi

The sky is clear, a crescent moon hangs low above the silhouetted outline of the lofty elm that stands in the garden of the imposing Victorian house that Truman now thinks of as home. He is at the top of the flight of tiled steps that sweeps steeply to the brass-furnitured door; whistling, singing, waiting for the taxi he's ordered.

♩ Rosie, oh Rosie ...

There was a change of plan during the day, of course, and he wasn't able to see her as he'd hoped. With Strachan suddenly appearing, he had to steer clear of the university after the demo, and he gave The Old Horse a miss at lunchtime.

Instead, he followed a zigzag route back to the flat, making sure the psycho wasn't behind him, and spent the afternoon with his feet up.

Well, he deserved that, didn't he, a spot of R and R? What

with all that running about in the park, all the marching on the demo and then the long walk back. He stopped for a couple of pints and a bite to eat at The Black Dog. He deserved that too. Set him up nicely for an afternoon doze in the armchair by the window with the sun streaming through. Perfect.

And now?

Now he's off to see Baxter at College Hall and he's given Rosie a call, asking her to join him.

Couldn't be better.

Truman reaches for his cigarettes, taps one from the packet, puts it to his lips, lights it, draws deeply.

Well, it *could* be better. It would be a whole lot better if he could be sure that Strachan has given up, that he isn't out there somewhere still waiting for him.

But what he doesn't understand is why Strachan has come after him, all this way and after all this time? It makes no sense. Going for him with the baseball bat on his home turf at The Salvation is one thing – but following him halfway up the country? It's not just about the money; there has to be something more to it.

Truman takes another long pull on his cigarette.

That's it! It's about Sally; it has to be. Strachan must have it in for Truman because of the thing he and Sally had all those years ago. And the psycho must have seen how she was with him at the bar, seen that she was still soft on him. All right, she was mad with him too, that's why she'd called Strachan down – but beneath it all, she must still be carrying a flame.

That has to be it, Truman thinks with a smile. Rosie, Sally: he hasn't lost it at all, has he? If he had another crack at Doll, he'd win her around too. Of course he would. And it will be the same with Christie – bound to be.

Tap. Tap. Tap.

It's all going like a dream.

♫ Rosie, oh Rosie ...

92

Baxter

Two hours later: The JCR

It begins innocently enough, quietly enough. A small curly-haired Cat Stevens lookalike wanders in with a set of bongo drums, squats on the floor in the corner of the JCR and starts softly patting out a rhythm. Baxter's father goes across to him and starts chatting. A few minutes later, he comes back to their table and dispatches Baxter and Josh to collect their guitars. By the time they return, an old upright piano has been dragged from the room at the rear of the bar.

And all at once the place is rocking, wild; suddenly it's a party, they are having a ball. And at the frenzied centre of it is Baxter's father, standing behind the piano, jacket collar up, thumping out the rhythm. Singing raw, Jagger-style.

'*Brown sugar, how come you taste so good?*'

In front of him, Baxter and Josh are side by side – Baxter with a bruise on his forehead, Josh with white tape across his nose – and they are reaching for the chords, following one another, giving it all they've got. Cat Stevens is to their right, slapping hard now at the drums. To the left, Georgie and two of her friends have taken up the backing vocals, their heads coming together over an imaginary microphone.

'*I said yeah, yeah, yeah, woo!*'

The floor has been cleared, tables and chairs are pushed to the walls, and everywhere people are strutting, punching the air, dancing, roaring along.

♫ I said yeah, yeah, yeah, woo!

At the door, a JCR JIVE poster has quickly been improvised and drawing-pinned to the wall: a cartoon Truman standing at the piano, collar up. An entrance fee is being charged.

Where his father leads, Baxter does his best to follow. He and Josh chase Bill Haley around the clock, Little Richard as he launches into 'Long Tall Sally', Van Morrison as he rocks his 'Brown Eyed Girl'.

♫ Do you remember when we used to sing
Sha la la la la la la la la la la-la te da

The queue at the bar is eight deep; pint-glasses are being lined up on the top of the piano.

When Abby went running to the telephone to talk to her mother, Baxter made his way back to his room, still up there, flying, flying high after the march, after walking up the hill with Abby by his side.

What he found when he turned his key in his lock brought him juddering down to earth: three notes had been pushed under his door, all dated the previous day. Someone had

433

scribbled on the top of one that they'd found them pinned to the noticeboard near the telephone and had thought he should see them.

Each note was more anxious than the last, telling him his mother had been trying to call him, that she was worried about him, that he should ring her. Urgently.

Ring her? Now? No way, he thinks. He can't face it. Not yet.

The three notes bring everything crashing back. The caution. The hearing tomorrow.

Putting the notes on his desk with the letter that Dr Paulizky gave him about the hearing, he shudders. He can smell the smell again. Rotten. No, he'll call her tomorrow: he isn't ready to speak to her yet.

Somehow, on the demo, being with Abby, he'd succeeded in putting everything else out of his mind. With a jolt, he realises that he's even managed to go hours without thinking about Nanna Bird.

How can he have done that? Two days ago he'd been able to think of nothing else. What kind of sorry loser is he?

He can hear her voice.

My busy Baxter Bird, she says. Disappointed.

But now he's flying again.

As Baxter plays, he scans the room. It's amazing, too much. Wherever his dad goes, it's a frigging riot – at The Old Horse, on the march, and now here.

He turns to look at his father: his hands are flying across the piano keyboard, there is sweat running down his face, he's dancing from foot to foot as he plays. Baxter is worried about the strain it must be putting on his heart. How does he manage to keep going like that in his condition? He needs to slow down. Baxter will have to find some way of getting him to slow down, but not now. Because there's no stopping him now.

♪ Sha la la la la la la la la la la-la te da

Everyone is on their feet, more people are crowding into the room and it's difficult to focus on individual faces, on *the* face he's looking for.

Abby.

Surreally, Dr Rosetta Paulizky is there, patting her hair into place as she dances with a boy wearing pixie boots. But he can't see Abby. Unless . . . ?

♪ Sha la la la la la la la la la la-la te da

She is standing alone, a little to the back, beyond what has become the dance floor.

Baxter smiles at her – a broad, delighted smile. She smiles back. Gives him a small wave. Shyly.

What was it Niloc said? *The season of failure is the time for sowing the seeds of success.* Well, he's certainly had his share of failure this week, hasn't he?

Van Morrison comes to an end, the room roars its approval and Baxter knows what he has to do. He shouts to his father, explains, puts his guitar carefully down and goes across to Abby.

'You came,' he says, stating the obvious.

'It's wild,' she says, looking around.

'My dad . . .' he says, shrugging, knowing that it's explanation enough.

'Would you like to dance?' he says.

She looks down, looks away, uncertain.

'I don't know,' she says.

The music starts up again. Baxter recognises it at once.

'Can you jive?' he says.

She smiles. Leans close to him.

'My mam taught me,' she shouts. 'At home, in the kitchen.'

Baxter grins. He remembers all the excruciating times *his* mother took him by the hand and made him dance with her, to the radio or to *Top of the Pops*. 'Oh, Mum,' he'd groaned. 'You'll be grateful one day,' she always said. He was. Now.

'Mine too,' he shouts back. 'Come on then.'

♫ See my baby jive ...

Baxter is the cool still heart of it: Abby circles, dips, windmills, sways, spins. She winds around him, unwinds; their hands meet, part, meet again. She steps, rocks, swings.

♫ See my baby jive ...

Somehow the dance floor clears, becomes theirs. Alone. A circle of people around them clap, cheer.

Abby turns, their hands touch, she spins faster, freer, and Baxter wants it to last for ever. This moment. This feeling.

Her hand is in his, he holds her. Loose. They move together. Step together.

♫ She hangs on to me and she really goes
Wo-oh, wo-oh, wo-oh

436

93

Truman

At the JCR Jive

Truman takes a long gulp of his beer, a longer drag at his cigarette. Smiling, he lets the smoke go, sending it spiralling towards the ceiling. It's been some night, some party.

And now here he is, a belly full of free beer, a warm glow of satisfaction and Rosie by his side. Couldn't be better.

The room has been restored – the furniture pushed back into place, the piano returned – but few people have left, it's still buzzing. He and Rosie are standing at the bar; Baxter comes across to join them.

Seeing Baxter approaching, Rosie takes a step backwards. Smart move, Truman thinks. She doesn't want the boy to know what they've got going on between the sheets. He doesn't need to know; it would only complicate things.

'Great night, Baxter,' Truman says, slapping him on the back.

'Amazing,' Baxter says.

'You remember Rosie, don't you?' Truman says. 'I just bumped into her – I've been talking to her about what I'm planning to say at the hearing.'

Truth is, he'd forgotten about it until he saw the boy coming towards him. It's tomorrow, isn't it? Never mind, he'll think of something to say when he gets there. Gift of the gab, see? Best change the subject though.

'Abby not with you?' Truman says.

Baxter looks away, looks at his feet.

'Gone to her room,' he mumbles.

Truman aims an encouraging punch at his arm.

'Never mind, son,' he says. 'Plenty more fish—'

At the far end of the room, there is loud applause as someone climbs on to a chair. It's Josh.

'Brothers, sisters,' Josh says, raising his hands to hush the room.

Truman takes a quick look at his watch. He finishes the last of his beer, signals with his eyes to Rosie. It's time to leave: he doesn't want to spoil the evening by listening to more daft student speeches. He's had enough, with all that smash, smash, smash nonsense on the march.

Rosie picks up her handbag; Truman nods a goodbye to Baxter and starts heading for the door.

'Whoa!' Josh shouts. 'Where you going, man?'

Truman turns, realises that Josh is speaking to him, sees that all eyes are on him.

'Time to go, Josh,' he calls back apologetically.

He taps at his heart by way of excuse, of explanation. He's a sick man. He needs his rest.

'No, no, no, Mr Birdman,' Josh says despairingly. 'Like, you can't go yet, my man—'

He is cut off in mid-sentence as Georgie climbs impatiently up on the chair beside him and pushes him down.

'Mr Bird,' she says sweetly. 'We'll be quick, I promise.'

Truman shrugs. He doesn't understand.

Georgie continues.

'We just wanted to say thank you, Mr Bird,' she says. 'Thank you for a totally amazing night. And thank you for what you did on the march too. It was ... it was totally ...'

'Far out!' someone shouts as applause rings out.

Truman gives the room a small bow of thanks, waves and makes again for the door.

Georgie picks up the words.

'It *was* far out, Mr Bird,' she says. 'And before you go, we want to show our appreciation.'

Truman stops. Appreciation? Interesting. Free drink? Bottle of Scotch?

Georgie is beckoning to him now. Leaving Rosie by the door, he goes towards her, pinning a smile on his face, a diffident smile.

The crowd around Georgie parts to let him through.

'We had a collection,' she says, as he comes close.

A collection? More interesting still.

'We hope you don't mind but we passed a bucket round in the pubs around city after the demo,' she says. 'And we charged people to come in here tonight.'

'But—' he says, frowning, pretending that he still doesn't quite understand.

Georgie interrupts him.

'We know you don't need the money, Mr Bird,' she says quickly. 'We know you've got your own company. That you're very successful.'

'The Charlatan Group,' he tells everyone. 'Import, export, record shops, a record label, nightclubs ...'

Well, a bit of expansion, a bit of diversification, does no harm, does it?

'But we also know about ...' Georgie says.

She stops. Taps slowly at her heart.

The golden key, he thinks. What's it going to open up this time?

Georgie continues, tears suddenly in her eyes, stumbling over her words.

'So we thought ... we thought you could give it to a charity ... A charity doing heart research, perhaps?'

A charity close to his heart, more like, Truman thinks.

'I don't know what to say,' he says, looking overwhelmed, overcome.

Georgie wipes away the tears, looks down at him from her chair.

'People have been very generous. It's more than six hundred pounds,' she says proudly, handing him a bulging cloth bag, bending down, planting a kiss on his cheek. 'But then again, you're a very special man.'

Bingo!

Six hundred quid. Tax-free. He couldn't earn that in half a year!

He takes the bag from her, to whistles and cheers; lets the applause continue, milks it. Finally there is silence. He hesitates, makes as if to speak, shakes his head. Tries again.

'I *really* don't know what to say,' he finally says, raising the bag aloft. 'But I can promise all of you that I'll make sure this goes to the cause that deserves it most.'

Well, it's like he always says: charity begins at home.

94

Abby

Later: Baxter's room

Outside, the echoing whoops and shouted farewells of the last of the stragglers from the JCR have long since faded into the night. It is late now and Abby is in Baxter's chair, feet tucked up, his greatcoat wrapped around her.

They find their familiar rhythm in the almost-darkness, rediscover the magic.

Baxter tells her about the speech Georgie made in honour of his father.

'There's a word for a speech like that,' Abby says, teasing and delighted.

She can almost hear him thinking: *Pantechnicon, paradigm, polyphonic ...*

'Panegyric!' he says triumphantly.

They talk about the dance. Their dance.

Abby had never danced with a boy before, never *been* to a dance. Warm beneath the coat, she closes her eyes and feels herself spinning, turning, their hands briefly touching, parting, touching again.

It's the dance, of course, that has brought her to Baxter's room: to apologise. When the music came to an end she'd rushed off without a word, leaving him standing there, confused and disappointed. Back in her room, she'd tried to sleep and found she couldn't: she knew she had to apologise. She went to his door, tapped hesitantly. It was only as the door began to open that she realised that all she was wearing was the widow Talbot's silk kimono.

Ridiculous.

Without waiting for a word to be said, she'd hurried in, grabbing the greatcoat from Baxter's bed as she went. To cover herself. To make herself decent.

Alice blundering again.

But why had she run from the dance floor? When Baxter asks her – was it something he did? Something he said? – she can't bring herself to explain. She can't tell him about Little Miss Mouse being kept safe at home by her parents, being kept pressingly close, hidden away. She can't say that running away is what she's always done. Can't talk about the dreams; the waking, fighting for breath.

'I didn't want you to go,' Baxter says dejectedly. 'I was going to sing for you.'

'For me?' she says, at once astonished and glad to move on.

'My favourite song,' he says.

'Can you sing it now?' she says.

In the half-light she sees Baxter sit upright and reach to the foot of the bed for his guitar.

'I've never played it for anyone before,' he says.

Abby holds her breath as Baxter begins, softly, low. Singing for *her* with an ache in his voice.

'Imagine there's no heaven ...'

Abby closes her eyes once more and all there is in the room is the music, the sound of his voice. And that ache of longing.

'It's easy if you try ...'

She'd always thought before that the song was a simple anthem for peace – haunting but naïve – but as Baxter sings it it feels more personal. Like a promise. It's as if he is imagining a different future, a better future, for himself. For both of them.

'That was so beautiful,' she says when he is done.

They fall silent. One of their drifting-in-and-out-of-sleep silences: long, reflective, sleepy, the notes of the music still playing in her head. It's Baxter who breaks it. Shocks her awake.

The question surprises her, coming from nowhere.

'Who are Dylan and Cissy?' he says.

Abby doesn't answer.

'Who are they?' he says again, gently, insistently.

He asks and then he waits; she can feel him waiting, feel the silence stretching, desperate for her to fill it.

And finally she does.

She begins where she always begins whenever her thoughts force her back to that day. She begins with the sun on the mountains.

It is one of those autumn Valleys mornings when the mountains, restless for the day to begin, push through the soft white blanket of fog that clings to the slumbering village below. On such days, the place to be is high on the mountain slopes in the chill dazzling light of dawn,

443

looking down, listening to the quiet, watching as the colliery chimneys emerge ghostly from the grip of the thick fingers of fog that wind themselves around. Down below, as those sinuous fingers work their way between the terraces of hunched houses, it is impossible to see even to the end of the street.

Abby knows about the shivering sun on the mountains because her father woke her one morning, two weeks before her eleventh birthday, and took her to watch it rise. She knows about the quiet too: her father put his finger to her lips, hushed her questions and made her listen. It was their mountain that day, theirs alone, and they had a breakfast picnic of chocolate bars washed down with tea poured into beakers from his everyday flask. Afterwards, and only when the mist had fully risen, they followed the steep twists of the snaking path back down to the village.

It had taken some coaxing from her father to get her out of bed that day – but two weeks later there is no rousing her at all. She's been hot in the night, feverish, her tummy aches. No school today, her mother tells her.

It's not fair, Abby moans. It's her birthday! And it's the last day before half-term, one of the best days. She's promised Dylan and Cissy they will play a special game. They are coming to her party later too.

There'll be no party either. Not unless she gets well, her mother says.

But I promised Dylan and Cissy, Abby says.

Dylan and Cissy, the twins, Uncle Bill and Auntie Emma's children, live next door and Abby has spent long hours of every day of her life with them; sharing adventures, running and rolling in the meadow on the hillside. She sits next to them in class; they are inseparable in the playground. Always together, they are more her brother and sister than neighbours and cousins.

Abby pauses, looks across the room to where Baxter is stretched on the bed. He hasn't moved for some time. It's as if he is holding his breath.

'Am I talking too much?' she says.

'What happened, Abby?' he says, his voice a whisper. 'What happened to Dylan and Cissy?'

The voices of the children on their way to school at the bottom of their street find their way into her dreams as she lies in her bed. She drifts feverishly in and out of sleep – and then something wakes her. There's a sound like thunder; but then it's quiet – quieter than it's ever been – and suddenly it's lonely in her bedroom.

Getting out of bed, she puts on her dressing gown and goes slowly down the stairs, gripping the banister, calling for her mother.

There's no reply; her mother doesn't come rushing, fussing as she normally would.

At the foot of the stairs, the door that leads from the front room directly to the street is wide open. Abby doesn't understand: the front door is never left open. In her dressing gown, without her slippers, she steps out. To look for her mother.

She walks along the street of squat, tightly terraced houses, rubbing at her eyes. Usually it's busy; there are always women on the doorsteps talking, children running and playing. Today there is no one. Nothing.

Abby walks on – feeling unsteady, drowsy, like nothing is quite real – to the corner of the street.

And there.

There she finds her mother. On her knees on the pavement. Bent forwards, her forehead almost touching the stone. And there are sobs coming from her. Choking tears that are being wrenched from some deep place inside.

Abby has to stop. She's never told the story before, never said the words aloud. Her mother's tears then are bringing tears to her now.

'What was it?' Baxter says, sitting up.

'I can't . . .' she says, her voice trailing away.

'But you mustn't stop now,' he says. 'You can't.'

He's right. She has come this far, she mustn't stop. She begins again. In a different place.

'Does Friday the 21st of October 1966 mean anything to you?' she asks.

Baxter thinks for a moment, shakes his head.

'I don't think so,' he says. 'Should it?'

'If you came from where I lived then,' she says, 'you wouldn't have to ask.'

'Lived then?' Baxter says.

'I haven't always been from Pontlottyn,' Abby says.

She begins again: it is quarter-past nine in the morning and the sun is on the mountain but, below, the village is still

446

shrouded in fog. The pupils of the junior school have arrived not long ago, for the last day before the half-term holiday. At assembly they sing 'All Things Bright and Beautiful'. Afterwards, Dylan and Cissy hold hands as they walk along the corridor. They always hold hands, Abby says. There is laughter as they go into their classroom. There's always laughter. Excited chatter.

Baxter is sitting on the edge of the bed now, leaning towards her. He is close enough to touch her, if he reaches out. He doesn't. Instead, he puts his head in his hands.

Even in the dimmed light of the room, she can see that he has begun to understand.

'This place, Abby, where you lived before?' he says. 'What's it called?'

She can hear in his voice that he already knows the answer.

She composes herself and speaks as steadily as she can.

'Aberfan,' she says.

The whole village had talked about the colliery tip high above the school: they'd worried about it, complained about it to anyone who would listen, even grimly joked about it.

For fifty years it had stood there, a mountain on the side of a mountain, accumulating waste and spoil. It isn't safe, they'd said, it can't be safe.

On Friday, 21 October 1966, after days of drenching rain, high on the slopes above the village, above the school, on the upper flank of the tip, something finally gives, breaks away.

447

A vast liquefied mass of water-soaked debris subsides, slips and begins to surge downhill.

Looking up through the fog, nobody in the village can see it. But everyone hears its roar.

It is a mountainous wall of black hurtling towards them.

By the time it reaches the outskirts of the village it is forty feet deep and travelling like a train. It obliterates a farm and a terrace of twenty houses – cuts through them, erases them.

And then it hits the school.

Within seconds the classrooms are buried deep in suffocating liquid mud and rubble.

And then the noise stops. And there is silence.

Silence.

On the street corner, Abby rubs at her eyes again.

'Mam?' she says, her voice small and frightened.

Her mother lifts her head from the pavement, looks up. Holds out her arms and pulls Abby to her.

Rocks her.

And as she does so, Abby sees over her shoulder. To where the people are running. To the school. Buried beneath the blackness. And all the children still inside.

At first, they tear at the debris with their hands.

From the village, and then from miles around as word spreads, people rush to the school. Mineworkers from local collieries start to arrive; open lorries carrying them grim-faced from their pits, shovels in hand. Among them is Abby's father from Merthyr Vale Colliery.

In the first hour a few children are pulled out; blackened, limp, but alive. They are carried off in the arms of coal-smeared men, their eyes dead with shock, their faces streaked with tears.

But after that there are only bodies.

One hundred and sixteen children and twenty-eight adults die that day.

And it takes a week before Cissy and Dylan are found. They are side by side. But their hands can't reach to touch.

'It should have been me,' Abby says. 'I should have been there.'

She hears Baxter react, gasp for breath.

'I dream about them,' she says. 'I dream I'm there, with them. In the blackness. Not able to breathe.'

Baxter doesn't answer. He holds out his hand towards her. For her to take.

She shakes her head, pulls the greatcoat to her chin.

'I didn't speak for nearly a year,' Abby says.

Her parents kept her from school for her year of silence. And afterwards, they kept her close. Pressingly close. As soon as they could, they moved from Aberfan.

And then the whole of Pontlottyn watched and worried for her: the small serious girl who should have been at school that day and wasn't; who lived halfway up the hill and was always on her own.

'It's all stupid,' Abby says bitterly, angry with herself.

'Stupid?' Baxter says

'The not-talking and the nightmares and the being afraid. Because it wasn't about *me*. It didn't happen to *me*.'

Baxter tries to say something.

'No, Abby—'

She won't let him.

'But I couldn't help it, see?' she says. 'And I still can't help it.'

The tears are running now. She pushes them furiously away.

'Stupid,' she says again. 'Stupid.'

Baxter tries again.

'No—'

She isn't finished.

'And my dad can't help it either, can he?' she says. 'He stayed at the school all week. Digging. Until they found Dylan and Cissy. And then he never worked again. Couldn't go back underground. All he could see were children, buried. And he still sees them. My poor dad.'

Abby can't keep the exhaustion from her voice. She pulls the greatcoat tightly to her.

She is done now.

She has told her story.

95

Baxter

His room

Afterwards, silence hangs heavily between them. There are no words Baxter can find; he knows there's nothing sufficient; everything would come out wrong, would sound like some inadequate platitude. So he stays sitting on the edge of the bed, his head in his hands, letting the quiet speak for him.

Then, finally. Banally.

'I've got a brother,' he says.

'I didn't know that,' Abby says, tiredness dragging at her voice.

'Harry,' he says. 'He's much younger.'

Again the silence.

Then.

'I had a sister too.'

'"Had"?' she says.

He doesn't know why he's doing this. He should be comforting her; or he should be thinking about the hearing, getting his mind straight, asking Abby what he should say.

But instead he's telling her about Megan. And suddenly it's

as if nothing else matters: he's been waiting to tell her this, waiting to tell someone.

He begins as she began, haltingly. He talks about the forest; about arriving at Nanna Bird's – *Let's all do the conga* – about playing cricket on the sand, Megan with a pretend-parrot on her shoulder. About the different schools, the drifting apart.

'You were just growing up,' Abby says, trying to make him feel better. 'You couldn't stay like you were.'

No, he says. There's more to it than that. He knew she was unhappy.

He tells her about Che frigging Guevara.

'You sound angry,' Abby says, alarmed, the tiredness gone now from her voice.

He tells her about the last time they talked, he and Megan. The conversation in her room. The night before.

He taps at Megan's door, half hoping she won't hear. His mother has asked him to try to talk to her, to find out what's wrong. He's put it off for days, knowing Megan will resent the intrusion.

The door opens almost at once.

'I've been sent,' he says gloomily. 'To find out what's up.'

She hurries him through the door, into her room, making sure they aren't seen, overheard.

She's pale, so thin.

The room has been tidied like he's never seen before.

'What's going on?' he says, looking around.

She hesitates, puts her hand to her mouth, makes a decision.

'I'll tell you,' she says. 'But you mustn't say anything to Mum. I don't want her to worry.'

Too late, he almost says. She's worried sick already.

She sits cross-legged on the bed; he stretches out on the floor. And she starts telling him about Che— About Jonathan.

But it's weird. Because almost as soon as Megan starts talking, it's as if Baxter isn't there. It's as if she's telling the story to herself, with a voice so quiet he has to hold his breath to hear it.

She first met Jonathan when she was working in Woolworths, doing her Saturday job. It was her birthday. He came to the Pick 'n' Mix and made her smile with some silly joke about a bag of jelly babies.

He was beautiful, she says. She's never seen anyone so beautiful.

An hour later, he was back – buying flying saucers. The next hour he came back again – for pink foam shrimps. And he carried on like that for the whole day: fudge, gobstoppers, Black Jacks, dolly mixture. He saved the Love Hearts until last. And that's when he asked her out.

From the beginning it was like nothing else that had ever happened to her, she says. Just being with him, hearing his voice, was enough. His eyes, she says – her arms wrapped around her knees, rocking – his eyes are the deepest brown she's ever seen.

Baxter interrupts from his place on the floor.

'That night,' he says. 'On Brighton beach?'

'Oh, *that* night?' she says quietly, with a shake of her head.

That night was the best, the most perfect night of her life. That was when Jonathan told her he loved her, when he kissed her, when they ...

453

Baxter sees her falling back into telling him as if she is telling herself, as if he isn't there. Suddenly she remembers. Stops.

'But you were alone on the beach when the police came?' Baxter says.

It *was* perfect, she says. But then suddenly it wasn't. They had an argument – about something silly, about nothing – and he left her in the dark on the beach. She didn't know what to do, where to go.

Baxter pictures her: sixteen years old, in her long black dress, sitting on the beach, her knees tucked to her chin. Cold. Frightened.

After Brighton, she says, nothing was the same. Jonathan lost interest, told her she needed to grow up.

'But you used to go out all the time?' Baxter says.

She'd get up early and try to see him on his way to college. After school and in the evenings she would hang around waiting for him: outside friends' houses, outside pubs, outside a disco. Whenever she saw him, she tried to talk. He ignored her.

Finally she got the message and stopped following him.

Baxter tries to puzzle it out.

'But what I don't get,' he says, 'is why your room's like this? So tidy.'

She looks around, as if surprised herself.

'You promise you won't say?' she says.

'Promise,' he says.

She pauses as if finally debating whether she should tell him.

'I'm going to meet him,' she says, with a quick nervous, excited laugh.

'We're going away,' she says, laughing again. 'Just the two of us.'

'But I thought—' he starts to say.

She cuts across him impatiently. There's suddenly something wild in her. Unpredictable.

'It's different now,' she says. 'Everything *will* be different. Once I tell him.'

'Tell him what?'

She doesn't answer. She's obviously got a speech worked out, Baxter decides. She thinks she can persuade him to come back to her. He has to tell her it won't work.

'But—'

She won't let him continue.

'No more buts,' she says. 'I'm sick of buts.'

She won't listen.

'But where are you meeting him?' Baxter says.

'On the beach, of course,' she says, with another quickfire laugh. 'I've sent him a letter, asking him to be there.'

Baxter stops talking.

'What happened?' Abby says.

'That was the last time I saw her,' he says.

'The last time?' Abby says, shocked.

All the time he's been talking, he has held his head in his hands. He lifts it now, looks across at Abby. He's close enough to touch her, to reach out to her. He doesn't. Best to hold tight to himself.

'Jonathan can't have turned up,' he says, his voice drained of emotion.

He can see Megan on the beach. Sitting. Waiting.

'She must have waited for him – and then she must have decided it was hopeless.'

'Hopeless?' Abby says, leaning forwards.

'Someone saw her from the esplanade,' Baxter says.

He stops again. He read the inquest report in the local paper – his mother had hidden it, but he'd gone looking.

'What did they see, Baxter?' Abby says.

He sighs. Shakes his head.

'He saw her as she went down the shore,' he says.

'No ...' Abby says, understanding.

'And as she walked into the water.'

Baxter can see it. Feel it.

The cold slap of the waves numbs her. She feels the drag of her long dress. The pull of the tide carries her on, carries her under.

'No!' Abby whispers.

'I think it's what she always intended if he didn't turn up,' he says. 'One way or another, she wasn't coming home.'

Baxter can still feel it. The pull of the tide. Carrying her under.

'My mum thinks it was some kind of an accident,' he says. 'But it wasn't. It was down to me.'

'No!' Abby says again.

He ignores her.

'It was down to me because if I'd told Mum that Megan was going to Brighton, she would have stopped her.'

'No, Baxter—'

'Yes, Abby,' he says. 'She would have stopped her and my sister would be alive today.'

456

FRIDAY 5 OCTOBER 1973

96

Strachan

Breakfast time: The hotel

Strachan is feeling better. He hasn't got rid of the poxy bug entirely, can still feel it dragging at him, but at least he's shaken off some of the tiredness. He stands for long minutes under the shower, letting the water rush over him; he then works his razor across his chin, his cheeks, the dome of his head; he smacks on aftershave; he dresses, unwrapping the new white shirt he bought yesterday; he knots his silk tie.

Not too dusty, he says cheerlessly to himself, standing in front of the narrow full-length mirror on the back of the wardrobe door.

He pulls at his cuffs, flexes his shoulders, feeling a new ache, a new stiffness as he does so.

Downstairs in the dining room he eats a dispiriting breakfast, pushing a shrivelled fried egg to the side of his plate. Then, for half an hour or more, he lets his coffee go cold as he stares through the window, watching the traffic pass.

He's going to be a father: he should be delighted, excited.

He should be with Sally. But instead he's in Leicester, pushing a greasy egg around his plate.

What the fuck's the matter with him?

He checks his watch: nine-thirty. By now, Sally will be on the train and well on her way. He'd rung early but couldn't stop her.

'I'll be home today,' he said. 'I promise.'

She wasn't letting it go at that.

'Too right, you'll be home,' she said. 'I'm coming to get you.'

'No, Sal—'

'Yes, Strachan,' she said. 'I need you home. Now. Where will you be?'

There was no point in arguing.

'At the university,' he said.

'OK,' she said. 'Wait for me there. Don't do anything stupid.'

The dining room is empty of customers, echoing to the scrape of chairs being pushed back under the tables by a bored-looking waitress. It's time to be on the move.

OK, Lewis. Let's do this before your mother gets here. Just you and me, son.

He hauls himself heavily to his feet, feeling a nag of tiredness again. He shakes it away and makes his way to the basement where the Capri is parked.

Easing himself behind the steering wheel, he hears Sally's voice again.

Don't do anything stupid.

He reaches across to the passenger seat. Picks up the baseball bat that has travelled all the way from Brighton beside him. Strokes it. Feels the weight of it.

Oh yes.

97

Christie

On the road to Leicester

They have spent a long time going nowhere, stuck in motionless traffic on the motorway, forty miles south of Leicester. An accident ahead has closed the road; a police car and an ambulance have raced by on the hard shoulder, blue lights flashing. Ray is drumming his fingers impatiently on the steering wheel.

'It's OK, Ray,' Christie tells him. 'There's no hurry.'

He looks at her, stops drumming.

'I just want to get you there,' he says. 'The sooner we can get all of this sorted, the better.'

Christie can't help a sudden prickling rush of irritation and concern. 'We'? When had they become 'we'? She's not sure she's ready to be part of a *we* with anybody. And, in all honesty, she's not sure she wants Ray there at all. He volunteered, *insisted* on driving her to see Baxter – his solicitude, as it always had before, starting to feel controlling, overbearing. A big part of her wishes she'd set off by train alone.

No, she's being unfair. He's doing it for her, because that's the kind of man he is. Not overbearing: loving and true.

She looks across at him, trying for a moment to understand why on earth he is with her, why he wants to be involved. He's seen so many tears in the days they've been together, and precious little laughter.

Ahead the traffic slowly starts to move off.

'Finally,' Ray says, turning the key in the ignition.

The *we* before was always the four of them – Megan, Baxter, Harry and her. It was the four of them against the world, she'd sometimes told herself.

And then they'd found Nanna; and four became five. They'd had no money and they'd lived crowded impossibly together, but they were times of adventure for the children, laughter with Nanna. Good times; safe times.

But now Megan has gone. Nanna. Baxter. And in not so many years, there will be no *we* at all. Harry too will leave home.

Of course he will, he has to; it's the order of things. But knowing that doesn't offer any comfort. It doesn't stop the empty ache inside.

As the car gathers speed towards Leicester, accelerating into the fast lane, Christie closes her eyes.

It's hard to imagine a life without any of the children at home. They have defined her; they've been her purpose. She knows she hasn't even begun to let go of Baxter – in her heart, she suspects she never truly will. She will do her best to hide it from him, of course, but even when he doesn't need her any longer, when she can do nothing more for him, he

462

will still live inside her. It will be the same with Harry. And it's the same, even now, with Megan.

'Nearly there,' Ray says.

Christie opens her eyes. The motorway has disappeared; they are deep in the heart of the city now. Soon she will be with Baxter, and just seeing him will ease that empty ache. At least a little.

She shivers.

Remembers. Her flesh creeping.

Baxter won't be alone. Truman will be there too.

98

Truman

Mid-morning: Victoria Park

It's hard to keep the limp going when there's a spring in your step, Truman thinks with a smile. But once you start with something, there's no choice. You have to see it through, don't you?

At the edge of Victoria Park, with the now-familiar red and white towers of the university against the grey clouds of the sky in the distance, he stops. Bends to rub at his knee.

'Still playing up?' Rosie says, coming to a halt beside him, tucking a loose curl of hair behind her ear, concern in her voice. She's wearing her black academic gown. Sexy.

'Think it's easing a bit,' Truman says. 'Like I said, it comes and it goes.'

She's a good sort, Rosie. Posh as Princess Margaret but with a heart of pure gold. Good between the sheets too: not so posh there, is she?

Lying on the bed this morning, head propped up on the goose-down pillow, first cigarette of the day between his lips, Rosie singing softly in the shower – '*Sha la la la la la la la la la la-la te* da' – Truman had come to a decision. She's far too good a thing to walk away from. He couldn't be with her full-time, of course; all that too-clever-by-half, la-di-da, post-impressionistic-whatdoyoucallit chat with her friends would do his head in. But a few days now and then? It would be rude not to.

And she seems to like it: having a good time, having a drink, a laugh, a dance, a bit of a sing-song; being picked up, carried to the bed, kicking her legs, squealing.

No, it would be a shame to just walk away and disappoint her.

So what he's decided is this. Once he's back with Christie, every so often he'll take a trip up to be with Baxter. After all, it's only natural for a father to want to see his son, isn't it? And it will be good, being with the boy, watching him grow. So, he'll have an hour or so every day with Baxter and the rest of the time he'll spend chasing Rosie around the flat. Perfect.

And with six hundred quid in his pocket, he can live the life of Riley for a good few months to come. He can be with Christie, see Rosie. He can even take a wander down to Brighton and see Sal at The Salvation every now and then – at least he can if he can figure out a way to keep clear of the psycho. He might even have that other crack at Doll that he's promised himself.

Yep. Truman Bird is back. Well and truly. You just can't keep a good man down.

As he and Rosie walk the final few yards across the park, side by side in satisfied silence, Truman reaches in his jacket pocket for his cigarettes.

The only small cloud on the horizon is the mad bastard,

Strachan. He needs to be sure he isn't still in Leicester, looking for him. But, in the great Truman Bird scheme of things, that's a small problem. He's given him the slip before, he'll do it again. And then he'll turn his attention to the next part of the plan. Getting back with Christie.

Truman pauses again, takes his lighter from his pocket, clicks it into life, cups his hand around the flame as he puts it to the tip of the cigarette.

He glances at Rosie as she waits beside him; smiles. There's no hurry: overhead, clouds are gathering but there's still warmth in the October sun. He stares back across the park, taking it all in, and then, turning full circle, he looks ahead to the foot of the Attenborough Tower.

And then he sees her. Christie!

Christie?

As they walk closer, Truman whispers to Rosie.

'Better make yourself scarce,' he says out of the corner of his mouth. 'It's the ex-wife.'

He had to tell her they're divorced, didn't he?

'Your wife?' Rosie says, alarmed.

It's too late for her to walk away: it would look suspicious. Although Christie hasn't seen them yet – she looks as if she's waiting for someone; facing the tower, checking her watch – she might turn at any moment.

Limping towards her, Truman spreads his arms.

'Christie!' he calls. 'What brings you here, princess?'

She turns, looks up anxiously. They're face to face now; Rosie is just behind. Truman bends to kiss Christie's cheek. She doesn't look happy about it, flinches; but she doesn't pull away.

'Christie,' Truman says, beckoning. 'This is Dr Rosie. She works for the university.'

'Rosetta Paulizky,' Rosie says, introducing herself, offering her hand, shaking Christie's.

Truman interrupts.

'I had no idea you were coming, Christie,' he says. 'Baxter didn't tell me.'

'He doesn't know,' she says. 'I need to speak to him.'

She looks pale, troubled.

Rosie takes pity, comes to the rescue.

'Shall I find him for you, Mrs Bird?' she says.

Christie manages a small smile, nods.

'Thank you. Tell him there's nothing to worry about,' she says. 'I just need to talk.'

Truman and Christie watch in silence as Rosie pushes open the glass door of the Attenborough Tower. When she's out of sight, it's Christie who speaks.

'You're limping,' she says, pointing to his leg.

She's noticed. Works a treat.

'It's nothing,' he says, brushing it aside.

'But why?' she says.

His hand goes to his heart, tapping.

'Your heart?'

'Something to do with the circulation,' he says. 'The doctors have some fancy name for it.'

She wouldn't know whether they do or not, would she?

'Thrombosis?' she says.

Thrombosis? Well, if she says so. He nods, changes the subject. There's no point in pushing his luck.

'What is it, Christie?' he says. 'You look upset.'

She shakes her head.

'Just things on my mind,' she says.

'Things?'

'I need to speak to Baxter, that's all. He's upset with me.'

Truman shrugs. Well, what did she expect? That's what she deserves for lying to him, telling him his father's dead.

'Well, that's—'

She cuts across him.

'I need to talk to you too,' she says.

Hello? This doesn't sound good, Truman thinks.

She looks around, as though making sure no one is within earshot.

'That Strachan came to see me,' she whispers urgently. 'He's after you again.'

So that's it.

'I didn't tell him where you are,' she says.

Didn't tell him! That's another lie, isn't it? How else did the psycho find him in Leicester?

'It's nothing to worry about,' he says. 'I'll take care of it, I promise.'

'I just don't want him anywhere near Baxter,' she says.

Too late for that, Truman thinks.

'Don't worry,' he says again, reassuringly, reaching out a hand to touch her shoulder. She flinches again, but lets it rest there. Progress.

'There's something else,' Christie says.

'What's that, princess?' he says.

She pulls away from him. But not angrily.

'It's . . .'

Something is really getting to her. She's biting her lip, finding it difficult to speak the words. Like she's wrestling with something.

'It's just ... just that I know you haven't got long,' she says, tapping briefly at her heart. 'And I wanted to say ...'

Yes?

She takes a run at it.

'I wanted to say that ... if it's what Baxter wants ...'

Yes?

'And I know it's what Nanna would have wanted ...'

Yes?

'You can come home ...'

Yes!

It's been even easier than he thought. No need for a plan, the magic key has worked like a charm. Like a bloody dream.

She doesn't look thrilled about it, but she's said it. She's swallowing hard now.

'I mean ... You can stay with me ... I'll take care of you.'

Bingo!

99

Baxter

Lecture Theatre One

The lecture theatre is rocking with laughter. The steel-haired Professor Arthur Humphreys is running late; in his place, a succession of guest speakers are taking the lectern, calling Baxter to his feet and summarily ordering him out.

John Cleese is first. With long, corkscrewing, swivelling, stooping strides, he makes his way to the front of the lecture theatre, points abruptly at Baxter, points mad-eyed to the door. Edward Heath is jolly about it, shoulders shaking; Harold Wilson puffs pensively on an invisible pipe; Richard Nixon talks hang-dog and oleaginously about it being a time for negotiation, not confrontation – but sadly Baxter still has to go; Tommy Cooper orders him from the room – just like that; Marlon Brando makes Baxter an offer he can't refuse.

They are jumping from their seats, forming a queue. Everyone is suddenly Mike Yarwood, everyone has an impression to deliver. And Baxter, the good-humoured butt of their jokes, is rocking with it, rolling with it – on his feet, applauding, bowing, laughing.

But even as he rocks and rolls, he can still feel it. The fear. That this could be his one and only lecture, the last day he'll be in this room.

After the hearing this afternoon, it will all be over.

Unless, of course, his father – who seems able to do most things – can talk them round, can work some of his magic.

How weird is that? At the beginning of the week his father was dead; now he's his only hope.

Eamonn Andrews is at the lectern, a red folder in one hand, pointing to the exit with the other: 'Baxter Bird, this is your life ...'

Baxter laughs again. Feels the churn of his stomach. The hearing is only hours away now.

100

Abby

Lecture Theatre One

They stop doing impressions and move on to songs. Two keystone cops chase a surrogate Baxter around the theatre and force him against the wall. The three of them begin to sing and everyone else quickly joins in.

♫ Please release me,
Let me go ...

Abby looks down to where Baxter is standing, shaking with laughter. He turns to face her, shrugs his shoulders in resignation. She smiles.

It's good to see him laugh, she thinks, this boy of hers with his long words and the terrible secret he keeps so close inside. This boy of hers with the weight of worry about the hearing bearing down on him.

He can't be sent down. It's not fair.

'This boy of hers'? Abby blushes. What is she thinking? She knows the answer.

It's the same thing as the previous night, after he'd told her about Megan; when she knew from the rhythm of his breathing that he was finally asleep.

'*Nos da, cariad,*' she'd whispered from beneath the greatcoat.

Abby's thoughts are abruptly interrupted: suddenly the door to the lecture theatre swings open, the singing stops and Dr Rosetta Paulizky comes rushing in, her black gown flowing behind.

She goes to the lectern and looks up. Baxter is still on his feet.

'Baxter,' she says, acknowledging him matter-of-factly, as though she'd expected to see him there, waiting.

Baxter had been standing tall amidst the laughter. Abby can now see a defeated slump in his shoulders. She's seen it before.

It's not possible, is it? Not again? Surely.

'Baxter,' Dr Paulizky says, holding out her hand as if to lead him.

There's a silence in the lecture theatre unlike anything Abby can remember. Not a breath is being taken.

Baxter doesn't budge. He's been called from the room on four consecutive days; this time he seems incapable of movement.

Dr Paulizky speaks again.

'Your mother's here. She needs to see you.'

Still Baxter doesn't move.

'It's OK, Baxter,' Dr Paulizky says gently, coaxingly. 'There's nothing to worry about. I promise.'

Abby breathes. The room breathes. There is nothing to worry about. Baxter's shoulders begin to lift and he starts to shuffle from the middle of his row.

And then, as he goes, the applause starts. The cheers and foot-stamping start. The whistles begin.

And this time.

This time, Abby bends to pick up her Biba bag and follows him.

At the end of his row, Baxter turns, sees her coming, waits. She is pushing her way towards him, treading on toes in her platform boots, clattering heads with her carrier bag.

She doesn't care.

Baxter climbs the steps to the end of her row. As she comes towards him, he holds out his hand.

And finally, Little Miss Mouse takes it.

101

Truman

Outside the Attenborough Tower

You can't bloody make them up. Women. One minute, there he is up there on cloud nine, home free, feet back under the table; there he is closing his eyes, seeing himself climbing between the sheets with his Christie, pulling her towards him, smelling her scent, nuzzling her neck. And the next, this lanky joker with a sorry moustache and mutton-chop sideburns shows up.

Her bloody fancy-man!

'This is Ray,' Christie says, sounding embarrassed.

At least she has the courtesy to blush.

'Ray?' Truman says.

'A friend,' Christie says.

Truman can hear the lie in her voice. Friend? Who does she think she's kidding?

Looking uncomfortable, guilty as sin, Ray offers Truman his hand. Truman ignores it and reaches instead in his pocket for his cigarettes. Lighting one, he sends an angry billow of smoke towards Ray. He then turns his back on the pair of them.

He doesn't get it. Does she want him back or not? He's not going to be messed around like this. A man in his condition.

He takes another irritated drag on his cigarette, looks up and sees someone walking towards him he doesn't recognise. Well, that's not quite true. He *does* recognise her. Immediately. He just can't get his mind around seeing her there, strolling across the campus in her best coat and stilettos.

Sal? Sal from The Salvation. What the . . . ?

She comes straight towards him.

'Truman—'

He raises his hands. Stops her. Turns to Christie. He can't resist.

'Christie,' he says, 'this is Sally.'

'Sally?' Christie says, her eyebrows arching.

'A friend,' Truman says with a smile.

Well, two can play at that game, can't they?

Sally nods at Christie, turns back to Truman.

'Truman,' she says urgently, 'I need to talk to you.'

She's come all this way to talk to him. He wasn't wrong, was he? She still carries that flame, burning hot.

He leads her away from the foot of the tower, towards the path that narrows as it runs to the park. A bit of privacy is called for: Rosie will be back soon with Baxter. Christie, Rosie and Sal together? That's too much for even Truman Bird to handle.

'What is it, princess?' he says to her with a lopsided smile, taking her by the arm. 'Can't keep away from me?'

She pulls her arm away, looks at him, cold as the slab his mother is lying on.

'Get your hands off me,' she spits.

476

He raises his hands in surrender. He's moved too quickly.

'What is it, Sal?' he says, renewing his smile. 'I thought you'd come to see me.'

'*You?*' she says disbelievingly.

Not him?

'I'm not here for you,' she says. 'I've come for *him*.'

'The psycho?' Truman says.

'Psycho?' she hisses angrily, menacingly.

He backs away. She's as crazy as Strachan. Crazier.

'So why do you need to talk to me then?' he says, alarmed.

She leans towards him. Hisses again. Through clenched teeth.

'Because wherever you are,' she says, 'he won't be far behind.'

Truman looks around, looks over his shoulder.

102

Christie

Outside the Attenborough Tower

A huddle of five students stroll across the broad paved area at the foot of the Attenborough Tower, talking animatedly, laughing, their books tucked under their arms. Three long-haired, long-legged girls confidently lead the way, two blonde, one dark, their eyes dancing; two boys follow, loping close behind. As she walks, the dark-haired girl turns, says something teasingly over her shoulder and skips quickly away before one of the boys can react and reach her.

Christie smiles.

If she could be anyone in the world right now, she'd be that dark-haired girl at the heart of that small group of friends, with the buzz of talk and laughter all around her and her books under her arm. She's got everything, that girl. She's beautiful, she's bright, she belongs here. She has everything in front of her too. All her dreams intact.

'Good for you, girl,' Christie whispers after her.

Ray interrupts her thoughts.

'Sorry it took me so long,' he says.

She resents the interruption, doesn't know what he means. 'The parking,' he explains.

She'd gone ahead; left him with the car.

'Did you speak to Truman?' Ray says.

She nods. She doesn't want to talk. She feels uncomfortable standing there, beside him. She *would* be better on her own.

Christie looks across to where the path narrows and the park begins. Truman has backed away from the woman in the stilettos who arrived so suddenly. The woman's name means something to Christie.

Sally? Surely she can't be *that* Sally, from all those years ago? One of the women Truman took up with while she was stuck in the caravan with the children.

No, it's not possible. She doesn't seem the type. In her black coat and high heels, she looks elegant, sophisticated. She makes Christie feel almost dowdy.

But if it *is* her, what does she want? What on earth is she doing there? Is she still with Truman? He said he's on his Jack Jones; alone and lonesome. Is that true?

She shakes the thought away, dismisses it. Baxter will join her soon; that's all she's interested in right now. Ray can go back to the car; Truman and the woman can wait where they are.

Her eyes return to the huddle of friends as they make their way across the campus. The dark-haired girl is laughing now. One of the boys has his arm around her shoulders. They are young. Carefree.

Christie tries to resist the thought; can't. That should be Megan. That should have been me.

103

Abby

Outside the Attenborough Tower

As the door of the lecture theatre closed behind them, while the cheers and whistles still rang out, Baxter put his arms around Abby, picked her up, lifted her and twirled her in a long slow circle. Like it was something he'd promised himself he would do.

The circle complete, he returned her to earth and they stood facing each other, slightly breathless, faces flushed. Neither of them said a word; they didn't need to.

Then he raised his hand towards her. For a moment, she was afraid he'd make the same mistake and lunge at her. But he didn't, he didn't try to grab her or kiss her, and she was relieved about that – well, relieved and a little disappointed too.

And then – with the lightest, softest, most sensual touch – he brushed her cheek with the back of his hand. As though making sure she was real.

After that they walked slowly up the stairs: they knew there was no need to hurry because Dr Paulizky had said there was nothing to worry about. It was as if they were just getting used to the feel of being together, the feel of his hand on hers, hers in his.

Finally they emerge through the glass door, blinking into the sunlight. Waiting outside is a woman standing next to a man with a drooping moustache. She is small, slender, young-looking, smartly dressed – not like Abby's mam, not nearly so comfortable and mumsy.

Baxter squeezes Abby's hand.

'Mum,' he says, 'I want you to meet Abby.'

His mother turns towards them. It feels strange to be standing hand in hand in front of her. Somehow illicit.

'You've got a bruise on your forehead?' she says to Baxter, reaching up to touch it. Gently.

'It's nothing, Mum,' he says, pulling away, embarrassed. 'Just a stupid accident.'

'Abby?' his mother says, turning to her. 'That's a lovely name. You must call me Christie.'

Abby decides she likes her already.

Baxter lets go of her hand and bends to kiss his mother on her cheek. He looks up to the man with the drooping moustache.

'Who's this?' he says.

'You remember Ray,' his mother says to him, looking awkward. 'Ray from work. He drove me here.'

Suddenly there is tension in the air.

Baxter straightens, stiffens. He shakes Ray's hand. Perfunctorily. He obviously hadn't known about his mother and this Ray, Abby thinks. All at once she feels like she's intruding, as though she should find an excuse to leave.

Hoping to find a way out, Abby glances towards the

park – and notices Baxter's father with a woman in a black coat and stilettos. He gives her quick, uneasy wave.

'And who's this?' Christie says.

Abby and Baxter look over their shoulders. Behind them are Josh and Georgie, side by side and grinning. They must have followed them out of the lecture theatre. Further behind is Dr Rosetta Paulizky, hanging back.

Baxter does the introductions. It's getting to be a crowd. A tense, edgy, uncomfortable crowd.

Christie bites her lip.

'I'm sorry, everybody,' she says. 'But Baxter and I need to talk.'

Abby begins to breathe more freely; she's grateful for the opportunity to get away. It's not that easy though. Baxter finds her hand again, squeezes it.

'It's all right, Mum,' he says. 'We can talk in front of Abby.'

Again Christie bites her lip.

'But I need to talk to you about your father,' she says, tapping at her heart.

'About Dad?' Baxter says.

'And other things,' Christie says.

Abby takes this as her cue.

'It's OK, Baxter,' she says brightly, trying to ease the tension. 'I'll wait in the Union coffee bar for you.'

She signals to Georgie and Josh and starts to move off. But at that moment a diminutive figure chooses to appear in the distance.

'Not now, Niloc,' Abby whispers under her breath. 'Not now.'

104

Truman

Victoria Park

Truman glances around nervously, his heart jumping, thumping, his eyes darting this way, that. Sal seems sure Strachan will arrive at any moment: Truman needs to be out of there. Fast. He'd been confident that he could give him the slip again if he needed to but now, with Sal there, watching his every move, clinging to him, he feels cornered. Now he'll have to shake her off *and* the psycho.

Bloody women!

But running is a mug's game. Safety in numbers, that's the trick, isn't it? It worked before, worked a dream, on the march. It will work again. The psycho won't dare touch him in a crowd. And there *is* quite a crowd gathering in a straggling semi-circle underneath the tower. Baxter and Abby have arrived and—

Who the bloody hell is that?

Some long-haired, pint-sized, barefoot, judo-clad joker is scampering busily towards them from the far side of the campus. It's the Maharishi Mahesh Yogi! Just back from tea with the Beatles.

Glad of the excuse to join the crowd, grateful for the opportunity to try to move away from Sally, Truman walks from the edge of the park towards the foot of the tower. Sally follows, clicking on her stilettos, staying limpet-close.

As Truman makes his way towards them, pointing towards the maharishi coming from the opposite direction, he calls to Baxter and Abby.

'Who the bloody hell is that?' he says.

It's Abby who answers, wearily, as Truman comes close.

'It's Niloc,' she says. 'I'll get rid of him.'

'Niloc?' Christie and Ray chorus, mystified, turning towards him and shading their eyes against the sun to see him more clearly. Josh and Georgie do the same, their grins growing wider.

'Colin,' Abby mutters. 'Backwards.'

'He's harmless,' Rosie contributes, taking a hesitant step forwards. 'Actually, he's something of a university character and he used to be ...'

Her voice fades away distractedly to nothing. She seems suddenly aware that all eyes are on her, that she has taken centre stage. She pats at her hair, steps back.

Despite himself, despite the fact that the psycho could appear at any second, Truman laughs. Well, you've got to. You can't look at this Niloc character and not laugh. Their own mini-maharishi.

Niloc is almost upon them – but a commotion from the edge of the park causes them all to turn the other way.

Strachan.

Bald head, dark glasses, black coat, he is striding along the path, carrying a baseball in his right hand, smacking the clubbed end of it into his left. He is being pursued by a portly security guard.

Seeing him coming, Truman edges closer to Baxter and Abby, closer to Christie, to safety. Sally moves with him.

'Hey, you!' the security guard calls to Strachan.

Strachan turns to face him, lifts the baseball bat. The security guard comes to a halt, puts his hands above his head.

'No, Strachan!' Sally shouts, alarmed.

She starts towards him. Without turning away from the security guard, Strachan raises his hand, stops her.

The guard speaks again.

'Now listen, Mr—'

Strachan breaks in. Deadpan. Icy.

'The name's Strachan,' he says.

'Now listen, *Mr* Strachan—'

It's a mistake.

Strachan steps towards him, swings the bat, short-armed, hard. The guard goes down with a strangled grunt that seems to come from deep in his guts.

'NO!' Sally screams, bending double, rooted to the spot.

Strachan ignores her.

'I told you,' he tells the prostrate guard. 'The name's Strachan. Just Strachan.'

Everyone else takes a step backwards as the blow strikes. Ray puts his arm around Christie. Pulls her to him. Baxter does the same with Abby, Josh with Georgie. Rosie's hand goes to her mouth. And Niloc is now amongst them.

Slowly Strachan turns to face them.

'Run, Dad!' Baxter whispers. 'Run!'

Truman looks around. Panicked. Run or stay? Run or stay?

A sudden bony grip on his arm answers the question for him. He looks down and finds Niloc staring up with startling blue eyes.

Truman tries to shake him off. Niloc holds tight, smiles and then speaks. His voice lilting, lisping.

'The yogi says …'

The yogi? What the hell is he on about, Truman thinks, trying again to shake free.

Niloc's grip is like a vice.

'The yogi says: remain calm, serene, always in command of yourself.'

What?

105

Strachan

Outside the Attenborough Tower

Strachan is shaking, sweating like a fucking pig. He'd thought he was feeling better; he isn't.

And he thought he would get there first – find the toerag, sort it – before Sally arrived: he hasn't. He had to pull over on the way from the hotel; the world was coming disjointedly at him, his eyes fighting for focus. He had to rest up in the car. He can't shake it: this poxy bug.

Finally, his head had cleared. A little. He turned the key in the ignition.

We're going to finish this thing, Lewis. Nothing gets in our way; not even your mother.

He didn't want her there to see it – but he can't do anything about that.

Not now.

Pausing, Strachan stares across to the small crowd gathered beneath the tower. Truman is at the heart of it, hiding behind his wife, his son. But he's going nowhere. Not this time.

Look and learn, son. Look and learn.

Strachan rests the head of the bat on the ground, props the handle against his leg. He flexes his shoulders, pulls at his cuffs. Leaving the security guard down and gasping for breath, he picks up the bat, slaps it in his hand and begins to move towards Truman.

He only takes two paces before he has to stop. His head throbs, the ground lurches beneath his feet. It's like being back on the tequila. He steadies himself, goes forwards again. Slowly.

He feels better, he tells himself. Yes, he feels better.

The sweat is running from his forehead, stinging in his eyes. He is close enough. He stops again and raises the bat; points it at Truman, calling him out.

Come on, toerag: time to play.

But Truman doesn't move. Instead it's the boy who takes a step towards Strachan. Stick-thin; he could snap him like a twig.

'Leave him!' Baxter yells defiantly. 'Leave my dad alone!'

The boy has balls, Strachan thinks. Balls but no brains. My Lewis will have both.

'Just leave him,' Baxter says, tapping frantically at his chest. 'He's a sick man.'

From a distance, Truman taps at his heart

'That's right,' he says. 'I told you in Brighton. One blow could—'

He snaps his fingers: they click dully.

Sally now intervenes. Pleading.

'Leave him, Strachan,' she says. 'Just leave him and come home.'

Christie joins the chorus.

'He's dying!' she says desperately. 'Isn't that enough?'

Strachan can't take any more. His face twists into a sneer.

'Dying, my arse!' he says.

He thinks of Doll as he says it. She would enjoy being there, seeing this, hearing that.

'*What?*' Christie says, shaking her head, confused.

'He's no more dying than I am,' Strachan says.

'But—' Christie tries again.

Strachan won't let her continue. He *is* feeling better now. His head clearer.

'He told Doll the same thing,' he says. 'Tapping away at his fucking heart. She called his bluff.'

'Doll?' Christie says, suddenly defeated.

'Ask him,' Strachan says. 'Just ask the toerag.'

Everyone turns towards Truman.

'I can explain,' Truman says, with a quick lopsided smile, eyes darting. 'I can explain everything . . .'

Strachan takes two more strides towards him. One swing of the bat now will end it.

This is who I am, son. This is what I do.

Everyone is suddenly talking, shouting at once.

'You can *explain*?' Baxter says to his father, frowning. 'What's to explain?'

He doesn't understand, doesn't want to understand, Strachan thinks. But Christie does. She gets it all right.

'So it's a *lie*?' she says slowly, tapping her heart, taking it in, her anger rising. 'It's all *lies*?'

'No, listen, princess . . .' Truman says, holding up his hands.

A woman with unruly hair steps forwards. Strachan hadn't noticed her before.

'All lies?' she says, bewildered, angry too.

'I can explain, Rosie,' Truman tells her. 'Everything.'

'*Lies?*' Christie says. '*Again?*'

A long-haired character in white pyjamas has been hanging on to Truman. He breaks free of him and Truman rounds on Christie, finger jabbing.

'Don't you bloody tell me about lies!' he says. 'You told the children I was dead!'

'All lies?' Rosie says. 'But I— But we—'

One hand goes to her breast, the other to her mouth.

'It's all right, Christie,' Ray says soothingly, his arm around her.

'It's not all right, Ray!' she yells at him, pulling away. 'It's not bloody all right!'

'The money,' Georgie suddenly shrieks. 'The six hundred pounds—'

'This is one bad trip,' Josh is saying to no one in particular. 'One freaking bad trip.'

'Let it go, Strachan, just let it go!' Sally is pleading.

'*All ... frigging ... lies?*' Baxter says to his father, incredulous.

'It's OK, Baxter,' Abby says, holding him. 'It's OK.'

'No, listen, son—'

Christie is standing in front of him now. Screaming.

'Your mother's dead ... your daughter's dead ... We're all falling apart, and you ... you ... you lie, about *this*!'

She taps furiously at her heart.

'All lies?' Baxter says quietly, distraught. 'The record label? Jack Charlton?'

'Jack Charlton?' Ray says, puzzled.

'The limp,' Baxter explains, pointing to his father's knee.

490

'Suez,' Rosie interrupts, pointing. 'SAS.'

'WHAT?' Christie says.

'He told me it was . . .' Rosie tries, gives up.

'He told *me* it was a thrombosis,' Christie roars. 'But then again, he once told me he loved me!'

'I do, princess,' Truman says, as if seeing a chance to make it all right. 'That's what this is all about, isn't it? I wanted a second go at it.'

'WHAT?' Christie screams at him, like he's lost his mind. 'WHAT?'

'This really is one freaking bad trip,' Josh is repeating.

Georgie swings a fist, hits him on the arm.

'Shut up, Josh!' she says. 'Think about the money. We gave him all that money!'

'Money?' Ray says.

Sally is inching closer to Strachan, talking softly.

'Put the bat down, Strachan,' she pleads.

Strachan blinks the sweat from his eyes. He can't stop. Not even for her. He grips the bat tighter.

He's heard enough. Enough talk from these sorry jokers to last a lifetime.

He braces himself, raises the bat higher.

This is who I am, son. This is—

The baseball bat falls clattering from his hand. He can't grip it, can't hold on to it. His arm, his hand, suddenly useless.

He sways. Staggers.

Sally screams.

'*Strachan!*'

A belt of pain grips at his chest, numbs his arm, makes the world black, drops him to one knee. But doesn't down him. Nothing fucking downs him.

Nothing ever has, Lewis. No one.

His head drops. Too heavy to hold upright. The pain settles quickly back but his breath is coming short. Not a bug then; but give him a moment and he'll be up again. That's all he needs. Just a moment.

Sally is at his side, kneeling, her hands at his face, cupping it, holding it.

'No ...' she's saying, 'no ... no ...'

The others have stopped talking, shouting. Strachan raises his head, tries to focus. They are all looking at him, frozen. Except for Truman Bird. And he's away on his toes, disappearing into the distance. Of course he is.

'Get help!' Sally screams at them. 'Get an ambulance!'

His head drops again.

Sally presses her face against his. He can feel the wet of her tears.

'No, Strachan,' she says. 'Not now ...'

Not now? He doesn't get it. Not for a moment. Then he does.

He finds his voice. The words slurring, coming from far away.

'Because of the boy?' he says.

'Boy?' she says.

'My son,' he says.

She laughs. Holds him.

'I love you so much, Strachan,' she says. 'Why have you never asked me to marry you?'

Somewhere in the distance is an ambulance siren.

Why? He's always known the answer to that.

'I was afraid ... you'd say ... no,' he says, fighting the words, fighting his eyes, fighting to keep them open.

Fight for the right things. Keep your mother safe, son.

Sally shakes her head, wipes at her tears.

'Ask me now, you big lump,' she says.

He's on one knee, why not?

He manages a smile, opens his mouth to say the words.

The pain grips again.

He goes over. Goes down.

Keep her safe, son.

Fuck it.

106

Baxter

Afternoon:
The Fielding Johnson Building

Baxter sits alone, waiting in a small windowless anteroom outside the formidable dark double doors of the University Council chamber. White-walled and dingy, the room reminds him of his cell at the police station.

He feels now as he felt then: a similar mix of numbed defeat, shame and rising dread. And he is waiting now, as he waited then, for his father to arrive.

Every rational bone in Baxter's body tells him he won't come. But a last small part of him can't finally let go of the thought that – despite all the lies, and his vanishing act when Strachan went down – his father will walk through the door at any moment with a lopsided smile and a ready word. He will come and set Baxter free. Save him.

Baxter hasn't told his mother about the hearing: couldn't bring himself to. His father is his only hope. He won't let him down. He promised.

He shakes his head in disbelief: how the frigging hell did

any of this happen? How could a week that began with such hope and anticipation end in this total car crash? On Monday his imagined life was beginning. On Friday it's over.

There's a clock on a table pushed to the wall. It is ticking down the last seconds towards the time when the double doors will open.

He shuts his eyes, feels the panic, his mind a blank.

What am I going to do, Nanna? What am I going to say?

My brave Baxter Bird, Nanna says to him. Disappointed.

Abruptly the double doors open. Light floods from the cavernous, high-windowed room beyond. Silhouetted in the doorway is a dark-suited man: tall, substantial, wearing horn-rimmed spectacles.

Baxter has seen him before. It's the same man who interviewed him when he first applied for a place at the university.

Every so often Baxter glances over his shoulder. Still he hopes his father won't leave him to face this alone. Will get him out of this.

His father doesn't come.

The horn-rimmed man reintroduces himself: he is Professor Gilbert Parbury. He also introduces the two people sitting either side of him. Baxter doesn't catch their names. One is the pinch-faced lecturer from the day that Strachan came; the other is a dark-haired girl, a student representative who keeps her eyes lowered and looks as nervous as Baxter feels.

They are sitting on high, cushioned chairs with their

backs to the tall windows. Baxter is separated from them by a wide mahogany table. The only other person in the room is Dr Rosetta Paulizky. She sits at the end of the table to Baxter's left, smiling anxiously, playing with her hair.

It's Professor Parbury who does all the talking. He looks irritated, as if he's got better things to be doing on a Friday afternoon.

'So, Mr Bird,' he says, wearily removing his spectacles, closing his eyes, briefly pinching the bridge of his nose. He has a buff-coloured file in front of him with Baxter's name on the cover. It is thick with notes that have been gathered over the past few days. An investigation has been carried out, information has been collected; students, university staff, the security guard have been spoken to.

'Mr Bird, at our previous meeting, when you talked your way into this institution, you told me your father was dead. Did you not?'

Baxter is thrown. He thought they would be questioning him about Josh. Not this.

'Yes, but—' Baxter tries.

The professor gallops on. It's as if he has the scent of blood in his nostrils; Baxter's blood.

'But it wasn't true, was it? Because your father is very much alive, isn't he?'

'Yes, but—'

'And you also told me you'd been brought up in the most straitened of circumstances. Some fanciful tale about a council flat and Pauper Bird.'

'Yes, and—'

'But it transpires that this was nothing but a tissue of lies, a web of deceit. Because your father is in fact a very wealthy man. With his own conglomeration of companies, no less – the Charlatan Group.'

Baxter suddenly sees: the clue was in the name.

'I put it to you, Mr Bird, that you are nothing but a liar and a fantasist.'

'No, I—'

Dr Paulizky tries to intervene.

'May I?'

Baxter's heart lifts. A little. In the absence of his father, Dr Paulizky is going to talk for him. Set the record straight.

Professor Parbury turns to face her. Acid in his voice.

'Dr Paulizky, I have no idea what you are doing here but I would recommend that you remain silent.'

He taps the buff-coloured folder. There is distaste, disdain in his voice now.

'Our investigation has revealed disturbing reports that you are involved in a relationship with Mr Bird's father of a clandestine and compromising nature. And that you have been using the accommodation reserved for visiting academics for these ... these illicit purposes.'

Baxter blinks. His head slumps. *No.*

'Your behaviour, Dr Paulizky, is therefore also under scrutiny. There may indeed be a separate hearing, at a later date.'

Baxter looks up to see tears gathering in Dr Paulizky's eyes. Another hurt his father has caused.

The professor turns again to Baxter.

'To resume, Mr Bird. I put it to you that not one word that issues from your lips is true. That you duped me and my colleagues and lied your way into this university.'

It's wrong, unfair: Baxter is the only person who *hasn't* lied. But try as he might, he can't say anything. The professor is talking, not listening.

'Furthermore, Mr Bird, I am informed that on Monday afternoon, at a hostelry known as The Old Horse – when you should have been attending lectures – you were incapacitated by alcohol. Is that true?'

'Yes,' Baxter says quietly. There's no point in trying to explain, to defend himself.

'In the *afternoon*?' Professor Parbury says. Appalled.

He carries on.

'I am also informed that you have failed to attend a single lecture all week. Have you, in fact, even bothered to pick up a book?'

Books? Baxter had forgotten about books.

The professor consults his notes, forges on.

'There are other matters here,' he says. 'Reports of an unauthorised dance at College Hall where you and your father profited from an admission fee. Reports of an assault on a university security employee. Of an unseemly episode outside the Attenborough Tower this morning.'

He leans forwards. His voice lowers.

'I am aware, Mr Bird that your grandmother passed away this week. You have my condolences.'

He straightens. His voice rises.

'But that in no way excuses your behaviour. I put it to you, Mr Bird, that before we even turn to the question of your unprovoked assault on a fellow-student, you are not a fit and proper person to be a member of this university. How do you answer that?'

Baxter is stumbling. He's about to fall. He's going to be

sent down. It's all got twisted, screwed up. He has to say something. Do something. It's not fair. None of it.

'I—' he starts to say.

In the anteroom outside the chamber, there are raised voices, there is a sudden pounding at the door.

Professor Parbury looks up, startled.

As Baxter turns, the door bursts open. And through it, in a rush, come Abby, Georgie, Josh.

And jostling, spilling noisily behind are a hundred students or more. There are faces that Baxter recognises from College Hall – Cat Stevens, the boy in pixie boots – there are people he remembers from the demo, including the megaphone girl with the giant afro hair.

Professor Parbury is on his feet. Outraged.

Baxter remains seated. Momentarily stunned.

'SILENCE!' the professor thunders. 'What on earth is the meaning of this?'

It is Abby who steps forwards and answers. She is flushed, angry; her eyes flashing.

'We've been listening at the door,' she says. 'And you've got it all wrong . . .'

Her voice drifts away; courage ebbing in the weighty silence of the room.

Dr Paulizky gets to her feet, goes to Abby's side, puts her arm around her.

'Professor Parbury,' she says forcefully. 'You must listen. What this girl is telling you is the truth. You *have* got it wrong about Baxter and you can't silence me – or these students.'

Applause runs through the crowded room.

'Right on!' someone shouts.

Baxter has a sudden picture in his mind of the demo. *Power to the people*, his father had sung. Maybe that much at least was true. The people can't be bullied, pushed around. Their voices have to be heard.

'I demand quiet!' the professor shouts again.

But Dr Paulizky refuses to be quiet.

'If you allow me, on Baxter's behalf I will answer all the unfounded charges you have made.'

The professor raises his hands. Unused to being challenged, he is flustered now.

'That won't be necessary, because regardless of the truth of the accusations I have laid before this hearing, there remains the substantive matter that the police have left to us. The assault on a fellow-student.'

It's Georgie who speaks now, brandishing a sheaf of papers.

'There's a petition,' she announces. 'It's signed by a thousand students. Asking for clemency on Baxter's behalf.'

She walks across to the professor, hands him the papers. He takes them, smiles thinly, shuffles through them to the end, begins to read.

'I see you have some distinguished supporters, Mr Bird.'

Baxter doesn't understand.

The professor continues.

'We have here: Nixon, Richard Milhous; Duck, Donald; Jagger, Michael; Python, Monty.'

Georgie turns to Josh. Glares.

'Sorry, man,' Josh says, raising his hands to Professor Parbury. 'I just needed four more names for the thousand.'

The professor lets the petition drop fluttering to the floor.

'With fabricated names, this is nothing but worthless paper. There can be no question of clemency. I will deal with this matter without further delay.'

He looks at Baxter. Unable to meet his eye, Baxter looks down at the tabletop.

'Mr Bird, you are accused of assaulting a fellow-student on the morning of Wednesday of this week. How do you answer that charge?'

Still Baxter doesn't look up. It really is over now. Nothing is going to stop Professor Parbury. Not Dr Paulizky. Not Abby. Not the petition.

'I—'

He is interrupted. By Josh.

'What assault?' he says.

Baxter turns to Josh, frowning. Josh is smiling, like he's suddenly solved a puzzle, found the answer.

'I beg your pardon, young man?' Professor Parbury says, pointing at the tape on Josh's nose, the bruises on his face; waving at them, his hands shaking in frustration. 'I understood that not only *was* there an assault, but I assumed that *you* were the victim. You *are* Joshua Hurlstone, are you not?'

'No assault, man,' Josh says with a widening grin. 'I tripped. Fell. Baxter came to help me.'

'Young man, I must caution you that—'

Josh doesn't let him finish. He turns, faces the crowded room, raises his hands, palms upwards, shrugs.

'No witnesses, no assault,' he says. Laughing.

The room roars its approval.

Everyone except Baxter.

He can't go along with it. It's a lie. Another lie. It's like frigging Watergate. Lies everywhere. He's had enough.

'No, Josh—' he starts to say.

Abby is suddenly beside him.

'Hush,' she says. Putting her hand firmly to his mouth.

The professor is scratching his head.

'No assault?' he says. 'But you told the police—'

Josh's mouth falls open. He'd forgotten about telling the police.

'Shit, man, I—'

Georgie steps in.

'He was concussed,' she says gleefully. 'After the fall. They misunderstood.'

'No, Georgie,' Baxter says.

No more lies. He's going to end this. Now. Be a man, face the consequences. He attempts to stand.

But Abby grabs him, claims him. Refuses to let him get to his feet. Won't let him say anything. Won't let him go.

Professor Parbury speaks.

'Mr Bird,' he says, exasperated, 'I am wearying of all this. I give you one chance to break the habit of a lifetime and tell me the truth of these events.'

There is a hush in the room and, in the midst of it, Abby relaxes her grip. Freed, Baxter rises to his feet.

He looks around the room, shakes his head. All these people are there for him. Fighting for *him*. They believe in him.

Something triggers inside.

And if they frigging *believe* in him, isn't it about time he started to believe in himself? About time *he* started to fight?

He draws hungrily from the thought – strength, confidence, excitement.

He stands taller, turns to face the professor.

'The truth?' he says, surprised at the depth and steadiness in his voice, the sudden fierce resolve.

'The truth is that I've made some terrible mistakes this week. I've done things that I'm ashamed of – that I will always regret.'

'No, Baxter,' Abby says.

'Yes, Abby,' Baxter says, reaching for her hand.

'The truth, Mr Bird?' the professor says testily.

'The truth?' Baxter says again, with mounting anger. 'Before this week, I'd never really thought about what truth was. I took it for granted. But now I know that you can't do that. Because there are lies everywhere. In families, between friends . . .'

He turns to Josh. Says thank you with a smile for his attempt to save him. Turns back to Professor Parbury. Meets his eye.

'And there are lies in this room too, Professor,' he says, hearing the challenge in his voice.

The professor bridles, starts to speak.

'Mr Bird, I—'

Baxter raises his hand. Stops him. Sees himself doing it: Baxter Bird, standing up for himself, standing tall.

'But there's an irony here,' he says. 'Because amidst all the lies – for all the good it's done me – I am the one who has told nothing but the truth.'

Again the professor tries to speak. But Baxter won't be stopped. Not now.

'When we first met, Professor, I told you about what it was like to be a boy growing up without a father, with second-hand clothes and no money for the meter. It was true, every

503

word of it. I had no father then. I don't think I've got a father now.

'I *am* that boy I told you about, Professor Parbury. I *am* Pauper Bird.'

He turns to the sea of faces behind. Shrugs. Unembarrassed. Unapologetic. Proud.

'Right on,' someone says quietly.

'But Pauper Bird got here!' Baxter continues. 'Despite everything, he managed to get to university. And I'll tell you something, Professor ...'

He pauses, gathers himself. Tries to control the emotions he can feel rising inside. Anger, pride, grief. But he can't control it. He is almost shouting now.

'I tell you,' he says, 'I *will* not let you take it away from me!'

The whole room is shouting with him.

He thumps the table with his fist. Leans forwards.

'I will fight you, Professor Parbury. I may have made mistakes – but I do *not* deserve to lose everything I've worked for. Try to send me down and I will fight you every step of the way.'

The room roars again.

'I will appeal to the Vice-chancellor,' he says. 'I'll write to my MP, to the Prime Minister – to the frigging Pope. I'll lead demonstrations ...'

He gestures to those behind him.

'And I won't be alone ... because these people here will fight with me!'

He's getting carried away now. He doesn't care.

'We'll occupy this building ... we'll call the newspapers, the BBC ... We'll write protest songs, go on hunger strike ... We'll fight and we will *not* be beaten!'

Power to the people, right on!

The crowd surges around Baxter. Someone raises his arm. Makes him punch the air. In the room there is uproar. Mayhem.

And amidst it, the professor removes his horn-rimmed glasses and polishes them furiously. He consults hastily with his two colleagues, whispering urgently into their ears.

And then he steps towards Baxter, reaches out, shakes his hand.

And manages to smile.

LATER

107

Truman

The following day: Margate

Truman is perched on a stool at the bar of The First & Last, elbows on the counter, nursing a pint and a hangover. Well, it was quite a night last night, wasn't it? A proper homecoming; a right old sing-song; plenty of laughter; Guinness and champagne on tap. And it *does* take him longer to bounce back these days, that's for sure. It isn't like the sixties: back then, he could keep going at it all night and still be right as rain in the morning.

And the thing with a hangover is there's always the chance it will leave you feeling down, feeling blue. So that's probably why he feels like this, isn't it? Down. Blue. Lonely. On his Jack.

Truman looks around the empty bar and raises his glass dispiritedly to his lips.

He shakes his head bitterly.

There's no justice, is there? Because by rights he shouldn't be lonely at all. By rights he should be spending every night tucked up in bed with Christie.

He'd been *that* close – he puts his glass down, shows himself, measuring the smallest gap between his thumb and forefinger – he was *that* close to having it all. Back with Christie, feet up, feet between the sheets; Rosie on the side, waiting for him up in Leicester. Perfect.

But then the psycho turns up and ruins everything. Everything. Selfish sod.

And what Truman doesn't get, what he doesn't understand, is why they were all so hopping mad with him at the end? It's not as if he's done anything *that* terrible. No one got hurt, no one died, did they? Well, his old mum died – but that's not down to him – and Strachan didn't look too healthy when Truman last saw him. But he can't be blamed for that, can he?

No, all he'd been trying to do was get that second go at it. And along the way, he just had a bit of fun; scratched that itch with Rosie. That's all. Where's the harm in that?

The truth is, there *is* no harm. In fact, there's *good*. It's been good for Baxter, being with his dad instead of being mollycoddled by Christie. He's been good for Rosie too. And he livened things up at the university, didn't he? On the demo, at the JCR Jive.

No, all in all they should be thanking him, not turning on him. OK, so he stretched things a bit with the heart business. But he was going to sort that. He was going to get a miracle cure, given the chance.

Once more, Truman looks around the deserted lunchtime bar. Feeling down. Feeling blue.

It's the boy he's going to miss most of all, he thinks. He shakes his head, smiles, a picture of him and Baxter playing in his mind, haring across the park with Strachan in pursuit. Another picture: Josh helping Baxter up the steps at College

Hall, the wounded hero being led from the battlefield. And then another: Baxter at the cool still heart of it, jiving with Abby as Truman thumps at the piano.

> ♫ See my baby jive,
> See my baby jive ...

A real chip off the old block, Baxter is. He'll miss him. In fact, he'll miss them all up at Leicester: Abby, Josh, Georgie, all the kids. They made him feel young again.

Truman raises his glass once more, puts it back down, drums on the counter and looks at his watch.

Where is she?

Lonely?

Well, lonely isn't quite right, is it? Not now he's back with Bella the belter. She's no Christie, no Rosie; but she's got a heart of gold. She'll do for now.

After he shook Niloc off and scarpered from the university, he went double quick back to the flat and picked up his stuff. He then thumbed it all the way down from Leicester and pitched up on her doorstep in the late afternoon. He couldn't think where else to go.

'*You?*' she squeals at him, just about to slam the door in his face.

'Bella, let me say just one thing,' he says.

She looks up at him with her eyes narrowed, the door held open just a crack. He speaks more softly.

'Bella,' he says. 'I've just come back to say ... to say goodbye.'

She opens the door a little more.

Bingo!

'Goodbye?' she says.

'The doctors . . .' he says.

'Doctors?' Bella says.

He nods. The door opens wider. Opens with the golden
key.

'They say it's just a matter of months,' he says, putting his
hand to his chest, tapping at his heart.

And that's enough. She can't resist that. No one can resist
that.

She doesn't say a word about the money he owes her; she
just opens her door and lets him right back in. Well, she
doesn't need to know about the six hundred in his pocket,
does she?

He looks at his watch, drums on the counter. Finally, the
door of The First & Last swings open and Bella comes
towards him, all smiles. He can hear the rustle of her
stocking-tops as she walks. Nice.

She hops up on to the barstool next to his, crosses her legs,
hitches her mini-skirt high and balances her red stiletto on
her toes.

'All right, lover boy?' she says, putting her hand to her
heart.

'Not so dusty, princess,' Truman replies.

With a brave lopsided grin.

108

Abby

Monday afternoon: The JCR

When the telephone rings, Abby snatches it from the receiver, hears the coins rattle and drop.

'Is that you, Abby love?' her mother says.

Abby laughs.

'Of course, Mam,' she says. 'Who else is it going to be?'

There's a moment's silence between them.

'What's the weather down there?' Abby says.

It's stupid but it's important for her to know, to be able to picture it.

'Oh, it's a much better day down here,' her mother says. 'Just that nice drizzle in the air.'

Abby closes her eyes and feels it cool and wet on her face.

'I've been thinking,' her mother says.

'Oh yes?' Abby says, with another small laugh.

'About that boy,' her mother says. 'I haven't been able to sleep.'

Abby's laughter dies. Her mam is going to tell her not to see Baxter; that she's worried, that her father is worried.

After everything she and Baxter have been through together, her mother is going to ruin it.

'You see, I told you something wrong, Abby love,' her mother says.

Abby doesn't want to hear it. But she knows she has to.

'What's that, Mam?'

There's another silence. She can almost hear her mother thinking, gathering herself, remembering a little speech she's prepared.

'I said you needed sensible, lovely.'

'You did, Mam,' Abby says uncertainly.

'But I was wrong, see?'

Abby doesn't understand.

'Wrong?'

They've never spoken like this before, mother and daughter.

'Sensible is safe, Abby,' her mother says. 'And . . . '

She doesn't finish; it's as if she can't.

'And?' Abby helps her.

'And you've had far too much safe in your life already.'

There's a catch in her mother's voice, tears.

'Mam? Are you all right?'

'No, Abby,' she says, laughing, crying. 'I'm not, lovely.'

'Don't cry, Mam. Please don't cry.'

'We've kept you too close, Abby love. I've always known that. Kept you safe, see?'

'I know, Mam. I know.'

Abby is crying too now. Tears from nowhere.

'After what happened, lovely.'

'I know.'

'We never let you grow up. Not properly. And now you're

514

on your own and you don't know anything about anything. You don't know about boys.'

It isn't true. She's learning. Fast.

Her mother isn't finished.

'And there's something else,' she says. 'I settled for safe, see?'

Abby isn't sure she's heard right.

'Settled?'

'Oh, I don't regret it,' her mother says quickly. 'Your dad's a good man. The best.'

'He is, Mam,' Abby says, wondering where this is leading, whether she wants to hear it.

'But I told you a fib the other day,' her mother says. 'Because there *was* someone else.'

'Someone else?'

'Another man. Before your dad.'

Another man?

'He wrote me poems, he did. Proper Dylan Thomas, he was. Loved his long words.'

Pantechnicon, paradigm, polyphonic, panegyric.

'He made me feel like I've never felt about anyone. He was a bit wild, mind. Unpredictable.'

Abby can hardly speak.

'Did you love him, Mam?' she manages to say.

'I did, Abby love,' her mother says. 'I did.'

'Oh, Mam ...' Abby says.

Niloc told her that she had come to rid the world of fear, that her tears would wash the past away. Well, she thinks, as she pushes at her eyes, trying to stem the flow, he was right about one thing. She has tears enough now. Enough to wash the world.

Still her mother isn't done. She is determined to say what she had to say.

'So don't forget, my lovely. Find a boy who loves long words, one who'll write poems for you.'

'I will, Mam,' Abby says.

Reeling. Wondering.

'And it's unpredictable you want, not sensible. Unpredictable is good,' she says.

As the pips sound, her money runs out and the line goes dead.

109

Christie

Ten days later: Brighton

Christie stands in front of the mirror by the door, smoothes away the creases in her skirt and adjusts her hat.

'Nearly ready?' she calls. 'The car's waiting.'

It's an unlikely friendship but there's no doubting the bond that has sprung up between them. And from the first they'd talked – as only women can so quickly talk – about what's important. About family, love, loss.

It's as if they recognise something in each other. Christie struggles to say exactly what it is, to put a name to it, but it's something like resilience. Whatever life throws at them, they find a way of dealing with it – and always for the sake of others, never for themselves.

For Christie, of course, it's been for the children. For Sally, for the past ten years it was for Strachan and now it's for the new life she carries.

Sally comes through the bedroom door of the flat above The Salvation in her black coat, shoes and hat. She joins Christie at the mirror, takes her hand.

'Thanks, Christie,' she says.

Christie can feel the shake in Sally's hand, the tremble that runs through her body.

'What for?' she says with a smile.

'Being here,' Sally says.

Why Christie was the one who went to Sally as she held Strachan as he lay on the ground, she can't quite explain. Nor can she explain why she and no one else volunteered to travel in the ambulance with Sally, sat with her in the hospital waiting room and held her when what they knew already was finally confirmed.

That it was too late. That Strachan was dead.

No one else moved when Strachan went down. But Sally looked up with such shock in her eyes that Christie found herself going towards her before she had time to think.

It was instinct. Pure and simple.

Much later that day, Christie insisted they make the journey back south together. Ray had waited for them outside the hospital and it was late in the afternoon before they set off. The sunshine of earlier in the day had long gone; clouds gathered, rain began to fall steadily.

By the time they got to Crawley, the night was dark and wild and Christie was determined that Sally shouldn't travel on to Brighton, that she shouldn't spend that night alone. Sally was too tired, too dazed and defeated, to argue.

Feeling uncomfortable, feeling excluded by the two women, Ray hesitated by the front door.

'I'll ring you tomorrow, Ray,' Christie said to him.

Relieved, he pecked her good-night on the cheek.

That would be the last kiss, Christie thought, with a parting pang of affection for him. What had happened that day had decided her: they could never be together. Whatever she felt for him, it wasn't something that would sustain them, that would endure. It wasn't enough. Perhaps part of it was that she *had* been too long alone, had become too much her own person. She didn't want or need a man who would erode the person she had become. The final straw had come in the car, driving back, when Ray had made a whispered suggestion that they should do the Open University course together. As if she wasn't capable of doing it alone.

She *was* better off on her own. She would tell him when they spoke on the telephone.

She was grateful to Ray, though – she always would be, for his kindness, his strength when she needed it. And his intervention had finally tipped her towards it: whatever else happens now, she *is* going to do that course. And she's not going to do it for Nanna and for all those Christies and Nannas who never had a chance. Not even for Megan. She's going to do it for herself,

At the kitchen table, she and Sally sat into the night. Still shocked and shivering from the day, with the wind rattling at the windows, they drank tea and talked long enough for Sally to move beyond tears and for Christie to find herself speaking about Megan.

And she'd never spoken about Megan, not about all of it, not even to Nanna.

But that night she shared Megan's secret with a near-stranger – with a woman who she'd met only that day, who Truman betrayed her with ten years before, who had shared her life with the man who stalked Christie in her nightmares.

It scarcely seemed possible.

But grief did that, Christie thought. It stripped everything else away and left only what was important. And what was important was not what should have separated them – Truman, Strachan – but what bound them together: what they had shared that day and what they recognised in each other.

In bed that night, Christie struggled to make sense of what had happened with Truman.

He'd just tapped at his heart and, like a fool, she'd believed him.

How could she have been so easily taken in?

She was vulnerable, of course – because of Megan, because of Nanna – but that didn't excuse her. She'd been naïve, soft.

But how *could* he do that? How could he lie about such a thing – with his daughter dead, his mother dying? Not for a moment had it crossed Christie's mind that anyone could be capable of doing that. It was too cruel.

And it was especially cruel on Baxter.

Truman had got to know his son. Lied to him. Broken his heart. Again.

He used people. That was the difference between them – or one of them. She'd lied only once, to try – stupidly – to help Megan and Baxter. He lied all the time, for his own sake.

One day, perhaps, she and Baxter would talk about all of

this. But not yet. The wounds between them needed more time to heal. He knew that she loved him and – however misguided – she had only ever done what she thought was best for him. That was all that mattered for now. Everything else could wait.

After that night, Christie and Sally spoke every day on the telephone.

During one long call, Christie told Sally that she had spoken to Ray, ended it. He'd taken it as badly as she'd feared; he was ignoring her at work, refusing to speak to her, the atmosphere was unbearable, everyone was talking about it. It was impossible for her to stay in the Planning office.

Sally immediately suggested a solution.

There was an attic floor to The Salvation; they could convert it to make another flat above Sally's. Christie could help with the bar work and still have plenty of time to study for the Open University. Harry would love to live by the sea, wouldn't he? And Sally would have Christie there for support when the baby came.

It was perfect.

Almost without thinking, Christie agreed. There was nothing for her in Crawley now – and it *would* be better for Harry. He was due to start at senior school anyway in the new year; that may as well be in Brighton, where his grandmother was. He'd soon make new friends. And it would be good to leave a house that held so many memories of Megan: all of the bad, none of the good. And it was about time she confronted all those ghosts in Brighton.

They could move in in just a few weeks, Sally said. Christie went home from the phone box that evening to the house at Pound Hill and started to pack immediately.

Christie is still holding Sally's hand, feeling the shake, the tremble.

'I'm not sure I can do this,' Sally says.

'You'll be fine,' Christie says. 'I'll be next to you every step.'

She lets go of Sally's hand and looks at her watch. It's time to leave.

'OK?' she says.

Side by side, taking care in their high heels, they go down the stairs of The Salvation, out through the bar and into the street.

Outside, a crowd of the regulars from the pub immediately gather around. One of them gives Sally a reassuring pat on the shoulder.

'He was a good sort, your Strachan,' he says. 'Underneath it all.'

'Thanks, Wally,' Sally says, forcing a brief smile.

Sally is holding tight to Christie's hand; Christie wonders for a moment how they will find their way through the crowd to the waiting car.

She needn't have worried because suddenly the crowd is eased apart by two bent-nosed, square-shouldered, dark-coated, crop-haired men in sunglasses.

'Move aside,' one of them says to Wally. He doesn't have to ask twice.

As the crowd parts, a small, elegant, white-haired figure in a long frock coat and a black-ribboned top hat theatrically appears and comes towards Sally and Christie.

522

'Mr Smith,' Sally says, holding out her hand, greeting him.

'Charmed, my dear,' Mr Smith says, removing his hat, bowing low.

Sally had told Christie that Mr Smith had insisted on handling all the funeral arrangements and that no expense was to be spared. He was Strachan's old boss, she'd explained with a shudder, back when Strachan was what Strachan was.

Mr Smith makes a pirouetting turn, replaces his hat and leads the way towards the car. He doesn't so much walk as glide across the ground, taking elaborately measured, graceful strides.

Christie and Sally follow. To Christie's surprise, the two crop-haired men who cleared the crowd have somehow become a dozen or more. They are standing square shoulder to square shoulder, chins jutting, forming a bulky, scarred and broken-nosed honour guard. At the car another of them welcomes Sally: with a flex of his shoulders, a tug at his cuffs, he opens the car door.

Brighton can never have seen anything like it, Christie thinks.

Mr Smith leads the way on foot, now carrying a black cane, gliding, striding, bowing. Behind him comes the hearse, a glass and varnished-wood Victorian carriage drawn by four black-plumed, high-stepping horses. Inside, Strachan's weighty coffin sits on a sea of white lilies. Propped either side of the coffin are long, stretched wreaths, with giant letters picked out in white roses against a background of leafy green.

On one side it reads: STRACHAN.

On the other: LEGEND.

Behind the hearse comes a procession of thirteen black

vintage Rolls-Royces – the first of which carries Sally and Christie. And every fifty yards, lining the route as the cortège makes its way out from The Lanes, along the seafront and then on up the hill that goes steeply towards the church and burial ground, are square-shouldered men in dark coats and dark glasses who bend their heads in respect as the hearse goes slowly by.

'Strachan would have been so proud,' Sally says, tears running hot. 'And my boy will be too, one day, when I tell him.'

'Boy?' Christie says.

Sally gives a small laugh amongst her tears.

'It *will* be a boy, don't you think?' she says. 'Strachan was sure it would be.'

After the service, at the graveside, Christie whispers to Mr Smith.

'Who are they?' she says. 'These men?'

All of those who travelled in the cars, and those who lined the route, are now gathered in the graveyard. They are greeting one another solemnly, shaking hands, speaking low, nodding. Christie and Sally are the only two women there.

Mr Smith looks around, spreads his arms wide as if to embrace them.

'They have come from all over the country,' he says delightedly.

'But who—?' Christie tries again.

Mr Smith smiles.

'They are Strachan's own kind,' he says. 'They have come to say goodbye – to the one who was the very best of them.'

Strachan. Legend.

In the graveyard that is so familiar to Christie, Strachan's grave is in the first rank, amongst the supplicating angels, in front of the forest of ornate crosses. In time, once the stone-masons had done their work and the ground had been prepared, the tallest obelisk in the graveyard would tower over it, Mr Smith explained. For now it is marked with a simple wooden cross.

Standing next to Sally in front of the cross, reading the carved inscription, taking a last few quiet moments before the car carries them back to The Salvation, Christie looks around. Tucked away, almost unseen behind the genuflecting angels, is her father's grave. She touches Sally's arm, points.

'My dad's buried just there,' she says.

Sally looks up, looks to where Christie is pointing and rubs away her tears.

'That's good,' she says. 'Strachan will keep him safe now.'

Together they turn back to face the wooden cross, their eyes going for a final time to the inscription.

A single word.

STRACHAN.

Just Strachan.

110

Baxter

The following afternoon: Crawley

The day isn't cold but among the small crowd gathered outside the squat, newly built yellow-brick crematorium there's much foot-stamping and hand-rubbing. More people are there than Baxter had expected and he can feel how jittery they all are, how wound up, as they wait for the hearse to arrive.

Friends from bingo, neighbours from the flats, Edie and the regulars from the Martletts café: they've all come to pay their respects to Nanna, to say goodbye, but they want this bit done – the hearse, the coffin, the curtains closing. It's too real.

Baxter and his mother stand waiting at the head of the small crowd. Baxter is feeling awkward, uncomfortable, angry. He doesn't want these people to speak to him; he doesn't want to hear their banal words of comfort. There is no comfort.

A solid crunch of tyres on gravel announces the arrival of the single car. As it approaches, Christie reaches for Baxter's hand, holds tight.

*

'Hold tight!' Nanna shouts. They are on the top of the helter-skelter on Brighton Pier. She is sitting on the mat, her long pleated skirt is hitched up, and she is holding Baxter between her knees.

'Whoosh!' she says as they speed down and round towards the bottom, as the light on the water dances all around them, as the girls on the nearby big dipper squeal.

'Whoosh!' Baxter says, feeling the rush of the air on his face, feeling her holding him.

'Don't let go, Nanna,' he shouts to her over his shoulder.

'Don't worry,' she says into his ear, her head close to his. 'I'll never let you go.'

Baxter and Christie lead the way into the crematorium chapel. They talked about Harry and decided that it would be better for him not to be here. He's too young, he doesn't need these memories. It feels somehow lonely without him, without Megan.

There is someone else missing too.

At the door to the chapel, Baxter pauses, looks into the distance. He'd been sure he would come. He'd been wrong.

After Strachan went down, Baxter had turned to find his father. He wasn't there: he'd just slipped away, vanished. For a moment, it was as if he'd been there, hadn't been real. The genie had disappeared back into the bottle and Baxter was left hurt, damaged, lonely, angry. Confused.

And the hurt was greater still when his father failed to appear to help him at the hearing.

Every night since, Baxter has been awake for hours, trying to puzzle it out. He just doesn't get it, can't understand: why all the lies? All the heart-tapping, the limping, the record label ... Everything.

Nothing was real. Nothing.

Except. Except there *was* this thing between them, wasn't there? This connection. That was real; he didn't make it up. And the music was real, and the laughter and ...

But then again, his father is a thief. He's stolen the six hundred pounds that Georgie and Josh collected for charity, taken it under false pretences. Frigging stolen it.

Tossing and turning in his narrow bed as Abby sleeps under the greatcoat in his chair, Baxter wrestles with it.

His father is a liar and a thief. But then again, it isn't as simple as that. Because he's also this totally far-out guy who brings everything to life around him – at The Old Horse, on the demo, at the JCR Jive. His father rose from the dead and everywhere he went was a party, a riot.

He'd been proud to be his son.

And that in turn had made him angry with his mother. Angry his father had been dead to him for so many years, about his mother's lie.

Baxter can't work that out either. Is her lie worse than his? Hers that he was dead; his that he was dying.

And his father's lie? However frigging stupid it was, and however much his behaviour with Dr Paulizky suggested to the contrary, if the intention was to bring the family back together, was it really *so* bad?

Does a right intention make a lie OK?

He doesn't know. Can't answer.

He knows, of course, that the motivation behind his

mother's lie was good too: she'd wanted to spare him and Megan any more pain. But his mother trying to spare them didn't make it right, did it? The lie may have may have stopped his nightmares, but it took something precious from him and from Megan. It denied them the choice of whether to try to see their father or not.

No, that's making it too complicated.

It's not really that at all: it's a simple matter of right or wrong. And the lie *was* wrong. Plain wrong. And the ceremony on the pier? The whole thing was wrong, a screw-up.

His mind goes racketing on.

Just like sending him to the wrong school was a screw up: the wrong-school-Pauper-Bird-no-friends screw-up.

But that too was a well-intentioned screw-up, wasn't it? His mother wanted the best for him, wanted the future for him she'd never had. And if he hadn't gone to the wrong school, he wouldn't have made it to university.

So she'd been right about the frigging school. And wrong. He doesn't know now whether to thank her or be angry with her.

But on the day when Strachan went down, he knew exactly what he felt about his mum.

He'd been so proud of her, seeing her go to help that Sally woman. It had been weird seeing her like that, being the only one to step forward, doing the right thing, however much she herself was hurting. That's a kind of courage, isn't it? The best kind.

Seeing her like that had helped him make a decision: he knew then that he would never tell her about Megan, about how she'd gone to Brighton hoping to meet Jonathan. Baxter would continue to carry that knowledge, that guilt, on his own. His mother doesn't need to know; she doesn't deserve more pain.

And, of course, he knows that keeping the truth from her is a kind of a lie too. And he also knows that part of the reason he's managed to stay on at university is because of lies – Josh's, Georgie's.

But hey: why should he be any different from the rest?

'Is everything all right, Baxter?' Abby says one night, hearing him turn yet again on his bed.

'Yes,' he says. 'It's just ...'

His voice fades away.

'Hush now,' she says, her voice a lullaby. 'Try to let it go.'

She's right: he has to let it go, move on. After all, he's no nearer finding real answers to any of it. All he knows is that he's proud and angry and ashamed of his dad – much more angry and ashamed than proud. And he's proud of, and just a little angry at, his mum. Between them they screwed a lot of things up. But, on her own – and with Nanna's help – his mother got most things right.

Who needs a Niloc, he thinks, yawning, finally finding his way towards sleep, when I can work this much out on my own?

'I'll never let you go,' Nanna had said.

But you have, Nanna, Baxter thinks. *You have let me go, and from now on I'll be going down the helter-skelter alone.*

The service is nearing its end. The eulogy is being read by a stooping, thin-haired man in a dog collar who never met Nanna Bird, his voice booming alarmingly in the chapel. If

Nanna was sitting beside Baxter, she would be nudging him and giggling like a schoolgirl.

Baxter closes his eyes: he wants it to be over. The whole service has been a joke; it has nothing to do with Nanna. The man doesn't know her, his words are empty and meaningless. In the chairs behind Baxter and Christie, people are growing restless, shifting; there is coughing, shuffling of feet.

The man in the dog collar booms again.

'We now come to our final hymn,' he says, 'which I am delighted to say is to be sung by a good friend of Mrs Bird's.'

Surprised, Baxter opens his eyes and watches as Edie from the Martletts café makes her way slowly, shyly to the front. She smiles nervously at Christie and Baxter, blows them a quick kiss. Composing herself, waiting for the coughing to stop and a perfect silence to settle, she closes her eyes, and then, unaccompanied and in a voice that is surprisingly young, surprisingly pure, she begins to sing.

♫ Sleep, my child, and peace attend thee,
All through the night.
Guardian angels God will send thee,
All through the night ...

And suddenly it's as if she *is* with them – Nanna, singing her favourite lullaby, and Baxter is eight years old and hearing it for the first time.

My brave Baxter Bird, she whispers to him as she kisses him good-night.

Baxter looks at his mother, sees her staring ahead, tears flooding her cheeks. He turns to those behind, Nanna's friends and neighbours, and sees their tears too.

She *is* there. With them. They can all feel it.

Baxter can feel it.

I'll never let you go, he tells her.

My brave Baxter Bird, she says to him again. Proudly.

Songs

♫ 'Let's All Do the Conga': origin unknown.

♫ 'Imagine': John Lennon, Apple, 1971. By John Lennon.

♫ 'You're So Vain': Carly Simon, Elektra, 1972. By Carly Simon.

♫ 'Hoochie Coochie Man': Muddy Waters, Chess, 1954. By Willie Dixon.

♫ 'Money': Pink Floyd, Harvest, 1973. By Roger Waters.

♫ 'Breathe': Pink Floyd, Harvest, 1973. By David Gilmour, Roger Waters and Richard Wright.

♫ 'Sleep My Child and Peace Attend Thee': music from a Welsh folk song. Words by Sir Harold Boulton, 1884.

♫ 'The Magnificent Seven': Elmer Bernstein, United Artists, 1960. By Elmer Bernstein.

♫ 'Let's Get It On': Marvin Gaye, Tamla, 1973. By Marvin Gaye and Ed Townsend.

♫ 'Paint It Black': The Rolling Stones, Decca, 1966. By Mick Jagger and Keith Richards.

♫ 'I'm Free': The Who, Polydor, 1969. By Pete Townshend.

♫   'Nutbush City Limits': Tina Turner, United Artists, 1973. By Tina Turner.

♫   'Life on Mars': David Bowie, RCA, 1973. By David Bowie.

♫   'Don't You Worry 'Bout a Thing': Stevie Wonder, Tamla, 1973. By Stevie Wonder.

♫   'Love Me Do': The Beatles, Parlophone, 1962. By John Lennon and Paul McCartney.

♫   'Yesterday Once More': The Carpenters, A&M, 1973. By Richard Carpenter and John Bettis.

♫   'Mad About the Boy': Noël Coward, 1932. By Noël Coward.

♫   'Walk on the Wild Side': Lou Reed, RCA, 1972. By Lou Reed.

♫   'Knockin' on Heaven's Door': Bob Dylan, Columbia, 1973. By Bob Dylan.

♫   'The End': The Doors, Elektra, 1966. By Jim Morrison.

♫   'Rosie': Don Partridge, Columbia, 1968. By Don Partridge.

♫   'Power to the People': John Lennon/Plastic Ono Band, Apple, 1971. By John Lennon.

♫   'Give Peace a Chance': Plastic Ono Band, Apple, 1969. By John Lennon and Yoko Ono.

♫   'Blowin' in the Wind': Bob Dylan, Columbia, 1962. By Bob Dylan.

♫   'My Ding-a-Ling': Chuck Berry, Chess, 1972. By Dave Bartholomew.

♫   'Brown Sugar': The Rolling Stones, Rolling Stones Records, 1971. By Mick Jagger and Keith Richards.

♫   'Brown Eyed Girl': Van Morrison, Bang, 1967. By Van Morrison.

♫ 'See My Baby Jive': Wizzard, Harvest, 1973. By Roy Wood.

♫ 'Release Me': Engelbert Humperdinck, Decca, 1967. By Eddie Miller, Robert Yount and James Pebworth (1946).

If you enjoyed
Imagine
go back to where it all
began ten years earlier with
Love, Love Me Do,
out now from Piatkus . . .

Acknowledgements

I am grateful to the University of Leicester, who took me as a student in 1971, gave me the experience of a lifetime, and unwittingly provided the backdrop for much of this novel. They invited me back in 2005 to award me an honorary doctorate and it was memories of that visit that first suggested the setting for *Imagine*.

I am indebted to the yogi Paramahansa Yogananda, whose *Autobiography of a Yogi* provided the spiritual wisdom that comes in the quotations uttered by Niloc. Niloc may be an improbable messenger, but the teachings are timeless.

The poetry quotation, meanwhile, has been borrowed from Emily Dickinson ('Parting': 'Parting is all we know of heaven/And all we need of hell').

As in my first novel, *Love, Love Me Do*, I have also borrowed liberally from the songs of the period. It is part of the soundtrack to my youth – one that I know I share with countless others throughout the world. Even when the music of that time was bad, it was unforgettable.

My extraordinary editor, Emma Beswetherick, and the talented team at Piatkus deserve special thanks. I have learned so much from Emma since we have worked together. She has no right to be so good so young.

I have learned a great deal too from my agent, Eve White, so ably supported by Jack Ramm. Without them, I would not be celebrating the publication of my second novel.

Finally, for my wife, Annie, thanks are not nearly enough. She has made my life what it is today. I owe her all my happiness.

JOIN
MARK
HAYSOM
ONLINE

For news, reviews, blog posts, competitions and more

www.mark-haysom.co.uk